Beyond the

Blossoming Fields

BEYOND THE BLOSSOMING FIELDS

JUN'ICHI WATANABE

*Translated by Deborah Iwabuchi
and Anna Isozaki*

ALMA BOOKS

ALMA BOOKS LTD
London House
243–253 Lower Mortlake Road
Richmond
Surrey TW9 2LL
United Kingdom
www.almabooks.com

Original title: *Hanauzumi*
Copyright © Jun'ichi Watanabe, 1970
Originally published in Japan by Kawade Shobo Shinsha
English translation © Deborah Iwabuchi and Anna Isozaki, 2008
All rights reserved.

This book has been selected by the Japanese Literature Publishing Project (JLPP) which is run by the Japanese Literature Publishing and Promotion Center (J-Lit Center) on behalf of the Agency for Cultural Affairs of Japan.

Jun'ichi Watanabe asserts his moral right to be identified as the author, and Deborah Iwabuchi and Anna Isozaki as the translators of this work in accordance with the Copyright, Designs and Patents Act 1988.

Printed in Sweden by ScandBook AB

ISBN: 978-1-84688-064-3

Beyond the
Blossoming Fields

1

The Toné is the largest river flowing through the Kanto Plain. By the time it reaches Tawarase in northern Saitama, it is a mighty and placid waterway swollen with snow melted from the rocky slopes of the mountains ringing the plain.

In the late nineteenth century, white-sailed boats glided gracefully along its surface. Standing on its banks looking out over its expanse, you could count up to fourteen sails at a time. With the chants of the head oarsmen too distant to hear, the scene seemed to stand still in the soft spring sunshine.

The river was edged by a thick swath of marsh grass, beyond which was a high bank of mounded earth. Fields of green wheat stretched from there to the tree-lined streets of Tawarase.

At the centre of the wheat fields lay the estate of Ayasaburo Ogino, the village headman. The imposing walled residence had a gatehouse in front and white storehouses behind it, enclosing a garden shaded thickly by zelkova and palm trees. From the river bank, it resembled a castle in the centre of the plain.

The area was populated with families bearing the name Ogino. All were descended, however circuitously, from the Ashikaga clan, and the family crest bore the same circle with two horizontal lines as the Ashikagas. Among the many Ogino families, the home of Ayasaburo was referred to as Upper Ogino. They, along with Lower Ogino, were the most venerable of the clan and, until modern times, they were one of the very few farming families to enjoy the privilege of a surname and the right to carry swords.

That year, Ayasaburo was fifty-two years old. He had been suffering from inflamed joints for three years, and spent most of his time in bed in an inner room of his house. His eldest son Yasuhei was twenty-four, still single, and showed little interest in farming. It was therefore left to Kayo, Ayasaburo's forty-five-year-old wife, to attend to all household matters.

Kayo was a small woman with beautiful eyes. She was a good wife and, not unduly influenced by her family's exalted status, she ran the home with a steady hand. At the end of the day when all the work was done, she made sure her husband had the first bath, followed by her two sons, and then all of the family servants down to the lowliest servant girl. It was only then that she would take a bath herself. Kayo considered it only natural that she should oversee every detail in this way. She had just two sons, Yasuhei and Masuhei, and her other five children were girls. All five daughters were clever like their mother, able to read and write, and known for both their intelligence and their beauty. They were all married.

"Learn from Upper Ogino" was a saying heard often in these parts. All the villagers loved and respected them. Recently, however, a rumour had started circulating about the family.

Three years earlier their fifth daughter, Gin, had married Kanichiro, the eldest son of the wealthy Inamura farming family in nearby Kawakami village. Now people were saying that Gin was back in Tawarase. But she was not there to give birth or to pay her respects to her parents. She had returned alone, bearing nothing but a single bundle in her arms. Two weeks had already passed since then.

Neither the Ogino family nor any of the servants had a word to offer on the matter, but no fewer than three villagers had seen her walking along the Toné River headed for her parents' home.

This was a country village that knew little excitement as long as the Toné did not flood its banks. Things were different in Tokyo, where the Meiji government had recently been established and the emperor newly installed from Kyoto, but the ripples of change had not yet reached northern Saitama.

The villagers here were bored and yearned for gossip. Little did they care if it was a new bride or a funeral – anything would do. The matter of a daughter of the area's most eminent family returning for an unannounced visit to her parents was sufficient to keep tongues wagging.

"Could it be a problem with her husband's family?"

"They say she shows no sign of going back."

"All the Ogino girls are beautiful, but she is certainly the most attractive – and I hear she's smart too."

"She completed the Four Books and Five Classics of Confucianism by the age of ten."

"What could possibly be keeping her here?"

"Of course I don't have it first hand, but there is talk that she is suffering from melancholia and has come back for rest."

"But there was no one to accompany her from Kawakami."

"Yes, exactly! That's what is so unusual."

"Was she not getting along with her mother-in-law? or her husband?"

"Well, it's undoubtably a household with exacting standards – the Inamuras of Kawakami were assistant magistrates for generations, and I've heard that her mother-in-law Sei is still strong and runs the home with a very firm hand."

"It couldn't be a divorce, now, could it?"

"In Upper Ogino? Certainly not. Her mother would never allow such a thing."

"They do have a reputation to keep up."

In a traditional, conservative village during the early years of Meiji it was unheard of for a young wife to run away from her husband and return to her parents' home. The rumours spread quickly and it was a matter of enormous speculation. Neither Yasuhei nor Kayo, however, gave the slightest indication that anything was amiss. They favoured people they met in the street, and the pedlars and tenant farmers who came to the house, with their usual good-natured smiles. Visitors were given no cause to suspect that anything was wrong.

"Maybe she's gone back to Kawakami. Nobody has seen her at home."

"No. Everyone knows that Gin is not in her husband's home."

"Perhaps she's gone to recuperate at a hot spring?"

"She's with the Oginos. If she had left, someone would certainly have seen her. She must be in one of the inner rooms."

Inhabitants of tiny farming villages were perceptive. No matter how well Kayo kept up appearances, the rumours refused to die.

Indeed, they grew with each passing day. Kayo must have known what people were saying. She could feel the eyes of the villagers following her with a mixture of pity and curiosity. There were even some who tried to coax information out of her gently in passing conversation. It had been thirty years since Kayo married into the Ogino family, and this was the first time anything like this had happened. But Kayo maintained her silence on the matter. She refused to risk any damage to the family name – after all, they had a duty to set an example to others.

2

"So, where is Gin?"

Tomoko dispensed with all but the basic niceties and got to the point as soon as she arrived. Tomoko was the fourth Ogino daughter, just four years older than Gin, and it had been five years since she had married the eldest son of a Shinto priest in Kumagaya. She had received a letter from her mother about an urgent matter, and had departed Kumagaya for Tawarase the next morning. The matter, of course, was Gin.

"She's in the inner room next to the hallway."

"Is she bedridden?"

"She gets up from time to time, but she still has a fever."

"Has a doctor been to see her?"

"Dr Mannen came."

Tomoko nodded. Mannen Matsumoto was a scholar of Chinese studies, who had come to Tawarase ten years previously, accompanied by his daughter Ogie, to open a private school for the villagers. As a child, Tomoko herself had been allowed to sit in on her brothers' lessons with him. As with many Chinese scholars of his time, Dr Mannen was also learned in Chinese herbal medicine, and served as the village doctor as well as a teacher.

"And what does he say?"

"Well..." Kayo glanced around to make sure they were alone, then drew closer to Tomoko and spoke in a low voice. "He says it is *norin*."

"*Norin*?"

Kayo nodded almost imperceptibly.

Norin was the term used in Chinese medicine to mean gonorrhoea. The patient suffered a high fever, severe pain in the infected area and pain when urinating. In modern times, gonorrhoea can be cured with penicillin and other antibiotics, but in those days even sulpha drugs were not yet available, and it was considered an incurable disease.

11

"How long has she had it?"

"From what Gin says, it has been two years."

"That means that her husband..."

Kayo remained silent.

"So she's had it since soon after she married." Tomoko was taken aback. "Did Dr Mannen say how long it would take to cure?"

"It's hard to tell, but from what he has told me, it may not be possible."

"I heard that a woman with *norin* may never have children."

"That's what Dr Mannen says." Kayo's voice was low and she sounded discouraged.

Tomoko sighed heavily. "What do the Inamuras have to say?"

"We haven't heard a word. Gin spoke to no one when she left except to tell a maid that she was going to Tawarase to get some rest."

"And what does she plan to do?"

"I don't think she has any intention of returning to Kawakami."

"She can't be serious." Tomoko sat up straight in surprise. "And you're saying that she came to Tawarase all by herself?" Tomoko could not imagine leaving her husband's home without telling anyone, and Gin had married into one of the wealthiest families in northern Saitama. "I can't believe she's done this to us!" A sister who had run away from her husband would cause repercussions for the entire family, including herself. "How can you let her stay here? You know you ought to send her back." Tomoko was quick to blame her mother for spoiling her youngest daughter and raising her to do as she pleased.

"I know that, but you should have seen her when she arrived. She was burning with fever and doubled over with stomach pain. It's only in these last two or three days that she has begun to feel better."

"That means she was ill before she got here."

"She says she's been bedridden since winter. She did write that she had a cold, but said nothing to worry me at all. At any rate, we gave her to the Inamuras as a bride, and it wouldn't have done to enquire about her."

12

Tomoko understood what her mother was trying to say, and listened carefully as she continued.

"Gin was humiliated, and hoped to recover before anyone noticed she was ill. She broke out in a fever in February, but continued to do the housework and other chores as usual. Then she got too dizzy to get up in the morning, and she's been that way ever since."

Tomoko was beginning to see why her sister had decided to run away. When Kayo had first been approached about the marriage for her youngest daughter, she had immediately agreed to it. Not once had Gin been consulted. Gin had done as she was told, and the entire process had taken place according to the social norms.

Kayo knew that Gin was not to blame; it was she and the go-betweens who had set up the marriage. "It's all my fault." She covered her eyes with her hand.

"It's just a stroke of bad luck," Tomoko began, intending to comfort her mother, but was unable to say more, as what it meant for Gin began to sink in.

Kayo quickly reached for the iron kettle and poured hot water into the teapot.

"What does Father say about all this?"

"He told me to send her back immediately."

"To Kawakami?" Now Tomoko did not know what to think. She was upset with her sister for running back to her parents, and now she was speechless at her father's command that she be sent back to the man who had given her the disease.

"Mother, what do *you* think Gin should do?"

"If she stays here, there will be all kinds of social complications. It would be best for everyone if she left as soon as possible…" Kayo hesitated. "But she probably has her own thoughts on the matter."

"Especially if the disease is incurable," concluded Tomoko.

"I asked you to come because I want you to talk to her and find out how she feels about it all."

Gin was the youngest child, and since Tomoko was the nearest to her in age, they had always been close. Tomoko had come home the day before Gin's wedding, and the two had spent the entire night talking. Gin had had no qualms about her marriage. Only sixteen years old, she'd been full of girlish expectations. It was hard for Tomoko to believe that just three years later, her cheerful, clever sister could have come back home in such a state.

"We will have to contact the Inamuras before too long."

"Who would have guessed he was a man like that?" Tomoko tried to recall the glimpses she had had of Gin's fiancé before they were married. He had lovely fair skin that was almost too good for a man and contrasted attractively with Gin's healthy wheat-coloured complexion. "I guess I'll never understand men."

It was the only thing she could think of to say.

Tomoko looked into the room down the hall from her father's, where Gin was lying down, reading a book.

"Tomoko!" Gin put down the book and sat up.

"No, don't get up," Tomoko protested, but Gin rearranged her sleeping kimono and sat up properly anyway.

"How are you feeling?"

When she left to be married, Gin had had a soft egg-shaped face. Now it looked like an upside-down triangle, her bones standing out sharply. Her complexion was the pale-bluish colour characteristic of gonorrhoea patients.

Instead of answering, Gin asked Tomoko, "What are you doing here?"

"I had business in the area, and I thought I'd stop in and see how Mother was doing. What a surprise to learn you were here too!" Tomoko tried to act nonchalant, but there was no fooling Gin.

"Mother asked you to come, didn't she?"

Tomoko was silent.

"She wanted to talk to you about me."

Tomoko finally nodded. "Yes, I suppose so."

"Do you have something to say to me?" Gin was ready. Her eyes, red-rimmed with fever, were sharp. Tomoko knew she had no choice but to be truthful.

"I've heard all about it from Mother. It's all so sudden, I don't know what to think."

"You're angry with me, aren't you?"

"No." The illness had made Gin look like an invalid, small and older than her years, and Tomoko was more shocked than angry. "But you must know that you can't just stay here. If you need time to convalesce, go to a hot spring like a proper convalescent. Or go back home and rest – you can't just hide here in a back room and expect no one to notice."

"And that is your opinion?"

"Well... you know I'm only thinking of your best interests."

"So you're telling me to go straight back to Kawakami?"

"No, no, that's not what I'm saying. Mother asked me to find out what you have in mind."

"May I be honest, then?"

"Of course, I'm your sister. You know you can."

"Then I will." Gin looked her sister in the eye and continued, "I won't be going back to the Inamuras."

"You mean?..."

Gin nodded determinedly. "That was my decision when I left."

Tomoko was once again speechless. Rather than looking ashamed, Gin was obviously relieved at having spoken, and she began to look almost serene. Now Tomoko felt like the younger sister.

"I'm trying to decide when to tell Mother and Father."

"Gin." Tomoko knew she had to say something, but she had no idea what. "So, are you planning to divorce your husband? Is that what you're saying?"

"Yes." Gin shook slightly when she heard the words put so plainly.

"And you know that if you do this you will probably never be able to marry again? You may be single for the rest of your life."

"I don't mind that." Now the relief in Gin's features was even more evident as she gazed out into the garden, where the sun was beginning to shine through the canopy of leaves. It was not an expression you would expect on the face of a young woman contemplating anything as life-shattering as divorce. Tomoko's shock began to be mixed with irritation.

"And you don't care about everything that went into making this match for you? No regrets?"

"Not at this late date."

"You're being selfish!"

"Me? Selfish?"

"Yes! You left your husband's home without his permission, came straight back to your parents' home, and just settled in as if you belonged here! That is not the behaviour of a respectable married woman!" Tomoko could no longer contain herself.

"I don't care about being respectable."

"What are people going to think?"

"My husband is the one lacking respectability. I have every right to abandon my duties to him, as he obviously first abandoned his to me."

"Gin!" Tomoko took a hard look at her sister. Gin's eyes were gleaming with determination. As a child she had always insisted on getting her own way, but Tomoko had never thought she would take it this far. There was a Gin inside that diminutive body who was entirely new to her.

"I want no more to do with men! I don't mind if I never get married again. Staying single would be the greatest relief in the world."

"Now, now, everyone makes mistakes. There's no need to make that sort of decision right now."

"No matter how small or one-time *his* mistake, the fact of the matter is that he gave me this disease."

"What a thing for a woman to say!"

"So if a woman gets a disease from a man and is unable to bear children, she should put up with it? Even if I have a fever, I should get out of bed, obey every order my mother-in-law gives me, and do everything I can to keep my husband happy?"

Tomoko was unable to reply. She had thought that she was more understanding than her mother, but now she saw that in spite of herself she too was trying to force Gin into an old-fashioned notion of what a woman should do and be.

"But you know how it will look." Tomoko tried to be reasonable.

16

"That's just too bad." Gin turned to look out at the white gardenia tree in the garden. It had grown larger since she had married and left home.

"And to think you were the bride of such a well-to-do family." Tomoko knew she was just complaining now. Of the five sisters, Gin had married into the wealthiest family. All of them had been a little jealous of the match, as anyone would have been. Sick or not, nobody would choose to leave such a family of their own free will. Tomoko was chagrined just imagining what the villagers would have to say.

"Why won't you even consider going back?" She knew she was pressing her luck with her sister, but she had to ask.

"I don't care how rich they are, I don't want to spend my life doing the housekeeping."

"Doing the housekeeping?"

Gin looked back out at the garden. The colour of the shiny green leaves reflected on her face made her complexion appear even more sickly.

Tomoko spoke again. "That's what young wives do."

"I don't want to." Gin turned back to face her sister. "Light the fire, clean the house, make rice – there's never any time to read."

"Do you mean to tell me you've been reading books? You won't find a farmer's wife anywhere who reads books! What were you thinking?"

"I'm talking about a few minutes after the day's work is done. I had to hide from my mother-in-law to do even that."

"Of course you did!"

"But why should I have to?"

"Stop talking like a fool."

"I'm not sorry I'm ill – I'm glad! Now that I know how selfish men are and how meaningless marriage is."

"Gin!"

"Don't worry about me. Just leave me alone." Gin sank back down onto her bedding and hid her face. She had used up all the energy she could muster, and now her thin shoulders were shaking. But then she added, "I'm never going anywhere ever again."

Looking at her emaciated sister lying there, Tomoko could see what three years of serving a huge household under a strict mother-in-law and being betrayed in marriage had done to Gin.

"Gin, don't give up. You'll feel better soon."

Tomoko rubbed her sister's back, and she could feel her sadness. That sadness grew and grew until Tomoko felt it as her own, as a fellow woman.

3

Gin spent the days in her spacious tatami room. Most of the time she stayed in bed, but whenever she was feeling good, she got up and sat on top of the bedding. From there, looking beyond the hallway through the windows that ran from floor to ceiling, she could see the garden. There were lanterns and a pond with a grove of palm trees at its edge. Gin had played there as a child and knew every inch of it. She could close her eyes and recite the name of every tree and shrub, and where each was planted.

Right now she could recall nothing of the Inamura home. All she could remember was the layout of their garden. It was similar to this one, and there had been one room in the house where she could sit and look out on it. Gin was sure she had spent more time there gazing at the garden than she had looked at anything inside the house.

Now at home, Gin spent all her waking time reading. There were as many books as she could read in the family study. When her father had been well, he had spent much of his time there, but now almost nobody used it. Gin had it all to herself. But there were times when she was suddenly seized with terror at the thought that someone might be watching her. Then she remembered that she was at home, far from her mother-in-law, Sei.

Dr Mannen Matsumoto travelled some distance on horseback to the Ogino house on the fifth, fifteenth and twenty-fifth of each month to teach Gin's brother Yasuhei and several of his friends from the area. One evening the breeze carried Mannen's voice into Gin's room as he read aloud. She did not recognize the words; it must have been a book she had not read. As a child, Gin had sat behind her brothers, listening in on their lessons. She wanted to do the same thing now, but Mannen knew the secret of her disease, and she was too ashamed ever to ask him to teach her again.

When the lesson was over, Mannen came in to see Gin.

"How are you?"

Gin briefly reported her symptoms over the last ten days to him. Mannen listened, prescribed a new medicine, and then let his eyes fall on the book she had been reading. "Reading complicated books like this must be tiring for you."

"I read a little at a time, when I'm bored."

"Is that so? I've written a book myself recently. I'll give you a copy."

"What's it called?"

"*Bunsai zassho*. It's a book of my thoughts on living in the countryside."

"I would love to read it!" As they spoke, Gin forgot that Mannen was her doctor. Once again he was her teacher and she was still a young girl.

"You know, you shouldn't stay cooped up in this room all the time. When you're feeling well, why not go outside for a walk?"

"Yes, thank you," responded Gin, but she had no desire to leave the house. There were ten servants in the house alone. If she ventured out onto the estate grounds, she would run into the tenant farmers and neighbours, and even visitors from Tokyo. In the house none of her family, let alone the servants, made any mention of what she was doing there. Her mother had told them only that she was recovering from an illness. They all greeted her silently if they passed her in the hall, but nobody asked after her health or how she was feeling, nor did they ask about the Inamuras.

The servants just quietly kept an eye on her. It was the most considerate thing they could do for a woman who had left her husband's home. Gin was grateful for their kindness, but it was also suffocating. The neighbours, on the other hand, were still looking for some decisive sign of what she was doing there. They acted as if they had only her best interests at heart, but Gin knew they were intensely curious. What would they say if they found out that a barren woman with gonorrhoea was back with her parents and just doing as she pleased? Even the strong-willed Gin was not prepared to go outside and face them.

"You must be bored, but people do talk. You're probably right to stay inside for now." Mannen looked affectionately at Gin, who sat so properly before him. "I have to admit that I don't mind having such a clever young woman nearby." He smiled. "Sulking can be poisonous. You should think about picking up your studies again."

"That would be wonderful!" These days learning was the only thing that lifted Gin's spirits.

"You'll recover before long. Then we can get back to work." Mannen knew better than anyone how long it would take to nurse Gin back to health. She was sure he was just trying to cheer her up, but she appreciated it anyway.

"I think I'll send Ogie over to see you. She's still as headstrong as ever. Still unmarried. I think the two of you would get along." Ogie was Mannen's daughter. Gin had met her several times. Ogie was eight years older, and she sometimes taught Mannen's students when her father was away. Naturally she had been taught by her father, and had even read the Confucian *Analects* by the time she was ten. "She's just like you – all alone out here in the country."

While an educated woman was an object of awe and respect, Ogie must have been aware that behind her back people said she was eccentric. Furthermore, she was still single well past her twenty-fifth birthday, and so would almost certainly never marry.

"She's been asking me about you."

"I'd very much like to see her."

Ogie always wore a stern expression on her face, but that may have been the way she maintained her appearance as a female scholar.

"I'll have her bring over your medicine."

"Please don't put her to any trouble on my account."

"Don't worry; if it makes both of you feel any better, it will be two birds with one stone for me." So saying, Mannen went off to inform Gin's father of the decision before leaving the Ogino home.

Summer came. Robust cicadas began their chirping early each morning in the Chinese parasol trees, serenading the earliest human risers as they were just beginning to move about.

Gin still woke up each morning fearful of being late for her chores. A voice in her head warned insistently that she had to be up before her mother-in-law, and that she needed to run out the kitchen door to wash her face. But while the voice urged her to hurry, her body was much too leaden to comply.

Now when Gin woke up and looked around in alarm, she could see the sun peeking through gaps in the storm doors that were closed each night, and a thin strip of sunlight stretching from her shoulders down to her feet. At the Inamuras, she remembered, the sunlight had come in at a different angle. Finally she realized she was in Tawarase and did not have to get up early. A wave of relief spread through her body and she took a deep breath.

Since returning home, Gin had begun to put on a little weight. The upside-down triangle of her face was slowly regaining its soft oval shape. Her illness was no better and she still did not have much of an appetite, so her improved appearance must have been due to being able to relax in her childhood home.

After supper, the maid, Kane, filled a basin with warm water and brought it to Gin's room. "Shall I wring out a towel for you?"

"I can do it myself." Gin put her book down. The white half-moon had begun to shine in the fading sky.

"You're feeling much better, I see," said Kane.

"Do you think so?" Gin had to admit that her reflection in the mirror each morning was showing improvement. The dull, slack skin on her face was gradually getting firmer.

"Tawarase water must suit you better." Kane had cared for Gin when she was small, and she had always doted on her. "Why don't you stay?"

"What?"

"I think it would be best for you." Kane laughed lightly, and Gin wondered how much she knew.

Gin sat up, soaked the towel in the basin and wrung it out. She still had a fever, so she could not bathe, but she wiped herself with a towel like this whenever she felt well enough. She had to do it at least once a day during the humid weather to rinse off the perspiration. She also aired her bedding once every five days to prevent her room becoming damp and uncomfortable.

22

Gin sat behind a screen to clean herself. Her mother helped her whenever she had time. "Let me do it today," she would say. Kayo wiped Gin's body thoroughly but gently. Gin had bathed with her mother-in-law before, and Sei had even washed her back for her, but that had felt entirely different. While Kayo cleaned her daughter, her hands would occasionally stop moving and Gin would feel anxious as she wondered what was preoccupying her mother. Afterwards, Kayo would go and throw out the water while Gin climbed back into bed. Gin had always been careful to thank her mother-in-law for any little favour, but such a polite exchange would have felt awkward with her own mother.

One night, it was already dark by the time Kayo finished. The night insects were chirping, and the moon was growing brighter. Kayo turned on a lamp and began folding the underclothes Gin had changed out of. Then she began to speak, almost as if she had just remembered something.

"I'm going to see the Inamuras tomorrow."

Gin lifted her head, startled at hearing the name of her husband's family. Neither of them had mentioned it once since Gin had returned home.

"Am I right to assume you have no intention of going back?"

Gin was silent.

"We can't just leave things the way they are."

Gin looked down. Of course she had no desire to return to Kawakami, but she wanted to know how her mother felt about it first. She was sure her mother wanted her to return to her husband.

"What do you want me to do, Mother?"

"I'm asking you what you want. I'm not the one who has to go. You are."

Gin cringed under her mother's gaze.

"It's all up to you." Kayo was determined.

"But—"

"Don't worry about what the neighbours say. I don't care what the rumours are. I want to know how you really feel."

Gin was about to speak, but then she remembered her father.

Kayo seemed to read her mind. "Leave your father and the others in the house to me." Kayo was being perfectly honest with her daughter. She felt responsible for what had happened and this was the only way she could express those feelings. She was not giving Gin special treatment just because she was sick. The marriage Kayo, Ayasaburo and the go-betweens had arranged had only wounded Gin, and Kayo felt obliged to let her daughter make a free choice.

"What is your decision?" Kayo persisted.

"Let me... stay here... please."

"So you won't be going back?"

"No." Gin looked her mother in the eye and spoke with conviction.

"In three days, your go-between is going to come with some-one from the Inamuras. We will ask them for a divorce."

"Divorce?" Gin was flustered to be finally using the term and discussing it directly with her mother.

"If we make the request, the Inamuras should have no objec-tion. And you agree to this?"

Gin was silent again.

"You will go ahead with the separation?"

Gin hesitated again, fear rather than uncertainty holding her back now.

"You'll do it?"

"Yes." Gin closed her eyes and nodded..

"Then I'll go and tell your father." Kayo stood without making a sound, and left the room.

Alone in her room, Gin contemplated for the first time the notion that she really was going to be a divorced woman. She tried saying the word quietly to herself, but it still did not feel as though it was happening to her. She spent the next few days in a state of anxiety. Waiting for the divorce she both wanted and feared was agonizing.

"We're starting formal procedures for the divorce," Kayo announced to her on the evening of the third day. It still sounded to Gin as though they were discussing someone else. She stared at the sunlight blazing through the paper of the shoji doors from the summer sunset, aware that her life was taking a major turn.

* * *

Ten days later, on a hot, dry summer day, Gin's belongings arrived back in Tawarase. She could hear hurried voices and the whinnying of horses. She tried to figure out who had come from the Inamuras, but she did not recognize any of the voices.

"We'll put everything in here. We can go through it all later and put anything you don't need in the next room." Kayo was directing two men who worked for the Oginos as they carried in Gin's things. They brought in everything but her kitchen utensils. Gin sat up and watched as the room began to fill with her dressers, chests and dressing table.

"We'll look through your clothes later. There's no rush," Kayo said briefly, and left the room again. Gin heard her speaking to someone, but she could not hear the other person's voice. She waited to see if someone from the Inamuras' would come in to see her or whether her mother would summon her out, but the bustle outside quietened down without anyone else coming into her room. Apparently neither Kanichiro nor Sei had made the journey.

Gin looked around the room, now full of furniture. She wondered if she would spend the rest of her life in this room surrounded by it all, as though walled into a corner.

It was past nine o'clock when Kayo finished her bath and came in to see her daughter. Gin had already been through most of her clothes.

"You can put the winter things in a storage box," said Kayo, bringing one in for her. There were kimonos that Gin had never even worn. They had been brought back exactly as she had taken them, having made a simple round trip from Tawarase to Kawakami and back again. She wondered if she would ever have an opportunity to wear them. Fragile silk crêpe and *ichiraku* weaves in brightly coloured patterns could only be worn for five or six years. Gin was sure that she would not be walking about in such finery within their lifetime. She felt almost as sorry for the kimonos as she did for herself.

"The Inamuras told us what they are telling people." Kayo spoke as she folded an under-kimono. Gin put her hand to her

25

hair and turned around to look at her mother. "The reason for the divorce is that you are frail and unable to bear children. We've agreed to go along with that. It will do for now. You understand that, don't you?"

Gin knew that it did not matter how she felt. It had all been settled.

"They've got their appearances to keep up too, I'm sure," Kayo continued, clearly indicating that appearances were something the Ogino family also needed to consider. "Anyway, it's all for the best."

Gin had to admit that she *was* frail. She had been unable to fulfil her duties as a wife and daughter-in-law because she was sick. But it had not been her illness to start out with. Her husband had given it to her. Gin was the victim. Saying she was "unwell" certainly blurred the reality of the situation. She supposed anyone who saw how thin and weak she had become would easily be convinced. She had to admit, the Inamuras had come up with a convenient reason for the divorce.

Nevertheless, Gin was pained to be branded as unable to bear children. She remembered reading in a book on feminine deportment entitled *Women's Great Learning* the phrase "a woman who bears no children shall leave her husband's home". In those days, the label "barren" was a common reason for divorce. But it was an insulting one that denied a woman any value apart from producing children. Gin wondered if she really was barren. The book had even given three years as the limit for producing a child. The more Gin thought about it, the angrier she became. Her husband had not only ruined her health but stolen her femininity. She could no longer be considered a whole woman by society.

"Well, they did apologize." Kayo spoke again. Gin took no comfort from those words. All men had to do was apologize. What were women supposed to do? Call it fate and give in?

"Mother." Gin spoke with a determined voice. Kayo put the kimono she had been folding to one side. "Mother, I never—"

"I know what you want to say, and I understand. But what's done is done, and this is the only way to settle the matter."

So, it's all a matter of honour, is it? thought Gin.

"This is something that men do. I understand he doesn't indulge himself more often than is usual."

"But—"

"He's the son of a rich family. It's only natural that he'd go to Kumagaya occasionally to enjoy himself. I'm sure he wasn't aware he had the disease."

"But that still doesn't mean—" Gin wanted to argue that it still hardly made getting an incurable disease from him something to just resign herself to. Gin had actually smelt other women on Kanichiro. She would never forgive him.

"It's a shame that it happened to you. As your mother, I apologize."

"Mother!" Gin had not spoken with the intention of provoking her mother to say such a thing.

"Just pretend it's all been a bad dream, and try to get over it as quickly as you can."

As a sixteen-year-old girl, Gin had dreamt about her future husband. Three years before, when she travelled up the river to her new home, that dream had been grand and detailed. She had been sad to leave her mother, but full of hopes for her new life. Gin looked back at that girl with scorn and disbelief now. How simple she'd been! How naive.

"Come on, it's time for bed." At Kayo's urging, Gin climbed into her bedding and pulled the comforter over her face. "Forget everything and go to sleep."

Gin cried for a while after her mother left. It was not sadness that provoked the tears, but they would not stop. The room was thick with the humid summer heat. She could see a faint light coming through the shoji from the night sky. Gin looked towards that weak light and thought how wrong it was that only women should be made to suffer in a situation like this.

4

Ogie came to visit Gin. Her hair was pulled back in a bun, and she wore a dark blue kimono with wide *hakama* trousers over it – a style similar to any male scholar's, and an exceptionally modern outfit for a woman to be wearing in a country village. She had the same wheat-coloured complexion as Gin, but was about half a head taller. She had a long, thin face atop her long, thin body.

People often voiced the opinion that Ogie was unfriendly and masculine, but Gin found her nothing of the sort when just the two of them were talking together. Ogie was a scholar, but she was also licensed as a teacher of tea ceremony, flower-arranging and even kimono-making. Gin thought she might be considered unapproachable merely because people were intimidated at how well she did everything she set her hand to.

"There are other ways for women to get through life than getting married and having children. There's no shame in a woman becoming a scholar and then using her knowledge to make a living." It was a bold statement, but Ogie brought up the subject of Gin's future the very first time she came to see Gin. Gin was slightly stunned, but she found herself looking at Ogie with respect.

"What good does it do to get married and follow the orders of your mother-in-law and husband, and then be completely tied down by children?" The gleam of passion in Ogie's eyes as she spoke gave her the look of an animal eyeing its prey.

Since she had returned home, everyone had been kind to Gin, treating her with sympathy. They all told her that she should put the bad memories behind her, but no one ever mentioned what lay ahead. There was no doubt that they considered her future miserable and devoid of hope. Everyone who saw her tossed a few pleasant words her way, and then left as quickly as they could manage. Gin had grown used to this, and Ogie's words were a refreshing surprise. She drank them down like a glass of cool water.

"I don't plan to ever marry again."

29

"I never intended to in the first place!" Ogie was not one to mince words. At twenty-seven she was already well past the marrying age. Her father said that she enjoyed studying so much that she forgot all about starting a family, and had now missed her chance. Apparently, though, that was not entirely true. As she was growing up, Ogie had carefully observed how young wives were treated in country homes, and she had been unable to find any meaning in it. She did not believe that merely following the rules of the house and the customs of a small, closed society had any value for her. It was not that she had forgotten about marriage, but rather that she had well-considered qualms about it.

"Maybe it was lucky for you that you got sick and came back home." Ogie had heard all about Gin's illness from her father, and did not flinch from mentioning it.

"Lucky?" Gin was startled.

"Of course. Now that you're rid of your ties to that household and all the limitations it entailed, you're free to make the most of your talents."

"My talents?" This was not a phrase Gin was familiar with. She had never thought of herself as having any talent. She had never studied with any real goal in mind – it was just something that she did because she liked it.

"My father said that it was rare for someone your age to be able to understand the books you read. There aren't even many men around who can understand them. He said it was a waste for a girl like you to have to spend your life keeping some man in good humour."

Gin was aghast at this.

"There's no reason for you to hide yourself away in this room."

"But I'm divorced."

"So?" Ogie laughed – it was the open-hearted laugh of a man. "Are you trying to say that getting a divorce has affected your mind? Has it affected your ability to read and understand? Have you forgotten anything you used to know?" Ogie leant forwards almost into Gin's face. "It's such a bore having to worry about whether someone is divorced or married. Being single means nothing in terms of how intelligent you are."

"Yes, I agree." Ogie had helped put into words the vague thoughts that had been floating around Gin's mind.

"There's no need for you to worry about what anyone thinks."

"But what others see is what I am. My existence is reflected in the eyes of other people – isn't it?"

"That's what you've always been taught," answered Ogie, looking at Gin with exasperation and compassion in equal measures.

"Is it wrong?"

"Times are changing, you know. The Tokugawas have lost power and the government has been completely reformed." Ogie had a faraway look in her eyes. "I've seen more of Tokyo than most people around here. Everything is moving and changing. It's breathtaking how fast it's all happening."

Gin thought about how the Toné River could be navigated down to the Edo River and on to Tokyo. If she followed the same course, she might find somewhere she could lead a new life.

Ogie continued, "The opportunity will come. Until then, you should spend your time honing your abilities."

"Me?"

"That's right. You're younger than I am. That means you have that much more potential." All of a sudden Gin felt as if she were in a dream, riding the wings of a bird and sailing into space. "The main thing is not to give up."

Gin nodded as she looked into Ogie's eyes, brimming with conviction.

Dr Mannen was over fifty and his wife had died five years before. Ogie took care of the house and looked after her father's needs. She also taught the young men who came to their home for lessons whenever he was out teaching or seeing patients. Even if she had wanted to get married, it would have been difficult for her to do so.

As busy as she was, Ogie still found time two or three times a month to visit Gin. She wore her mannish attire of wide *hakama* trousers over a plain-weave kimono. And she always came with a new book tucked under her arm for Gin to read.

31

"The lady teacher is on her way to the Ogino home to see their divorced daughter," the gossip-loving villagers whispered among themselves as they watched Ogie stride by. "They are both quite clever. And single. I'm sure they have *plenty* to talk about."

"I'm back again." Ogie always came through the garden instead of the front entrance. Spotting her there, Gin felt as happy as if all of the flowers in the garden had burst into bloom and the sun had brightened.

And it was much the same for Ogie. Gin was younger, but she was the only woman she had ever met with whom she could chat freely, spicing up the conversation with lines of classic Chinese poetry. With anyone else, Ogie had to carefully compose herself to project a certain image and, despite her position as Dr Mannen's daughter and as a teacher and scholar in her own right, she was unable to speak openly with men either. With Gin, however, she was free of such constraints.

On her visits, Ogie spent the first hour teaching Gin new kanji characters. Next she would talk to her about new books and what was happening in Tokyo. Later their talk would turn to more feminine topics, like sewing.

When Ogie was with her, Gin was animated and cheerful, as if a spell had been cast over her. As soon as Ogie left, however, Gin drooped back into lethargy. Anyone who happened to glance at the two women chatting and saw Gin full of life and overflowing with confidence would have been shocked to see her so listless and gloomy a short while later.

Left alone, Gin tormented herself with thinking of the ways a woman in her position could be described: chronically ill, barren, divorced and a parasite. She would stay in that melancholic state until Ogie's next visit some ten days later.

She did not have to concern herself with her parents, brothers or any of the servants. She could get up when she pleased and go back to bed whenever it suited her. She was served meals whether she asked for them or not. It certainly looked like a comfortable life, but Gin did not enjoy it. She needed a direction, some purpose in her life, and she cared little whether it was hard or if she had to suffer for it. The present was peaceful and uneventful, but Gin needed a goal to work towards. Living each day in bland comfort without any hope for the future was more than she could bear.

It was only during her time with Ogie that Gin had a glimpse of the light and could feel as though once it had found her it would continue to shine on her. But as soon as Ogie was gone, Gin would wake from the spell of her friend's inspiring speeches and look around to see that nothing had changed. She was still in the countryside, in a room in the house she had been born in. The energy of Tokyo life had yet to arrive here. Gin began to think that she would waste away with disease and old age before she ever had a chance to experience it.

Summer passed, and autumn was upon them. Gin still came down with a fever several times a month, forcing her to take to bed for four or five days each time. Pain and discharge persisted. In late October Gin found herself in bed again. The warm autumn sun had felt so welcoming that she had rolled up her bedding for three full days. She had wiped down the tatami in her room too, but even that small effort had taken its toll. Gin was amazed at her lack of stamina.

My body is still tainted by the disease he gave me. Heavy with fever, Gin dreamt that poison was eating away at her, turning her into a single black pillar full of holes. She woke up to hear a raging wind. It was the middle of the night, and the house was completely still. Every few minutes a sideways blast of wind and rain slammed into the storm doors, and she could hear the zelkova and palm branches being whipped back and forth.

Kayo was asleep in the next room. "Mother?" Gin called out quietly, but her small voice disappeared in the sound of the storm. She tried to remember her dream, but it had lost its coherency in her mind and only the eerie feeling of it remained. *What will I do if anything happens to my mother?* Gin's mind filled with anxiety about the future, and she was awake for several hours before falling into a light doze just before dawn.

When she awoke later that morning, the wind and rain were even stronger. The hurried sounds of footsteps and frantic voices signalled an emergency. Gin got up and opened the shoji to see the downpour accompanied by a gale-force wind. Rain was leaking through the cracks in the windows into the hallway.

Water had already begun to fill the garden, and the ground was no longer visible.

"Are you up?" Kane, the maid, came running down the hallway. The hem of her kimono was pulled up and her feet were bare. "It's a terrible storm!" she continued in the local dialect.

"Is the river bank holding?"

"Your mother and brother have gone out to check the Dokanbori River."

Gin watched the trees swinging crazily in the wind.

"They say the river burst its banks in Ono early this morning. That means the same could happen here by noon, so we've been told to get everyone up to the second floor of the house. I'll carry your bedding."

Gin changed out of her nightclothes. She was still chilled from the fever, but there was no time to waste.

The village of Tawarase was in fact a small triangle of land bordered on the east by the Toné and to the south by the Fuku. The Dokanbori, a tributary of the Fuku, also flowed through Tawarase and emptied into the Toné. From the end of the Edo period through the early Meiji years, a raised bank ran along the opposite bank of the Fuku River, but this had been built to protect the area on that side of the Fuku, and for Tawarase it had meant an increased chance of damage from floods. There was nothing in the form of a protective embankment on the Tawarase side of the Toné. For this reason Tawarase was known to the surrounding villages as "the watering place".

At noon, neither the rain nor the wind showed any sign of abating. Ensconced on the second floor, which was usually used only to keep silkworms, Gin looked out over the fields and roads covered uniformly with white water. The roads were devoid of people except for occasional groups of four or five hurrying towards the river bank. Some held long poles and others shouldered sandbags. Their figures, clothed in straw raincoats, quickly disappeared into the distance.

"Gin, you should lie down." Gin turned to see her mother, her hair still wet from the rain.

"Tell me how things are."

"I think we'll last until evening." Kayo turned her anxious face

34

to the window. The estate was surrounded by fields of water. "If it doesn't let up soon, though..." Raindrops continued to beat against the windows. It was almost as if the sky had gone mad. "Now get back into bed. You'll get a fever again!"

"But—"

"Don't worry. Everything will be fine." Her words offered Gin some relief. "Have you taken your medicine?"

"Yes, a while ago."

After Gin lay down again, Kayo gently patted down the edges of the covers and then stood up. "There may only be rice balls for dinner."

Just then there was a clatter downstairs and a voice called up, "Mrs Ogino, ma'am! Another couple of feet and the banks will flood!" It was Gensuke, one of the farmhands.

"There should be some more sandbags in the storage rooms. And get the boat ready," Kayo called back to him as she hurried down the stairs.

Night fell and the rain continued. They were unable even to hear the bell of the temple just beyond the canal. The cooks had begun preparing emergency rations early in the afternoon, cooking up rice and forming it into balls, enough to last for two days. By early evening, the entire household was up on the second floor crammed in among the silkworms.

The Dokanbori burst its bank just after eight o'clock that night. Despite the darkness, they could all see the turgid waters swirling on both sides of the estate, headed for the village.

The rain continued all the next day, and only began to let up that evening. By then the back-flow of the Toné had added to the flood, keeping Tawarase underwater. The first sunset in three days drenched the flooded fields in red. Kayo looked down at the sea covering the fields. Ears of corn and single *geta* sandals floated here and there. The entire household gathered at the windows, but no one had a word to say.

Gin's brother, Yasuhei, finally broke the silence. "There goes the work of an entire year. What did I do in my past life to deserve being born here?" Gensuke nodded in forlorn agreement as Yasuhei continued bitterly. "What a waste. All that work – knowing this could happen at any time."

"What are you saying?" Kayo turned and chided them. "How can you complain about being born in the watering place? It's water that gives us life."

Yasuhei and Gensuke were silent. In a strange way, what Kayo said made sense. Nobody could accuse the Toné of being all bad. It flowed through the centre of the Kanto Plain, a major artery that merged with the Edo River to link the northern prefectures to Tokyo. The crops grown on either side of its banks were taken to the markets of the capital city in large sailing boats that anchored regularly at ports along the river, filling the towns with crowds of merchants and travellers.

Summer crops were occasionally damaged by flooding, but in the years when there were no floods, both spring and summer crops were bountiful thanks to the fertile soil that was carried downstream by the river. The Tawarase area was one of the very few regions that were able to make their entire living from crops – vegetables, grains, indigo and silk. This was why it was difficult to condemn the river for the damage wrought by infrequent floods. Kayo was convinced that it was the fate of the people born here that both joy and sorrow were inextricably tied to water.

As soon as the rain stopped, the villagers got out their boats and visited homes isolated by the flood to deliver food and chicken feed. No matter how accustomed they all were to such disasters, some people were left hungry and sick, or an expectant mother would have gone into labour.

Gin spent that night on the second floor with her family and the servants. The house was built on a slightly raised piece of ground and was safe from being washed away, but the first floor was in no condition for them to move back downstairs. Gin and her father were the only two given the space to stretch out and sleep. All the rest slept wrapped in quilts, leaning against their belongings or the wall. During the day too, to Gin's intense shame, only she and her elderly father were lying down and resting, while the others were up and working.

A cloudless blue sky greeted them all the next morning. The water quickly receded in the warm autumn sunlight. The crops that had been standing high and green a few days before were now covered in mud, sediment and rocks. The household stared at the devastation in silence.

"All right, let's get the tatami mats back downstairs," Kayo called out to the stunned men.

Some time after noon, Gin heard that the first floor had been cleaned and so began to fold up her bedding. She was free of fever, almost as if the storm had chased it away. She was determined to take care of her own bedding at least, and she turned towards the window. All she could see were muddy fields sprinkled here and there with puddles in which the afternoon sun was reflected.

Out there in the fields, she saw a figure working away; she could see it bending over and then standing up over and over again. It was her mother. Kayo was dressed in cotton work clothes, a white scarf tied to shield her face from the sun, and was picking up stones that had been carried inland from the river. She was tiny, but she worked ceaselessly. Every once in a while Gin saw her stand and point, clearly instructing the men working alongside her. She could also see in Kayo's posture that she was not discouraged; in fact she looked positively animated.

I am my mother's daughter. Gin remembered that she, like her mother, had been born and raised in the watering place.

"Maybe I should go to Tokyo to find a doctor who might be able to cure me." In early November, about the time life had begun to settle down after the flood, Gin told her mother what was on her mind.

"I've wondered about that myself. I'll talk it over with Dr Mannen." Kayo was sure that he was doing everything he could for Gin, but she went to see him a few days later anyway.

Mannen welcomed Kayo and listened attentively as she explained what she was there for. "Was this Gin's idea?"

"Has she ever mentioned such a thing to you?"

"I can't say it's a complete surprise." Mannen smiled. "As a matter of fact, I've been thinking she should go to Juntendo Hospital to be seen by Dr Shochu Sato."

"Dr Sato?"

"Yes, he is the Chief Imperial Physician, and one of the best doctors in the country."

"But would such a grand doctor agree to see Gin?"

"If you'll allow me, I'll be glad to provide an introduction. I met him when I was in training."

"I'd never be able to thank you enough if you could get him to take a look at Gin." Kayo was anxious not to discourage this spark of energy in her daughter.

"Let me make one thing clear," continued Mannen. "Even if Dr Sato agrees to treat Gin, she may never fully recover from the disease."

"I understand. But we would all be able to accept the outcome if we knew she had been seen by the best doctor in Japan."

"Good. I'll write to him directly, then. You can plan your departure as soon as we hear from him."

"But she's still so weak."

"Don't worry. Her fever is like a volcano that explodes from time to time. She'll be fine in ten days or so. She'll be well enough to go by then."

"All right, then," agreed Kayo, "I'll leave the decisions to you." Indeed, Mannen was the only person she could depend on when it came to Gin.

"It pains me to see Gin closed up inside her room with no hope of a cure. She has always been one of my favourite students, you know."

"She'll be so pleased to know you feel that way," smiled Kayo.

"I'm not sure how much all of this will cost," Mannen warned.

"I'll take care of that. It will all be worth it if she regains her health." Kayo, of course, had no idea how much money Mannen was talking about, but they were the wealthiest family in Tawarase, and she knew her husband would agree to pay the expenses.

"OK. I'll let you know as soon as I get a reply from Dr Sato."

"Thank you so much. I'll be waiting to hear from you." Whatever the results, Kayo felt she should allow Gin to go to Tokyo. If nothing else, it would at least be a gesture of how much she wanted to make amends for the miserable state to which Gin had been condemned.

5

Gin was admitted to Juntendo Hospital in Tokyo in mid-December 1870, accompanied by Kayo. It would have been more convenient all around to have started treatment after the New Year festivities, but the two had departed the moment they heard of a bed that had become available.

The head of the hospital was Dr Shochu Sato, a surgeon known and respected throughout the Kanto area. The son of a court physician, Shochu had been born in 1827 and was forty-three years old by the time Gin came to him.

He had come to Edo – modern-day Tokyo – at the age of ten to learn Chinese classics and medicine, and at sixteen he had started studying Western medicine under Daizen Sato. When in 1843 Daizen Sato moved back to his home town of Sakura to build the Sakura Juntendo Hospital, Shochu went with him. Daizen came to love and appreciate the outstanding talents of his pupil, and ten years later named him as his successor, adopting him into the Sato family, despite already having five children of his own. Shochu became the legal head of the Sato family, and in 1864 was ordered by the clan to go to Nagasaki to study under the renowned Dutch doctor Johannes Pijdius Catharinus Pompe van Meer der Voort, known familiarly to the Japanese as "Pompe". There he studied night and day along with the other apprentices. Even among such distinguished company, his talent was evident. It is said that when Shochu returned to Sakura, Pompe presented him, and him alone, with several medical books written by Dr Georg Stromeyer, one of the most progressive physicians of the day.

On his arrival back in Sakura, Shochu reformed the clan's medical system, with the construction of a hospital and the establishment of a department of health. His most significant achievement, however, was the abandonment of Chinese herbal cures in favour of Western medicine – a revolutionary move.

Even the Edo shogunate had heard of Dr Shochu Sato and ordered him into its service – an order that the doctor's home clan politely but firmly refused. The new Meiji government also bestowed Dr Sato with a number of titles, including that of Chief Imperial Physician. The following year, however, he resigned his elite posts following a run-in with a high government official, and instead turned his efforts to setting up his own Hongo Juntendo Hospital in north-eastern Tokyo.

It was on her second day at Juntendo that Gin met Dr Sato for the first time. He was a small man with a stern face and piercing eyes, his hair almost entirely grey. After reading the letter of introduction from Dr Mannen, he scanned the records from the preliminary examinations by his staff, before turning to face Gin herself. Behind him stood ten or so medical students under his tutelage. Nervous in front of so many men, Gin kept her eyes on the floor.

"How is Dr Mannen?" asked Dr Sato.

"Fine," Gin eventually managed to stammer.

"I'm glad to hear that." The niceties thus completed, Dr Sato nodded, held out Gin's records for the students to see, and began speaking in a foreign-sounding language she could not follow, although she was sure that they were discussing her symptoms. She stayed perched tensely on the examining stool.

When Dr Sato had finished his explanation, he turned back to Gin. "Let's take a look."

Gin had no idea what he meant by this. She looked up to see a man approaching her, his sleeves rolled up, and gesturing silently for her to come. Gin followed him into a small room curtained off with a white cloth.

"Climb up onto this," he said.

Gin gasped as she saw the leather-covered table with black leather stirrups attached to it.

"The doctor is going to examine you," the man said tonelessly. "Come on, now."

Gin climbed hesitantly onto the table and hunched over defensively. She heard the doctor's footsteps approaching and coming to a halt beside her.

"Let me examine the infected area."

Gin closed her eyes and bit her lip until she tasted blood. She was certain it would be better for her to die than to be exposed here to these men. Were doctors actually allowed to do things like this? If the doctor had been a woman it might have been different, but it was unthinkable for a woman to show herself like this to any man.

"All I want to do is to see what's wrong with you." Dr Sato folded his arms and waited. She was going to have to do this of her own free will. Gin looked over at the man who had brought her in, pleading with her eyes for him to come to her aid.

"Let the doctor examine you," he spoke up. "You want to get better, don't you?"

Gin felt the last bit of energy leave her body. Her arms and legs slowly unfolded as if they were under some sort of spell. Her knees parted, and her pale thighs appeared from out of her underclothes.

"A little more, please."

Gin's legs refused to move another inch.

"You'll have to forgive me, then."

As the doctor spoke, Gin felt the cold palms of a man's hands on her knees. She automatically tried to close her legs and sit up, but by now she was being held down by several strong men, and was unable to move.

The next few minutes were completely erased from Gin's memory, as her mind went blank from shock and humiliation. When it was all over, the first man lightly tapped her feet to rouse her, but she continued to lie there with her eyes closed. She was shaking when she finally managed to rearrange her clothing and get off the table. The doctor's assistant helped her down and back onto the examination stool. Gin's face was drained of colour.

"You've been in a great deal of pain, haven't you?" The doctor who had seemed so cruel a few moments before now spoke in a gentle voice. "The treatment is going to take time, I'm afraid. You'll have to resign yourself to it if you want to get better."

Then Dr Sato turned back to the group of students and spoke again in that incomprehensible language. They listened attentively, shifting their gaze from the doctor to Gin. Now Gin was faced with the awareness that all of these young men, about

the same age as herself, had most likely been standing behind
Dr Sato when he examined her. She no longer cared about
being treated; she just wanted to go back to her room. *Why
me?* she screamed to herself. *Why do I alone have to endure this
punishment?* She was sure that death could not be any worse
than what she had just been through.

Back in her room, Gin collapsed in tears the moment she
saw her mother's face. "What happened?" asked Kayo. "The
doctor examined you, didn't he? What did he say?" Gin only
sobbed harder, wrapping her bedding tightly around herself.
"Did he scold you? What went wrong?" Kayo was at a loss as
Gin refused to answer her questions. She turned to one of the
women sharing the room with Gin. "I'm so sorry about all this
fuss she's making."

The woman was in her mid-thirties, the wife of a kimono-
shop owner from Nihonbashi. "This is her first visit to a
hospital, isn't it? I'm sure it must be a shock to her," she offered
understandingly.

"We've come all this way to put her in this grand hospital
and she's had the famous doctor see her – so what on earth is
she crying about now?" Unaware of what Gin had just been
through, Kayo was irritated by her daughter's behaviour.

"I can't say for sure," continued Gin's room-mate, "but she
might be crying because she has never had such a distressing
examination before. No matter how much she wants to be cured,
there can't be many women who can take being held down like
that. It must have been horribly embarrassing. I couldn't eat for
two days after my first time."

The woman was recovering from a difficult childbirth, and had
been hospitalized with a persistent fever. Having experienced
such examinations herself, she had little trouble guessing the
cause of Gin's distress.

"Is that so?" Kayo looked over at her, and then back down at
her daughter sobbing in the bedclothes.

"You'd best leave her alone awhile. Comforting won't do any
good right now. She'll get used to it before long."

Kayo finally understood that Gin had been humiliated before
the great doctor, and it made her feel sorrier for her than ever.

"The wife of a doll-shop owner I know was having terrible bleeding, but she couldn't bring herself to have the doctor examine her. She was taking a Chinese herbal cure from a neighbourhood practitioner, but she just wasted away. By the time she finally plucked up her courage to go to a hospital, it was too late. She died less than a month later."

Despite her continuing fever, the kimono-shop proprietress obviously enjoyed chatting, and her forthright manner clearly placed her as being from the progressive Tokyo mercantile class. She raised herself a little, the better to converse with Kayo. "You know, with Western medicine, doctors have to see the problem to treat it. It's not like with Chinese medicine. But I don't care what anyone else says, it's hard to get over having your knees held down by some young doctor."

"Is that what they do?"

"How else are they going to get a look?"

Kayo had lived her entire life in the countryside, and could not begin to imagine such a thing. "Is there nothing else that can be done?" Western medicine was beginning to seem like some sort of demonic business to her.

By evening, Gin was worn out from weeping and, as the early winter night crept into the room, she finally lifted her head.

"Come on, eat now."

"I don't want anything."

In the light of the lamp, Kayo could see how bloodshot her daughter's eyes were. "You can't fret like this. You'll just have to bear the embarrassment if you want the doctor to cure you." Kayo was trying to convince herself as well as Gin. "You have to take your medicine after eating, so at least try a few bites." Kayo filled Gin's bowl with the rice gruel she had just made.

Gin was lying on her bedding laid out on tatami mats, while Kayo sat on the wooden floor. The kimono-shop proprietress was lying to Gin's left, and beyond her was a woman of about fifty suffering from joint pain. The room was a little over twenty square yards in size, and seemed rounded and bright in the lamplight. Kayo suddenly wondered what she and her daughter were doing in this strange place.

Gin managed to eat a bowl of gruel. She lay watching her mother's shadow against the sliding wooden door growing larger and then suddenly smaller again, as Kayo moved about the room.

"Here's your medicine." Kayo passed Gin a grey-coloured powder in its white paper wrapper. "This is supposed to be Western medicine."

The powder was odourless, utterly unlike the black colour and burnt smell of the herbal medicine that Gin was accustomed to.

"Come on, now."

At her mother's urging, Gin gulped it down, and a bitter taste spread throughout her mouth. The next moment, though, the powder had dissolved and was gone.

"How was it?"

Gin tilted her head to one side as she considered Kayo's question. A hint of the bitter taste remained in her mouth, and she knew the strange, foreign matter was flowing throughout her body. Gin felt as though the tide of Westernization that had been flooding the capital city had now finally begun to seep through her own being too.

6

Ten days after their arrival in Tokyo, Kayo was satisfied that Gin had settled into life at the hospital sufficiently for her to hire a girl to take care of Gin's daily needs, so that she herself could return home to Tawarase. It was 25th December, and the year was coming to an end. For patients, though, New Year held little meaning. No matter what the date, Juntendo Hospital was crammed with people waiting to see the great Dr Shochu Sato. Gin herself had only been admitted so quickly because of her letter of introduction from Dr Mannen.

Dr Sato saw outpatients in the morning and made the rounds of his hospital patients in the afternoon. He checked on them daily, visiting each room in turn. Once every three days, Gin was examined on the leather-covered table in a separate room. As each third day approached, she grew quiet and lost her appetite. No matter how she thought about it, she could not reconcile being a woman in that position in front of a man.

"Gin, the *karinto* vendor is here! I'd love something sweet. Would you go buy some for the two of us to share?" The kimono-shop proprietress who shared her room noticed Gin's morose mood and did her best to distract her and cheer her up. "Stop worrying about those examinations! The doctor is only trying to treat you. He's not doing it for his own enjoyment."

However, it was not such a simple matter for Gin. "Why do *I* have to do this?" Why had she, not her former husband, been thrown into this hell of humiliation? It was not fair. Fresh rage pricked at her, rousing her from the depths of her sadness.

"It doesn't do to think about it too seriously."

"But I hate it. I just can't stand it."

"Yes," her room-mate was forced to agree. "If the doctor were a woman, then at least it would be easier."

"A woman?" Gin lifted her head.

45

"I mean that it might not be so bad if a female doctor were doing the examinations."

"A female doctor..." Gin turned the unfamiliar phrase over in her mind. *Yes, if only the doctor were a woman and not a man. That's it! If I were being seen by a woman, I would gladly undergo any form of treatment!*

But the proprietress continued with a laugh, "Of course, you'd never find a woman doctor if you searched the entire country!"

Gin was no longer listening. *If there were women doctors, I and countless other women like me would be saved from such terrible shame.* Then another idea occurred to her. *Why don't I become a doctor and help those women?*

The sudden thought reverberated to the centre of Gin's being. It filled the emptiness in her nineteen-year-old heart, that of a girl whose marriage had failed and who was faced with a future devoid of hope.

The New Year arrived, and Gin spent it in her hospital room. She ordered soba noodles to eat on New Year's Eve and had *zoni* soup on the morning of 1st January, but that was the extent of her celebration. On 2nd January, however, a package of special New Year's *osechi* delicacies arrived from her mother in Tawarase. Gin was filled with nostalgia with every bite. Her room-mate shared some salted salmon sent from her home too, and although Gin was lonely, she ate well.

The hospital was closed to outpatients for the first three days of January, during which time Dr Sato also rested from his hospital rounds. Through the leafless trees of the hospital garden and surrounding alleys, Gin could hear the voices of children playing their New Year games. Gin knew her girlhood was over, but she enjoyed listening to them nonetheless.

On 4th January, the hospital resumed its normal routine, including examinations. By now, the dream that had been planted in Gin's mind had begun to take root. To begin with, she had wistfully aspired to becoming a doctor, but now she was absolutely determined to become one. Indeed, it was all she thought about. She had no idea how to accomplish this ambition, nor was she confident of success, but she would try her best. She could no longer hope for a normal woman's happiness, and that left her free to focus entirely on pursuing her dream.

"Open your legs." The cold voice of the doctor sent a chill through Gin. She kept her eyes squeezed shut, and thought of something that would take her mind off what was happening. She felt a man's hand on her knees and then inside her, opening her up as though she were a machine of some kind.

Previously, Gin had recited to herself, *Mother, Mother, please make it all end as quickly as possible! –* repeating it over and over until the examination was finished. She felt no pain, but her eyes were always wet with tears. Now, though, things were different. The doctor's voice was the same, but Gin no longer mentally implored her mother to rescue her. Instead, the instant she felt the hand on her knees, she screamed to herself, *I'm going to be a doctor! I'll show you!*

She heard the sound of metal on metal, she felt the liquid used to disinfect the diseased area, and she felt that part of her body being cleaned by a man. *I'm going to do it! And you'll be sorry!*

Her anger was not directed at anyone in particular – not at her husband, who had given her the disease, nor at the callous doctor, nor at the villagers who smirked behind her back. Perhaps it was directed at the woman inside her. But she was in no state to calmly analyse her feelings, and simply focused her entire concentration on her goal.

"Try to relax, please." The doctor's voice sounded impatient.

All that was alive was her mind; the rest of her was dead. In her humiliation, Gin did as ordered with her body, but her conviction continued to grow. The examination seemed to take an eternity, although it was no more than a few minutes.

"That'll be all."

As soon as the words were spoken, Gin's legs snapped shut as if operated by a spring. Her long prayer was over for now. Gin got off the table and rearranged her clothes. While pulling the front of her clothing together and retying the sash, she could feel her desire to be a doctor had grown, as if it were a baby inside her waiting to be born.

* * *

In mid-January Gin's eldest brother, Yasuhei, married Yai Takamori, the second daughter of a rich farming family in Nibu. Yai was twenty, the same age as Gin.

Of course, Gin was unable to attend the wedding, and would not have had the confidence to go even if there had been a palanquin to take her. It would have been inappropriate for someone with a disease like hers to attend anything as celebratory as a wedding. She told herself that it was better for everyone that she was in the hospital rather than at home. It was not long, though, before she regretted her decision. At the end of January, while the family was still in a festive mood, Gin's father suddenly died.

It took an entire day for the news to reach her. It was late at night and Gin had just fallen asleep when the brief note arrived informing her that Ayasaburo had suffered a heart attack during the early morning hours. Ayasaburo's health had been declining steadily over the past few years. In 1868, the first year of the Meiji era, he had quit as village headman, a position that had been in his family for generations. He had spent much of his time in bed, so nobody had expected him to live to an old age, but neither had they expected to lose him so suddenly and so soon.

The last time Gin had seen her father was when she and her mother had said goodbye to him before they set off for Tokyo. It was not as if Gin had ever had anything other than formal conversations with him, but he was her father and she knew that he had been concerned about her. Even in the few words he spoke, she had understood that much. *I wasn't even with him when he died!* Never had Gin felt so keenly how her illness had affected her ability to carry out her filial duty.

Spring in Tokyo arrived a little earlier than it did in Tawarase. Gin felt better as the weather got warmer. By April her fever had abated, and she was finally able to urinate without pain. The examinations that she hated so much were reduced to once every five days. She was still not allowed to leave for overnight visits, but she began taking walks in the streets around the hospital on sunny days.

In mid-April her room-mate, the kimono proprietress, was sent home. "Take care of yourself. Do your best to make a complete recovery, won't you?" She gave Gin an ornamental hairpin made of boxwood to remember her by, and added firmly, "No more crying, now."

"I've decided to become a doctor." Gin decided this was a good time to tell her what had been on her mind.

"A doctor?" She turned to look at Gin as she finished dressing. "Really?"

"Yes."

The woman gave Gin a long, searching look, and then smiled. "If you make it, you must remember to let me know. I'll be your first patient."

Juntendo Hospital was no more than a collection of wooden terrace houses. The other side of the street was lined with similar homes, all occupied by local residents. By day, the street was visited by vendors, street performers and sometimes beggars too.

Gin listened to a vendor hawking his wares. "Seedlings, seedlings! Morning glories! Corn! Cucumbers!" The morning started out with the tofu seller, followed by pedlars of sweet beans, steamed sweet potatoes, pipe-stem replacements and cooked beans. Then there was the *kamaboko* fish-paste hawker, and eventually she heard "Flowers! Flowers! Freshly cut flowers here!" Gin could not resist buying fresh flowers to decorate her room every few days. There were even vendors who, apparently unaware they were passing by a hospital, sold remedies for cracked skin, chilblains and other skin irritations. The noodle carts came out at night. Gin enjoyed them all. She could get a taste of the swirl of activity in Tokyo just by poking her head out the window.

The following February, a little over a year and two months after arriving at Juntendo, Gin was released to go back home to Tawarase. During her time in the hospital, she had not had surgery of any kind, although the infection had spread through her urethra to her bladder and ovaries.

Dr Sato's approach had been to keep the external infected area clean, something Chinese remedies did not do, and treat the infection with something more advanced than herbal medicine. Today Gin's hospital stay would seem extraordinarily long, but in those days it was not an unreasonable length of time to treat a serious case of gonorrhoea.

Dr Sato was well aware that Gin's disease was not actually cured, but had merely been tamed into remission. "There's no telling when the symptoms will return. Keep taking the medicine for the time being, and be careful to avoid fatigue or getting chilled," he told her frankly. It had been two months since her last bout of fever, and she had almost no pain when urinating. The only lingering symptom was a feeling of heaviness around her lower back; she was much better than she had been in the December when she had been admitted.

"Will I ever be able to bear children?" Gin wanted to check one last time.

"I regret to say it's impossible."

It was just as she'd guessed, but Gin was no longer thrown by this sad fact. The emptiness that it had left in her heart had long been replaced by her goal of becoming a doctor.

7

It was only a little more than a year since Gin had left, but in that brief time her family home had undergone a transformation. Her father, who for so many years had been laid up in the inner room, was no longer there, and his absence had wrought changes in the family.

For the years Ayasaburo had been incapacitated, Kayo had done both her own work and that of her husband. Now she suddenly looked older. Gin had been sure that things would be easier now that her mother was no longer at the beck and call of her father, but she was wrong. As with so many couples, the loss of one meant a loss of courage and youth in the other.

A brand-new memorial tablet for her father had been placed in the centre of the family altar, between those of Gin's grandparents. It was engraved with a posthumous name that suited her father well. Gin kneeled before the altar, brought her hands together, and thought about her father. He had often spent his time writing or reading books Gin knew nothing about. She could hear him clearing his throat as she tiptoed past his room, always careful not to disturb him. That was her only impression of him. She could not remember ever having enjoyed a friendly conversation with him.

Her mother had always occupied a position higher than Gin's own, and her father had been higher still. That was what her father had meant to her. They had lived in the same home, but otherwise he had seemed unconnected to her in any way. That was why she had always resented everything her mother had done for him. Even so, Gin was soon to learn the influence his presence had had on her position in the family.

"It's time to greet your brother. He's in the inner room," announced Kayo as she entered Gin's room.

"Yasuhei?"

"Come with me." Kayo led the way.

51

Gin had always greeted her father first whenever she came home, as a matter of courtesy. She had never gone to any trouble to greet her brother, however. Even on visits home after having married, Gin had done no more than exchange a simple greeting with him when they met for meals. Now, however, greeting Yasuhei had suddenly become the first order of business, and her mother was accompanying her. For the first time Gin realized that her brother had succeeded to the title of head of their family. It was only natural, but it felt strange.

Yasuhei's new wife, Yai, had a lovely complexion, but was tall and heavy. The Oginos had always been small and fine-boned, and Yasuhei was no exception, being of average height but thin and narrow-shouldered. In contrast, Yai was large-boned. That might have been why she looked a few years older than Gin, even though they were both the same age.

"I've just come home." First she formally greeted Yasuhei. He was five years older than Gin and she had never had much to talk about with him. As his father's heir, he had always been treated with preference. Even the food he ate had been different from the other children's. Yasuhei nodded briefly, and averted his eyes from Gin, although she was not sure whether this was merely embarrassment on his part. Raised with five sisters, he had never had a strong personality.

Next Gin bowed to Yai, who sat next to Yasuhei. "I am Yasuhei's youngest sister, Gin. I'm honoured to meet you."

"I'm Yai. Yes, it's an honour." Yai spoke in a leisurely tone that seemed to match her girth, but Gin felt a spark of tension between them. It was only a matter of time before Yai took over her mother's role as mistress of the household, although this did not occur to Gin at the time. "So, are you cured of your illness?"

"Yes, thank you." As Gin responded, she wondered why she found herself acting with such deference to someone who had so recently joined the family.

That evening she felt even more confused. Until now, her father had sat at the head of the table, and had eaten from a separate tray. His sons, Yasuhei and Masuhei, had sat on either side of him. Kayo and the other women occupied the lower end of the table. This was the way it had always been. Now, however, Yasuhei occupied his father's seat, and ate from his father's lacquer tray.

From her own place near the kitchen, Gin felt like she was looking at a family entirely different from the one she had been raised in. Everyone else, though, already appeared comfortable with the new arrangement.

The room Gin had used before she left for Tokyo was now occupied by Yasuhei and Yai. Gin slept in a smaller room next to the study, which had previously been used to store things like cushions and hibachi braziers when they were not needed. Once it had been cleaned out and furnished with her own things, Gin found it to be neat and cosy. The room's location in the corner of an L-shaped wing close to the bathroom was hardly ideal, but she did have a view of her beloved garden.

She knew that it made sense for the family's eldest son and his wife to occupy the largest room while she, the divorced younger sister, had a smaller one. She found herself resenting the other small changes that Yai was already beginning to make, though.

Just as before, Gin spent most of her time in her room. She cleaned and did her laundry, but otherwise she stayed inside, absorbed in her books. Kayo kept an eye out to make sure she did not get too depressed, but that was because she was unaware of the promise Gin had made to herself.

Ogie came to visit Gin a month after she arrived back in Tawarase. Instead of coming through the garden as before, she entered the house from the front door. Even Ogie, it appeared, was showing deference to the new wife.

"You look so much better." Ogie was amazed to see Gin's rounded, rosy cheeks. "So, you're fine?"

"The doctor told me that I still have the disease, and that I have to be careful to keep the symptoms from recurring."

"Really?"

Gin had to laugh as she nodded in answer to Ogie's undisguised disbelief. She was well enough to do that.

"Well, you look just fine to me," Ogie returned.

"I made a decision while I was in Tokyo." Gin had been waiting for a chance to share her secret with her friend.

"What is it?"

"Promise not to laugh." Gin looked up at a calendar she had posted in her room. On it she had written the subjects she planned to study that day: Chinese classics, history and maths. "I want to be a doctor."

"A doctor? You?"

"Yes, me."

"Really?"

Gin nodded again. Ogie took a closer look at Gin with her short-sighted eyes.

"I thought about it while I was in the hospital. I decided that someone has to be there to take care of the patients, the women... like me."

"Like you?"

"That's right. Women who have diseases in places that cause embarrassment." Gin could finally say this without flinching. "Do you think it's strange?"

Ogie looked at Gin's face for a few seconds longer, and then shook her head.

Gin went on. "There must be lots of women who have diseases like mine. But that doesn't mean that they are all seen by doctors. Who knows how many go without treatment because they are too ashamed to be examined? I want to do something for them. The way things are now is just not right. I mean, women are not to blame, but they are the ones who suffer most."

Ogie had never seen Gin glow like this before. Her father, Mannen, had said she had beautiful eyes, and now she saw for herself the brilliance with which they could shine.

"Can you understand what I'm trying to say?" Gin asked Ogie.

"I understand."

"I can see that you're shocked."

"That's not true."

"Yes, it is. I can see it in your eyes."

Ogie shrank back. "No, I'm not."

"So, you will support me?"

"Of course." Ogie had no problem saying this, but once the words had left her mouth, the realization of what Gin was proposing to do struck her with renewed force. All of a sudden Ogie was unsure whether willpower and effort alone could make a woman into a doctor. "What does your mother say?"

"I haven't told her yet. This is the first time I've told anyone in Tawarase."

Ogie was honoured that she was the first to know. At the same time, it was no small secret to be responsible for. "Will your mother let you do it?"

Kayo was a wise woman, but conservative. It was already a source of embarrassment to her that Gin was so interested in books, and Gin knew she would never allow her to go to Tokyo to try to become anything so unbecoming as a doctor. It would most likely be impossible to convince her mother that she was serious. This was an age where schooling, let alone an occupation, was considered unsuitable for women. On top of that, the profession of physician was so exalted that even few men could aspire to it.

"I wonder what I should do?" Gin had made her decision, but she didn't have the first idea about how to pursue it.

"Wait." Right now, it would mean nothing even if she got her mother's permission. Ogie herself did not know what Gin should do to become a doctor, but she could safely assume that she would have to become more accomplished in scholarly pursuits first. "There's no way for a woman to become a doctor of Western medicine."

"I know that, but I would like to talk to Dr Mannen about this."

"I'll let him know when I get home."

"If he won't mind talking to me, I'll visit him immediately."

Ogie nodded, still unconvinced there was any possibility of Gin realizing her dream.

In those days there were only a few paths to a medical degree, especially when the field was limited to Western medicine. In the whole of Japan there were just three institutions able to award degrees in medicine: one each in Tokyo, Nagasaki and Chiba.

In Nagasaki was Seitokukan, a teaching hospital for apprentice doctors run by the government. The faculty included teachers from Holland who mentored students in medical research as well as practice. Tokyo was home to Daigaku Higashiko, which later became the University of Tokyo School of Medicine. In Chiba, there was Sakura Juntendo, the private medical school established by Daizen Sato, which was considered the top school when it came to surgery. Gin had been treated in its Tokyo branch, established by Daizen's successor, Dr Shochu Sato.

None of the schools took more than twenty or thirty students at a time, and youths throughout the country competed fiercely for each one of the coveted places. It was well known that only men who had contacts in the new Meiji government were ever admitted, and even after graduating they had to pass a two-session licensing examination in order to be allowed to practise medicine.

In Gin's case, there was an even greater obstacle: neither public nor private institutions admitted women, and no one could ever hope to take the licensing examination without graduating from one of them. All the possible routes to becoming a doctor were completely and irrevocably closed to women.

In view of this, Gin's conviction seemed little more than a declaration of insanity on her part.

Over time, Ogie and Gin discussed the matter further, and Gin eventually told her mother of her dream late that summer. Predictably, Kayo was dumbfounded.

"Are you mad?"

"Of course not. I'm only asking that you let me go to Tokyo." Gin's eyes were bright as she pleaded.

Kayo had been concerned about how Gin kept herself shut up in her room, and now she was sure that Gin was suffering from a delirium caused by depression. With a sinking feeling, she looked down at her daughter kneeling before her. "Please don't talk like a fool."

"I'm not a fool."

"In the world we live in, some things are possible, others are not. Just look at the reality." Kayo thought perhaps Gin had been possessed by the spirit of a fox that had bewitched her into this confusion. Time would surely work this out and return her daughter to her right mind.

But Gin showed no sign of acquiescing. "How do you know what can and cannot be done if you won't even let me try?"

"No."

It was not seemly for women even to open a book. During the divorce proceedings, Kayo had been sympathetic to the Inamura family's complaint that Gin was fond of studying. Kayo decided not to mention it, but just now she sympathized strongly with her former in-laws. Gin had ruined her chances for marriage, and not only was she unapologetic, now she was proclaiming that she wanted to be a doctor!

"Where's the shame in wanting to help people who are suffering?" Gin persisted.

"That's what male doctors are for. Cutting off limbs and looking at blood are not things that women should do. There are other things that only women can do."

"Like taking care of the household and raising a family, I suppose?"

"Yes, that's one thing."

"And that's something I'll never be able to do."

Kayo was temporarily at a loss for words.

"You know it's true."

"But that doesn't mean that you can do anything else you please. You're a woman!"

"There is no law that says women can't learn."

"Yes, and the more you learn the less feminine you become in stating your opinions. No one will ever love you."

"I have no need of men."

Kayo looked sharply at Gin. "You do not live alone and there is more to consider than your own personal desires. There is your family to think of, along with all of the people we come into contact with. There may be no law preventing you from doing as you please, but there are social customs. Think of how the villagers would laugh if they ever heard that you planned to go to Tokyo to study and become a doctor. They'll point their fingers at you, and talk about 'that madwoman'.

"Once you leave here, no one will ever have anything to do with you again. You'll never be able to come back. That might be fine for you, but think of your brothers and their wives. Everyone will whisper about how the Oginos had a madwoman in the family who did nothing but read books. It will affect the spirit of your dead father and every one of our relatives. Will you still insist on doing this?"

Gin was silent. She knew that what her mother said had some truth in it. It was really no more than common sense. But the truth was rigid and uncompromising. It was too much for Gin to bear. She thought about the glimpses of the hustle and bustle of Tokyo she had had from her stay in the hospital. It was a world very different from that of her home town.

"Your brother will tell you the same thing. Women have their own place, and they should stay there. Society would fall apart otherwise. Stop this nonsense, and resign yourself to staying here."

"No!"

"Gin!" Kayo finally raised her voice, but she stopped herself and returned to her usual soft tone. "Look, I beg you to stop making me worry like this." Kayo looked down, and Gin could see that her mother's ageing shoulders were shaking ever so slightly. It hurt her to see her mother so sad. "Please try to understand," Kayo pleaded, her voice now lost to tears.

But Gin was not willing to give in. Her mother did not know the extent of the shame she had endured. Retaining a thread of hope, she went and spoke to her brother, but alas, Yasuhei had the same opinion as their mother. Gin knew it had been a mistake to have any expectations of her unremarkable brother.

Now that Kayo knew what was on Gin's mind, she kept an even closer eye on her. Her demeanour towards Gin did not change, but Gin knew she was being observed. She could tell that Kane, the maid, was also reporting back to her mother. Gin, for her part, acted as if she had no notion of any of this, but her relationship with her mother was different now.

Up to now Gin had taken at face value everything her mother said and obeyed her unquestioningly, but no longer.

My mother and I are as different as night and day.

This discovery left Gin feeling more alone than ever.

* * *

Now that Gin knew the door to her dreams was not going to open just by talking to her mother, she found an opportunity early that autumn to discuss the matter with Dr Mannen.

"My mother refuses to allow it," she blurted out, her eyes brimming with tears as she filled him in on the discussion she had had with Kayo. "Would you please talk to her?"

"You're asking me?" Mannen was surprised.

"Yes, she'll be convinced if she hears it from you."

Mannen groaned. He wanted to help Gin. Of his many students over the years, she had stood out as both brilliant and beautiful. And she was still so young – her health had been restored and she was just over twenty now.

"I'm begging you! I'll never ask anything of you again!" she pleaded.

Mannen had to admit that he had encouraged her to have lofty hopes. At the same time, he was deeply concerned about Kayo's reaction. She would never forgive him if she thought he had put Gin up to this. And he could not ignore the fact that women were essentially barred from becoming doctors. Gin's request was in no way practical, but coming back full circle, he knew he could not just turn her down.

"It might be a good idea to give up on becoming a doctor for the time being."

But Gin was desperate. Mannen was her last resort. "I'd rather die! My motives are not selfish. I was sick for so long and I found out at first hand how much female doctors are needed. I've *got* to study medicine. I want to help women like me who are ill, but for whom being treated by a male doctor is almost as cruel as the disease itself. That is all I want to do. Nothing more, nothing less. What is wrong with that?"

"No woman has ever become a doctor before. It's not allowed. What you propose to do amounts to breaking the law. I'm not surprised that your mother refuses to allow it. If you go to Tokyo now, saying you want to become a doctor, you've still got no way forwards; you have no connections and there's still no road open for a woman even to begin medical studies."

Mannen was right. Gin did not have a clue what she would do when she got to Tokyo. Mannen continued, "To become a doctor, you'll have to know lots of things. If you stick to your books for a while, you'll never be in danger of learning too much. Why don't I ask your mother if you can go to Tokyo to study? She might agree to that."

Gin realized this was sage advice. Even the goal of becoming a female academic was eccentric and barely within the range of social acceptability. She had only to look to Ogie as an example of that.

"Right now, your mother is not going to want to agree to let you go. You are much healthier than you were, but there is no telling when you'll become ill again. I can't blame your mother for not wanting to send you to Tokyo. She doesn't want you to be a doctor or a scholar. She probably hasn't given up hope of finding a good match for you, and she wants you to stay put until then."

"I'm not fit to be anybody's wife, and even if a man agreed to take me, I have no intention of getting married again."

"I understand your feelings, and I think you are within your rights. But your mother is different; she'll never be able to stop worrying about you. She wants you at home where she can keep an eye on you."

"But I'm going to have to leave there soon."

"Why is that?"

"My brother is the head of the household now, and it won't be long until his wife, Yai, claims her position as mistress. It won't be easy for an unmarried sister-in-law to live with them."

"But your family holds a prominent position."

"That's what I don't like about it."

"All right, I understand. Don't say anything more about becoming a doctor. Let's get your mother to let you go to Tokyo to study. Your mother understands your talents more than anyone, and you are dear to her heart. You're her youngest, and I can see how she feels when she talks about you."

"No matter what she says, I plan to leave home." Gin was trying to convince herself as well as Mannen of her determination. It was difficult for her to go against her mother, to whom she was so deeply attached.

"Now don't be rash. You've got to convince your mother if you expect to get the money you'll need to live on."

This was Gin's weak point. She was well aware that she had never earned a penny in her life by her own hand.

"Let's hope for the best. Once you get to Tokyo, you can watch for your chance to study medicine."

"I wonder if the day will ever come." As she began to calm down, Gin found herself acknowledging the near futility of her situation.

"I think it will take more than a day and a night, but anything is possible. The Tokugawa government fell after three hundred years, and there's no telling what else might happen."

Gin thought about the riotous commotion of Tokyo. She momentarily wavered between determination and uneasiness, then steadied herself. "When will you speak to my mother for me?"

"Tomorrow would be fine."

"Then I'll bring her here."

"No, let me go and visit her. I haven't seen your mother in a while. And it's over six months since the first anniversary of your father's death."

Gin wondered what would happen if her father were still alive. Would he object? No, he might give in more easily than her mother.

"Who should I apply to study under in Tokyo?"

"Hmm, there used to be quite a few teachers, but most of them have spread out into the countryside. I've heard of some new schools being opened since the government reforms began; why don't we wait until we have your mother's permission?"

Gin realized she had to quell her impatience, so she humbly agreed and took her leave.

Dr Mannen had become a father to Gin as well as her teacher.

8

Gin finally received her mother's permission and left for Tokyo in April 1873, the spring of her twenty-second year. It had taken over a year, but Kayo had finally given in to Gin's persistence and Dr Mannen's arguments on her behalf. But her permission was still grudging; Kayo had been surprised and angry at her daughter's relentless determination even in the face of Kayo's repeated tears and entreaties to give it up. It was as if Gin had ceased to be her daughter and had become a different person.

Gin made her departure at eight o'clock in the morning. She said goodbye to her brother inside the house, but received just a curt, silent nod in response. Not a soul in the household supported her – not even Kane, the maid, who had doted on her.

Gin wore a sober *kasuri*-patterned kimono and white tabi on her feet. She had been as excited as a child setting out on an excursion until the palanquin had arrived and her wicker trunks had been carried out from the house. Then she began to feel uneasy for the first time. She had been in Tokyo for about a year, but had seen most of it from the window of her hospital room. Now suddenly regrets crept in, and she felt irritated with herself for her own recklessness and afraid of what was awaiting her.

Kane, Yai and her sister Tomoko accompanied Gin as far as the gate of the estate to see her off. Tomoko had come from Kumagaya to spend the last night with her.

"Well, it's time," said Tomoko.

"Thank you for coming all this way."

Tomoko had been the only one to support Gin's determination to go to Tokyo. It was thanks to her sister that Kayo had finally relented, thus allowing her to leave by the front door rather than having to sneak out in the middle of the night.

"Take care of yourself."

"And please look after Mother."

"Don't worry about anything," Tomoko reassured Gin as she looked up at her. "I hope you know how lucky you are."

"Me?"

"Yes. You're the one that gets to go off on the path you've chosen for yourself." Tomoko found herself almost jealous of her sister, who had managed to bring the rest of them round to accepting her.

Kayo appeared belatedly at the gate. Gin said goodbye to all of them, and then turned her eyes once more to her mother. Kayo seemed to want to say something, but then just averted her eyes. Gin thought she looked pale, but shook off her worry and climbed into the palanquin.

"Goodbye. Take care of yourself!" Tomoko and Kane called after her. Kayo stood to the right of the group, disappearing into the shadow of the pine trees as soon as Gin had rounded the corner.

When the palanquin reached the main road, Gin took out the purse she had tucked away in the breast of her kimono. Yasuhei had given her thirty yen in his capacity as head of the Ogino family, indicating that he considered it enough to live on for about a year – the extent, he intimated, of any remaining responsibility he felt for his sister. Gin was leaving home under the assumption that she would never return. She knew that her mother was behind the money she had received from her family before they washed their hands of her. She had received further small gifts of money from Tomoko and Yai, as well as from Dr Mannen and Ogie. There was also the small packet, creased and folded over and over again, that her mother had silently handed to her as she left the house. Nothing was written on the outside. But inside the tightly wrapped white paper was five yen.

Deeply moved by this generous gift, Gin held the coin tightly in her hand as though to reassure herself of its tangible presence, and recalled her mother's pale face. In the bottom of the little packet there was something else, also wrapped in paper. It was small and hard. Gin opened it and found a protective amulet embossed with "Tawarase Shrine" in silver and gold.

"Thank you, Mother," she murmured. Rocked by the movement of the palanquin, Gin wondered what her mother had wanted to say to her as she was leaving.

* * *

Gin rented a room in the Hongo Kanazawa district, not far from the school of Yorikuni Inoue. At thirty-five, Yorikuni was still young, but he was already one of the top scholars of Japanese literature in Tokyo. He lived in a solid two-storey wooden house.

On her first visit there, Gin was led by the maid directly to Yorikuni's study on the second floor. In the centre of the room littered with books and papers was a large cypress desk with a single cushion in front of it. The maid calmly shoved some of the clutter aside, pulled out another cushion from under several books, placed it in the space she had made, and motioned for Gin to have a seat.

Gin settled herself on the cushion and then looked around. There were books everywhere, stacked in piles that snaked halfway up the walls. While she waited for Yorikuni to come up the stairs to the study, Gin tried to read some of the titles. They were all new to her.

She heard sounds of movement deep in the study, and all of a sudden a large, round, somewhat stolid-looking man appeared. Gin found it difficult to believe that this was the learned Professor Inoue, but smiling widely, the man plumped himself down on the cushion before the desk. The hair on the top of his head was thinning, but his eyes were engagingly childlike. Gin decided that this, indeed, must be Yorikuni. She sat up straight and then bowed deeply to him in greeting.

"I am Gin Ogino."

"Yes, I see. You've got a letter from Dr Mannen." Yorikuni read through the letter of introduction written by Mannen, and then brusquely set it on his desk. Gin had never seen anyone so artless and unassuming. "And how is he?"

"Quite well, thank you."

"I'm glad to hear it. I haven't seen him in years." So saying, Yorikuni began pulling books out of the front of his kimono. Gin realized that that was why his kimono had been so dishevelled. He piled four books on the desk and spoke again.

"I hear that you want to be a scholar. Are you really that fond of books?"

"Yes. I've come here to learn everything you have to teach me."

"Well, there is quite a bit I don't know. There's so much I don't know that I'm never sure where to begin. It seems scholarship is like that – the more you study, the more you realize there is to learn."

Gin was silent. Yorikuni was a different sort of scholar from the temperate Mannen. Keeping her eyes on Yorikuni's large, open face, she wondered if it was because Tokyo was such a big place.

"You'd be my first female pupil."

"And I ask that you please accept me as such." Gin bowed her head again. He was the only person she had to turn to in Tokyo.

"Such a pretty girl. It's unusual for someone like you to turn to academia."

Gin turned red with embarrassment, and she kept her eyes firmly down. She was unsure whether she should take him seriously.

"You're sure this is what you want to do?"

Gin did not understand his meaning.

"You don't think it would be a better idea to get married?"

"No, that's not what I want."

"I see. You do speak your mind, don't you?" Yorikuni laughed, showing his yellowed teeth. Gin wondered if she should tell him that she had already been married and divorced, but she decided that it had nothing to do with studying.

"All right, then. We won't decide whether or not you're staying yet. We'll start you out with this book." Yorikuni turned and pulled a book off the shelf behind him. It was entitled *Nihon gaishi*, a book of Japanese history. "First and foremost, you've got to read. Books have a lot to teach us. And they tell us the things that people in ancient days didn't understand yet, as well. It's our job to solve at least some of those remaining puzzles during our lives. That is what scholarship is all about."

Yorikuni, now speaking in earnest, folded his arms across his chest, his offhand attitude gone. Listening to him talk, Gin forgot about how messy he looked.

* * *

Ten days later, Gin was officially accepted as a student at Yorikuni's school. He had about thirty regular pupils, ranging in age from twelve or thirteen to almost fifty. There were former samurai retainers of the Tokugawa shogunate, townsmen, youths and even some who looked more like ruffians than budding scholars.

In the midst of this motley group, Gin's talent quickly began to show. She had come with an excellent background in Chinese classics, thanks to the tutelage of Dr Mannen and Ogie, and now had the opportunity to polish her skills in a more demanding environment. The abilities she had been refining since childhood blossomed all at once.

Yorikuni's teaching, too, was just what she needed. He taught Gin that scholarship was to be not merely absorbed and memorized, but also questioned. It was as though an enormous barrier had been removed from her mind. This, however, was not the only reason Gin thrived in Tokyo. She also experienced tolerance for the first time, in this big city. She no longer had to hide from the prying eyes of a stifling, small community, or read books furtively in an oppressive and disapproving environment. She was free to study, or do whatever else she felt like. No one stood in her way. There was nobody to stare and point fingers at her should she even decide to dress in the navy-blue kimono and trousers of a male student. She was free, body and soul.

Gin was able to forget that she was a divorced woman. Everyone considered her a young, single girl. No questions were asked, and she was under no obligation to explain herself. Learning had the highest priority. All she had to do was study. Another factor behind her renewed vigour was that her disease was in quiet remission. Everything was working in Gin's favour.

When she had first arrived at the school, the other pupils had looked at her with curiosity. As time passed, however, their curiosity grew into respect for her intelligence. "It's a waste to have so much talent in a girl." Even Yorikuni praised her without reserve. Gin was indeed talented, but she also worked hard. The better she felt, the harder she worked, and the harder she worked, the greater her confidence grew.

In a matter of months, Gin had surpassed all the others in her class. She was one of the top students in the school. Not only that, but with intelligence illuminating her elegant features and wheat-coloured skin, she was beautiful. By the time she had been there half a year, the name and reputation of Gin Ogino had spread throughout Tokyo's academic world.

In 1874, early in the New Year, Gin had a visitor to her lodging house. An imposing woman in a *yuki*-weave kimono beneath a bold striped *haori* jacket stood in the entrance as Gin came down the stairs. She looked to be a few years past forty. As soon as she had ascertained that it was indeed Gin she was speaking to, she introduced herself as Masuko Naito, the Head of the Naito School in Kofu. Gin had heard of her reputation as a great educator of women.

"I came to see for myself that the rumours I've been hearing were true. I'm delighted to meet you." Masuko, obviously at ease with another woman, spoke as familiarly as if the two had known each other for years.

Finding it difficult to drop all formalities, Gin apologized for having only a boarding room in which to entertain her guest.

"I'll get right down to business, then," Masuko said. "I've recently lost one of my teachers who had to come back to Tokyo due to family matters. I'm searching for a replacement. I met someone from the Inoue School who told me about you, and I'd like to have you come back with me and teach at my school." Masuko looked at Gin with the sharp, clear eyes of a woman who had devoted her life to learning.

"I'm sure I couldn't..." Gin was flustered. She had not even been in Tokyo a year. She knew she was making progress, but until six months ago she had been living a secluded life in the Saitama countryside. She was certain she was not yet ready to teach at any school.

"And I'm sure you're wrong. Professor Inoue himself has been singing your praises. He's a strange man and difficult to please, so if he's impressed, there can be no mistake. And you're such a lovely girl too. My students will be delighted to study under someone like you."

"So you've spoken to Professor Inoue about this?"

"No, of course not. He'd never agree to let me run off with you, so I won't say a thing until you agree. He seems quite attached to you." Masuko showed a hint of a smile and went on. "My life's work is to improve the status of women. I'll be satisfied with any progress at all. Won't you help me?"

At this, Gin wavered. She knew from personal experience the need to raise the social status of women.

"If you have any conditions, please don't hesitate to tell me. I'd like you to supervise the school dormitory as well as teach. This would make living expenses less of a strain and we'd all benefit from the arrangement."

Gin realized that Masuko, after a look at her lodgings, had seen the limitations of her finances.

"What do you think? Will you come to Kofu?"

Gin was honoured, but felt the praise Masuko Naito heaped on her was undeserved. Still, she was tempted to agree to go, but then a voice deep in her heart called her up short.

Didn't you come to Tokyo to become a doctor? For that you fought with your own mother and abandoned the home you were born and raised in. Have you forgotten the humiliations you suffered? The best way to become a doctor is to stay in Tokyo, continue studying and watch for your chance. Everything you've done up to now, everything you've fought for, has been so that you could study medicine.

However, Gin was not yet ready to talk about her ultimate goal to anyone, and did not wish to waste her energy evading the questions that would inevitably follow. "I'm sorry, but I regret to say that I have just begun my studies and I couldn't possibly presume to teach."

"I'm sure you'd be fine, and since I'm the head of my school, you can trust my judgement."

"I really don't have the confidence for that responsibility."

"Is there some reason why you can't leave Tokyo?"

"No." Gin knew she had missed her chance to be honest with Masuko. She stared silently down at her feet.

Masuko pressed her a little longer, but finally gave up. "I'll be on my way, then. But I'll write to you again soon, and I do hope you'll reconsider." Masuko took her leave, looking regretful.

In addition to being an exemplary scholar of Japanese classics, Yorikuni Inoue was schooled in Chinese medicine. This was also true of Gin's first teacher, Dr Mannen. In the late Edo era, scholars generally read Chinese medical books as well as the classics, which meant that they all had some knowledge of medicine.

Since the beginning of the Meiji Restoration, however, the tide had turned towards Western medicine. In reaction to this, the Movement for the Restoration of Chinese Medicine had been started. On the surface, Western thought appeared to be welcomed into Japanese society with open arms, but the reality was that in certain sectors it was fiercely opposed by those who refused to accept anything that had not been nurtured in Japanese culture. The Movement for the Restoration of Chinese Medicine was a part of this anti-foreign sentiment, and its purpose was to promote Chinese medicine, which had been a part of Japanese culture for centuries.

At the time Yorikuni was teaching Gin, he had been noting with dissatisfaction the encroaching predominance of Western medicine and was considering joining the Movement for the Restoration of Chinese Medicine. One day in class, he happened to comment on the Westernizing trend. "All you hear about these days is Western thought. Even in medicine, doctors are accepting it wholesale and calling it the New Japanese Medicine, but it all comes from barbarians, you know."

Gin immediately stood up and asked, "But isn't it true that Western medicine is both superior and more logical?"

Yorikuni responded, "Japan has medical practices that suit its climate and customs," and continued with the only knowledge of Western medicine that he had at his disposal. "I hear that Western medicine does autopsies on corpses to study them. Only barbarians would conduct autopsies. It will never be allowed in Japan."

It was not surprising that Yorikuni, a leader in the field of

Chinese classics and medical theory, would take this conventional stance. But Gin, young and strong-willed, had encountered a side of her teacher that she could not accept.

Spring came. Gin changed into a lighter-weight kimono. She had left Tawarase with four kimonos, and had not had any new ones made since arriving in Tokyo.

The matter of food was much more urgent than that of clothing. Despite the troubles she had had before, hunger had never been a problem in either her parents' home or that of her husband – both had been wealthy. But now things were different. She ate frugally, generally having miso soup and a vegetable dish for breakfast and lunch combined, and dried fish or a vegetable dish for supper. Gradually, however, money for even these foods was running out.

She had spent half of her funds setting up house in Tokyo, and now she had less than a third left. Her brother had promised to look after her for a year, but she had heard nothing from him, and she was growing increasingly uneasy. Gin knew well that, having left in spite of her family's objections, she would have no grounds for complaint even if she never heard from anyone at home again.

Along with the shortage of food, Gin was also plagued by the cost of the rapeseed oil that she used to heat her room as she studied late into the night. To cut down on costs, she began using fish oil, which she bought by the cup. One cup would last her for two nights.

"You must be up late every night," the friendly oil vendor commented. "Are you busy with needlework?" Anyone who bought oil once every two days was using more than usual.

"Ye-es," Gin responded vaguely. Tokyo or not, she was not comfortable admitting that she, a single woman, was up studying each night. She did not want to have to answer awkward questions or avoid curious stares.

"All that work, night after night. I'll give you a little extra."

"Thank you very much." The daughter of a well-to-do family, this was the first time Gin had benefited from a stranger's charity.

One day, as Gin was tying up her notes in her *furoshiki* cloth wrap and getting ready to go home after lectures, Yorikuni came over to her.

"Would you mind staying a little while longer? I have something to talk to you about."

After everyone had left, Gin tied back her kimono sleeves and began sweeping the floor. Even if she was Yorikuni's brightest pupil, this kind of thing was expected because she was a woman. Yorikuni had lost his wife to an illness two years before. He had not remarried, and an older woman came daily to take care of his two children and the housekeeping. The students who lodged with Yorikuni were supposed to do the cleaning, but Gin occasionally helped out too. As she finished, Yorikuni showed up, as if on cue.

"Why don't we go out for dinner tonight?" he suggested.

"Are you sure?"

"Why not?"

Yorikuni, his arms folded across his breast, left the house first. They walked several blocks to a restaurant that specialized in a hotpot of goose meat. Gin had been there with him once before in December, when he had taken her and ten other students. This time, though, it was just the two of them. Gin felt slightly concerned by this, but Yorikuni was apparently unfazed. When they arrived, the lights were already on in the shop, illuminating the words "hotpot" written in red under a picture of a goose.

"You've got rooms on the second floor, haven't you?" enquired Yorikuni, casually indicating the stairs with his chin.

"Go right ahead."

The first floor was crowded with diners. Gin was relieved to get away from the crowd and followed Yorikuni as he headed upstairs with the air of someone who came here frequently. The two settled on the tatami floor, facing each other at a table partitioned off from the rest of the room by a wooden screen.

The meal was a treat for Gin, who had had little to eat recently. While encouraging her to eat as much as she liked, Yorikuni nursed a glass of sake.

"How about a drink?" he asked her, picking up a second small cup.

"I can't drink," she said, refusing.

"Just a cup won't hurt. Come on, now."

"I'm sorry, I can't tolerate liquor at all."

"I see." Yorikuni put down the second cup reluctantly.

Gin could hold a little sake if she had to, but Dr Sato had made it clear that it was not good for someone with her disease.

After he had finished two flasks of sake, Yorikuni rearranged the collar of his kimono and sat up a little straighter. Gin had to smile, because she had never known him to show the least concern over his appearance.

"I've got something I'd like to discuss with you," he began.

"Yes?"

Yorikuni crossed his arms across his chest. "It's nothing you have to take seriously, but…"

"Hmm?"

"I mean, I'm serious about it, but…" The usually unflappable Yorikuni suddenly seemed unsure of himself.

"Is something the matter?"

"Well, it's about my *nochizoe*."

"*Nochizoe?*"

"I mean, my second wife."

"I see."

"I think I would be better off if I had one."

Gin nodded. She agreed completely with him.

"And," Yorikuni kept his arms folded, coughed, turned to one side and nodded to himself before continuing, "I'd like it to be you, if you wouldn't mind."

"Me?"

Yorikuni opened his small eyes as wide as they would go and continued, "I'm asking you to be my second wife. Will you marry me?"

Gin stared at him, speechless.

"With a head as good as yours, I'm sure the house would run smoothly if you were managing it. How about it?" Gin was still unable to speak, so Yorikuni pressed on. "I'd appreciate an answer right away."

"Professor…" Gin had to admit, he was quite daring. This was still an age when almost all marriages except for those in the lowest classes were arranged through a go-between. Although he did not have a government position, he was one of the top Tokyo scholars of the day. He was also much older than she was, and he had children to care for. He was either very brave, or unforgivably audacious.

"Well?"

Gin did not know how to react. Yorikuni's proposal was too much of a shock.

"I know we're more than twelve years apart in age," he said, trying a new tack, "and that might bother some, but it's no reason not to get married." At this point, he appeared to think he'd covered the essentials, and picked up a new cup of sake. "Well then, promise me you'll think about it."

"I – I..."

"Say what's on your mind."

Gin had been about to refuse him, but she closed her mouth. He was her teacher, after all. Was it acceptable to turn down a teacher like that?

"So, you'll do it?"

"Well..."

"I can take care of all your needs."

"But I'm not ready—"

"You wouldn't have to move in right away."

Gin nodded, and this seemed to assure Yorikuni that all was going according to plan.

"I couldn't... not right away."

"I'm sure you've had other offers."

"That's not it." Gin did not know what to say. Yorikuni knew nothing of her past. "I'm sorry, you'll have to excuse me."

"I can wait for your answer."

Gin had lost her appetite. She left the restaurant and fled back home. She was unable to sleep that night. She could hardly believe what had happened, and began to wonder if Yorikuni had actually meant what he had said. Then she remembered the sincerity she had seen in his eyes.

Gin had never considered Yorikuni a romantic prospect, but she could say the same thing for every other man she knew, too. She knew she could never have special feelings for a respected teacher. Quite apart from that, she had no desire to take care of a man, raise his children or meet social obligations of any kind.

The repellent memories of her husband came back to her, though she had thought she had forgotten him for good. As far as she knew, all men were tyrannical, selfish and spoilt. She had no desire to sacrifice herself for any of them.

I'm going to be a doctor.

Gin's mind was made up. Now all she had to do was think of a way to turn Yorikuni down.

The next morning, as the sun rose, she began to write.

Dear Professor Inoue,

Thank you for dinner last night. In regard to the subject you brought up afterwards, I can only say that while I was honoured, I was taken by complete surprise, and I know it was rude of me to have left so abruptly.

After returning home, I gave the matter much thought. I do have some knowledge in academic matters, but in all others I am no more than a child, and I would never have the confidence to serve you in any other capacity than as a student. Not only would I cause you much trouble and confusion, I would be in danger of damaging your good name.

I must ask you to forgive my many weaknesses and beg you to act as though last night's conversation never took place.

Sincerely,

    Gin Ogino

Gin gave the letter to her landlady's housemaid to deliver, and then closed herself up in her room.

Two and then three days passed with no word from Yorikuni. In the afternoon of the sixth day, a maid from the school arrived. "Have you been ill?" she asked Gin.

"Just a little," she replied.

"Have you seen a doctor?"

"I'm fine now. How is Professor Inoue?"

"He's been in a very bad mood and all of us are trying to stay out of his way. We have no idea what could have caused it." Despite this profession of ignorance, it was clear to Gin that the maid was checking her closely for any clues as she continued, "I'm sure you are aware that you can be expelled for unexcused absences. Why don't you come by and apologize?"

"I'll go tomorrow," Gin agreed, but she was irritated that she should have to be going through this torment at all.

In those days, it was extremely rare for a teacher to declare himself to a pupil. It may have been easier in a larger, public school, but Inoue ran a small, private operation, and distinctions between teacher and student were strictly observed. Nevertheless, it was even rarer for a woman in such circumstances to turn down an offer of marriage.

Now Gin was confronted with the question of whether she really should go back or not, and spent another three days in indecision. On the tenth day, she finally went to the school. When she arrived, the other students began to gather about curiously, but Gin brushed by them and went straight to Yorikuni's study on the second floor. As usual, Yorikuni was sitting at his desk, surrounded by books, his back against the wall as he gazed out the window.

Gin spoke up without preamble. "I'm sorry for being absent so long. Please forgive me." She looked at Yorikuni and then dropped her head.

Yorikuni was silent for a few moments before answering, "Were you worried about what happened?" Gin lifted her face. Yorikuni nodded slowly. "Don't worry."

Looking at those round eyes in his big face, Gin suddenly felt like crying. The eyes of the man who had always been so fierce and strict with her were now friendly and forgiving. *So this is what happens after a single declaration of love*, thought Gin, surprised at her own change of heart.

"It was thoughtless of me to approach you like that. Let's forget it ever happened."

Gin was silent. She felt as though she had let something important slip through her fingers. Up until now she had only been irritated with the necessity of apologizing to Yorikuni, angry that such a disaster had befallen her. Now that Yorikuni had apologized, she suddenly felt a kind of loneliness. She had been so heartless.

Gin now came face to face with another side of herself, a side that wavered despite her outward show of confidence. She continued to vacillate during the day's lectures. She was impressed at the way Yorikuni could teach as though nothing had happened. She was envious of his ability to do that. Meanwhile her thoughts raced uncontrollably. What would have happened if she had accepted his offer? How would the other students have reacted? What would her mother have said?

She and her teacher, now sonorously reading a passage aloud from a book, shared a secret. It would gradually stop being a burden, turning instead into a warm memory. But for now, Gin was unable to keep her mind on her lessons.

Her confusion continued into the next day, and the next. She did her best to stay away from Yorikuni while she wavered. Before, she had blithely gone in and out of his study, borrowing books. She had never hesitated to clean or do small mending jobs for his children. Now she was unable to do any of these things. Everything led back to that night at the restaurant. She felt herself acting unnaturally; nothing came easily.

After about a month, Gin realized that her studies had ceased to make any progress. Yorikuni must have been aware of this too, but he did not scold her. *Men are such a hindrance to academic pursuits.* Gin knew she could not carry on like this. She finally concluded regretfully that a teacher and his students could not indulge each other like this, and that she had no recourse but to leave Yorikuni's school.

At the end of July, about two months after Yorikuni's proposal, Gin moved to Kofu to teach at Masuko Naito's school. Gin could hardly believe that, having turned Masuko down flat six months before, she was now appearing on her doorstep asking to be taken in.

Yorikuni merely nodded when Gin told him she was leaving for Kofu.

"I've decided to work for the sake of women's education," she declared.

"That might be a good idea," he replied. Whatever excuse Gin might offer, Yorikuni knew why she was leaving and there was little he could say.

"Please forgive my selfishness," she continued.

"Take care of yourself." So saying, Yorikuni turned back to the book in his hands.

Gin was taken aback at his apparent lack of concern. But then, she decided, perhaps that is what separates a teacher from his pupils. It also struck her as further evidence of the strength and arrogance of men.

The Naito School was a small version of a modern-day private girls' school. There were about one hundred students in all. In addition to academic subjects, the school taught sewing, flower-arranging, tea ceremony and koto music – the traditional skills for well-bred women.

Most of the students were unmarried girls of sixteen and seventeen who lived in the school dormitory, while a few married women commuted from home. Gin taught Chinese classics and history, and also served as the dormitory supervisor. As Masuko had predicted, her wholesome beauty and extensive knowledge quickly made her popular among the students. Within a month, they had nicknamed her "Princess".

While Princess was popular in the classroom, her strictness in the dorm meant she was feared by its residents. The dorm curfew was seven o'clock, even during the summer months, when darkness descended later. Gin refused to pardon lateness, even by a minute. Missing curfew meant losing privileges, such as permission to leave the school grounds, and gaining the duties of cleaning the hallways and toilets for a week. Students complained that the punishment was too harsh, but within a couple of weeks lateness had become a thing of the past. Gin meanwhile paid their complaints no attention, aloofly sticking her nose in a book and reading well into the night. The students muttered among themselves that she was fussy and impossible to please, but gradually the grumbling subsided as the girls saw that Gin was simply conscientious.

In early autumn, two months after Gin took over the post of dorm supervisor, a student by the name of Ai Kanazawa climbed back over the wall after eight-thirty in the evening. Unhappily for the young woman, her return coincided with Gin on her evening rounds. To make matters worse, Ai's jacket and kimono trousers were covered in mud and straw. Gin's sharp female intuition immediately told her exactly what the girl had been up to.

"What do you think you're doing?" Gin demanded. Ai stood stock-still. "You're Miss Kanazawa, aren't you?" The other girls in the dorm were watching from the windows, keeping as still as they could. It did not look like this infraction would be overlooked, given that it was Gin she had run into.

"And where have you been?"

Ai was silent, but her pretty lips began to quiver.

"So you can't say it. In that case, come with me." Gin dragged Ai by the sleeve of her kimono into her own room, and made her kneel on the floor.

"Women are different from men. No matter what the situation, you must always protect yourself. A woman who cannot protect herself will not be treated as a human being."

To Ai, Gin's fine features looked more like the face of a cruel executioner.

"You know what this means?"

A week before, Ai had received, of all things, a love letter, and it had caused quite a sensation in the dorm. Her pale, childish features were attractive to men.

"You'll have to stay here until you decide to talk." So saying, Gin turned to her desk and picked up a book.

An hour passed, and then two. Gin maintained a proper sitting position, holding her book to the lamp so she could read. Ai's room-mates did their best to wait up for her, but they finally fell asleep. Both Gin and Ai, however, were up all night, both sitting up straight. Gin was used to doing this, but it was no small feat for Ai.

"I'm sorry!" It was almost sunrise by the time Ai finally gave in. "I went to Shingen Levee."

"And what did you go there for?"

Ai fell silent again, unable to say the words.

"You went to see a man, didn't you?"

Ai nodded, her mussed hair falling over her eyes.

"I knew it." Gin's eyes gleamed. As young as this girl was, she had gone out to meet a man, and had returned late, climbing over the wall to get in. What was it that had made her want to see him so badly? She had given in to a man, and had thereby shamed all women. "You are being misled. He is trifling with you."

Ai had no response.

"All men want is your body, and they use sweet words to get you to acquiesce. But really they're all selfish creatures, and they don't even think of you as a woman. They're horrid!"

"No!" Ai raised her face, her mussed hair falling aside. "No, it's not like that. He's different. I'm sure of it!"

"Be quiet! You know nothing of men. They make women suffer without a twinge of conscience. How many women do you think have cried at the hands of men?"

"It's not true. He would never—"

"I'm in charge of this dorm, and I'm older than you. I know more about these things than you do."

"But... but he..." Ai burst into tears. As she held her hand to her eyes, the sleeve of her kimono hung open to reveal her skin. Gin could smell the scent of passion coming from it. She was filled with an intense hatred, and she exploded.

"You are a student! You are in training, and you have no business carrying on a romance." Gin was also trying to convince herself, since she sometimes found herself thinking about men. It infuriated her to think that she and Ai shared the same female weakness. "Is this what makes life worthwhile to you, doing filthy things with men, over and over? Is it?"

Gin suddenly felt a pain in her lower abdomen. She knew that losing a night's sleep could aggravate her disease, and the dull pain there enraged her further. "You are supposed to be getting an education," she continued. "With a good education you can become the kind of woman no one will talk about behind her back. Do you understand? What do you mean by sneaking out at night, running off to do disgusting, dirty things with a man? Is that what a woman of quality and sophistication does? Can you really call yourself a student of the Naito School?"

Gin found it hard to go on. She almost wanted to cry herself. Why did she have to scold students when it made her feel miserable too? What was she doing in a position like this anyway? The thought made her more impatient than ever. "Stand up," she commanded roughly. Her usually bright, large eyes were narrowed into slits, and she pushed Ai, who struggled unsteadily to her feet. "Get rid of the shameful things in your heart."

The early morning sun from the east had begun to seep into the hallway. Gin led Ai down it, looking for all the world like an executioner leading a prisoner to the gallows. At the end of the hall was a large, formal room that was usually used for lectures on morals and talks by special guests. The huge room was silent in the light of dawn.

"You will spend the day in this room reflecting on your behaviour." Ai no longer had the energy to protest against Gin's harsh treatment. "I will not forgive you until you rid yourself of that black shadow in your heart." With that, Gin closed the door and locked it from outside, leaving Ai sitting in the large room like a sacrificial lamb. The pain in Gin's abdomen had grown worse, and she headed for the toilet.

A new year began. It was 1875. Over five years had passed since Gin had divorced her husband, and she was twenty-four years old.

Soon after the holidays, Gin received a letter from her sister Tomoko. Gin had always respected her most of all of her siblings. If Tomoko had been allowed to continue her own studies, Gin was sure she would have been the more accomplished of the two of them.

In her letter, Tomoko complained that the family home in Tawarase was losing its vitality. She said that their brother Yasuhei was much too nonchalant in his dealings, while Yai devoted more time to her own expensive pursuits than she did to managing the household. Tomoko was sure that this was why the family seemed increasingly isolated. Gin was reluctant to take everything Tomoko told her at face value, but since people rarely criticized their own families, she imagined there must be some truth in it. Gin thought back to the way Yasuhei's wife had so quickly put down roots after their marriage. Although it was only natural for the wife of the eldest son to take over the household, Gin had never recovered from the feeling that her home had been invaded by an outsider.

There was never any danger of me taking over the Inamura household, she thought. *I was never in any position to do so.* Yai's boldness was all the more remarkable compared to her own weakness. *I'm just not the sort of woman to manage a household.* Gin was struck with unease at the realization that she was not suited, either physically or mentally, to womanhood.

In the middle of her letter, Tomoko noted: "Kanichiro is still single". The name of her former husband stood out on the page, catching Gin's eye. The family Tomoko had married into ran a Shinto shrine, and had connections with most of the powerful families in the area. Gin realized that her sister must still have frequent contact with the Inamura family. However, Gin had ceased to think of Kanichiro as a man who used to be her husband, the man she had given her virginity to. It seemed like the name of a stranger. *Has it already been eight years since I got married?*

"Keep up your studies and become a doctor. I know it's not much, but please accept the five yen included in this letter."

Tomoko's family was well off, but Gin knew that Tomoko would certainly have had to get permission before sending such a sum to her sister. Tomoko was the only member of her family who had stood beside Gin from the first. She did not understand why she got along so well with her sister, but she guessed that Tomoko had desires that she had never confessed to anyone and that she had given up to get married. Maybe she had entrusted to Gin some of the things she had wanted for herself.

The letter continued, "Mother has suddenly become weaker and hardly goes out any more. When I went to see her at New Year, she tried to get me to stay longer and tell her what I knew about you. She seems to worry about you and, although she didn't say so, I know she has forgiven you everything."

Gin looked up from the letter. She recalled Kayo's face as she had stood slightly apart from the group that saw her off at Tawarase. *How could I have wanted to be a doctor badly enough to make my own mother so unhappy?* She felt a chill wind blowing through the cracks in her determination.

Summer again. The zelkova and ginkgo trees around the school were in their leafy finery, reflecting the sparkling hot sun. The students changed into lighter kimonos.

Gin sat in the grass, narrowing her eyes slightly against the light breeze, and watched them as they ran through the greenery. She realized that she had been married at the exact same age. Time was undoubtedly doing its work; it was getting easier for her to recall her past without feeling so sad.

A student came running towards her. "Miss Ogino, there's someone from Tokyo to see you."

"Tokyo?"

"A very tall woman. She's standing at the main entrance."

It was unusual to have guests from Tokyo in Kofu. The last had been in autumn, when five of Yorikuni's pupils had come to pick grapes, the local speciality. Gin hurried around to the front gate.

"Ogie!" Gin broke into a run as soon as she caught a glimpse of her old friend and mentor. There stood Ogie Matsumoto, a parasol in her right hand and a parcel wrapped in cloth in her left.

"Gin!" The two embraced. It had been three years since they had last met. The students watched in surprise – it was rare for Gin to show such exuberance.

"You look wonderful. Thank you for coming so far to see me." Gin brought Ogie to her room.

"What a lovely, relaxing place," said Ogie, looking around as she settled down comfortably, after rinsing her hands and feet.

"How is your father?" asked Gin.

"He's fine and sends you his regards."

Gin recalled Dr Mannen's gentle face. She even thought nostalgically of his large, round eyeglasses. The two talked for a while about Tawarase, before Gin finally thought to ask, "But why have you come all this way?"

"I came to see you." Ogie smiled mischievously.

"You came all the way from Tawarase just to see me?" It would take a woman three days to get this far; Kofu was two days' travel from Tokyo.

"I live in Tokyo now; Father and I live there together."

"I had no idea."

"To tell the truth, I also came to talk to Miss Naito about a new school." Now Gin was truly confused, and seeing this, Ogie was obviously further amused. She finally gave Gin the entire story. "Did you know a teaching college for women is being established in Tokyo?"

"Yes, I've heard about it from Miss Naito."

"I'm going to teach there."

"You are?"

"That's right." Ogie smiled shyly.

Gin looked Ogie up and down with widened eyes.

"You must wonder what's possessed them!"

"Not at all – you'll be a wonderful teacher."

Gin herself passed as a teacher in this country school, and she had discovered in Tokyo that the academic background she had received from Dr Mannen was better than most. If she had achieved this much, how much more Ogie must have to offer.

Gin took another look at Ogie. With her hair tied back and wearing a simple Oshima kimono, she retained the bloom of youth that most women lost in their thirties. Her zest for life was what made her shine.

"Now about this school..." began Gin. "They're building it in Hongo. Classes will begin this autumn."

"Is it government-run?"

"Yes. They've finally decided to open up teaching to women. Women who graduate from this school – the Tokyo Women's Normal School – will be able to have jobs."

"That's a big step."

"Rumour has it that an educational advisor for the Ministry of Education, an American named David Murray, recommended it to Vice-Minister Tanaka. Tanaka himself has taken observation trips abroad, and I hear he is very progressive. They say that he is the one who submitted the petition to Grand Minister of State Sanjo."

Gin thought of everything that was happening in Tokyo, and felt suddenly anxious. She knew she could not stay in this quiet backwater for ever.

Ogie spoke again. "I came to see you because I want you to come and study there."

"Me?"

"You've got to. They're taking applications for the first class now, and you've still got time."

Gin's eyes shone. Ogie had come all this way just to tell her this.

"Don't worry, I know what your final goal is. It's only a matter of time until a medical school is opened to women, but you can't just sit around waiting. When you do get the chance, it will be an advantage to have graduated from this new school, and you'll have a chance to learn more while you wait. Don't tell Miss Naito, but I hate to see you stuck out here. It's time to come back to Tokyo and look for opportunities."

Everything Ogie said rang true to Gin. No matter what had happened between herself and Yorikuni, she had realized already that it was not prudent to stay here in Kofu. This was just what Gin had been waiting for, an opportunity to take her back to Tokyo.

"You're sure to be accepted. Come to the Women's Normal School, get your teaching qualification, and strengthen your academic knowledge."

"Yes, ma'am," Gin responded formally.

"Come now! No matter what happens, you and I are sisters. We made a promise in Tawarase. Don't you remember?" Ogie gave Gin a friendly, boyish clap on the shoulder.

9

In November 1875, Tokyo Women's Normal School – today's Ochanomizu Women's University – opened in Tokyo's Hongo Ochanomizu.

In the first class, there were seventy-four women, including Gin. The opening ceremony was attended by the Dowager Empress, who composed a poem for the occasion:

Glass balls and mirrors
Are worthless unless polished
The same is true of our minds

Previously there had been just one other institution for women, the Tokyo Girls' School in Takebashi, which was established in 1872, around the time education nationwide was centralized by the Meiji government.

The directive governing education stated that "except for elementary schools, males and females must be educated sep arately". This was a throwback to the Tokugawa era's stricture that "boys and girls should not remain together after the age of seven" – a measure to keep females subservient to men that was written into the new Meiji government policy with little change. It remained in force until the current Japanese constitution was established after World War II.

In an atmosphere so hostile to women's education, it was almost a miracle that a normal school, or what would now be called a teachers' training college for women, could successfully be established. Yet the school did open, although to begin with there were no uniforms or badges for the students and most attended wearing everyday clothes of cotton or common silk, carrying their belongings in cloth wraps.

Without exception, all of the young women who attended in those early years, including Gin, braved some degree of opposition from their families. The times were hailed as the age of civilization and enlightenment, but this was only evident in certain parts of Tokyo and Yokohama society. Throughout the rest of Japan, the old ways of thinking were still deeply entrenched.

The mainstream attitude towards women's education was evident in sayings such as "Giving birth to a girl who likes studying brings shame on the whole family", "Service rather than study" and "Women belong in the home". A school to train women educators would therefore necessarily produce a type of woman that was hitherto unthinkable.

For these and other reasons, all the girls had come against their parents' wishes, and some had even been disowned by their families as a result. Each one of them was proud and strong-willed. They were spirited pioneers, with the firm belief that they were shouldering the future of Japanese education for women. They could also be described as a prickly bunch of young women: all shared a strong competitive spirit and were highly motivated. Gin, needless to say, felt quite at home among them.

On entering the school, Gin seized the opportunity to change her name to "Ginko", thus becoming Ginko Ogino. She had been dissatisfied for some time with the way women were given names that were short and easy to call, almost as if they were dogs. She disagreed with the current thinking that the only need for women to have names at all was that they were handy when a husband or mother-in-law needed to give them orders.

"Women's names should be written with the same dignified Chinese characters as men's."

Her opinion on this had been reinforced when she had read the roll of the students at the girl's school in Kofu. It was pitiful how they all had simple names like "Yai" or "Sei". This was just another example of the dominant idea of the time, that men should be looked up to and women despised. The more she thought about it, the angrier Gin became. The name "Gin" had no impact; it was not the name of a woman who was going to forge a new path for society. So, ten days into the semester, after thinking about it long and hard, she started writing her name as "Ginko".

"Well, which one is it?" her teacher asked, perplexed, when she tried to correct him.

"In the family register it is 'Gin', but 'Ginko' fits me much better now. I'm turning over a new leaf and want to move forwards as a new woman."

"I see."

The Tokyo Women's Normal School had a five-year curriculum and the courses were divided into ten levels covering a great many subjects, including geography, history, physics, chemistry, ethics, general reading, calligraphy, dictation, composition, mathematics (arithmetic, algebra, geometry), economics, natural history, educational theory, book-keeping, health, handicrafts, singing, gymnastics, teaching methods and practical training.

The large number of subjects meant there was a lot to memorize, which was typical of curricula at the time. Furthermore, the teachers were all hard-working scholars burning with the desire to fill their students with knowledge, and so the resulting load for the students was considerable. It was not uncommon for the maths professor to assign the students two hundred algebra problems for homework, but they patiently persevered. Ginko's natural intelligence and superior effort soon saw her outpacing the others and at the top of her class. But no matter how diligently they all worked, there was never enough time.

In the dormitory, the women slept five to a room. Their bedding was lined up at both ends, with their desks in the centre, set in rows facing each other. For illumination they had only a lamp with a wick that burned in rapeseed oil. Ginko faced constant competition from her classmates, and soon realized that the allocated study time before lights out was not enough for her to maintain her lead. At the head of each girl's bed was a three-foot cupboard for stowing bedding during the day. Deep in the night, she would therefore rise and slip stealthily into her cupboard, taking with her a single wick for light, before which she crouched, huddled over a book, while her roommates slept on unaware. Her small frame silhouetted against the cupboard wall, the only part of Ginko clearly visible would be her sparkling eyes reflecting the light.

The single wick lasted for two hours. Ginko did this every night for a fortnight before her room-mates began to catch on and follow suit. The habit quickly caught on in other rooms, and within a month Ginko was called in to see the dorm headmistress.

"You're the one who started it, aren't you? I don't wish to complain about studying, but you need to remember that night is the time to sleep. More to the point, what if you fell asleep with that lit wick in such a small enclosed space and started a fire?"

"I'm sorry."

"I do understand your desire to study, but I must ask you to stop doing this." Rather than scolding Ginko, the dorm headmistress seemed to be asking for her cooperation.

"I promise I won't do it again," Ginko apologized, alarmed at the competition among her schoolmates her harmless little habit had sparked off.

For a while Ginko did nothing untoward at night; she simply slept. But she would often find herself wide awake after a nightmare, unable to go back to sleep. The harder she tried, the more completely awake she would find herself, and so she devised a new scheme. When she awoke at night, she would pick up the book she had left by her pillow and head to the bathroom. It was perfectly quiet at night, and had a lamp burning in the centre of the room. It was somewhat malodorous, but Ginko would nevertheless stand under the lamp reading her book, and wait for sleepiness to return to her.

At the beginning of 1876, when Ginko was accustomed to life at the school, she paid a New Year visit to Yorikuni Inoue. Though they had parted on somewhat uncomfortable terms, she knew it was a matter of courtesy to update him on her activities.

She waited until ten days into the new year, aiming for a time when his other visitors would have dwindled, then purchased some of Yorikuni's favourite sweet-bean-jam wafers from Shitaya's Eisendo confectioners and set off for his house.

The hedges had lost their vibrant green in the winter cold, but otherwise his garden and home were unchanged. Ginko opened the front door and called out, "Hello?" There was no reply, and an uneasiness came over her as she called out again.

This time a woman's voice replied, "Yes?" The old housekeeper appeared. "Oh, it's Miss Ogino!"

"I'm sorry to have been out of touch for so long."

"I heard you were in Kofu?"

"Yes, that's right. Is Inoue-sensei here?"

"Oh yes, he's here. I'll just tell him you've come. He'll be so pleased to see you."

She hurried off all a flutter, disappearing into the back. Silence returned to the hallway.

Beside Ginko in the spacious entrance was just one pair of *geta* sandals – the big ones Yorikuni wore. There was no sign of anything pretty that might belong to a woman. He must still be single. Ginko felt a faint sense of relief.

Yorikuni was still big and round. Even though he was wearing a nice kimono, the collar was hanging loose at his neck, just as always.

"So you're in the Women's Normal School?"

"You already knew?"

Yorikuni nodded. "Academia is a small world," he laughed, teasing her.

Ginko flushed. While he was no longer her teacher, he had been once. She should have come to inform him sooner. But he showed no sign of having been offended.

Yorikuni called out to the maid, "We've got some of those *karinto* sweets that Miss Ogino likes, haven't we?"

"Please don't trouble yourself—"

"Not at all, not at all. We just bought some this morning. It's not really my favourite, but when the hawker comes around I always end up buying some in spite of myself," he chuckled.

It had just been once that he'd asked what she liked and she had answered *karinto*, yet he had remembered all this time. Just as she had remembered and brought Eisendo's sweet-bean-jam wafers for him.

"I bet they're keeping you busy."

"There are a great many subjects."

"But I'm sure you're managing just fine. 'Scuse me a moment – I'm just going to the bathroom." He rose, and the stairs creaked as he descended them. Nothing had changed about this house or the people in it.

"Here you go," said the old housekeeper, bringing in the sweets on a tray and setting a small plate in front of her.

"Professor Inoue's not remarried yet?" Ginko asked her. She wanted to make sure.

"Not yet, no."

"Are there any likely candidates?"

"Well, there have been some discussions, but he says he doesn't like them, or he'd rather not bother. He doesn't seem the least bit interested."

"Is that so? But it would be better if he hurried up and found someone, wouldn't it? It must be a strain on you too." Ginko said this with an air of concern, but inwardly she felt satisfied that he was still alone.

While their studies were challenging, the students of Tokyo Women's Normal School did find time for other activities. After dinner, or on days when their homework load was light, like Sunday afternoons, classmates would get together and discuss the latest moves by the Meiji government or the role of women in society. Unlike the conversations of most young women, they rarely touched on subjects such as fashion or men.

One of Ginko's room-mates, a petite woman by the name of Shizuko Furuichi, was quiet and reserved in comparison to the other generally outspoken students. At twenty-five, Ginko was one of the older students in her class, and since Shizuko was twenty-three, Ginko felt a little closer to her than the younger women. Ginko sometimes tried to make conversation, but Shizuko never replied with anything more than the bare essentials. Her face was always pale, and in her habitually downcast eyes were the traces of some deep anguish.

One Sunday afternoon, Ginko had gone to visit Ogie to borrow the first volume of Yukichi Fukuzawa's new, much-discussed *An*

Encouragement of Learning. She had then returned to her room to find Shizuko there alone, sitting at her desk.

"You're working hard, aren't you?" Ginko approached to see what she was studying on a Sunday, and Shizuko raised her face quickly in surprise. There were shadows beneath her eyes and tear streaks down her face. "What's wrong?"

Ginko was worried that something had happened while the others were all out, but Shizuko just shook her head and turned to gaze out the window. The zelkova tree, which had been green with leaves when they had entered in the autumn, looked bare and shrunken in the weak winter sun.

"I'm worried about you. Tell me what's wrong." Gazing down on Shizuko's slender neck, Ginko suddenly felt like an older sister to her. "If there's anything I can do, I'd like to help."

"It's impossible."

"How can you decide that without even giving me a chance?" Her refusal made Ginko all the more determined to find out what was behind this young woman's distress. Despite her single-minded devotion to study, there was another, almost forgotten, gentle side to Ginko.

Persuaded by Ginko's concern, Shizuko began to explain. A former envoy to the United States, Arinori Mori, had returned to Japan. He would later become the Minister of Education and begin a revolution in education, but at this time he was an up-and-coming politician. He had progressive views and ideas that he had brought back with him from overseas, and had recently surprised many by deciding to break with Japan's long-standing marriage traditions and instead make a marriage contract with a woman named Tsuneko Hirose. The marriage contract read thus:

Tsuneko Hirose of Shizuoka prefecture, who is nineteen years and eight months old, hereby creates a marriage contract with Arinori Mori – age twenty-seven years, eight months – from Kagoshima prefecture. With the permission of the parents of both parties, today – 6th March in the 2535th year following the accession of Emperor Jinmu – in the presence of Tokyo Governor Ichio Okubo and their friends and relatives, the

*two parties vow to be married. The set details of the marriage
contract are as follows:*

*Article 1: Arinori Mori shall take Tsuneko Hirose as his
wife, and Tsuneko Hirose shall take Arinori Mori as her
husband.*

*Article 2: As long as the two parties of the contract remain
alive and do not abandon the conditions herein, they shall
love and respect each other as husband and wife.*

*Article 3: As for the possessions of Mr and Mrs Arinori
Mori, none shall be lent or sold to another party without
mutual agreement.*

*If any of the conditions of this contract are broken by
either of the parties, the other shall be free to demand legal
redress.*

6th March 1875, Tokyo
Arinori Mori and Tsuneko Hirose
Witness: Yukichi Fukuzawa

It was not so different from the oath of most marriages nowadays, yet in those days it was an impressive innovation, and the
fact that they had a witness – Yukichi Fukuzawa, no less – made
it all the more intriguing.

This marriage had taken place in the spring of the previous
year, so Ginko had heard about it. Most marriages that failed in
Japan usually did so from male infidelity, tyranny or selfishness,
as Ginko knew well, having had her own youthful idealism and
ardour snatched from her. She fully supported the sentiments of
this contract, and was also impressed with the courageous stance
and integrity of Arinori Mori. However, in the background was
apparently something quite different.

"I'm embarrassed to say this, but he and I were once engaged
and we had physical relations."

"Is that so?"

Ginko was taken aback, but she could not believe Shizuko
would ever say such a thing unless it were true. Who would
have known that in the shadow of this much-discussed event
there was a woman who had been tossed aside and, resigned
to remaining single, was now studying to become a teacher to

support herself? It came as a shock to Ginko, who had considered Arinori Mori a statesman of the new era.

"No matter what his high government position might be, it's unforgivable for him to treat someone like that. Does his new wife, this Tsuneko, know about you?

"I think she probably does."

"Then she's appalling as well." Ginko voiced this as vehemently as if she herself had been wronged. She had borne her own divorce in silence, convinced that she had no options and that it was her burden as a woman, but things were different now. Six years had given Ginko self-confidence and courage.

"Let's go. I'll go with you."

"Where?"

"To see Mori."

Shizuko was speechless. What would be the purpose? He was already married in the eyes of the whole world.

"You don't have to just put up with what's happened and bear it alone. We'll meet with him directly and negotiate terms with him."

"But isn't it too late?"

"Well, he's wrapped up in Tsuneko now, so there's probably no way to get his affections back. But we should still ask for something to prove his good faith."

"Good faith?"

"If that doesn't work, then at least he should give you some money by way of apology. In Western countries they do that as a matter of course."

"But that…" Shizuko could not yet muster Ginko's clarity about the situation. She was still in love with him and could not convince herself to hate him, despite what he had done.

"If you can't bring yourself to go, then leave it to me. I promise I won't make the situation any worse."

Ginko was so worked up that, having decided on her course of action, she was unable to sit still. Twice she visited Arinori Mori's official residence fruitlessly, but the third time she succeeded. His secretary had initially brushed her off when she introduced herself as a student of the Tokyo Women's Normal School who wanted to meet Mori to discuss a personal matter, but on her third visit he was forced to give in and announce her to Arinori.

"I wonder what this is about? Well, yes, see her in."

The secretary had mentioned that she was petite and beautiful, and this had piqued Arinori's interest. Wearing a new kimono of woven silk, and reddish-brown *hakama* trousers fastened at her chest, an outfit she had purchased from the money she had earned in Kofu, Ginko stood before Arinori.

"Well, take a seat," said Arinori, himself quite the dandy in a navy-blue suit and bow tie.

After giving her name, Ginko looked him in the eye and got straight to the point.

"I haven't come to see you about myself, but about a friend I'm sharing a room with."

"Your friend?" Arinori asked guardedly, pulling out a Western-style cigarette.

"Shizuko Furuichi."

"Shizuko?" Arinori winced.

"You don't need someone like me to tell you about her, as you, sir, know her best, I believe."

"And what do you mean by that?"

"She is still thinking of you, sir, and crying. She gave you everything she had as a woman, and is now withering away. She will be alone for the rest of her life. She is withering because of you, sir." Ginko completely forgot the station of the man in front of her. She was chiding her own ex-husband and all other men like him as well.

"Shizuko has decided that she'll never marry anyone else. She thinks only of becoming a teacher so that she'll be able to support herself, a lonely single woman. You have destroyed her life. And in contrast, you, sir, have proceeded with hardly a care in the world to build and keep a love nest with another woman, covering up the lie behind your contract marriage."

Arinori stared in astonishment at this ball of fire delivering her passionate sermon. Ginko never even gave him an opening for rebuttal.

"You are a disgraceful hypocrite. An enemy of all women." Having said this much, Ginko paused to draw breath.

Her cheeks were flushed with feeling, and Arimori was bewitched. She was the kind of woman he liked – he would have been drawn to her just by looking at her face. *If only I could see her naked, she'd be even more attractive*, he thought. Though she had just showered him with invective, he was not at all offended. On the contrary, he admired her courage and passion. If she were a man, she would be thrown out on her ear, or even thrown in jail for insulting him like this. Beauties had an advantage with him.

"So what do you want me to do about it?" Arimori asked, coming back to his senses.

"Please help Shizuko."

"Help?"

"Marry her."

"I can't do that – as you know very well."

"Then at least offer some financial assistance."

"I see – consolation money." He had no relationship with Shizuko now, much less was she his mistress, and there was no law that could force him to honour a verbal agreement.

"At the very least I hope you will agree to support her until she graduates from the Women's Normal School."

Gin may have been ferocious, but in reality she had not asked for much. Arinori Mori was at the height of his career, and Shizuko, an insignificant female student, had little standing in comparison. Still, he had to give Ginko credit for her pluck.

"All right. I'll agree to that." Arinori shrugged in the exaggerated American way, and gave her a small smile, betraying his youth. *It's nice to have something pretty come dancing in here for a change, instead of a starchy bureaucrat with a boring report*, he mused as he extracted a nose hair.

Ginko decided his travels in the West had influenced him well after all. "In that case, I'll leave you now. Please accept my apologies for the strong language."

There was no use in staying now that the conversation had been wrapped up. Ginko rose and bowed politely.

Ginko had seen to the school expenses of her friend, and from then on she and Shizuko were like sisters. Ginko herself, however, was in financial straits too. The demand for tuition fees for the next several years for her friend had occurred to her so quickly because the matter of her own expenses had been on her mind.

Ginko had supported herself while working at the Naito School in Kofu. Her salary had not been large, but as the dorm supervisor she had been able to save two or three yen a month. When she had resumed her studies, Ginko had spent more than half of her savings on her new kimono and books. She had considered taking up some kind of work that she could do at home, but her school work left her no time for that. She received a scholarship for tuition and only needed two yen a month to live in the dorm, but there was no leeway to buy new clothes or expensive books. Now, six months into her first year there, she had almost nothing left.

If she asked her family in Tawarase to send money, she could probably count on them sending three to five yen a month. But Ginko had left home all but disinherited. She hated to think of her brother and his wife grumbling to each other "Didn't we say this was coming?" Her pride would not allow her to ask them for help, yet she had nowhere else to turn.

Eventually she decided to write and ask her sister Tomoko in Kumagaya to send three yen a month for the next three years. Since Tomoko had married into a Shinto priest's family, it would not be beyond her means. Tomoko immediately sent a reply agreeing to this, and telling Ginko to go at the end of each month to collect the money from the Kinos, a family they did business with in the Monzen-Nakacho district.

Tomoko concluded her letter with "Never give up your dream!" Ginko felt a tightening in her chest. Tomoko had never forsaken her, and even now was looking out for her, protecting her.

The strain of the heavy workload resulted in a drop-out rate of about ten students a year. Most of the students had graduated from elementary school and had then studied classical Chinese at home with their fathers or older brothers. Not all of them actually wanted to become teachers; a great many had entered simply because there was no other place for women to study.

These were from wealthy homes, and did not have an urgent need to either graduate or get their teaching licences. Dropping out part-way through would have little effect on their lives; in fact their parents often welcomed the opportunity to marry them off as quickly as possible.

Becoming a teacher was not Ginko's goal either. She was as determined as ever to become a doctor, and was building the educational foundation for her medical studies. This distinguished her from the less serious-minded women at the school, whose eventual escape into marriage was not a route open to her. Ginko had no alternative but to push forwards.

In February 1879, Ginko graduated from the Tokyo Women's Normal School at the top of her class. The class had originally numbered seventy-four, but only fifteen had made it to graduation.

At their graduation, the principal, Professor Nagai, asked them one by one about their future aspirations.

"I want to be a doctor."

Ginko had been too embarrassed to say this aloud when she was studying with Yorikuni, but she had no problem voicing it now. It was partly that she had grown stronger, and partly because times had changed enough for a woman to be able to have ambitions and not be treated with scorn.

"Is that so? A woman doctor?" said Professor Nagai thoughtfully, stroking his moustache. "How do you intend to go about it?"

"I want to go to medical school."

"I see."

The first public universities were being established, and there were a few private medical colleges as well, but all of these were closed to women.

"All of my studies to date have been undertaken with the goal of becoming a doctor."

"But you know you run the risk of being disowned by your family if you pursue that goal."

"I already have been."

"I see."

"Isn't there any way for me to proceed?" For Ginko, this graduation was not the end of her studies – far from it. But she was almost twenty-eight, and the pressure of time was on her.

"The problem is with the government, so an academic like me won't be of much use. But I do know one person who might be able to help. I'll arrange an introduction for you – would you go to meet him if I do?"

"Would you really do that for me?"

"I'll have a letter of introduction ready for you by tomorrow. I don't know if it'll be of any use, though."

"I'm very grateful, thank you. I'll definitely try."

"With a mind like yours you probably could become a doctor. It's a shame that you happen to be a woman." Professor Nagai regarded Ginko's intelligent face and sighed.

Professor Nagai's introduction was to Tadanori Ishiguro, the Director of the Army Surgical Hospital and an influential person in the medical world of the day. Ginko hesitated to visit him in his office, which was in the Ministry of Military Affairs, and was sure to be busy with members of the military coming and going. She settled instead on visiting his private residence. He was at home on her second visit, and she finally had the opportunity to meet him.

Ishiguro was a strong-jawed, stern-looking man. He read through the letter of introduction from Professor Nagai, muttered, "I see," and nodded. "So you're Ginko Ogino?" Fittingly for a man who had survived the upheaval of the Meiji Restoration and had come out on top, his deep voice rang through the house. "I'm pleased to meet you."

His imposing demeanour unnerved Ginko. He was quite a contrast to her professors at the Women's Normal School.

"I have to agree with you. Generally speaking, women are shy, and particularly dislike being examined for gynaecological conditions. I've been at a loss about how to deal with the matter. It would be tremendously beneficial to have a female doctor for these kinds of problems. There's nothing taught at medical school that a woman wouldn't be able to learn, so there's no reason for women not to become doctors."

Ginko realized with relief that he accepted new ideas readily, having studied the fairly new field of Western medicine himself.

"By the way, which medical college are you aiming for?"

"I'd happily take a place at any school that offered me one."

"As you know at the moment, all medical schools are closed to women. I don't know that I can find you a place quickly, but I will check around."

"Do you think there might be one?"

"I don't know. But since I don't know, I'll have to start looking."

Ginko, greatly appreciating his straightforward attitude, thanked him and left.

It was a week later, at the beginning of March, when Ginko heard back from him. She went straight to meet him, and in his usual booming voice he told her, "I tried a number of places but none would accept a female student."

Ginko absorbed this in disappointed silence.

"There was just one, Kojuin in Shitaya, that said they'd let you enter."

Ginko jumped up from her chair. "Really?"

"Whether you stand or sit, what I have to say is the same, so please sit down!"

Ginko hurriedly reseated herself.

"At first they refused, bringing up the issue of moral discipline for the male students and other inconveniences for a woman, but they said that since the request was from me, they had no choice but to give in." Ishiguro was clearly pleased with himself, and justifiably so.

"Thank you so much."

"I know the President of that college well. Tsunenori Takashina – an exceptional man. A bit hard to please, though."

At last Ginko was moving a step closer to becoming a doctor. Feeling almost dizzy, she looked up at Ishiguro with bright eyes.

"You should go and see him about it within the next few days."

"I'll go right away." Ginko bowed very low.

* * *

Ginko went to see her former teacher, Yorikuni, to report on her plans to enter Kojuin. It would only be a matter of time until he found out on his own, since the President was the Imperial Court physician, and Yorikuni himself had frequent business at the court. But she was not going to see him only for the niceties of exchanging polite greetings and to let him know about her commencing medical training – she also wanted to know how he was.

"Is that so? You're going to become a doctor of Western medicine?" This was the first time she had told Yorikuni of her aspiration to be a doctor, and he listened gravely, with his arms folded. Even an advocate of Chinese medicine like Yorikuni had to admit that Western medicine was fitting for the times. "But it's going to take so long," he muttered.

"Pardon?"

"I mean, you still have years of study ahead of you." Once Ginko had graduated from the Women's Normal School, Yorikuni had intended to propose to her again – in fact, to keep at her until she agreed – but now he knew any chance of that was even further off than before.

"Yes, but I'm prepared for that," said Ginko

"Right," Yorikuni groaned.

Ginko had never seen Yorikuni look so troubled before. *I think that's for me.* Ginko felt a mixture of contrition and pleasure – he was a great man, but she was the one he wanted.

Kojuin Medical College was in Shitaya-Neribei, not far from Juntendo, where she had been hospitalized, so the area held many memories for Ginko.

The President had agreed to accept Ginko, but he made no special accommodations for a single female student – nothing in the way of facilities, equipment or adjustments to the rules. If she wanted to attend, her presence would be tolerated, but that was all. From day one, Ginko was in for nothing but rude shocks.

Places in medical colleges were generally limited to the sons of well-known former samurai families or those who had introductions from persons of note. Students ranged in age from under twenty to those in their forties, and many were rough characters who had fought in the recent upheaval of the Meiji Restoration. They were no longer permitted to carry their swords around, but the college atmosphere nevertheless tended to be that of a gathering of ruffians, all with chips on their shoulders.

The first day, after completing her registration papers, Ginko looked around wondering what to do next, but not a single person offered any guidance or directions. When she asked the office staff where she should go, the reply was a cold "Hmm, no idea". It was clear from their expressions that for them her mere presence besmirched the reputation of the school. With no alternative, Ginko set out alone to look around. The school consisted of nothing more than a white-walled, tile-roofed house with a handful of classrooms and labs lined up off the hallway. She looked in through the doorway of one classroom, where a large number of students were gathered.

Suddenly someone called out, "A doll!" The entire room stood up, clapping and stamping their wooden *geta* sandals on the floor. Ginko found herself surrounded by ten or fifteen unkempt men with stubbly beards. They looked like outlaws. Ginko flew back out of the room in fright, but the whistling students trailed after her. Boys and girls were educated separately from the age of seven, so even grown men were incapable of handling a female presence. The scent of a marriageable young woman in the vicinity was enough to create an uproar.

"Pretty, isn't she?"

"Mmm, and she's going to be taking the pulses of men."

"And seeing them naked too!"

Teasing and insults washed over Ginko. She felt like fleeing, but if she ran home now she would have wasted all of her efforts thus far. The memory of the brightly lit examining room of Juntendo Hospital, with her pale body on the table and her legs being forced apart, flashed through her mind. Ginko's cheeks burned. The humiliation she was undergoing now counted for nothing compared to what she had endured back then. She raised her head resolutely.

103

Ignoring the men, Ginko headed for a seat near the back of the classroom. As she moved, they stuck close behind, like a pack of starving wolves following a single lamb. The seating consisted of benches for four or five students to share, with a long board set up in front to serve as a desk. When Ginko sat down, the students herded around her. Then suddenly a large, swarthy man with unruly hair jumped to the teacher's podium and, fist raised, began to rant.

"Gentlemen, it is truly unbearable – unspeakable – that our glorious medical college, run by the Imperial Court's designated physician no less, has today admitted a female medical student. Why? Our honourable profession is being degraded to the work of women and children. It's not enough that educated women are breaking up the home – now they are proceeding to crush the medical profession. It's outrageous!"

The other students immediately began clapping and roaring their approval. Ginko wanted to cover her ears. Next a man in a full beard leapt up.

"Gentlemen, today we are faced with a female student. We will have to study medicine with women, listen to lectures and do experiments alongside women. In other words, we have been demoted to the level of women. Who's to blame?"

At this the hairy guy pounded his desk violently. "Hear! Hear!"

Nearly fifty students raised their fists in the air all together, shouting along with him. Ginko sat with her hands on her knees and her eyes closed, waiting for this to pass.

From the next day, Ginko left her home in Honjo at six in the morning in order to arrive early enough to secure a good seat near the front of the lecture hall. She had rethought her clothing and, instead of a casual kimono, she wore her reddish-brown *hakama* over a kimono and *geta* on her bare feet – a style similar to that of the male students. Naturally she eschewed any make-up, face-whitening powder or lipstick, and she wore her kimono neck pulled tightly closed and her sleeve openings firmly restrained. She meant to erase any femininity from her appearance.

The attempt, however, was not entirely successful. Her attractive features and wheat-coloured complexion made her appear several years younger than her true age, and the intelligence shining from her face made her all the prettier. In addition, with her *hakama* tightly tied, her small waist was accentuated and it made her figure even more eye-catching for the men.

Whenever Ginko appeared, the students would pound their desks and stomp their feet to harass her. There were also scattered hisses of "Woman, go home". Another favoured trick was to shake her desk or keep it pulled so far from her bench that even the men had trouble reaching it. Ginko then simply piled her books on her lap and took notes on top of them. The professors were not as openly hostile to her presence as the students, but neither did they hold a positive view of a woman becoming a doctor. They were men of progressive opinions, but that did not extend to accepting a woman into the exclusively male medical profession.

Ginko had been accepted into the school based on the personal, albeit reluctant permission of its president. He had only agreed because the request had come from Tadanori Ishiguro, and was frankly displeased by the friction it created with the other students. Integrating a medical college of students who had been segregated by sex since childhood seemed fraught with hazard.

There's no one who will help me

At the fringes of the lecture hall, Ginko bore it all in solitude. And the single cause of her isolation was that she was a woman. She had never felt more bitter about her fate. It was an era when women waited to eat until men were finished, walked a few paces behind men and always spoke respectfully when addressing them. When a man had something to say, a woman's response was expected to be "Yes, I understand". Women's concerns were supposed to be confined to housework and child raising.

It was in this context that Ginko, a woman, had suddenly appeared in a classroom full of men. Not only that, but it was a class in the medical field, where only men were allowed. Most people would have sided with the shocked and angry male students, who had always been taught that women were far beneath them.

Ginko's disease was relatively under control during this period, and she did not get fevers, but she did suffer from cramps and a frequent need to urinate. She always headed for the bathroom during breaks between lectures. At Kojuin, though, there were no facilities for women. The only toilet was a single stall in the men's bathroom, right next to the row of urinals. The men would line up at the urinals, talking and laughing. For Ginko, this was the worst time of all. She would try to slip by the men as unobtrusively as possible. At first the men were confused, and they just turned and stared curiously when she appeared in the bathroom, but as they got used to it, the harassment began.

In mid-May, a month and a half after Ginko had started attending lectures, she hurried as usual to the bathroom at the end of the midday lecture. About ten men were ahead of her, lined up and talking loudly. Ginko quickened her steps to pass them and head for the stall, when suddenly one of the men turned to face her. Noting the movement, she looked up and found him exposing himself.

"Oh!" she gasped involuntarily and covered her eyes with both hands, dropping into a crouch on the spot.

"No, *look*! I'm a man!"

The men's vulgar laughter filled the bathroom.

"Oh my, it seems to have upset Miss Female Scholar." So saying, he waved his penis in front of Ginko's face and tightly shut eyes.

Revealing her shock had only encouraged the men, and their disgraceful behaviour continued to escalate. She realized that she would have to remain unruffled and simply sail through their ranks no matter what they did. Thus resolved, the next day she composedly passed through the crowd of men and headed for the stall.

As she went to open the door, however, she saw that it had been freshly painted with the words "The Honourable Ginko Ogino". She maintained her composure and went in. But the men waited with folded arms outside the door. When she finished her business and came out, they all clapped and whistled.

There were even some who carefully put their ears to the door of the stall to listen. Or worse, they would occupy the stall until the end of the break simply out of spite. There were even those who would rush in as soon as she vacated it, and then attach a sign to the door announcing "Miss Ginko's got her period".

There was no one to whom Ginko could complain. She had chosen this path for herself. But it was hard. On returning home in the evening, she was unable to eat and simply laid her head on the desk and wept through the night. Little did she know, however, that the worst was yet to come.

Behind Kojuin ran a long stone wall where a firehouse had once been, beyond which was a mulberry field now gone to ruin. Rumour had it that, long ago, a man had hung himself from one of the trees, and most people were too frightened to pass by it at night. The mulberry field, however, was a shortcut home for Ginko, and she used it frequently.

At the beginning of July, at six-thirty in the evening, Ginko was hurrying home through the field, through weeds almost as tall as she was. About halfway across, as she approached a grove of tall zelkova trees, her path was suddenly blocked by three men. All three were square-shouldered, bearded student-types.

Ginko stopped short for a moment, then tried to walk past them as if she had not noticed them. The man in the middle spread his arms to block her way.

"Who do you think you are?" Ginko yelled as fiercely as she could, but the men just smiled scornfully and remained silent. The one in the middle had a walrus moustache and carried a cane in his right hand. It was dusk, and the shade of the trees made it even more difficult to see, but she had seen his face somewhere before. In the dim light, Ginko recognized the men as Kojuin students.

"Do you want something?" Ginko knew she should not show any weakness, so she glared squarely at the one directly in front of her.

"What do you *think* we want?" baited Walrus Moustache, his left hand tucked inside his kimono.

"Don't all men want the same thing from women?" added the one on his right, with a thin smile. He was exceptionally tall, with a stoop – Ginko barely came up to his shoulder. They had clearly known that Ginko used this path, and had lain in wait for her.

"You know very well, don't you, Miss Female Scholar?" She could hear their ragged breathing.

"So whaddya say?"

"About what?" They planned to assault her like common thugs. If she broke down in tears, it would be all over for her right there. She desperately pulled herself together and stared back at them.

"We're asking to take turns, got it?"

She turned again, but they were blocking the path behind her.

"We won't tell anyone, so there's no need to play hard to get."

She looked past them as far as she could, but there was no one in sight.

"Take your clothes off!" roared Walrus Moustache, his eyes bloodshot. They were going to gang-rape her.

"Hurry up!"

Ginko suddenly crouched, feinted to the right, and then darted to the left under the arm of the one in front of her.

"Help!" Ginko ran as fast as she could, her cloth-wrapped bundle of books under her arm. But her legs were no match for theirs. They quickly caught up and pulled her back by her collar.

"NO!" she screamed as she was yanked back.

The men had become beasts, and fought to pin down her flailing limbs.

"Wait! Just wait a minute, *please!*" Ginko had had an inspiration.

"What?" Struck by her vehemence, the men released her momentarily. She quickly pulled her dishevelled collar and front together and held them closed with both hands.

"You can't run away."

"Wait..." Ginko took a deep breath and fixed the three men with a stare as she mustered her courage.

"So, *what?*" demanded one of the assailants impatiently.

"You really want my body?"

"You got that right."

Ginko took a deep breath again and said, "Fine. Do as you like, then."

The men were taken aback.

"Well, you've got guts," the one on the left said as he reached out towards her.

"But…"

The man yanked back his hand.

"I've got gonorrhoea."

"What did you say?"

"My husband gave me gonorrhoea and then divorced me. I want to become a doctor so I can cure it."

The men were silent.

"I'm still infectious, but if you want this body, it's all yours."

The sun had set, and dusk was shrouding them fast. Her small pale face floated like an ornament in the dark. She remained with her eyes closed and her mind blank. She could neither run nor fight them off. But the three had lost their bravura and were glancing questioningly at each other.

"Is that true?" asked Walrus Moustache, finally breaking the silence. He seemed to be the leader. "There's no mistake?"

At the second question, Ginko nodded firmly.

Walrus Moustache signalled the other two with his eyes. "We'll let you off for today, then," he said in a low growl.

Ginko slowly opened her eyes. The three were looking at her as though they had never seen her before. The night gathered more closely around them, bringing with it the scent of the mulberries.

"Slut," he spat as he turned away. The other two followed suit and their figures weaved uncertainly as they disappeared off down the path.

Ginko's legs gave out and she sank to the ground. The light from the yellow moon shining in the west grew stronger. Sitting in the almost unnerving quiet, she could feel neither hate nor anger as tears rolled down her cheeks.

Ginko said nothing of what had happened to either the President of the college or the police. It had been her decision to study with men, which could be viewed as a dangerous undertaking from the start, and she could not say that it had not been a mistake to take that isolated path in the evening. Women were supposed to stay home, and the outside world was made to suit men. Any attempt she made to punish the thugs would merely damage her own name, and it might even endanger her hard-won opportunity to study medicine.

Ginko's fears were well founded. Some years later, around 1887, private medical colleges started letting female students informally attend classes without putting them to all the trouble Ginko had gone through. Even then, though, there were no more than one or two fully registered female students. And even though these were medical colleges, the rough times of the Meiji Restoration were not yet over, and the atmosphere in the classrooms was still threatening. Unless they were possessed of outstanding strength of will and strong nerves, most women were unable to hold up; they developed nervous disorders and quit their studies part-way through.

Even at Saisei Academy, which had the highest number of women attending classes in 1895, there was one problem after another with moral discipline. When one of the incidents resulted in a criminal case, all the female students were forced to quit the school. Bitter struggles for female medical students continued until Yayoi Yoshioka founded Tokyo Women's Medical School in 1900. For Ginko, struggling all alone among these men twenty years earlier, the odds were unquestionably stacked against her.

Ginko stayed home for two days while she gathered the strength to return to the classroom. The terror she had felt, along with the cover of dusk, had combined to leave her without a clear image of her attackers, and she could not be sure she recognized them at school. She thought they might have been from a group of hotheads who always encamped themselves to the right of the classroom and spent the breaks criticizing and reviling the new government. She had the feeling they were watching her. When she sat down, she stole a few glances at them, but the one she remembered best of the three, the one with the walrus moustache, was not there. She knew that every year twenty to thirty per cent of the student body dropped out, and she wondered if the attack on her had been his parting shot.

Ginko intensified her efforts to look unfazed by anything. Whenever she recalled the incident, she flushed with fury and shame, but no matter what rumours the men circulated, she was sure that her undaunted attitude would cast doubts on anything they might say. She knew she had to ignore them.

She did her best to think of the whole episode as a natural disaster, a whirlwind she had walked into, and tried to convince herself that she had not somehow invited it. The body that one man had sullied, other men still wanted to use. The body that she herself hated was still attractive to men. As far as Ginko was concerned, men were no better than beasts, and it was not worth wasting her time thinking about every little thing stupid animals did. Like sand caught in her teeth, the repulsiveness of the men was something she wanted to spit out back at them, but she had to keep it locked inside.

Ginko recalled her time at Juntendo Hospital, as though carefully re-examining a fold-up picture book. The shame she had felt then was far more vivid than any other picture in her life that she could compare it to. Against the background of that, any other trouble she had experienced seemed light and ordinary, like a glass bead with its colours faded and paled into insignificance.

Ten days later, Ginko went to visit Yorikuni. Whenever she was closed up in dark thoughts, Yorikuni's round, kind face would come to her. He would never let her down. Even now, if Ginko changed her mind and said she would marry him, she knew he would take her in an instant.

Ginko did not have the minutest intention of marrying Yorikuni. He was her teacher, and she thought of him only as a kind father, or older brother. Even so, if worse came to worse, she knew she could run for protection into his arms, and she counted on that. She had no intention of doing so, but it was a comfort to her to think she could. For Ginko, Yorikuni was a safe harbour to flee to in a storm.

Climbing the familiar slope to his house, she could see the woven brushwood fence around his garden. It was closely cut and very neat. *That's unusual*, she thought, amused by how little attention Yorikuni generally paid to his garden's appearance. She followed the garden steps, almost dancing along.

"Hello? Anybody home?"

She would poke her head inside the door and surprise him. That full-moon face of his would crumble into a pleased smile.

"Hello?" Ginko called again, her feet coming to a halt at the entrance. On the floor, instead of Yorikuni's usual big *geta*, there was a pair of pretty bright red-strapped sandals.

Ginko's breath caught in her throat and she looked around. On the shoebox was an arrangement of summer daffodils. Next to it, a slender paper parasol was set in the umbrella stand. One glance was sufficient to see that it was a woman's.

"Coming!"

Before Ginko could decide what to do, she heard footsteps coming from the interior of the house.

"Well, hello, Miss Ginko! It's been a long time!"

Ginko had been about to duck out and flee, but she stopped when she recognized the old housekeeper.

"Come in! Professor Inoue is out at the Imperial Household Agency, but we're expecting him home soon."

"Miss Ise," Ginko asked her. "Is there another guest here too?" Her gaze fell again to the pretty sandals.

"No, no. Oh, you didn't know? He's found a second wife."

"He's remarried?"

"Three months ago! She's fifteen years younger than he is and just like a little doll."

Astounded, Ginko could not muster a reply.

"I'll call her now. Isn't this nice? You'll finally have a chance to meet!"

"Wait!" Ginko called after Ise's rapidly retreating back. "There's no need to bother."

"But you've come all this way…"

"I'll come back again later."

"But it'll only take a moment—"

"No, it's *fine.*"

Under the puzzled eyes of the flustered housekeeper, Ginko hurriedly closed the door and practically ran out the gate. And without pausing or breaking stride, she went directly to Ogie's home in Takemachi.

"What are you doing here, in the middle of the day like this?"

Without bothering to answer, Ginko launched straight into a full account of the boorish and misconceived behaviour of Yorikuni Inoue.

The largest of the lecture rooms at Kojuin could seat fifty people at most, but there were almost one hundred students in the school. Sometimes students would be absent, or they would be divided into two groups to take the lectures, but practical seminars were rare opportunities, and for these all the students crowded in together.

At these seminars, students took turns summarizing the medical conditions of the patients they had each been assigned to examine. It was near the end of September when Gin's turn to do this came around. The patient she had been assigned was a compactly built man of fifty-two, who was said to have been a magistrate's assistant in the shogunate. He had an open wound on his right upper arm the size of a pomegranate, and the pus from it soaked through three bandages a day. His arm dangled uselessly whenever it was removed from its sling. It looked as though the bone had been broken and left to putrefy.

It had been fifteen years since he had been injured, but it was clear from the wounds on both the front and back of his arm that he had been shot, the bullet passing right through him He absolutely refused to give an honest account about what had happened, however, and instead insisted relentlessly: "I fell from the roof." At this late date, even if he were exposed for what had formerly been considered illicit political activity, he was in no danger of being punished or censured, but he obdurately refused to alter his account. Although the wound's infection had gone through a period of remission, it had recently worsened.

Ginko knew the man, because she had attended the Professor's examinations of him. Several days before her clinical practice, she studied the upper arm, referring to Stromeyer's book on human anatomy and Celsius's book on surgery. Fairly confident that she had familiarized herself with his case, she went to see him in his room the afternoon before she was scheduled to treat him.

"My name's Ginko Ogino and I'm a medical student here. I'll be coming to treat you tomorrow as part of my student practical training, so I've come to examine you today." Ginko addressed him in the politest of tones, but the man kept his face turned to the wall and refused to acknowledge her. "I have to examine you now to prepare your treatment in time for tomorrow. Please bear with me."

This did elicit a reply, and the man growled, "I've no need for a woman."

The other patients in the large room stared suspiciously at Ginko.

"Yes, I may be a woman, but I've been properly trained, studying the same materials as everyone else. It isn't relevant to your examination, and I would like to proceed if I may."

Ginko bowed her head in respectful request once again, but the man showed no signs of relenting. Next she tried her trump card. "I am here to examine you on the orders of the President of this college. He instructed me to examine you and report back to him." Her voice was clear and pleasant.

The man shook his head, still bearing a samurai topknot, and clucked at her disapprovingly. "Whether it's the head of this college or anyone else doesn't matter. There are just some things that a woman shouldn't see."

"But you are a patient of this hospital."

"I may look bad now, but I'm from a samurai family. If it got out that I'd been examined by a female doctor, I'd never be able to show my face to my ancestors. If you force me, I'll have to slit open my stomach instead. Then you'll be free to examine me all you want."

He made as if to pull out a dagger from a hiding place under his bed. Ginko sighed. There was no way she would be able to examine him. She thought of appealing directly to the college President, but that would be tantamount to admitting that women were inherently unfit for the medical profession. It could be seized on as an opportunity to ban her from lectures, and she would lose everything. Nevertheless, she realized there was nothing to gain from forcing the matter while the man's feelings were running high, so she left the room.

Lacking any further inspiration, Ginko gazed out the window, wondering what to do. It occurred to her that she might appease him with a present. Leaving the hospital, she walked east half a block to a confectioner's shop. There she bought some country-style sweet-bean-jam-filled cakes, and returned to the man's room.

"I'd like to ask for your cooperation once more. I'm sure there are a number of things that don't meet your approval, but I will do my absolute best. So please consider allowing me to examine you."

Ginko bowed her head and offered the wrapped package of still-warm cakes to the man. This was a complete reversal of the usual doctor-patient relationship. But she was neither ashamed nor interested in putting on airs. *This may be undignified, but it's inconsequential*, she told herself as she kept her head bowed.

"Please, that's all I'm asking," she bowed her head once more.

"Leave me alone, you stupid woman!" shouted the man, hurling the cakes at her feet. "I said I won't show you and I won't. Leave me alone now!"

His face was pale with anger, but Ginko's was even paler. Glancing at the cakes on the floor, and just barely controlling her frustration, she left the room.

After the last lecture of the afternoon, Ginko headed for the hospital room a third time. The man was eating his dinner with his good hand.

"I've come again."

The student practice was the next morning. If she failed to gain the man's acquiescence this evening, she would not be able to prepare in time. The man looked at her and, without a word, turned his back.

"I'm begging you. Please let me examine you."

No response.

"This is not something I want to do just for me. It is also for the progress of Western medicine. Gender aside, please let me study."

The others patients in the room watched the proceedings with fed-up expressions.

115

"In the past I also had a serious illness and was hospitalized in Juntendo Hospital. It was there that I learnt the suffering of a patient and made my vow to become a doctor. I swear my request is not just for myself. I think there are fields within medicine where women doctors may be able to contribute too."

Ginko leant forwards, both hands on his bed, almost touching his bed cover with her forehead as she bowed down. "An examination in the name of medicine is the same whether it is conducted by a male or female. Please let me examine you."

If he did not grunt an assent now, Ginko intended to sit by his bed all night. She waited, her head bowed. The man continued to eat, with his back to her, in silence. The others in the room were silent too. It seemed like a long time passed, then Ginko noticed the man's upper body shift out of the corner of her eye.

"I'll show you." The man sat cross-legged on the bed, and fixed Ginko with a direct stare.

"Really?"

The man nodded leisurely. "Yes, I can't refuse someone with your determination."

"Thank you very much!"

"But," the man recrossed his legs, and looked up at the ceiling as he continued, "I won't have a woman touching it, and I won't take any orders from you. That's my final offer."

Limited to just looking, Ginko would be unable to assess the depth of the wound or the extent of the infection, much less judge whether his joints could move. But, considering that this was a former samurai, it was probably the biggest concession she could expect of him.

"I see. Well, that will have to do, then."

The man, unsmiling, slowly began to unwrap the bandages.

Ginko put up with many bitter experiences at Kojuin, but she gradually began to get used to life there and even to enjoy it.

Jostled about by the men, attired in her usual simple style with her hair pulled back in a bun, her habitual will to succeed grew even stronger. Occasionally, though, she questioned herself, and wondered whether she was losing her femininity. *But if I wanted to have the same life and loves as other people, I wouldn't be able to achieve what other people can't. What I'm trying to do is as different from what ordinary women want as heaven and earth. So this is the way it should be.* Sometimes, however, the loneliness would creep in like a cold wind seeping through the cracks in a wall.

A year passed. During the second year of study at Kojuin, the medical students were occupied with clinical medical studies, including internal medicine and surgery. Human anatomy was part of these studies, but for the most part it was confined to lectures based on diagrams, without any practice dissecting a real human body. Even anatomy books were scarce. The top schools had one or two of the best-known books by foreign authors, but Kojuin had only a single book, hand-copied by an expert artist.

Ginko tried to imagine the inside of a human from the red-, yellow- and blue-coloured lines of the diagrams of organs lying below the skin.

From the vicinity of the solar plexus, the stomach hangs down in a hook shape, gently curves upwards, and connects to the duodenum, which extends for the width of twelve fingers. This then connects to the small intestine, which extends in many folded layers for twenty to thirty feet or more, and then to the fat large intestine with its dramatic constrictions, which runs up, across and down, then reaches the rectum, which opens out at the anus.

It was half-discomfiting, half-interesting to just look at the illustrations, but as a medical student, Ginko had to commit every minute detail to memory. In the middle of the night she would stealthily examine her own reflection in the mirror, using her finger to draw imaginary lines around where the internal organs should be.

To the left and the right of the trachea and covered by the ribs are the two lungs, and, as though hidden under the left lung, the fist-sized heart. To the right in an umbrella shape is the liver, then in the abdomen on the left, bordered by the diaphragm, is the spleen. At the lower part of the stomach there is the pancreas, then the egg-sized kidneys to the left and right, behind where the small intestine is wound. In women, there is then in the centre of the lower abdomen, in the shape of a samisen's plectrum, the uterus. From the uterus, as though pulling it up to the left and right, are the Fallopian tubes, which extend to the ovaries. To the front of the uterus is the bladder, which connects to the urethra, and then to the outside.

With black ink, Ginko marked the placement and size of each organ on her own body. Before long, her pale, nude figure was covered in ink. Anyone seeing her would have assumed that she was insane.

"Stomach, liver, kidneys." She spoke the words aloud as she looked at the places on her body in the mirror. She envisioned the illustrations in the books she had read during the day layered on top of her naked body, and felt as though she was looking past her skin and inside herself.

"Uterus, bladder, urethra." Ginko's voice stilled. "And the internal membrane here…" She regarded her ink-painted lower abdomen solemnly. "And the inflamed Fallopian tubes, blocked by the build-up of infected material in them, will not let an egg pass from the ovaries through the tubes. This results in lifelong infertility."

The pictures of this flew through her mind: the inflammation throbbing unnaturally in red, with blue for the pus building up and obstructing the insides of her tubes. "The bacteria thrive and multiply, squirming around." Without thinking, Ginko lifted the brush in her right hand and painted the whole stretch of her lower abdomen entirely in black.

"Dirty, dirty, dirty!"

Shaking her head back and forth as though possessed, Ginko covered herself in ink. If she could, she would have ripped off her skin and torn out the infected organs with her own hands, shaking off the blood and flinging them away.

"Ugh!" She collapsed before the mirror, her energy spent.

Gradually Ginko calmed down and returned to her senses. Reflected in the mirror was the female body a man had touched for three years after she turned sixteen. Now it was marked all over with patterns in black.

Despite the insanity that Ginko experienced whenever she visualized anatomy, she craved the opportunity to see a true human anatomical dissection. Chances were few and far between, however, even at the top medical schools. Any time a dissection was announced, the most famous doctors of the time would crowd into the hall, so it was nigh on impossible for the likes of medical students at a small school such as Kojuin to ever see one.

"A hundred people a day die in Tokyo, yet we can't even get one body to dissect." Ginko had invited Ogie out to a newly opened milk hall in Ueno. She enjoyed the somehow Western scent of the milk, but her favourite thing about the place was its white walls and chic atmosphere. "People are generally treated miserably, like cats or dogs, but as soon as the body is dead it suddenly commands great respect – what a contradiction!"

"But that's because anyone can become a Buddha after they die, isn't it?"

"What a strange way to think! Wouldn't it be better to treat people well while they're still alive? It's ridiculous."

"It's all very well saying that now, but if you died and your body was taken apart, you wouldn't be too pleased about it, would you?" Ogie could not bring herself to agree with Ginko.

"But I'm not talking about cutting off heads or arms and legs. I just want to be able to see what's inside! After looking inside and taking out the inner organs, we'd sew them up neatly again, so that from the outside they'd look exactly the same."

"So the body would be hollowed out?"

"Yes, just like they do in taxidermy."

"I don't much like the idea of stuffed humans."

"But that way the dead bodies last longer. And after two or three days they're cremated anyway. Whether a body has been dissected or not beforehand, either way we still have the bones to bring home."

It may have been just as Ginko said, but Ogie could not accept Ginko's pragmatic view. When she talked like this, she seemed like a completely different person.

"You need the government's permission to touch even one finger of the deceased, let alone carve them up for dissection," continued Ginko, as she delicately lifted her milk cup with her little finger crooked.

"But dissections by doctors are allowed," Ogie retorted confidently.

"That's true. But you still need permission from the family and the police to touch even the most ordinary dead person's body."

"Well, of course."

"Do you think there are *any* families out there who will agree to have their loved one dissected?"

"I don't suppose there are."

"So we never get the opportunity!"

Ogie felt somewhat repelled by Ginko's gimlet-eyed view of other humans, and would have liked to convince her friend that her cause was hopeless.

Ginko, however, set her now-empty cup aside and went on, "Seriously, though, the reason Western medicine is ahead of Eastern medicine is because it accepts human dissections. It's a waste of time to memorize old-fashioned names for internal organs out of books, when just opening someone up and looking for yourself will tell you everything you need to know. *That's* the basis for the scientific development of Western medicine."

Ginko waved her hands in the air for emphasis, as was her habit when worked up, and now she smacked her hand down on the table for good measure. Hair pulled back in a neat bun and dressed in *hakama*, anyone seeing the two friends engrossed in this heated discussion in a milk hall would know at a glance that they were female scholars, and the sight would not strike them as particularly odd. But no one would have imagined that their subject of discussion was human dissection.

"But there are some bodies with no one to claim them, aren't there?"

"Yes, exactly. But you know what? That's no good either. When there's no one to claim a body, it means there's no one to give permission."

"I see, so it's that kind of logic…"

"The officials are such thick-headed sticklers for the rules!"

"I suppose you have a point, but…" Ogie couldn't help thinking it would be sad for someone who died in an accident, whose family could not be found, to be suddenly left in the hands of some medical students. Ogie herself, unmarried and without children, could not say for certain that she would not end up like that. Indeed, it was the same for Ginko – but judging from her blasé attitude, she could not care less about the fate of her body after she died.

"So our only hope is for someone to bequeath their body to medicine while they're still alive," Ginko pressed on.

"As in, 'Please dissect me'?"

"Yes, for the purpose of the advancement of medical science."

"Does anyone do such a thing?"

"Yes, but only one so far."

"A former samurai?"

"No, they're no use! They have their honour and name to uphold, and always find some excuse."

"Then who?"

"A prostitute."

"A woman?"

"Yes. She was in Koitogawa Sanatorium and died of tuberculosis. Apparently though, three days before she died, she said that since she'd never done anything of use for the world, they should use her body for dissection."

"Poor thing," said Ogie, deeply moved.

"Well, she was certainly the exception."

"Yes, I guess so." Ogie was sure she would never have the courage to do that herself.

"Well, at this rate I'll probably never get to see a dissection while I'm at Kojuin."

"I've heard that at Daigaku Higashiko they do them occasionally. How do they get the bodies?"

"Oh, those are executions."

"People who got the death penalty?"

"Yes. If no one claims the body, the authorities dispose of it by selling it off. That's how the university gets hold of them."

"Dispose of?" Ginko's manner of speaking was so matter of fact. She hadn't been like this before she'd entered Kojuin. Could just one year of medical study have changed her this much? For Ogie, the change in her friend was unnerving.

"Actually, you know, I've got an idea – but it's a secret."

"What do you have in mind?"

"You won't tell another soul?"

"Of course not."

Ginko leant so close to Ogie that they nearly bumped foreheads. "I want some human bones." Ginko quickly glanced around before continuing, "I'm thinking of getting some from the Kozukkapara execution grounds."

"Kozukkapara?"

"Shh! Keep your voice down!" Ginko's finger was at her lips, but her eyes were smiling as she went on, "They say there are human bones lying exposed there. I know bones make most people shudder, but for us they're more precious than gold, so it seems like such a waste."

Ogie stared at Ginko, speechless.

"We asked at Ekoin Temple if they'd share some of their bones with us, but they turned us down flat, so there's nothing for it but to—"

"Are you serious?" Ogie's voice was hoarse.

"Of course! Why wouldn't I be?"

Kozukkapara been used for executions throughout the Edo era. The new Meiji government had abolished decapitation, and Kozukkapara was no longer used, but the bones of those executed there remained, and people still reacted with horror to the name.

Just inside the tall wooden fence surrounding the grounds, there was an "execution *jizo*", a stone image of a Buddhist guardian, to console the souls of the prisoners who had died there. Ekoin Temple was just to the right of this. The chief priest-in-residence said daily prayers for the dead, but the grounds were unkempt and overrun by weeds. The area was carefully avoided at night, and there were few brave enough to make visits even during the daytime.

Ginko had seemed to be teasing Ogie about her plan to gather bones there, but in fact she was serious. A month later, towards the end of October, she invited four fellow Kojuin students to join her. Of course these students were men. Ginko had chosen them because, like her, they were passionate about their studies, coming early to all the lectures and occupying the front-row seats.

At first they were taken aback by Ginko's suggestion, but after thinking it over they all agreed. Involving too many students would be risky, so the four agreed to meet Ginko in the field behind the school to finalize their scheme.

"What'll happen if we're caught, I wonder?" asked one student nervously.

"The first thing to do is get in the good graces of the head priest. Then if he sees us, he might let the matter pass." Ginko looked at them each in turn as she continued, "Tomorrow we'll go offer prayers at the temple. Remember to take some coins to make an offering too."

"But won't it look suspicious? I mean, we don't have any connection with the place."

"We can make up a reason. For example, we could say that a body donated for medical study had been buried there, and we came to offer prayers for his soul. We could then take the opportunity to make a larger than usual donation to the temple."

"Good thinking." The men all nodded. Ginko was the instigator, so they would go along with her on the details as well.

"And we can get a good look at the layout of the grounds in daylight."

"OK. Then what?"

"Let's meet in front of Ryusenji market at eight tomorrow evening. We'll have to carry the bones in bags on poles balanced over our shoulders. We can't come all the way back here like that, though, so from Imado we'll hire a boat to take us as far as the Izumibashi Bridge in Shitaya."

Ginko spread out a map she had brought along and pointed out the streets. The men looked a little green as they stared first at Ginko, then at the map.

"Once we're in the execution grounds, one of you stand guard by the front gate. I'll watch the temple. The rest of you dig. If someone comes, everyone run. We'll meet up afterwards at the Imado dock."

The men looked at each other, then nodded in silence. They were like a gang of thieves, with Ginko as their leader.

"What if we're caught?"

This was from the largest of the men, who sounded none too sure of himself. They were all young, and it was clear they had never done anything like this before. Neither had Ginko, for that matter.

"Surely they won't just let us off?"

Nobody knew what, if any, the penalties were for stealing bones. Even if the law did not punish them, however, they would most likely all be expelled.

"It's too risky."

"We shouldn't worry about it now. If we're caught, we're caught, and we'll deal with it then," Ginko retorted bracingly. "If that happens, we'll just tell them the truth – that we're medical students and we only wanted to study some bones. We might get a lecture, but they won't kill us, I'm sure."

"Of course not," the large student hurried to agree.

"And anyway, if we are caught, the first one they'll catch will be me, so *you* have little to fear."

At this the men finally relaxed, letting out their breath and chuckling.

The next day, the five gathered and set off for Ekoin Temple. They delegated the most earnest and studious-looking one among them, a student by the name of Hashimoto, to announce them to the chief priest. The priest betrayed no hint of suspicion as he took them to see the large stone monument behind the temple.

"The bones of prisoners who had no one to collect their bodies are all buried together under here," he told them, further explaining that while some were criminals, others were merely victims of the changing times. Some were vicious and brutal robbers, murderers, arsonists and wife-beaters. At the other end of the spectrum were zealous patriots who, on the wrong side of the authorities of the day, had died there as well. Reduced to bones, however, their value was all the same.

Perhaps in a good mood because of the students' donation to the temple, the priest gave an extra-long Sutra reading in front of the monument. Standing behind him with their heads bowed, the five covertly surveyed the area. The monument itself was a large stone engraved only with "Grave of the Nameless". The black earth around the stone was overgrown with weeds, and the ground, perhaps softened by rain, was sunken in places. It probably would not take much digging to yield a quick pile of bones.

Later that evening, the group met at eight o'clock in front of the Otori Shrine. Laden with rakes and hoes, and carrying poles, they headed for Imado. They may have resembled a group of farmers, but they felt more like loyal samurai embarking on a raid. Having come this far, there was no turning back now, and the five of them walked in silence. The sky had been completely overcast, but as they neared Imado a chill autumn wind began moving the clouds along. By the time they reached Kozukkapara, the moon had come out to illuminate the temple grounds in bluish-white light.

The five crouched down as they moved forwards through the thick autumn weeds. Behind the execution area was a raggedy low fence, through which they could see the rows of wooden grave-marker sticks inside, white in the moonlight like withered trees. Past them, a solitary light shone inside Ekoin Temple. The wind had picked up now, and the undergrowth crunched faintly underfoot. Insects hummed and chirped around them, and in the distance they could hear dogs howling.

The five intruders looked at each other, their faces pale and set, before proceeding. The first man clambered over the fence, followed by Ginko and then the remaining three. Before them lay the execution site, but it was just as overgrown as the rest of the grounds. Earlier they had pinpointed a zelkova tree as the place where they should turn right in order to reach the monument. The temple light wavered, half-hidden between the low trees. The five moved into single file and proceeded along the narrow path. Wooden memorial boards of every size sprang up whitely around them in the moonlight. It was like a scene from the end of the world.

They were just approaching the zelkova tree when suddenly there was a growl, then barks rent the air.

"Uh-oh! Dogs!" The leader backed up in alarm and fell down.

The stillness of moments before was gone and the night was filled with howling and barking. It was as though the dogs had been lying in wait.

"Run!"

The group scattered and ran for their lives. Later, all Ginko could remember of her flight was the silhouette in the moonlight of a huge dog, half as tall as she, running as swiftly as the wind.

By the time the five regrouped at the reservoir to the south of Kozukkapara, they were too winded to speak. The *hakama* trousers of two of the men were in shreds, while another had been bitten in the rear. Ginko and one other student were unscathed, but all were completely covered in evening dew and mud from the waist down.

They beat a hasty retreat home, but Ginko refused to give up. As for the men, they had seen more than enough of the execution grounds, but they could not be outdone by a woman.

"We'll bring some fish to keep the dogs happy. As long as they don't bark, we won't have any problems. No one came out of Ekoin last night to check, did they?"

The bones had been tantalizingly within reach, and Ginko couldn't bear to give up on them. Encouraged by her enthusiasm, the men agreed to a new plan. In addition to a lookout and diggers, they appointed one of their number to be in charge of the dogs, providing him with food to throw to them.

The overcast night threatened rain at any moment. This time they succeeded in distracting the dogs, and in those bought moments they dug frantically. With each blow of the hoe, the earth yielded something, and they pulled up one round skull, arm or leg bone after another, white even in the darkness. Their raid successful, they gathered two bags full, and journeyed back from Imado to Izumibashi Bridge. By the time the sky began to lighten at four in the morning, they were each back in their respective lodgings.

The next day they washed the dirt off the bones, only to find that few were satisfactory specimens and most had rotted away. But at least they were authentic. Ginko fitted bone fragments together at her desk, painstakingly comparing them inside and out, sketching them and, for the first time, really feeling the shape and weight of human bones.

"Learning medicine takes more than just study," she would sometimes say in later years, with a hint of pride.

Having got her hands on human bones, Ginko's desire to learn was stronger than ever, but one pressing problem remained. This, of course, was money. Kojuin required fees for everything. Tuition alone was six times what she had paid at the Tokyo Women's Normal School. As a woman, she was ineligible to stay in the school dormitory, and thus could not benefit from its lower rent. There were no scholarships available for private colleges. Furthermore, the cost of medical textbooks was exorbitant.

The most highly valued books of the time were in foreign languages, such as Handenburg's *Science*, Wagener's *Chemistry*, Bock's *Anatomy and Anatomical Diagrams* and Stromeyer's *Surgery*, most of which were originally written in German and then translated into Dutch. The students further required quadrilingual dictionaries in English, French, German and Dutch, as well as Kramer's *Dictionary of Technical Terms*.

Ginko's predicament may be better appreciated through the story of Guntaro Kimura, a Western-studies scholar. When Kimura's home was destroyed in an earthquake, all he had of worth to sell was his copy of Kramer's *Dictionary of Technical Terms*, but the money he received for this tome enabled him to build a new house. Such were the prices commanded by medical books and dictionaries. Of course, books like these were far beyond Ginko's reach, and so she patiently waited her turn to copy the few volumes in the school's library.

Though Ginko had long since graduated from the Women's Normal School, she was still relying on her older sister Tomoko for three yen a month. Tomoko never uttered a word of complaint or even hinted that their original promise had been for a much shorter period of time. Unfortunately, however, three yen was still nowhere near enough for Ginko to get by on. The tuition for the first semester at Kojuin was one yen thirty *sen*, the second semester was one yen fifty *sen*, and there were also fees amounting to fifty *sen* a month for microscopes and experiments. On top of that, Ginko paid three or four yen per month in rent, so expenses for the first semester were actually seven or eight yen a month, rising to ten yen a month for the second semester.

At this rate, Ginko would never be able to continue her medical studies. After considerable thought, she went to see Ogie to ask her to keep an eye out for home-tutor positions. She was not sure she could teach and keep up with her studies, but it was too late to worry about that.

In less than a month Ogie had found three students for Ginko. "Each of these are respectable families, and are excellent positions for a home tutor." Two visits a week to each of the three homes would provide Ginko with the living she needed.

"The Maeda family is headed by a secretary of the Ministry of Agriculture and Commerce, Mr Takashima is the foremost import-export trader in Japan, and Mr Arakawa is a teacher at the Naval College."

"Do you really think they'll agree to have someone like me in their homes?" Ginko asked, intimidated by such illustrious names.

"You are going to be teaching them academic subjects. You're not looking for profit or involved in war-mongering. In academic subjects you are second to nobody, so do try to be more confident." Ogie was as brisk as always. "It's also fortunate that you're a daughter of the leading family of Tawarase."

"What do you mean by that?"

"I mean that your background helps them feel comfortable hiring you."

"Surely not!" Her family background was irrelevant to her

academic training. She hated Tawarase, and thought she had left it behind.

"That is how society works, at least for now. Being from a good home can be an advantage, and there's no harm in using it." Ogie offered this with breezy confidence, and Ginko really was in no position to complain.

"These jobs will help me greatly."

"But will your health hold up? One of the homes is in Hongo, one is in Honjo and the other is in Azabu."

"It'll be fine. I like to walk around town."

"But it will be quite far, over two miles, and you'll have to do it no matter what the weather."

"Let me do it – I want to try." At the prospect of being able to support herself, Ginko's outlook brightened immediately.

Of the three homes Ginko began to visit, Takashima's was the largest, as befitted a wealthy merchant. Takashima had had his hand in a number of businesses and was well known, but when Ginko met him, he was nearly fifty and in the process of handing his business over to his son, while he devoted himself to studying the divination lore of the classic work known as the *Donsho*.

Ginko made her rounds in kimono and wooden *geta*, footwear not known for comfort when walking distances. She had brushed off Ogie's concerns about the weather, but rainy days did indeed make the daily trips even more difficult.

Often when she got home she was too exhausted to review her school work and would fall asleep instead. But even so, she would wake in the middle of the night. The habit had lingered on from her days at the Women's Normal School, when she had studied by lamplight in the cupboard. She was starting to feel a difference physically, though, now that she had passed twenty-five. Her motivation was as strong as in her early twenties, but even though she planned to study until morning, she would sometimes fall asleep at her desk before dawn broke.

When copying a medical textbook that had to be returned quickly, she would slap herself to stay awake. If that had no effect, she would soak a facecloth in cold water, apply it to her face, and then turn once again to her book.

One other problem with her new job as a home tutor was finding a place to change clothes. When attending classes at Kojuin, Ginko dressed as plainly as possible to avoid attracting the interest of the men there – no make-up, hair pulled back in a bun, her kimono covered with *hakama* trousers. However, each of the houses she visited as a tutor were respectable, and it would not do for a woman to go dressed like that. The attire of female students was considered boldly Westernized, and it would have been scandalous to wear it in polite society. At worst, it could offend her employers, who might wonder who indeed they had hired to look after their children's education.

So, when Ginko went to her tutoring jobs after school, she had to find some place on the way where she could remove her *hakama*. At school, the curious eyes of the men followed her everywhere, and she could not just step out of her trousers on the street. A public toilet would have been helpful, but no such facilities were available. After considerable thought, Ginko finally settled on the thicket behind Yushima Temple, where nobody would see her. She would rush into the shelter of the thick trees and shrubs, hurriedly take off her *hakama*, and quickly tuck them into the carry-all cloth wrap she had brought with her. Then she would straighten her clothes and hair, and dash out from behind the temple. It soon became part of her daily routine.

Just as her financial worries began to subside, a new problem surfaced. During the summer of the year Ginko had started at Kojuin, she had occasionally experienced some light pain in her lower abdomen. By the start of her second year, the incidence had increased to once or twice a month, and the pain was stronger. By the summer of her second year, she spent several days a month in bed, when the pain became worse near her period. Discharge had also increased, as well as a feeling of heaviness and general lethargy. The disease that had been in remission for so long had flared up again.

She tested her urine herself and, with its muddy appearance and protein deposits, the results were unequivocal. Her body had weakened. Ginko nevertheless kept to her usual schedule of classes and teaching, secretly preparing and dosing herself with a Chinese medicine of sandalwood oil and bearberry.

It was in the autumn of her second year that Ginko finally broke out in a fever and collapsed. She was confined to bed and was delirious with fever for three days and nights. The heat and cramping pain in her lower abdomen was the same as before too. She knew that in her current condition, simply taking medicine would not lead to a complete recovery.

I wish I could go back to Tawarase. In the encroaching chill of winter, as Ginko lay alone in her room, she dreamt that she met her mother on the bank of the Toné River.

On the morning of the third day, she was bathed in sweat as her fever finally broke, and after three more days to recover, she headed back to school. It had been a six-day absence. She had lost weight, and looked as though she had suddenly aged. She decided to quit one of her three tutoring jobs.

The programme of study at Kojuin was a three-year curriculum, although some students took four or five years to complete it. Ginko had entered Kojuin in 1882 and, despite all the difficulties she had experienced, graduated three years later. Her difficulties had in no way affected her grades – as usual, she was ahead of the rest of her class. Her main problems had been supporting herself and being the only woman in the school.

Supporting herself had not been too hard, with cutting back and living frugally, and the families she tutored had all been kind to her too. Even Mr Takashima, who at first had seemed remote and unfriendly, had warmed to Ginko and encouraged her ambition to become a doctor.

Ginko's main difficulties had stemmed from her gender. She had been the only woman in an all-male school. While European influence had affected a certain class of the population, it had no relevance at all to the lives of ordinary people. Three hundred years of conservative thinking cultivated during the Tokugawa era would take many years to change. The difficulties Ginko had experienced were the same as those faced by all other modern female pioneers, although in her case, the discrimination could be described as active persecution.

It was because of that humiliation that I was able to bear it here.

Walking through the now-familiar Neribei area, her Kojuin graduation certificate in hand, Ginko recalled the shame of the physical examinations she had endured at Juntendo Hospital. As time passed, far from fading, the memory came back ever more vividly to her. She no longer looked back on that time with hate, but neither had she forgotten it. It was a fact, and she wanted to ensure it was engraved firmly in her heart. That humiliation had in a way become her spur, urging her on.

She was proud of herself and what she had accomplished. But her battles were not over yet. They were only just beginning.

10

After graduating from Kojuin, Ginko continued her tutoring work, while waiting anxiously for a chance to take the medical licensing exams.

On 23rd October 1883, the Grand Council of State had decreed a new system of medical licensing regulations to take effect from 1st January 1884. From this date, anyone wishing to establish a medical practice would have to sit the government's licensing examination, and only those who passed would be permitted to practise medicine. Graduates of imperial and prefectural medical universities were exempt from this rule, as were doctors licensed by medical universities abroad – they could request to have their licences converted upon inspection of their qualifications.

Until this decree, all doctors had been licensed to practise by the prefectural authorities. Now, however, all licensing was to be undertaken by the Home Ministry. This centralization enabled the Ministry to create a national registry of medical doctors and lay the groundwork for a modern, standardized medical licensing system, although it was 1906 before the system was reformed to require all doctors to take the medical licensing examination. In the meantime, practitioners of Eastern medicine tried to create a parallel licensing system, but the focus of the times had shifted from Eastern to Western medicine, and their energetic campaign foundered.

Ginko graduated from medical school just as these first medical licensing regulations were going into effect. None of the exemptions applied to her, so she would have to pass the examination – except that women were not permitted to take the test. Indeed, Ginko was the first woman to apply.

The examinations were held in two parts, the first in the spring and the second some weeks later, in the summer. With nothing to lose, Ginko sent off her application. As expected, it was curtly refused with the note: "No precedent of a female receiving a medical licence".

The next year she reapplied. Again she was rejected.

The following year she reapplied to take the examination in her native Saitama prefecture, enclosing a formal letter outlining her qualifications and stating that her reason for wanting to become a doctor was to help women who might otherwise avoid seeking treatment.

However, this application was rejected as well. She was getting nowhere. She decided to go over the heads of these administrative bodies, and petition directly to the Home Ministry.

Earlier that year she had read in the *Choya Shinbun* newspaper that "Women have until now been restricted to midwifery, but there is currently some discussion of the possibility of proficient women, upon passing the requisite examinations, obtaining the same licences as men to become doctors and pharmacists".

Nevertheless, the result of Ginko's appeal to the Ministry was the same, the notification stamped with the single word "Denied". For Ginko this was like a sentence of death. All the fanfare about women's thirst for knowledge and the potential benefits of education for women was merely hollow bombast. Nothing had changed.

Ginko decided that there was nothing for it but to go in person to the Home Ministry and speak with the official in charge of the medical licensing examination. This, however, was easier said than done. Public officials were nothing like civil servants these days. They were former samurai who had simply assumed the title of "public official", while their haughty, arrogant way of wielding authority had not changed a bit.

The Home Ministry was the most powerful and authoritarian of all the ministries, and its imposing air was sufficient to dissuade most ordinary citizens from making casual visits. Nonetheless, Ginko went. She was convinced that she had a better chance by taking action than by sitting around and waiting.

The Home Ministry was located in Otemachi, not far from the Imperial Palace. The Lord Minister was Aritomo Yamagata, but as Head of the Bureau of Public Health, it was Sensai Nagayo who oversaw the licensing of medical practitioners.

Standing before the Home Ministry, which was surrounded by uniformed guards, Ginko felt weak in the knees. On her left, a number of horse-drawn carriages were lined up on the cobblestones, at the ready for use by high officials, and bearded men in official garb were busily entering and exiting the building. Ginko had twice before met public officials: Arinori Mori to discuss his affair with her friend Shizuko; and Tadanori Ishiguro, to whom she had taken a letter of introduction from the President of the Tokyo Women's Normal School, asking for help in finding a place in a medical school. On both occasions she had gone to their homes. This was the first time she had come to a government building, and the person she wished to meet was in a much higher position than they had been.

"I would like to meet the Head of the Bureau of Public Health."

"You?" One of the two guards at the reception desk looked her over from head to toe without a trace of respect or manners. It was unheard of for a woman to arrive alone and ask to see a top official. She did not even have a letter of introduction. "What for?"

"I have come to beg his favour with regard to the medical licensing examination."

"The medical licensing examination?" The guards looked at each other. Their expressions indicated that they might have heard the term some time or other, but had no idea what it meant. Clearly reflected in their eyes, however, was the conviction that Ginko was not a normal woman.

"If you want to meet the Head of the Bureau, you should come after arranging a proper appointment. But he is extremely busy and doesn't have time to meet some woman about insignificant matters. Who do you think you are?"

This haughty brush-off made Ginko angry. She knew her efforts were foolhardy, but there was no other way. "I am only asking for a moment of his time."

"You're carrying your little joke too far." One of the guards leered at her, gesturing lewdly to intimate that Ginko must be carrying on an affair with the great man.

"I am not here to provoke humour," Ginko insisted. "I have come about a serious matter."

"So *we're* saying that if it's so serious, first you should get an appointment, and then you should come back."

"Well, then, all I would like now is for you to find out whether I may meet him or not."

"No. Get out of here. Go home."

Having come this far, she could not simply back down. "You are mere receptionists, am I right? All you are expected to do is announce visitors who have come to see the Head of the Bureau!"

"Who do you think you are, telling us what our job is? We don't need to be told what to do by some woman!" The younger guard's face changed colour. "You don't just insult us and get away with it!"

"Wait, wait! What's going on here?" came a deep voice suddenly from behind Ginko.

Turning around, she saw a large man with a long moustache. He did not look yet thirty, but judging from his business suit, he must have been quite high up in the Ministry. She also noticed how the demeanour of the guards changed the instant they caught sight of him.

"What are you doing, threatening a woman like this?"

"Well, uh… actually, she just showed up trying to push her way in without an appointment, demanding to see Mr Nagayo immediately," explained the older guard, a man in an official navy-blue uniform with a single gold-lace braid.

"On what business have you come?" the man with the long moustache asked Ginko.

"Actually, I've come to respectfully request that the Ministry consider allowing women to sit the medical licensing examination." Maybe this man would understand, thought Ginko, as she bowed her head politely.

"Does that mean that you want to take it, then?"

"Yes."

"And then become a doctor?"

"Yes, that is correct."

The man roared with laughter, slapping his hairy cheeks in amusement, and then the guards followed suit. Ginko fixed them with a steely gaze. "What is it that you find so funny?"

"Isn't it funny to you too?" asked the man, finally regaining control of himself. "I've never heard of anything like it. A woman becoming a doctor? It's enough to make anyone laugh!"

Ginko did not respond.

"So, you're married?" he asked.

"No, I'm not."

"Then you're single. You don't look so young. Why don't you forget those notions of yours and get married? You're certainly pretty enough to find a decent husband."

Ginko bit her lip and glared at him. "That is not what I came here to discuss. I would like to see the Head of the Bureau of Public Health, please."

"If you want to talk to him about becoming a doctor, I can tell you right now that there's no point. You might as well give it up right now."

"Why is that?"

"If you thought about it you'd understand. Women have the burden of pregnancy. They would have to abandon their patients when pregnant, and we can't entrust patients to that sort of instability. Besides, every month on certain days, women are... dirty. Aren't they?" The guards leered at her. "Isn't that right?" he demanded once again.

Ginko could not answer. Being surrounded by such men discussing her body so explicitly was too much even for her.

"And besides, the licensing exam is difficult. Even quite intelligent men have failed it. Supposing you did obtain permission to take it, you would never be able to pass. Save yourself the strain by giving it up sooner rather than later."

"I would like to see the Head of the Bureau of Public Health, please." She did not know who this man was, but it was clearly a waste of time talking to him.

"The Chief of the Bureau is not in today."

"Tomorrow, then."

"Impatience won't get you anywhere. I'll convey to him that you came to ask a favour. I'm Noriyasu Hirao, Head of the Disease Prevention Section."

So this is a section chief, thought Ginko, looking up at the man once again. Even his moustache seemed no more than an empty, ostentatious display, she thought bitterly.

"But really," he continued, "I'm telling you that you should just give up on it."

Staying any longer would only invite more insult. Without a word, Ginko turned her back and hurried almost at a run towards the gate.

By the time she reached home, the short autumn day was already approaching sunset. Ginko sat at her desk without lighting a lamp. All the way home she had been shaking with fury as she recalled the men's words, but now she no longer had the energy even to be angry. The voices of women preparing dinner came wafting in through her window from the alley below. Dusk fell on another day, the same as always.

Letters were no use, nor were personal visits. Ginko had no idea what to do next. If there was anything she could do, then do it she would and simply bear any hardships it might entail. With no recourse left, however, she was completely at a loss. She had not expected the walls of the Ministry to be quite so unyielding. She had underestimated how hard it would be. Years later Ginko wrote about her frame of mind at this time:

I applied yet again, and yet again my application was rejected. I have never experienced anything as trying in my entire life, and I don't expect I will ever experience anything worse. It was early autumn, time to change into warmer clothing. Who was I to complain that my clothes were so thin? On the night of the full moon, I climbed the hill and looked down in anguish at the smoke of cooking fires in the city below. There was no one who would offer me even a single meal. It had been ten years since I left the home where I was born. I had wandered and suffered as much as I could bear, but society still refused to accept me. My family and friends had shunned me, and I had tried everything I possibly could. I was losing weight and growing old, and I was despairing. Couldn't anyone see me there? I felt like a rock in the middle of a river engulfed by waves and whirlpools.

For the best part of two days Ginko stayed in her room eating little. She did not want to see anyone, and even if she had seen someone, she lacked the energy to speak to them.

On the second night, someone came stamping roughly up the stairs and banged on her door.

"Miss Ogino! Miss Ogino, are you sleeping?"

It was the voice of the landlord's wife. *She's come to check on me again*, Ginko thought. Heavy with lethargy, she turned her face to the door and asked, "What is it?"

"A telegram has just arrived. May I come in?"

Ginko hurriedly roused herself, pulled on her kimono, and lit a lamp.

"It's from Tawarase."

Ginko was gripped with a sense of foreboding. Twelve years before, the news of her father's death had come at night, also by telegram. News of such importance as to warrant a telegram could not be good. Nonetheless, as she opened the envelope she found herself praying that it was nothing serious. Her foreboding was justified, however.

"Mother critically ill. Tomoko." Ginko read the words several times, but their meaning remained patently clear.

"Has something happened?" The landlady looked at Ginko, still clutching the telegram and trembling from head to foot.

"My mother... she's ill..." The telegram was not summoning her home. Tomoko clearly meant to leave that decision to Ginko. But Ginko's mind had been made up as soon as she read the message. "Do you think there's a rickshaw nearby?"

"It's already half-past five, you know." The landlady was using the old way of telling time – by today's timekeeping it was nine o'clock at night.

"Would you please look for one anyway? It doesn't matter what it costs. I'll be ready to leave in a few minutes."

"You're going all the way to Tawarase?"

"Yes, of course."

"But if you start off now, you'll be travelling through the night!" Even the main roads were dangerous at night, and all the more so for a single woman. Riding in a rickshaw was no reason to feel secure. The landlady glared at Ginko in exasperation.

"What if something happens to you? You'd be better off going first thing in the morning."

"Don't worry about it – please just help get me a rickshaw."

The landlady eventually nodded reluctantly. "I'll ask around to see if there's anyone willing to take you that far."

"Quickly – please!"

The landlady trotted down the stairs. Alone, Ginko read the telegram once more. The message remained unchanged.

Moments later she was in a rickshaw, but it would be morning by the time they reached Tawarase. *My mother's dying.* Ginko finally faced up to this thought. Two months ago, Tomoko had written that their mother was weak and had begun to have some swelling in her hands and feet, yet even then she had been describing her mother's condition on her previous visit three months before. Ginko wondered if the swelling had got worse after that. It could indicate kidney or heart trouble. If it was her kidneys, then she might possibly have fallen into a renal coma, but if she had suddenly collapsed, it could be her heart.

But maybe it hadn't been so sudden. If it was heart disease, her legs would have been more swollen than her hands. If her hands were more swollen, it was probably her kidneys. A renal coma could still be reversed after two or three days. She might not be too late. Jostled in the rickshaw, Ginko ran through the medical knowledge she'd accumulated. Either condition was possible – or it could be something else altogether.

Before long the rickshaw had crossed the large bridge over the Arakawa River. From there they would travel through Urawa and Konosu before reaching Kumagaya and heading east. There was hardly anyone else on the road. The few people they passed looked in astonishment at the rickshaw hurtling from the city into the countryside.

Ginko could not shake off her swirling thoughts. Had her mother been seen by a doctor? The Ogino family had always been taken care of by Dr Mannen, but he and Ogie had long since moved to Tokyo. As far as Ginko knew, there were no other well-known doctors in the area, only some local old-fashioned Chinese-medicine practitioners. With her knowledge of Western medicine, Ginko had no faith in their abilities.

"Mother's dying," whispered Ginko to herself – though even after saying this, it did not seem real.

Kayo would be fifty-eight this year. It was not unusual for women in their late fifties to die, as Ginko knew only too well. Nevertheless, it had never occurred to her that her mother might die so soon. Of course she had known that it had to happen some day, but she had never worried much about it. In a way, that very fact revealed how much she still depended on her mother.

"She really is going to die," Ginko told herself aloud, but in the next instant she retreated back into denial – maybe she wouldn't die yet. She *had* to live.

Ginko could see the autumn moon through a small window in the hood of the rickshaw. They had to be in the Omiya area by now. Lights from homes were now few and far between. Shadows from a forest of evergreen trees lay blackly across the road. Up ahead she could make out the flat farm plots spreading out before her. The moon was high in the sky. The rickshaw driver was panting as though he were fleeing the terrors of the night, and autumn insects chirped from both sides of the road as if to urge him on.

Mother, please don't die. Ginko pressed her hands together in prayer.

As they left Omiya, the sky was beginning to lighten and the fields were clearly visible. It was a little after eight in the morning when they reached Tawarase.

"Please turn right where that large gate is."

"All right," the driver answered, gasping for breath as he turned through the white-walled gate.

"Thank you. Just here is fine."

As Ginko descended from the rickshaw, she could not believe her eyes. Just to the right of the wide front door, there was a sign on which had been painted the words "In Mourning".

Ginko stared at it, wide-eyed with shock.

"We didn't make it in time, did we?" said the driver regretfully, as he mopped the sweat from his face. "I'm so sorry."

His voice sounded as if it were coming from far away and directed at someone else. Ginko's feet were unsteady as she approached the entrance.

* * *

Kayo's body was laid out in the large room at the back of the house, her head on a pillow facing north, as was the custom. A white cloth had been laid over her face, and incense and a candle had been lit beside her head. Yasuhei and Tomoko were kneeling on either side of her.

"Gin!" Catching sight of Ginko, Tomoko raised herself to greet her.

"Mother!" Ginko collapsed at her mother's side. Beneath the white cloth, Kayo's small face was pale with some slight swelling, but still well proportioned and pretty.

"Mother!" Ginko burst into tears. "Why did you have to die when I was trying so hard to get back to you in time?" She gripped her mother's shoulders, trying to put her arms around her, shaking with sobs. Her mother's stiff, shrunken body rocked with her as Ginko called her again and again. The others in the room waited in silence.

Her face wet with tears, Ginko looked once again at her mother's face. She did not look dead. She looked almost as if she were taking a quick nap and would soon be up and about again. Ginko tried calling her once more; she knew it was no good, but she could not help hoping for a miracle that might bring her back.

"Well, let's let Mother rest now," Tomoko broke in gently, and took the white cloth from Ginko's hand to place once more over Kayo's face.

Ginko now saw that there were four or five other relatives seated in the room. She could feel their curious eyes on her as she put her hands together in prayer over Kayo's body.

"When did she pass away?" Ginko finally felt calm enough to ask.

"In the Tiger hour, just before dawn," Tomoko replied.

Tiger hour meant four o'clock in the morning. Ginko's rickshaw had been passing through Ageo and she had been gazing out at the road shining under the blue light of the moon.

"What was wrong with her?"

"The doctor said it was kidney disease, isn't that right?" Tomoko looked to Yasuhei for confirmation. Yasuhei only nodded silently, his arms crossed over his chest.

Ginko thought of the bluish-black swelling on her mother's face. *So that's what it was after all.*

"You came very quickly," Tomoko observed quietly. Yasuhei and the other relatives still said nothing, but they were all listening carefully to the conversation.

"Why didn't anyone tell me sooner?"

"It was only yesterday morning that she suddenly lost consciousness. Until then she'd been in bed but she hadn't seemed so seriously ill."

"But she was bedridden?"

"Yes, for about a month, wasn't it?" Once again Tomoko directed her words to Yasuhei for confirmation.

"Then why didn't you call for me?" Ginko reproached them.

"Because Mother said not to tell you," Yasuhei muttered gloomily. "She said, 'This is an important time for Gin, so don't go worrying her.'"

Ginko met Yasuhei's eyes for a moment. Unable to bear it, she looked away.

"She was calling your name just before she died."

Ginko bit her lip in chagrin and her eyes blurred with tears. She quickly raised her hands to cover her face, but it was too late to regain control.

"Come now!" Yasuhei looked embarrassed at the scene she was making. His sister had not been home for over ten years, yet here she was now, thirty-two years old and sitting in their midst crying like a child.

"*Mother! Mother!*" Ginko was still screaming inside. She had wanted to meet her mother once more while she was still alive, to beg her forgiveness. With all the time that had passed, if they had had a chance to talk now, her mother would have understood. Her mother had probably already in her heart forgiven Ginko. Before Ginko had left for Tokyo, Kayo had said that she never wanted to see her face again, yet on the morning of her departure, her mother had given her a protective amulet and money from her own savings. Although

143

she never said so, it was possible that she had already forgiven Ginko even then.

Ginko had always had the feeling that she could go see her mother any time she liked, and that even though they never spoke, there was some kind of understanding between them. She had always imagined that they would meet and talk and make their peace. *That's where I was wrong.*

Kayo had been calling for Ginko right before she died, at the same time that Ginko had been calling to her mother in the rickshaw. Ginko had no doubt that during those moments, their hearts had been in communion.

If they had been so close, though, why hadn't she come to see her mother while she was still alive? It would not have been difficult. It was a mere day's trip from Tokyo to Tawarase. She could have come any time. Ginko was filled with regret and anger at herself for having left this important task undone.

Tomoko tapped Ginko lightly on the shoulder. "Some guests have come to pay their respects to Mother, so let's retire to the back room." A long line of people had begun to arrive to pay their respects and give condolences. The first family of Tawarase had prospered under Kayo's good management, and it was only natural that there would be many calling on the family when she passed away.

"Here, take this." Now that they were alone together, Tomoko passed Ginko a fresh hand towel and said, "Crying's not going to change anything."

Ginko looked up and realized that they were now in her old room. Kayo had always kneeled and carefully slid the door open and shut whenever she entered. Never, at any time, had Kayo deviated from proper form.

Ginko and her mother had talked during the time she had spent there recuperating. Whenever her mother had managed to find a spare moment, she had spent it at Ginko's side, sometimes bringing along her needlework, all so that Ginko would not feel lonely. She had chatted to Ginko about goings-on in town, the crops in the fields, the neighbours – anything and everything. Listening to her mother, Ginko had had a general sense of what was happening outside, even though she was confined indoors.

Yet not once had Kayo mentioned the Inamura family into which Ginko had married and then run away from. Even when her belongings had been returned after the divorce, Kayo had said no more than was necessary. Everything had been handled with the utmost consideration for Ginko's feelings. Looking back, despite Ginko's illness and isolation, it had been a happy time, because she had spent it with her mother.

"When did the telegram reach you?"

"Late last night."

"It must have been a shock."

"Yes, it was."

They could hear the sound of children playing in the living room. A large gathering of people was always a cue for children to have a good time, regardless of having been occasioned by a death.

"Was it a nuisance?"

"Not at all. Why?"

"I sent it against the others' wishes."

Come to think of it, it had been signed by Tomoko, not Yasuhei.

"Yasuhei said we should wait and contact you after she died. Since you were basically disinherited when you left the Ogino household, he was sure you wouldn't come back home for the funeral."

Ginko stood and looked out at the garden. The hemp palm and nandin bamboo were in the same places as always, but both had grown taller.

"He thinks that you're selfish and that all you think about is becoming a doctor."

"How cruel!"

Tomoko came and stood next to Ginko. She was just a shade taller. Ginko watched as a flock of sparrows came and settled in the top of the nandin tree.

"It's not just Yasuhei. All the relatives are saying that."

Ginko recalled the coldness in Yasuhei's eyes just now. He was nearing forty, and age was showing in his face. *You left, and never came back to help nurse her – what's the point of crying now?* That's what his eyes had said.

"But that's the sort of person Yasuhei is," Tomoko continued, "so try not to worry about it."

The sky spread out beyond the top of the palm tree, devoid of all summer warmth. Her mother was dead. Ginko was astonished the sky could remain unchanged, clear and bright as ever. Their mother's death, Yasuhei's cold eyes – all these things were trivial beside that bright sky.

"You've come to look just like Mother."

Ginko turned to see that her sister, now leaning against the door frame, was looking intently at her.

"Exactly like her when she was young," continued Tomoko.

"All her daughters do."

"No. I've seen Sonoe and Masa recently, but neither of them look as much like Mother as you do."

"Oh?" Ginko faltered a little under Tomoko's intense gaze. Ever since she was little, she had often been told the same thing, although she herself had never really understood what it was about her that reminded others so much of her mother.

"Mother's love all went to you."

"Her love?"

"Yes. You were the baby of the family, and she always cared most for you."

"But that's not fair! We were all her children."

"Yes, but you worried her the most."

Ginko had often heard the saying that the child who gives the most trouble is also the most loved. She was beginning to see what Tomoko was saying. "Was that true, just now?"

"What?"

"What Yasuhei said about Mother calling for me as she was dying?"

"Yes, it's true. She waved her hands and called for you in a low voice."

"Then?"

"I said you were coming and would be here soon. I asked her to wait. I don't know if she understood or not, but she repeated it two or three times, then she went quiet."

Ginko was silent as she took this in.

"She only breathed for a few minutes after that."

Ginko turned her face away. The self-reproach she had managed to suppress was welling up once again and threatening to overwhelm her.

"You were on her mind to the very end."

Ginko gazed at the Chinese parasol tree. A brown-eared bulbul had settled in its upper branches and was calling sharply. She had the sudden illusion that it was pecking at her with its long, hard beak.

The next morning Ginko offered prayers at her mother's side once more, then gathered her things to leave.

"You're going already?" Tomoko had dropped by her room, a young child in tow, and noticed the preparations.

"I'm sorry for imposing on you all."

"That's not what I meant! Stay one more night anyway."

"But I've seen Mother."

"You should at least attend the funeral."

That night there would be a formal wake, and then Kayo's body would be taken from the house the next morning. Ginko's four older sisters and the other relatives would be staying for another four or five days.

"I don't have any mourning clothes."

"That doesn't matter. You came rushing here because you heard she was critically ill, so of course you don't have any with you."

"But—"

"Is there something you have to hurry back to Tokyo for?"

"No." Several days had now passed since her disastrous visit to the Ministry, and her latest hopes to take the licensing examination had been dashed.

"Then why don't you stay? We don't know when you'll be able to make it back again, do we?"

"No, but I already got to see you, and we've had the chance to catch up on everything. There's not much for me to do here now." Ginko glanced around at the room and its old furniture, and realized that she might well never come back here again. "And if I start off now, I can reach Tokyo before nightfall."

The child had gone out into the garden and was plucking red fruit off the coral berry shrub.

"Do you mind if I use Mother's dressing table?" Ginko was doing her hair in front of it as she spoke. She was the only mourner with her hair in a modern Western style, and although no one had said a word, Ginko had felt their interested eyes on her.

"Gin," Tomoko turned to address Ginko's reflection in the mirror. "Are you leaving because of what Yasuhei and the others were saying?"

"No, not really." Ginko forced a cheerful expression and shook her head.

"You shouldn't let what loud-mouthed country folk say bother you, you know."

"I know." As always, Tomoko could see right through her. "But anyway, I've got to go."

"Once you've made up your mind to do something, there's no stopping you, is there?"

Ginko raised her eyes and met her sister's gaze in the mirror. They shared the faintest of wry grins.

Ginko left by the back door to avoid being seen by the relatives and villagers. She did not feel up to being pointed at or hearing them discuss her: *Oh, that's the daughter who left home, saying she wanted to become a doctor.* Tomoko accompanied her on the footpath between the rice fields as far as the main road.

"Here, take this." Tomoko had come to a halt by the edge of the footpath, and held out something small, wrapped in paper.

"But Tomoko—" Ginko started to protest, but Tomoko overrode her.

"Don't worry about it; just take it." Tomoko quickly slipped the little packet into the breast of Ginko's kimono. "Take care of yourself."

"Thank you for everything."

"When I die, I want you to be there to see me off. Promise?" Tomoko gave a cheerful laugh and added, "Now, go!"

The sun was still touching the tops of the pine trees to the east. It was probably only just past seven in the morning. It suddenly occurred to Ginko to go and see the Toné River. If she took the shortcut between the fields, it would take less than ten minutes.

Just past the barley fields, she mounted a gentle incline which brought her to the river bank. When she was a child, that river bank had seemed so high, but it was no more than a few steps. Beyond the grasses on the bank lay the expanse of the Toné, with the sun reflected on its surface. Further still was the hazy bank on the opposite side of the river. The landscape all looked the same – the river muted everything around it.

Ginko squatted on the top of the bank. She could recall playing in the shallows here as a child. Later she had travelled up this river to get married, and later still she had come back down it alone. She remembered the floods as well. It could all have been long ago, or it could have been yesterday.

The last time she had gazed at this river was the day she left home to go to Tokyo. That time too, she had been alone. Ten years had passed since then. What had she done? During that time she had lost her father, caused her mother heartache, and then lost her too. What had she gained from her single-minded efforts? To be sure, she had never rested once. Looking back now, though, what could she say that she'd gained? When she pressed herself for an answer now, the only one that came to mind was: *It's all been for nothing.*

Ginko looked around. A light breeze rustled the expanse of miscanthus reeds used for thatching houses, and the deep blue autumn sky spread out above her. Ginko closed her eyes.

Has it all been a mistake?

This misgiving surfaced in her mind like a small bubble. She felt it expanding to a whirlpool, twisting and pulling her down. *Why did I do it, then?* The things she had hoped for had been too difficult, too much of a revolt against her family and society. *Why, why?* Ginko kept asking herself, but the answer wouldn't come.

This hasn't all been a mistake. I'm not wrong.

A vision suddenly floated up of her smooth, pale limbs being pressed and bent, her knees pushed almost into her stomach, and a huge force pulling her knees apart. She recalled the momentary incandescent pain in her knees, as though she were being restrained by branding irons, and the marks that those hands had left behind.

149

Those men's hands!

The memory of that brightly lit examining room of thirteen years before replayed itself in Ginko's mind. Her whole body burned. Her shame rolled like a red-hot ball round and round her head.

That really happened to me. I experienced that with my own body. There's no question about it. Murmuring this to herself, Ginko opened her eyes to find the sparkling sun reflecting off the Toné River into them.

The path I've taken is the right one, she told herself once more as she rose to her feet and started off down the river bank to the south.

11

On her return to Tokyo, Ginko was once again overwhelmed by the frustration of not being allowed to sit the medical licensing examination. Still disconsolate over Kayo's death, her frustration was exacerbated by her renewed determination to become a doctor in honour of her mother's memory.

Maybe I should apply once more, she thought, although she knew the result would be the same.

A number of her Kojuin classmates had already passed both sessions of the examination and had subsequently opened their own practices. They had the right to do so merely because they were born male. Yet Ginko had clearly surpassed them in terms of academic ability. If this had not been the case, she might have been able to resign herself to the situation, but the fact that it was blatant discrimination based solely on her gender was intolerable.

Would women ever be treated equally to men? There was no indication that such a day would ever arrive, and the more she thought about it, the further she sank into gloom.

A year and a half had already passed since Ginko had graduated from Kojuin. Without the opportunity to use the knowledge she had gained there, she would soon begin to forget it. On top of that, she had turned thirty-two, an age at which it would be impossible to go back to the beginning and try something new. The more she thought about it, the more her irritation mounted. At a loss and with nothing else to do, she found herself pacing her room.

At the end of October, about a month after her mother's death, Ginko went once again to visit Tadanori Ishiguro, the official who had found her a place at Kojuin. It had occurred to her that she might be able to ask for his help as a last resort, and she did not see any alternative now.

The autumn sky was a beautiful clear blue in the wake of a

typhoon that had just passed through Tokyo. Ishiguro was not at home, so she asked his secretary for an appointment and was told to come back the following Sunday afternoon, three days later. She was scheduled to tutor at the Takashima home then, but she cancelled the lesson and turned her steps to the Ishiguro residence instead.

Ginko found Ishiguro wearing traditional Japanese garb, a rare and relaxed style for him. They were not exactly familiar with each other, but she did not feel particularly nervous about meeting him either. She brought him up to date on her circumstances since their last meeting, and on her current straits in not being allowed to sit the medical licensing examination.

"They had the nerve to refuse you?" He was outraged when Ginko told him what had happened at the Home Ministry.

"I have no idea what to do or where to appeal," Ginko told him frankly. "I don't know why I was born a woman. It has frustrated me at every turn."

"I can see your point," Ishiguro responded, himself unsure how to assist her. This time they were up against the national system itself, a seemingly impenetrable wall.

"I'm thinking the only way may be to enter a medical school overseas."

"You're thinking of going abroad?" Ishiguro asked, his big eyes widening further to stare at Ginko.

"Yes. The fourth article of the medical licensing rules clearly states that graduates of foreign medical institutions will receive licences upon request."

"But that would cost a tremendous amount of money! Besides, you'd first have to master a new language and get used to the customs."

Ginko had thought of this possibility after being driven out of the Home Ministry, but it was such an enormous undertaking that she did not yet have any concrete ideas about how to proceed. "I don't see any alternative if I want to become a doctor."

"I understand your feelings, but I don't think you have to give up on Japan yet. Our country isn't populated solely by narrow-minded bureaucrats, you know."

"I've always gone under that assumption, but…" Ginko was filled with an empty sadness.

"First of all you should meet Commissioner Nagayo. I'll write a letter of introduction for you. Bureaucrats base everything on precedent – that's just the way they are. Whatever the matter at hand, the safest way to proceed is to do it the same way as it has always been done. They may begin their careers with generous hearts, but even the softest of them get hardened over time."

"But how can I get around the law?"

"As long as a country is ruled by laws, we have to follow them, but in the matter of a woman doctor, it's just that they're troubled by the idea. There isn't any written law that says a woman cannot become a doctor. And as long as there isn't, then you should be able to take the examination, and if you pass, it follows that you should be allowed to start practising. If they want to prevent women from becoming doctors, they should write a clause that specifically states that women may not become doctors."

Ishiguro had entered the government halfway through a career in medicine, so his way of thinking was more flexible than most career bureaucrats. His broad view of the situation gave Ginko a new inkling of hope. "There's no need to turn you down just because there's no precedent."

"If it were a matter of simply finding the words 'woman doctor', I have read them somewhere."

Ishiguro leant his large frame towards her, interested. "Where?"

"In *Ryo no gige*, the ancient law book."

"Is that so? It's been listed in the *Ryo no gige* all along?" Ishiguro was impressed that Ginko's literary scholarship had extended to such erudite lengths. "When and where did you read it?"

"It was more than ten years ago, but I studied it under Yorikuni Inoue."

"Oh? You studied with Professor Inoue?"

"Are you acquainted with him?"

"Just slightly."

153

The two men had been on opposing sides of the conflict occasioned by the Movement for the Restoration of Chinese Medicine. Any bad feelings, however, had long since dissipated, and Inoue was known to Ishiguro not so much as a practitioner of traditional medicine, but as a top-level scholar of Japanese classical literature, and he respected him as such. "Well, then there can't be any mistake about it. That's a useful bit of information to have remembered."

"I had already resolved to become a doctor, so when I came upon it by chance, I wrote it down."

How was Yorikuni doing these days? Ginko suddenly recalled the pretty red-strapped sandals that had been set at the entrance of his home on her last visit.

"Then that will be our precedent. Do you have a copy of the book on hand?"

"No, I'm afraid I only transcribed it. I expect it is still in Professor Inoue's library, though."

"Could you borrow it from him and bring it to me?"

"From Professor Inoue?"

"Right."

This was a dilemma. She had wanted to put Yorikuni, living with that unknown woman, out of her mind permanently. "I wonder if he still has it..."

"Do you think something could have happened to it?"

"What would you use it for?"

"The first thing I want to do is go to Commissioner Nagayo and make the case for women being able to sit the examination, so I'll need to show him the book as evidence."

"So the book itself really is necessary?"

"It would make our case all the more credible if we had Professor Inoue's signature along with the book. Since you're a former pupil of his, he should be willing to write a few lines for you." Oblivious to the awkward circumstances, Ishiguro continued enthusiastically, "Do you think you could get it in the next few days?"

Refusing was out of the question, and Ginko hesitantly nodded her assent.

It was three days later, at the beginning of November, that Ginko mustered the courage to visit Yorikuni Inoue. A cold autumn rain had been falling in the morning, but it cleared up in the afternoon. Ginko dressed in a fine kimono she had ordered on her graduation from Kojuin and put her hair up. While attending Kojuin, she had tied her hair back and had dressed in a way she hoped would let her be mistaken for a man. After graduation she had abandoned this habit, returning to a more typical feminine style.

So young, and just like a little doll. Ginko recalled the old housekeeper's description of Yorikuni's new wife and, suddenly self-conscious, looked at herself critically in the mirror. Her skin was not as youthful as it had been. Meticulously, she covered her face with white face powder. That finished, she applied lipstick, and then decided the make-up was too thick, so she took it off and started all over again.

As she painted, wiped off and repainted her face, she asked herself, *Why?* She had never harboured any affection for Yorikuni in the past, nor did she now. She respected him as a teacher, nothing more. Why was she going to all this trouble? *I don't want to look bad in front of that woman.* It was a matter of pride, having once been the object of Yorikuni's love.

Her make-up finished, Ginko called a rickshaw and pulled up the hood to guard against the wind, as she headed for Yorikuni's house. She felt as if she were on her way to mount a raid on enemy territory.

"Oh, Miss Ogino. How nice to see you again! Will you please wait upstairs?" The old housekeeper, Ise, had come to the door. Ginko followed her up to the familiar study.

"Is Professor Inoue here?"

The study, which had been a cluttered mess in the past, was now as neat as a pin. Even the ashtrays had been wiped clean, without a speck of ash to be seen.

"He's just stepped out to the hospital, but he'll be back before long."

"Is something wrong with him?"

"No, no, it's not him. It's his wife – she's expecting."

"They're having a baby?"

"Yes. She's five months along now and it seems she's having some swelling."

155

"Is it serious?"

"Well, to my old eyes it doesn't look too bad, but the Professor was terribly worried and had her admitted to the hospital ten days ago, just to be on the safe side."

"And so, today?..."

"Oh, he goes out to see her for an hour every day about this time," Ise laughed.

Ginko looked around again. Yes, the study was perfectly tidy, and complete silence reigned. It did not look like the room was being used at all. Preoccupied with his new wife, Yorikuni must be neglecting his studies. Ginko's dislike for the new wife now turned to disdain for Yorikuni.

"So that's keeping him from his work, is it?" Ginko observed aloud.

"Well, he was alone for such a long time. He's probably earned the right to think about other things sometimes. Oh, I forgot to get tea. Just a moment, please, and I'll bring some." Ise stood up and hurried out.

Ginko meanwhile glared at his bookcases as though they were putting on airs, muttering to herself, "What an idiotic way for a scholar to act!"

Yorikuni returned about thirty minutes later. "Oh! Nice to see you again." Yorikuni looked at the immaculately dressed and made-up Ginko with curious eyes.

"It really has been a long time. I must apologize for falling so far out of touch."

"I haven't seen you since you graduated from the Women's Normal School – so about four years now. But I heard you came by once when I was out."

"No, I don't believe so."

"Oh? I thought I remembered Ise saying something about it... well, anyway, even so it certainly has been a while, hasn't it?"

Yorikuni was relaxed and smiling with nostalgia, but Ginko's expression remained stiff. "It was rude of me not to have kept in touch enough to hear that you'd remarried."

"Oh, it's nothing, no big news or anything." Yorikuni scratched his neck, looking embarrassed.

"And now she's expecting?"

"Where did you hear that?"

"Ise told me just now."

"What a chatterbox. She's going to send me to an early grave."
His words were aggrieved, but looking at his gentle, round face,
Ginko noticed that his colour was good and he looked younger
than when she'd seen him last.

"Marriage suits you well."

"Oh, it's nothing special. Being single is inconvenient, and it
seemed easier than hiring another maid... was there anything
special you came to discuss, by the way?" Clearly embarrassed,
Yorikuni abruptly changed the subject.

Ginko forced down her irritation and filled him in on
developments since they'd last met, and her present difficulty.

"And that's what Mr Ishiguro said about it?"

"Yes, he told me to request a letter directly from you."

"Well, if you really think my offering an interpretation would
be useful, I could do that right away."

"Would you really?"

"Of course. Your memory of the text is correct."

Yorikuni lightly picked up his brush, and Ginko watched
appreciatively as the beautiful characters flowed from it. It was
a sight she had not seen in a long time. He placed the letter in
an envelope and handed it to Ginko. Then, as if struck by an
afterthought, he asked:

"So, are you still single?"

"Yes."

"I see," he nodded deeply and dropped his eyes to the desk.
"Well, I hope you become a good doctor."

Ginko raised her face and said firmly, with a trace of bravado,
"I will."

Ishiguro's plan worked out just as he had predicted. It had been
conceived from the wisdom of his experience, and might never
have occurred to Ginko, who had spent so many years devoted
to her studies.

The Commissioner of Public Health was Sensai Nagayo,
whose grandfather had been a renowned scholar of Dutch
studies. Along with other progressives in the Meiji government,

Nagayo had helped build the foundation for a modern medical administration based on the German system, the most advanced in the world. He was also known to be well disposed towards women's education.

It took Ishiguro three visits to the Ministry to finally meet the Commissioner. At first Nagayo thought it was a joke, but with Yorikuni Inoue's letter as supporting evidence of the existence of female doctors in the past, and after a long discussion, he was brought around to considering the matter seriously.

"Having talked with her, I would say she is of upright character and has a good head on her shoulders. It would be a shame if she was barred from becoming a doctor merely because of her gender."

As Director of Daigaku Higashiko, Ishiguro's status was below that of the Lord Commissioner of Public Health, but the two men had worked together on numerous occasions in various ministries and were able to speak straightforwardly with each other about medical matters.

"It is written here in the oldest medical law book in Japan – the *Ryo no gige* clearly refers to women doctors." That the pre-eminent Japanese classical scholar of the time, Yorikuni Inoue, had vouched for this helped Ishiguro present his case confidently. "All the advanced Western countries have women doctors. Japan will be a laughing stock if we refuse to let go of Edo-era policies."

"I have always felt we should allow women to sit the exam. It won't require a revision of the law, but a modification of one of the established procedures. If public opinion is in favour of it, there should be no problem granting permission."

"But public sentiment is already in favour, isn't it? There are at present a number of qualified women waiting to become physicians. I have come here to make a personal request, and I beg you to make the change."

Nagayo looked somewhat taken aback by Ishiguro's vehemence. "I understand that, but there is still a great deal of prejudice against the idea, and many will still insist that women are unfit due to pregnancy and childbearing."

"Women aren't always pregnant. And if they do have children, they can simply take some time off, can't they?"

"Then what would their patients do?"

"Western medicine is different from Eastern medicine. There are clear principles of diagnosis and treatment. If a patient changes doctors, it does not mean that the treatment will therefore change."

The idea that changing doctors would create difficulties undoubtedly came from the insular tradition of Chinese medicine. Nagayo had pursued Western studies, but he was not a doctor himself and so he most likely still felt some of the traditional discomfort on this point. "But most ordinary people still object to a woman practising medicine."

"Is it not the work of leading figures in the progressive government such as yourself to break down that prejudice?"

"All right, all right." Nagayo gave in.

Six months after this meeting, a formal directive was issued to the effect that women should be allowed to sit the medical licensing examination.

Ginko learnt about this landmark revision from her morning newspaper. For a while she was struck speechless, but once she recovered from her astonishment, she could feel joy slowly spreading through her being. Now she would be able to become a doctor simply by studying.

Ginko offered the news at the memorial tablet for her mother that she kept atop the dresser in her room, and then wrote about it to Tomoko. Finally there was a lit path ahead of her.

The medical licensing examination consisted of two parts: the first session testing physics, chemistry, anatomy and physiology, and the second covering surgery, internal medicine, obstetrics, gynaecology, ophthalmology, pharmacology, bacteriology and clinical medicine. Once again Ginko resumed studying through the night. During the days, in addition to tutoring at the Takashima and Maeda residences, she added the family of Vice-Consul Shohei Ota, who happened to be the son of her father's cousin. She visited each home twice a week.

After completing her lessons each day, she returned home and took up her own studies. On the days when she had walked especially far, she would begin to nod off at about nine o'clock.

159

It was harder for her to study all night than it had been during her years at the Tokyo Women's Normal School. Dark circles formed under her eyes. Names of medicines, which she'd previously memorized simply by repeating them to herself as she paced the corridor, were now easily forgotten. Chemical formulas likewise eluded her.

At the age of thirty-three, both her mental and physical strengths were beginning to decline. Yet now that she had her goal in sight and her task was clear, Ginko considered her difficulties to be the lightest she had had to bear thus far.

Ginko took the first stage of the medical licensing examination on 3rd September 1884. Three other women took the exam, including two who had graduated from the precursor of the Navy Medical College.

The results were posted on the wall outside the front gate of the Home Ministry at the end of the month. Ginko had passed with flying colours, and she was the only one of the women to do so.

The next big hurdle was the second session of the examination, six months later. Her success would be meaningless unless she passed both sessions, so Ginko kept her joy and relief in check. Her achievement created a sensation with the rest of society, however, and newspapers and medical journals took up her story: "First Woman to Pass the Test!"

The Takashima family, who had been among Ginko's most loyal supporters and employers, now asked her to teach another of their children, their daughter Hanako. This meant that as long as Ginko did not overspend, she could cover her living expenses by working for the Takashima household alone. Furthermore, the wife of a Navy College instructor, Juhei Arakawa, whose family she had also been teaching, offered Ginko a room in their house to use freely as a study. She also continued to teach at the home of Shohei Ota. The Vice-Consul was being posted to Mexico, and he asked Ginko to direct his wife's studies during his absence.

Now that Ginko's financial difficulties had thus been eased, she could even afford to hire a rickshaw when too exhausted to walk. However, all this goodwill served to remind her how great the expectations of her now were. It was imperative that she pass the second half of the exam, if only to maintain her reputation.

A new year began. Ginko continued to study through the holidays, and the mental and physical strain she was under was beginning to take its toll. In mid-January she broke out in a light fever, and in early February another fever forced her to bed for two days. Still she was determined not to waste any precious time. With the fevers came sharp pain in her lower abdomen. It was like a demon, reminding her that her disease would never be cured.

The night of 5th March, Ginko came down with chills. The examination was two days away. Ginko asked the housemaid to buy her some medicine at a pharmacy nearby, drank it down, and snuggled up in bed. The chills eased but the ache in her lower abdomen remained. Lying there, she continued to read, occasionally reaching down to rub her stomach. Each time it responded with a throb of pain.

There was no improvement the next day. The test would begin at nine o'clock the following morning whether she was better or not, so she continued to study, curled up under the covers.

Ogie appeared late that afternoon. Ginko had asked the maid to call for her friend when it had passed noon and she still couldn't rise.

"You've got quite a fever," Ogie observed, as she put her hand to Ginko's forehead. "What does the thermometer say?"

"I haven't got one."

"You, who are going to be a doctor!" Ogie was exasperated. "How about ice?"

"I asked the maid to buy some for me yesterday, but I think it's all melted now," Ginko answered, her eyes still on her book.

"OK, I'll go buy some then. How about medicine?" Ogie suddenly noticed, appalled, that Ginko's small desk was piled to overflowing with red and white packets of medicine, and the wastepaper basket next to her pillow was full of empty wrappers. "Should you be taking this much medicine?"

"It doesn't matter – none of it is having any effect at all!" Ginko retorted, raising her fever-reddened face. "Would you pass me some of that on the right, there?"

"You need to rest, not just medicate yourself!" Medicine might have been Ginko's speciality, not Ogie's, but this much was clear to anyone.

"There's no time! You know the test is tomorrow."

"That's what I mean. You won't be able to take the test if you don't get better, right?"

"Just give me the medicine!"

Between her fever and anxiety over the imminent test, Ginko was not her usual self. Ogie reluctantly passed her one of the packets, judging it most important for Ginko to calm down.

"Really, why does medicine have to be this bitter?" Ginko complained, as she downed the smoky-smelling powder in one swallow and, still on her back, took the water Ogie offered her. "I'll get better, you'll see!"

Ogie silently picked up a washbasin and went out to buy ice.

Later, as the sun was sinking, Ginko said she had no appetite and refused dinner.

"I'll make you an egg-nog. That'll warm you and you'll be able to rest."

"But it might make me sleepy."

"But you *should* sleep!"

"No, I can't. There are still books I've got to read."

"With that fever, nothing you read will stay in your head!"

"It's better than not reading them at all."

Ogie decided the only thing to do was to make Ginko sleep, so she whipped up the egg-nog and forced her to drink it.

"Will drinking this make the fever go down, do you think?"

"Definitely. It's what my father always made me drink whenever I caught a cold."

Ogie changed the cold towels on Ginko's forehead every ten minutes, but they still came away lukewarm. "Let's cool the back of your head as well," Ogie suggested.

Ginko suddenly sat up. "You know, if I can't sit the exam tomorrow, I'll die wretched." She was staring, her eyes fixed on some point off in space like a woman possessed. "I must take the exam. I must, I really must!"

"I know, I understand."

"I *will* get better, I'm sure I will. Won't I?"

"I'm telling you, you've *got* to rest now!" Ogie insisted, taking Ginko by the shoulders and pushing her back down.

"What bad luck!" Ginko muttered and started to doze off, then suddenly got up and weaved unsteadily over to the single chest of drawers.

"Gin!"

She looked dizzy, and her left hand was pressed to her temple, as she searched with her right through the top drawer for something.

"What are you doing?"

Ginko didn't answer. Clutching something in her hand, she hastily dived back under the bedclothes. "I'm cold."

"That's because you keep getting up! Here, get the covers over yourself properly now." Ogie tucked Ginko in and asked, "So what did you get just now?"

Ginko poked her hand out, still holding the object. Ogie took it from her and saw that it was a walnut-sized brocade bag. Inside was a small piece of white folded paper that read: "Tawarase Shrine".

"It's the charm Mother gave me when I left home. I'll hold it while I sleep."

"That's a good idea."

Ginko gave up the book and lay facing the ceiling. Under the cold towel on her forehead, her long eyelashes cast slight shadows over her cheeks. After a little while, her eyes still closed, she said, "You should go home when I fall asleep."

"Do you want me to?"

"I like to be alone when I sleep. I've got used to it and I relax better that way."

"Then that's what I'll do."

It looked like the egg-nog had worked. At any rate, it took less than ten minutes for Ginko to fall into an exhausted slumber. Ogie made sure her sleep was sound and wrung out one last towel from the washtub of ice water. As she placed it on Ginko's forehead, Ginko's eyebrows furrowed slightly and she sighed.

"Mother…"

Ogie sat watching Ginko's childlike face a little longer, then quietly slipped from the room.

The next morning Ginko's fever had subsided, thanks to her sound sleep the night before. Her joints still ached and she felt lethargic, but she washed her face and arranged her hair. At seven she drank down some medicine with two raw eggs, called for a rickshaw and headed off to the examination centre.

The test began at nine o'clock, with the first subject being surgery. The final written examination ended at two o'clock after a short lunch break. The practical in clinical medicine began at three. She had ten minutes to examine a patient, and then had to answer interview questions about her conclusions.

"From what disease is today's patient suffering?"

Ginko's questioner was one of three examiners sitting across from her; a large man with a moustache. Ginko instantly recognized him as Gentoku Indo, a professor at Daigaku Higashiko.

"Heart disease, I believe."

"And your basis for that judgement?"

"Soundings taken on his chest indicate that his heart is swollen, approximately one finger-width to the left and right, and I believe I heard unnatural noise above the aortic mitral valve during the stethoscope examination."

"How about the pulse?"

"Yes, I forgot to say – it is somewhat weak and irregular, suggestive of heart disease."

"In what way is it irregular?" the examiner to the right, Professor Kenkichi Urashima, spoke up.

"It's systolic, I believe."

"And what do you think about his oedema?" This was from Professor Tomotake Morinaga. These men were three of the most revered names in the Japanese medical world. Ginko was trembling from nerves as she answered. The interview was no more than ten minutes long, but to Ginko it felt more like an hour.

"Are you ill?" Gentoku Indo asked her when the formal questioning was over.

"No, I'm fine."

"Really? You look a bit feverish. You had better take care of yourself. You may go home now."

Ginko practically fled the room. This was the end of the exam session. Once outside she caught a rickshaw and headed straight to her lodgings. As soon as she got into bed, the chills once again ran through her body. A hand to her forehead quickly revealed that the fever was back with a vengeance. *At least it's over*, she thought, and fell into a restless sleep.

The list of successful candidates was posted on the twentieth of that month. Ginko found her name: "No. 135: Ginko Ogino". The paper rustled slightly as it fluttered in the early spring breeze. Gradually the characters of her name grew larger and more blurred until she could no longer see them clearly. She clenched her fists as the tears fell from her tightly closed eyes. Ginko whispered, "Mother."

Others around her were jumping up and down whooping, or dashing off down the street. Some were clapping their hands and yelling, "Hooray! I'm a doctor!" Ginko simply stood there, jostled by the crowd, whispering, "Mother, look! See, Mother?" She was still standing there stock-still as the others drifted off.

It was March 1885, the spring of her thirty-fourth year.

12

So it was that Ginko became the first female doctor to be certified by the Japanese government.

This is not to say that no other women were practising medicine at the time. Ineko Kusumoto, daughter of the Dutch doctor Philipp Franz von Siebold, married one of her father's students and opened a maternity clinic in Tokyo in 1870. Yet she was a quarter-century older than Ginko, and in her day there was no government examination. There were also records of women practising obstetrics, particularly as midwives, going back to ancient times. In 1884, however – just before Ginko received her licence – of the 40,880 doctors practising in Japan, only 3,313 had passed the licensing examination and were officially qualified to practise.

To mark the occasion, Ginko bought a formal gentlewoman's dress with lace at her breast and sleeves, and white frills at her collar and cuffs. She also bought a hat with a feather and a broad brim, and sat for a commemorative photograph at the Acakuoa Tawaramachi Photography Studio. This photograph shows Ginko sitting on a stool, hat in one hand and her body turned slightly to the right, clearly expressing her pride and spirit.

The first woman to receive a licence to practise medicine, Ginko became a celebrity overnight as her story was carried in newspapers and magazines, all praising her academic talent and effort. Ginko had hitherto been widely derided as an eccentric and a woman who did not know her place, so this sudden shift in public opinion was slightly alarming and the praise rang somewhat hollow.

People Ginko had never met now offered to lend their homes or the use of their land. Uncomfortable with the idea of receiving charity, however, Ginko politely refused them all. Instead she borrowed twenty yen from Mr Takashima, in whose home she had tutored for years, in order to lease a modest single-storey house in Yushima. She had got this far by virtue of her own efforts and she was determined to continue in the same way.

In May 1885, she thus opened the Ogino Obstetric and Gynaecological Clinic in a humble building indistinguishable from the wooden houses and shops surrounding it. The small room by the entrance served as a waiting room, while the slightly larger one adjoining it was the consultation room, sparsely but adequately furnished with a chair and desk, an examination table and a chest full of tiny drawers for medicine. The remainder of the house included a small room for the nurses to rest in, and a single room and kitchen for Ginko's personal use. It was as small as a clinic could be and still serve its purpose.

The clinic was on a tiny alley several blocks off the main thoroughfare, not a place that would usually draw attention. The very unobtrusiveness of the location, however, made it an ideal location for an obstetric and gynaecological practice.

Once the refurbishment of the waiting room, examination room and pharmacy had finally been completed and the clinic was due to open the following morning, Ginko went outside to look at the building from the front. Over the sliding-door entrance was a freshly painted sign that read: "Ogino Obstetric and Gynaecological Clinic". To the right of the door hung another sign that proclaimed: "Female doctor, Ginko Ogino".

All it took was two signs to change the building from a modest home to a hall of medical science. It was not large, but it had a feeling of substance. Ginko gazed at her clinic, full of joy that this day had finally arrived. She could have stood there all day looking at it, such was the affection she felt for it. *This is my castle.* Ginko closed her eyes, and then opened them again to make sure it was still there. This was her clinic and she was the head doctor. Her dream had finally come true.

Ginko's only regret was that she was unable to show it to her mother. *I wonder what Mother would say if she could see it?*

That night, Ginko held a celebration at a restaurant in Shinbashi, inviting all of the people who had helped her over the years. There were her friends Ogie Matsumoto and Shizuko Furuichi, her teachers Mannen Matsumoto, Yorikuni

Inoue, Professor Nagai of the Tokyo Women's Normal School, President Takashina of Kojuin, and everyone else from the government official Tadanori Ishiguro to her benefactor Kaemon Takashima. It was the first time that all of them had been together under the same roof.

"Thank you for everything," Ginko said. "I'll do my very best." That was as far as she got before she was overcome with emotion and unable to continue. It was the high point of her life so far.

Tokyo natives are known for their curiosity and love of new things, and twelve or thirteen patients were lined up at Ginko's clinic the next morning before it opened. It was a good start.

On the first Sunday after it opened, however, Nurse Moto Kodama, who had gone out to sweep the entrance, came running back in to find Ginko. "Doctor, someone's been writing on the wall!"

"What does it say?"

"Umm..." Unable to go on, the nurse headed back to the entrance. Having just woken up and not yet had time to dress, Ginko quickly tied back her hair and dressed before following her nurse outside.

The owner of this house is a wanton woman who revels in blood. The words scrawled all over the walls were accompanied by a caricature of Ginko with a scalpel in one hand and a demonic face half-obscured by long, dishevelled hair.

"Clean it off," said Ginko simply, and headed back into the house.

The graffiti was duly removed, but two days later there was more. *The end is near when a woman takes your pulse. Doctoring is not an occupation for a woman!*

"Shall I call the police?" asked the nurse.

"Don't bother," replied Ginko.

"But it's dreadful to think that some strange man is coming in the middle of the night and doing this."

"We'll remove anything we find on the wall. Making a fuss about it is just what this person wants us to do. The only way to deal with prejudice is to show them who can hold out longer."

This is how Ginko had dealt with the persecution and hardships she had faced at Kojuin. Plus, she did not have the leisure to spend fighting mere graffiti artists. When it had become known that she had been certified as a doctor, the newspapers had been filled with articles singing her praises. These were rapidly followed, however, by editorials arguing whether or not women were suited for the medical profession. Readers then joined in with letters stating their own opinions. The majority agreed with the conventional view that women could never make suitable doctors. In reply, Ginko wrote to a magazine specializing in women's matters:

> Not only are women suited to medicine, it is a profession for which women are uniquely suited. Japanese men should be ashamed of themselves for the condescending way they examine the health of their patients. The talents of the Japanese man are much better suited to the battlefield.

This statement swayed many opinion leaders of the day, who were impressed by her innovative way of thinking. Nevertheless, this was a battle waged on the pages of newspapers. Whether or not women ought to be allowed to practise medicine, or even take the pulses of men, was not something those in need of a doctor had the leeway to contemplate.

There were only two other medical clinics in the Yushima area. In other words, there were not enough doctors for patients to pick and choose from. In the downtown areas populated by merchants and common people, the superiority of men over women was not a hotly debated topic and did little to interfere with Ginko's medical practice.

Indeed, within a month of opening, the Ogino Clinic was overflowing with patients. Ginko was astonished at the prevalence of venereal disease. It was as if all of the women who had been silently bearing their symptoms until now had come forwards at once. Each morning the waiting room was full of women with the pale complexion characteristic of gonorrhoea, including some whose disease had progressed so far that they had difficulties walking. Familiar as she was with their agony, Ginko gave each patient a gentle but thorough examination.

This was an age when doctors had extraordinary authority and status, and male doctors were known for questioning their patients in a condescending fashion. Ginko, however, treated her patients with respect and spoke to them politely. She was so small and slight that she looked more like the next-door neighbour's daughter than someone who had passed the national medical examination. As she listened and nodded sympathetically, patients found it easy to talk to her and often told her everything else that was going on at home in addition to their symptoms.

The sign over the door clearly stated that it was an obstetric and gynaecological practice, but in time men with injuries began to appear in the waiting room. One afternoon, the nurse gently reminded a man with a bleeding finger who the clinic was for, but the man, a labourer with a large voice and even larger body, retorted, "I don't care who it's for! A doctor is a doctor. Look how I'm bleeding," thrusting his bloody finger in the nurse's face.

"All right. I'm sure the doctor will see you, but please try to be mindful of all the ladies here and wait quietly."

"What're you on about? Just get the lady doctor to see me, will you?"

The man did require attention, but he was also curious about the doctor. Having faced the ruffians at Kojuin, Ginko was not afraid of treating men. She looked both beautiful and commanding with her kimono and black overcoat, and the very sight of her could make a man forget his pain.

"What happened?" she asked, when he walked into the examination room.

"I cut my finger with a hatchet."

"I'll disinfect it and then we'll have to sew it up." Ginko moved quickly to wash her hands, and took his enormous hand in her own tiny one.

"This will sting a little," she said, as she poured alcohol on the cut.

"Ow!" the patient howled in pain, but Ginko continued her work unperturbed.

"I'm going to make three stitches. It will only take a few moments, so I won't use anaesthesia. You'll have to bear the pain."

"You're just going to sew it like this?"

"It will hurt a little, but it will be much easier to bear later on."

In those days, anaesthesia generally meant inhaling chloroform to induce unconsciousness. Patients were in pain until the chloroform took effect, as well as during the time it took for the effects to wear off. There was also the danger of suffocation if any food remained in their stomachs.

"Well, try to be gentle."

"I will. Don't look while I'm sewing." Ginko suddenly sounded stern and the man quickly squeezed his eyes shut. He was discovering, possibly to his chagrin, that the lady doctor was not to be taken lightly.

Ginko tucked back the sleeves of her jacket, disinfected her hands again, and picked up a needle. "Now, I want you to count slowly. I'll be finished by the time you get to thirty." She looked up to see him nod that he understood, and then plunged the needle into a patch of skin.

"Ouch!"

"Don't move!"

"Ahhh!" The patient tried to yank his hand back, but the large, matronly nurse kept it securely in place. The fingertip is a sensitive spot on the body, and having it sewn without anaesthesia is a painful experience. The man in his work clothes went several shades paler and was howling, sweating and swearing there in the examination room. Men, especially Tokyoites, were expected to bear pain without showing it, and he must have tried mightily to keep the tears from flowing, yet a few drops found their way out of his tightly shut eyes.

"I told you not to move!"

"OK, OK!"

"Keep still!" The man's cries of agony and Ginko's sharp commands must have startled the patients in the waiting room. The two men who had accompanied the injured man stood, arms folded, exchanging nervous glances.

"One more now." Ginko neatly slipped the needle through the man's skin and pulled the thick thread through while the man cringed. "Now stretch your finger out once more."

Ginko never hesitated – she even appeared to be enjoying herself, looking at times more mischievous than comforting. She was not aware of this, of course. The only conscious thought that passed through her mind was, *Even though I'm a woman, seeing blood doesn't really bother me. Maybe I should have been a surgeon.*

Incidents like this only served to reinforce her confidence in her skills as a physician.

One of the patients at the Ogino Clinic was a woman called Sue Imura. Her chart listed her as twenty-three years old, the wife of Kokichi Imura of Naka-Okachimachi, yet she looked closer to thirty with her pale, careworn face. On her first visit, she brought with her a boy of seven or eight.

From Sue's description of her symptoms, it was clear to Ginko that she had gonorrhoea, but she examined her to make sure. Sue had climbed onto the examination table without a hint of hesitation.

"This isn't the first time you've seen a doctor for this, is it?" asked Ginko, following the examination. Sue shook her head as she rearranged her clothing.

"You must rest when you have a fever," Ginko instructed, unsure if Sue understood what she was saying. She watched as her patient drew her son, who had been waiting quietly, to her side. "If you exert yourself, the disease will spread into your abdomen."

"The last time I had this, it got better in about ten days." It was evident that she did not realize she was undergoing waves of a disease that had not been cured.

"You really must rest when you're ill. If you don't, the medicine won't have any effect. When you get home, cool the infected area with ice water, and then rest." No matter how she urged, however, Sue refused to respond. Looking at the mother and child, it occurred to Ginko that their lifestyle might not allow for bed rest. "And you must take your medicine."

"How much will it cost?" Sue suddenly looked uneasy at the mention of medicine. Her complexion was much too pale, yet her face had aristocratic features. Her dirty, unkempt hair hung limply over the dry and unwashed skin of her face, but Ginko could see that with a little cleaning up, she would be quite beautiful.

"Twenty-five sen for five days' worth." This was half of what Ginko normally charged.

Sue thought for a moment, and then answered, "I'll take three days' worth."

"You can pay me later. Go ahead and take enough for five days," said Ginko, jotting down "No payment required" on the woman's chart. "Now, do you understand? Keep the infected area clean, and get as much rest as you can."

"Thank you." Sue bowed to Ginko, grabbed her son's hand, and rushed out of the examination room.

It was not easy for Ginko to run the financial end of her practice. Not only did she have to repay the loan from Mr Takashima, but she also wanted to return at least some of the money her sister Tomoko had provided over the years as soon as possible. There were also small amounts she had received from Ogie and the Arakawa family she had tutored. None of these people had ever put conditions on their loans, saying only, "Pay me back whenever you can", and this had made their kind-hearted gestures all the more touching.

The truth of the matter, though, was that not all of Ginko's patients were well off. Yushima was located between the crowded downtown area and the estates of the Yamanote district, and among those who came to see her were labourers, street vendors, musicians and even beggars, as well as the wives and mistresses of wealthy merchants. The poorest rarely saw doctors, relying on remedies and potions available without a prescription, but even they would seek help from a doctor when desperate. This was especially so when they knew the doctor was a woman, and a kind woman who refused to pick and choose her patients at that. Sue Imura, a poor man's wife, had surely brought every cent available to her when she set out to Ginko's clinic.

A once-popular saying held that "Medicine is a benevolent art", and this applied very much to Ginko, despite the unimaginably high status afforded Meiji-period doctors. In those days, there were no set prices for either examinations or prescriptions, and the more unscrupulous could mix a little starch with flour and pass it off as "a special formula I made myself". There were no rules or regulations to prevent them from doing such things and charging outrageous prices for them.

At the opposite end of the spectrum were the doctors who were kind to paupers, telling them, "You can wait till summer to pay," or "I won't charge you for this medicine." These were few and far between, but the news of them would spread quickly. Common folk had many acquaintances, making word of mouth the most efficient form of advertisement. Some doctors even counted on this, adjusting their prices accordingly.

It is hard for us nowadays to appreciate fully the awe in which Meiji-era doctors were held. No matter how high a temperature a patient was running, when he heard that the doctor had arrived he would sit up, loosen his clothing and respectfully wait for him to enter the room. He would suppress his dizziness to greet the doctor with the proper formalities, and keep his head lowered while having his pulse taken. Doctors were much too imposing to invite conversation, and their patients did not chat or ask questions, but would merely follow any instructions given: "Show me your back. Now your side. OK, that'll do." Sometimes it would only be after the doctor had departed that patients would belatedly realize that they had not received any explanation of their symptoms or treatment. Their families, too, took pains to avoid any hint of disrespect. In those days, a doctor was more god than human.

Ginko, however, was different. She was not kind in order to ingratiate herself, nor was her kindness capricious. Every time Ginko treated a patient, she remembered how it felt to be sick. It was unclear whether she did this consciously, since she moved and acted naturally. Possibly it was the result of the empathy that people who have suffered feel for others.

Ginko would greet her patients whenever she saw them in town. Patients who saw her coming and prepared to pass quietly by would be astonished when Ginko stopped them to chat. "How are you feeling these days? Are you taking your medicine?"

"Yes, thank you. I'm feeling much better lately."

"I'm glad to hear that. But you mustn't try to do too much yet."

"Thank you very much."

Doctors customarily made their rounds in palanquins or rickshaws by the mid-Meiji years, and so it was very rare to run into your doctor on the street. For most people, Ginko was the first doctor they had ever seen in town, doing her own shopping no less, and greeting people she knew. Ginko's reputation grew by the day, and she was hard at work from nine in the morning until eight at night seeing patients in her clinic and making house calls.

Sue Imura, who had paid for three days' worth of medicine and taken home five, still had not come back ten days later. "Doctor, you shouldn't let the patients pay later," grumbled Nurse Moto as she straightened up the patients' charts at the end of the day. "I knew from the minute I saw her that she wouldn't come back to pay."

"I'm sure she has a lot to do, and will be back when things settle down," Ginko reassured her, although she did not expect to see Sue again and did not plan on taking money from her if she did.

"You can't keep doing this," insisted Nurse Moto. "All these patients owe you money," she continued, indicating a pile of twenty or so charts. Many were patients who had debts going back several months, and some of them had moved and were impossible to contact. This was despite the old adage that no matter whom else you owed, it was bad practice to be in arrears with your doctor, because you never knew when an emergency might arise.

"I'm more concerned that she only had five days' worth of medicine. That won't be enough to cure her symptoms. I wonder how she's doing?" Ginko felt sorry for this woman, who surely would have come back if she had the money.

"The wife of the rice merchant in Mannencho is a neighbour of hers. She told me she's a *yomiuri* in the Asakusa area."

Yomiuri were people who stood on busy street corners reading out verses composed to communicate current events, and they made their living selling books of the poems to passers-by.

"With her husband?"

"And her son, I hear."

"Is that so?"

"I've talked to people who've seen them. Her husband recites the poems and she passes out the books."

It pained Ginko to think of a woman with gonorrhoea standing on the street with her husband and son. She was certain that Sue and her family barely scraped by on the money they made day to day, and that medicine was a luxury she could not afford.

"I never should have let her pay in the first place."

"But she offered to pay for three days."

"Only because I suggested that she pay what she could."

"Doctor, you're not going to be able to make a living cither."

Ginko understood what Nurse Moto was saying, but still she found it difficult to take money from people who could not afford it. Ginko herself had been raised in a wealthy household, and her lack of a head for business was probably due to this. But she knew too that she would never get rich from insisting on Sue paying her bills.

Nurse Moto went on, "She was wearing *geta* and her clothes weren't so bad. With people like that, they start expecting you to let them get away without paying. You must be more careful."

Ginko knew that Moto, who had been raised in the area, knew more about the people who lived there than she did, but it was difficult for her to change the way she felt about these things.

Almost as if she had known they had been talking about her, Sue Imura showed up at the clinic that evening.

"Where have you been?" Ginko demanded as soon as she saw her. "I've been worried about you."

Sue looked down, ashamed. Her hair was dry and lank, and her complexion as pale as it had been the last time Ginko saw her.

"Anyway, what can I do for you today?"

"It's my boy." Sue pushed her son forwards. "This morning when he woke up—"

"Oh my." Ginko breathed in sharply. The boy's eyelids were so red and puffed out that he could not open them. Pus was dripping out of the corners of his eyes onto his cheeks.

"What happened?"

"Nothing. Last night, he started complaining that his eyes hurt, and he cried all night long." Sue's voice was so low Ginko could hardly hear it.

"Did you touch his eyes with your hands?"

Sue looked up as if trying to remember. "Yesterday it was windy and he got dust or something in his eyes, so I wiped them for him."

"What time was this?"

"In the afternoon."

Ginko looked at the boy's eyes again. He began crying again as soon as the light hit them. "Try to be strong," she implored. She washed her hands and touched his eyelids. Then she quickly gave his mother instructions. "I'm going to wash out his eyes. I want you to hold him on your lap. You must hold him so he can't move."

The boy cried even harder when the cold liquid flowed into his eyes.

"Nurse Moto, hold him from behind."

Ginko steeled herself against the boy's sobs, and opened his eyelids with her clean fingers. She rubbed in the cleansing fluid and it flowed down his cheeks along with the pus. The insides of his eyelids were infected and they had swollen up as large as strawberries.

"Cream." Ginko dabbed some cream onto the end of a glass stick, and applied it to the insides of his lids. "He's going to have to wear a patch over his eyes. I'll give him an injection, and he'll have to take medicine."

"But—" Sue began to object.

"I'm sorry. You have no choice."

The boy continued crying, but he had so little energy left that it was nothing more than a thin wail in the examination room. After the eye patch was in place, his mother hesitantly asked, "Is it trach... trach..."

"Trachoma? No. Anything that comes on this suddenly has

got to be *fugan.*" *Fugan* was the old name for gonorrhoeal conjunctivitis. "You infected him with your hands. There are germs on them. That's why I told you that you must be careful to keep your hands clean at all times."

Sue glanced down at her hands. They had many more wrinkles than you would expect on a woman in her early twenties. She looked as if she could not believe that her hands were covered with such frightening germs.

"I'll give you medicine for compresses. Use them on his eyes as often as you can. And make sure he takes this medicine four times a day. Every six hours. Do you understand? If you don't do this, he'll go blind."

Sue looked frightened.

"I'm not saying this just to scare you. This is a very serious disease, and lots of people have lost their eyesight because of it." Mucous membranes were highly susceptible to gonorrhocal bacteria, and many people were infected by rubbing their eyes after touching other infected parts of the body. "Do you understand?"

Sue only nodded, her mouth hanging slightly open. She seemed badly shocked at the prospect of her son going blind. "And how are *you* feeling, by the way?" Ginko asked, changing the subject.

Sue did not answer.

"How is your health?"

Sue looked down, as if she were a child being scolded. Her long eyelashes cast shadows on her thin face.

"Do you urinate frequently? Come on now, speak up. You're still in pain, aren't you?"

Sue nodded ever so slightly.

"Is there something that looks like pus in the urine?"

Sue thought a few moments and then shook her head.

"You really must rest. I'll give you some medicine too. Make sure you take it."

Sue raised her eyes with a look of fear. "This is all I have," she said, pulling two ten-sen coins from the collar of her worn kimono. She would never have come if it hadn't been for her son.

"I won't be needing that. Don't worry about the money – just make sure you come here regularly. You must bring your son back again tomorrow."

Sue nodded, took her son's hand, and shuffled out of the examination room. Nurse Moto followed them both with her eyes, then heaved a great sigh and shook her head as she called in the next patient.

Ginko was unable to free herself of the images of Sue and her child, and fretted over them for the rest of the day. When Sue turned up the next day around noon, she felt a flood of relief. The boy's left eyelid was looking better, but the right one was still badly swollen and he was unable to open it. The pain of the inflammation had begun to ease, however, and he was not crying the way he had been the day before.

"Are you keeping a cold compress on his eyes?"

Sue blinked in a way that could have been taken as either yes or no. If she had spent all day attending to her son, she would not have been able to be out on the street with her husband making a living. Had she left him at home alone? Ginko wanted to tell her that she had to take care of him when he was this sick, but felt she had no right to say anything except "You must keep his eyes cooled all the time". The whole situation made Ginko sad.

Sue and her son obediently arrived at the clinic each day for four days running. After that, though, they stopped coming. Sue had paid twenty sen and no more, and still owed Ginko for her first visit. On the upper right-hand corner of her chart, Nurse Moto had written: "Owes twenty-five sen".

"We haven't seen Mrs Imura lately, have we?" Ginko tried to bring the subject up with Nurse Moto in an offhand manner, hoping to hear they had come while she was out making house calls.

"No, they only came for those four days. I wonder how the boy is doing?"

"He must be better," said Ginko with an air of optimism she did not feel. The boy was going to lose his eyesight, and Sue's gonorrhoea was only going to get worse. Ginko was unable to get them out of her mind.

The next day, while out making rounds, Ginko decided to look them up at their backstreet home near Tokudaiji Temple. It was in a single-storey wooden building divided into a number of dwellings. Women getting water in preparation for making the evening meal had gathered at the well, making the alley seem all the more narrow. Ginko asked one of the women for directions, and finally located Sue's home. The paper doors were torn, and an old scoop and bucket for the well had been left carelessly in the doorway.

"Hello?" Ginko called out as she slid the front door open, but there was no answer. She called out again and waited.

"Who is it?" She heard Sue's voice from inside the house. It sounded as though she had been asleep.

"Is this the Imura home?"

"Yes. Who's there?"

Ginko saw the shadow of someone coming to open the door.

"Oh!" Seeing who the caller was, Sue shrank back and quickly tried to straighten her clothing. Ginko could see that she was clad only in a grubby slip, the kind worn under a kimono, and her hair was dishevelled.

"I was in the neighbourhood making house calls, so I thought I'd drop by and see how you were."

Sue was silent.

"How have you been feeling?" Ginko eyed the sink by the entrance, which opened onto a room with a wooden floor. She caught a glimpse through the shoji doors of bedding laid out in the room beyond. "How about your son?"

Sue still would not speak.

"Are his eyes better?" No matter what Ginko asked, Sue still refused to say a word. "Well, is he at home?"

Just then, a deep male voice called out, "Hey! What's going on?"

Startled, Sue looked back towards the inner room.

"Is someone here?" The voice sounded drunk.

"Is that your husband?" asked Ginko.

Sue looked petrified. She looked back at Ginko and nodded. Having seen the bedding laid out in the middle of the day and Sue in her underclothes, Ginko summed up the situation. "You're still sick, aren't you?"

"Yes," she whispered.

Just then the man's voice boomed out again, "Hurry up and come back to bed!"

Ginko was filled with uncontrollable rage. Later she was unable to recall how she had summoned the courage brazenly to enter someone else's home. Sue and her husband were just as startled.

"Are you Sue's husband?"

"And who the hell are you?" The man had been lying on the bedding in his loincloth, but sat bolt upright in surprise when Ginko suddenly appeared.

"My name is Ginko Ogino. I'm the doctor in Yushima."

The man stared up at her, his mouth open.

"And this is my patient." Ginko indicated Sue, who had sunk to the floor behind her, her legs apparently having given out.

"Did you call her?" the man asked Sue. Sue just shook her head.

"I must apologize for showing up so suddenly." Ginko looked around, as if finally realizing how absurd she must have looked standing there in front of a man who was all but naked.

"What do you want?" demanded the man.

"Your wife is ill. She has gonorrhoea, an extremely serious disease."

Still seated, the man began sluggishly to pull on his cotton kimono.

"And the disease has spread to your son's eyes. He is in danger of losing his sight."

"So what are you saying?" he demanded, the kimono now half-slung over his shoulders.

"Your wife and child are seriously ill. What do you think you're doing lazing around like this in the middle of the day?" The man did not answer, but his displeasure was palpable. Ginko pressed her point home. "Instead of working, you're drunk and in bed. How can you call yourself a father?"

The man suddenly glared past her at someone outside and yelled, "It's none of your business! Get out of here!"

Ginko spun around to see the faces of numerous neighbours craning through the open front door. She felt ashamed of her imprudence and flushed bright red. Lowering her voice, she added, "All I'm asking is that you start acting like a father."

The man remained furiously silent.

"I expect to see you at the clinic tomorrow!" She said to Sue, who was still seated on the floor like a wilted plant, and quickly exited. The neighbours drew back as she passed them, but Ginko saw them looking at her and nodding. She hurriedly made her way back to the main road.

The events of the afternoon spread like wildfire throughout the area. Some praised Ginko, saying, "Some doctor, that one!" and "She told him all right! He'll have to change his ways now!" Others, however, were more critical, with "The nerve!" and "From a woman, at that!"

For her part, Ginko feigned ignorance of the furore. In private to Nurse Moto and her other staff, however, she grumbled, "A bad husband means a life of misery for his wife," and "I've never seen such a lazy man before," then "You have to keep an eye on men. There's no telling when they'll turn on you!" Suddenly she realized she was speaking from her own experience, and fell silent.

Sue showed up with her son the next day, just as Ginko had ordered. It was during a time when there were few other patients. Ginko apologized for her intrusion the day before. It was not that she felt she had done anything wrong, but she felt a need to apologize before she could proceed with the examination.

"That's all right." Sue appeared unable to say anything else.

"Now, let's take a look." Without further ado, Ginko pulled the boy hanging onto Sue's right hand towards herself. "Let me see."

Ginko sucked in her breath the instant she saw his eye. The swelling was down on the right eyelid and he was able to open it, but the entire membrane over his eye was grey.

"Look over here," Ginko prompted him, holding her finger just beyond his right eye. The boy turned his face as if trying to find the finger, and looked diagonally up at it. His right eye, however, did not move at all.

"Now over here." Ginko moved her finger to the left. Once again, the boy turned slowly towards it. The right eye still refused to move. The gonorrhoeal bacteria had damaged both the membrane and the cornea.

"He can't see," Ginko spoke to Sue. "He has lost the sight in his right eye."

Sue finally seemed to realize the seriousness of what Ginko was telling her, and she looked down at her son.

"What are you going to do?" Ginko asked her. "It's because you didn't bring him in, you know." Ginko knew it would not help to get angry at Sue, but she could not force herself to stay silent either. "You and your husband are his parents. It's your fault."

"His eye is gone for good?"

"Of course it is. It's too late to save it now." The little boy was startled by the doctor's stern voice, and buried his face in his mother's knees. Sue put her hands on his head, and her own head drooped. The sight of the two huddled together made Ginko even angrier.

"This boy will be blind for the rest of his life. And *you* made him that way!" The veins in Ginko's forehead bulged and her eyes glistened. "How can you call yourself a mother? You gave birth to him, you..." She found it impossible to go on, and just shook her head.

"Doctor?" Nurse Moto tried to intervene.

"You've got to understand!..." Ginko tried to go on, but she had forgotten what she wanted to say.

"You must do what the doctor tells you," Nurse Moto continued for her, trying to smooth over the situation.

Sue and her son were clutching onto each other as if trying to brave a storm. The rage drained from Ginko as suddenly as it had filled her, and she sank down on her chair. Loneliness silently washed over her.

"Let's have the doctor take another look." Moto gently detached the boy's hands from his mother, and brought him over for Ginko to examine him again.

Ginko's rage was replaced by a wave of regret. The way she had just acted was not worthy of an adult, let alone a doctor. This was a side of herself that she had not known before. She could not remember clearly what she had said or done. Now that the storm had passed, she was once again a doctor examining a patient, someone entirely unrelated to the furious woman she had been a few moments ago. Ginko closed her eyes. What had come over her?

"Doctor, please."

Ginko opened her eyes at Nurse Moto's words. The boy was sitting patiently on the stool, while his mother sat with her head in her hands. Ginko could not yet say with certainty that the damage to his eye was permanent.

"We might be able to save part of his sight." Ginko spoke more gently, as if to make up for her anger a few moments before, but Sue didn't say a word. After Ginko had dressed the boy's eye, she turned to Sue. "Now let's take a look at you."

Sue walked slowly over to the examination table, loosened her sash, and climbed up on it. Without having to be told, she pulled up the hem of her kimono and bent her legs. The infected area was inflamed again.

"You mustn't have relations with your husband," Ginko warned her, thinking how her disease was so closely connected to the man who had been lying on that bedding.

Every day for the next ten days, Sue diligently showed up at the clinic with her son. She paid for each visit. Ginko wondered what had become of her husband, but she knew it was not her place to ask. The regular and consistent care for her son's eyes paid off as a small degree of sight returned, and it looked as though the eye would heal after all. Sue's condition began to clear up too and the infection to abate.

The rainy season came to an end, and Ginko's clinic welcomed its first summer.

"Change your underclothes frequently if you sweat, and keep the infected area as clean as possible. And no sexual relations for the entire month of July."

Sue was now able to look Ginko in the eye and nod when she spoke to her. Ginko was relieved. She had thoroughly embarrassed herself by barging into Sue's house, but now she was glad to see that some good had come from it.

Then, in mid-July, Sue failed to show up at the clinic for three consecutive days. Ginko wondered if she had gone back to work or just did not feel like going out in the heat. Whatever the reason, Ginko was satisfied that her condition was almost completely cleared up for the time being. As long as Sue was managing to keep herself clean, the infection would remain at bay.

Sue turned up at the clinic on the fourth day.

"No change, right?" asked Ginko.

Sue looked away and nodded slightly.

"Did something happen?"

"No."

"Well, then let's take a look." Ginko indicated the examination table with a nod of her head. Sue looked flustered and hesitated, but pulled herself together and climbed onto the table. This was the first time she had ever hesitated, and she seemed to be moving reluctantly.

"Bend your knees, please." Ginko had finally grown accustomed to giving this kind of instruction. "A little more."

Sue's white thighs trembled slightly as she parted them.

"A little more..." Ginko stopped short. Four days before, Sue's infection had been almost completely dry. Now it was red and raw, and there was a green discharge. "What happened?"

Sue snapped her legs shut.

"Sue!" Ginko tried to stay calm. "It's much worse today."

Sue refused to answer.

"We're right back to where we started." She peered into Sue's face, but Sue only blinked, her breath ragged.

After Ginko had cleaned the infection and applied fresh medicine, Sue slowly rearranged her kimono and returned to the stool, stealing glances at Ginko. Ginko washed her hands and sat down at her desk. On her chart, Ginko wrote *Red, some ulceration, discharge.* Then she looked up at her patient.

"Why don't you tell me what happened?" She wanted to know why the infection was so much worse. Had she failed to keep herself clean? Was her resistance to infection down? Or... Ginko looked more closely at Sue. "You broke your promise, didn't you?"

Sue looked up, startled, and then looked down again.

"Tell me the truth!"

"The day before yesterday—" Sue started.

"Didn't I tell you to wait until the end of the month?"

Sue looked up again and moved her mouth as if she was about to speak.

"What?"

"My husband..." Ginko had to strain to hear Sue's voice.

"What about your husband?"

"He said he had to."

"Did he force you?"

Sue nodded slowly.

"Why didn't you refuse? You're sick! How many times do I have to say it?"

"But—" Sue made a rare attempt to answer back.

"But what? Was there some other reason?"

"It had been a whole month." Sue's eyes were sad. Her long eyelashes almost covered her eyes.

"Why couldn't you keep a promise for that long? Why couldn't you make him wait?" Ginko was irritated at Sue's lack of resolve. "You are a woman. A woman should be able to protect herself!"

Ginko stopped speaking when she caught Sue looking at her. Her unkempt hair covered her eyes, but Ginko could see that she was staring at her. Her eyes did not flinch, no matter how she was scolded. At last Ginko understood.

"It wasn't that you couldn't refuse him. You yourself couldn't wait. So that's the kind of woman you are!"

Sue was silent.

"I give up. Do whatever you like!" Ginko finally realized that Sue had another side to her, one that was brazen and shameless.

Ginko's clinic also attracted the wealthy wives of successful merchants, as well as some geisha and mistresses. Katsu Nakagawa was a geisha with an attractive home in nearby Ueno, and the mistress of a shipping-warehouse owner. Katsu was thirty-two years old, but with her clear complexion and tiny figure, she looked more like twenty-five. Her exquisite beauty would normally indicate a delicate constitution, but having been so long in the pleasure quarters, she had become a spirited and strong-willed woman.

One of Katsu's maids arrived at the clinic with a note on a scrap of paper. *The pain is back. Would you mind paying a house call?* Ginko spent the mornings seeing patients at her clinic, and made her rounds in the afternoon. Sometimes she would not be finished at the clinic until four or five in the afternoon. She would then set out after the briefest of midday meals, walking to nearby homes or taking a rickshaw to those further away.

About half of Ginko's patients had either gonorrhoea or *shokachi*, a bladder infection caused by sexually transmitted disease. Katsu was one of the former.

"It's back," Katsu told Ginko. "I was out walking around in Mukojima in the rain before it healed fully from the last time." Katsu had had gonorrhoea for ten years, ever since she made her geisha debut, and she related this setback with resignation rather than surprise. "It's like a ship that comes to port every six months."

Ginko washed the affected area and gave her a prescription of sandalwood oil and bearberry. After Ginko had prepared the medication, Katsu asked, as if suddenly remembering something, "It will clear up by the end of the month, won't it?"

It was already 25th July, so that left six days. Though this was just an inflammation of a chronic disease, it would certainly take longer than six days to push it back into remission.

"Isn't there anything you can do?"

"Are you planning a trip?"

"No, no..." Katsu looked coquettishly at Ginko out of the corner of her eye. "Come now, you must know what I mean."

Ginko realized that it had something to do with a man.

"He'll be back from Osaka for the first time in a month."

"It's much too soon."

"But, it won't do to—"

"Tell him you're ill."

"He's not one to take no for an answer. He makes demands of me even when I've got a fever."

188

"That's despicable."

"He's not normal. He'll get what he came for."

"So, his only purpose in coming is to give you pain?"

"That's right," agreed Katsu, her eyes sparkling with humour.

"Well, then, if *you* can't refuse him, I will have to do it for you."

"No, please don't! He only comes to see me about twice a month these days, so I can handle that much." She spoke as if it were only natural.

"Then it will only get worse, you know."

"I've got to make sure he gets what he wants when he comes to see me."

Ginko had to admit Katsu had a point. It was how she made a living. Yet Ginko hated the fact that the man was merely using her as a plaything, even if he was providing for her. "This is not a disease you were born with. You were infected by a man."

"Yes, I know. I was eighteen, and it was my second man."

"And you've suffered from it ever since. This suffering is all from men!" Ginko wanted to spur this innocent woman to put the blame where it belonged.

Instead Katsu responded cheerily, "When I first learnt I had it, I cried from the pain and the fever. But then Tamamoto – she's an older geisha who's gone back to Senju now – explained to me that it was all for the best."

"Why was that?"

"Because, although it would be painful for a while, it would make it impossible for me to have children. After a month, when I was able to see customers again, the woman who ran my house held a celebration for me. Sure enough, I've never had to worry about getting pregnant since then."

Ginko was speechless. She looked into Katsu's eyes. They were so black and clear that you would never guess she was a prostitute who had slept with so many men.

"Please let me, just this once."

"I'm sure you don't need my permission."

"It's cruel of you to tell me not to do something that feels so good. Don't you agree?" Katsu teased.

Ginko washed her hands and grabbed the handle of her medicine box.

"Doctor, you must know what I'm talking about, surely?" Katsu fired her parting shot, still laughing.

Ginko did not say a word, but stood up and headed for the door.

"The doctor is leaving," Katsu called, and a maid came running to see her out.

As Ginko left, she thought that with its black fence, the house almost announced itself as the home of a mistress. She no longer felt pity or outrage as she walked down the narrow lane – she simply felt hopeless and empty.

At the end of July, Ginko paid a visit to Yorikuni. Three months had passed since she had opened her clinic, and she had now settled into her job. Though she had got used to the work itself, emotionally she was anything but settled. Truth be told, she was feeling more turmoil now than when she had opened her practice. She was visiting her mentor ostensibly to thank him for attending her clinic-opening celebration, but she also wanted to discuss with him certain things she had on her mind.

It was a hot day, so she took a rickshaw. As it climbed the hill to his house, Ginko thought about how Yorikuni had taken a young wife and now had a child. The last time she had visited, she had learnt that his wife was pregnant. On that occasion, Ginko had spent an hour applying make-up and choosing a kimono to wear, not wishing to compare unfavourably to his young wife. This time, however, she wore her usual black kimono and did no more than dab a little powder on her cheeks and at the corners of her eyes where wrinkles were beginning to show. *I'm a doctor now*, she thought. She had a new confidence in herself that exceeded the boundaries of youth and good looks.

Ginko's sudden visit took Yorikuni by surprise, and he hurried to the door to greet her himself.

"It's wonderful to see you. Come in, come in." Instead of calling for his wife or a maid, he himself led her into the tatami room where he received guests. His entire manner had changed towards her. Before she had been a mere medical student, but now she was a fully fledged doctor, and he saw her much more as an equal.

After they had exchanged their greetings, the shoji slid open and a woman appeared.

"Let me introduce my wife," Yorikuni said.

Ginko looked over at her slowly.

"My name is Chiyo, I'm pleased to meet you." Kneeling on the tatami floor, Yorikuni's wife bowed politely to her.

"I'm Ginko Ogino. Nice to meet you too." Ginko bowed in return, quickly sizing up this woman. She was small and slight, about thirty-one or two, and gave the impression of being quick and intelligent. She wore a dark reddish-brown kimono, and had her hair tied up in a large chignon. All in all, her style was quite youthful for her age.

"I've told you about her," Yorikuni said to his wife. "She's the first woman doctor in Japan."

Ginko dropped her head in a show of modesty, but the praise felt good.

"Yes," said Chiyo, "my husband speaks of you often."

Husband, thought Ginko. If she had accepted Yorikuni's proposal all those years ago, that would have been what she would have been calling this large, balding man. She smiled to herself.

"Is something funny?" asked Yorikuni quizzically.

"No, not at all. You've got a beautiful wife."

"What are you waiting for? Go and get Dr Ogino some fruit to eat, will you, Chiyo?"

"Right away." As Chiyo stood up to leave the room, a toddler appeared on unsteady legs. "Look who's here!"

"I'll hold him." Yorikuni held out his arms to the little boy, then plopped him down between his crossed legs.

"Your child."

"Yes, yes. He's just learnt to walk and is always getting into something."

"He looks just like you."

"That's what everyone says." Yorikuni broke into an enormous smile. This child had to be especially dear to him, having come to him later in life. Yorikuni no longer looked like a stern professor. Ginko smiled in return, although the whole scene felt somehow odd.

Chiyo brought in cold tea and summer oranges, then left the two alone, the child still on his father's lap.

"You seem to be doing very well."

"Thanks to you," Ginko replied automatically.

"Doctors are lucky. People are grateful to them and pay them money too. There can't be a job that's any better than that."

"I wouldn't go that far."

"Anyone who has people's lives in her hands is going to get respect."

"I don't know. I'm beginning to have my doubts."

"What do you mean?" Yorikuni held his cup of tea to the boy's mouth, who then gulped it all at once, giving a little shiver as it went down.

"All of a sudden, being a doctor seems like glum work."

"What a thing to say!"

"There isn't much a doctor can do for her patients."

"That's not true. When they're in need, people always count on their doctor. How many people are only alive today because of a doctor?"

"It's not the doctor. People's lives are saved because of their own physical strength and the environment they live in. Doctors merely provide a bit of assistance."

"It doesn't matter as long as it saves the patient, does it?"

"But there are times when I can't even do that."

"You're doing everything you can."

"I'm doing everything I'm capable of, and it's still not enough."

"You're just one person."

"I'm not complaining about a lack of doctors or limitations to my physical strength. What I mean is, I can't do anything at all if the patients won't come to me. Even when they come, they won't always follow my instructions. Or sometimes the patients want to obey me, but others around them prevent them from doing so."

"I see."

"No matter how simple and common the disease, it's still complicated by everything else in the patient's life. And it's that which determines whether the disease is cured or not, or whether they live or die."

"But there's no end to it once you start reasoning like that."

"Not at all. There are any number of cases where it would be better to improve the environment surrounding a patient rather than provide medical care. It would be much quicker and more efficient."

The child had fallen asleep in Yorikuni's arms. He gently stroked his son's plump little arm.

"What I mean is that matters of poverty, social systems and customs are more urgent than making advances in medical care." Having said what was on her mind, Ginko picked up the cup of tea and took a sip.

"But is that the responsibility of the medical profession?"

"Of course not. It's a much more basic, fundamental problem than medicine."

"So, what do you plan to do?" Yorikuni sniffed the child in his arms. "I think I smell something... Chiyo!" Ginko heard his wife's footsteps hurrying down the hall. "He needs to be changed."

"Let me have him, then." As Chiyo moved to take the child off Yorikuni's lap, he woke up and began to cry.

"It's all right, it's all right," said Yorikuni, patting the boy's hand.

"Excuse us, then," said Chiyo as she hurried off.

"Children do what they do no matter who they're with!"

Ginko realized she was seeing a new and unexpected side of Yorikuni.

"Now, what were you saying?"

But Ginko had lost the energy to go on.

"You were talking about social problems?"

"That's right."

"You're a doctor! You shouldn't have to think about that sort of thing."

As Ginko drank up her tea, she could not help regretting that Yorikuni no longer seemed to have the will or the mettle to aim for a higher goal.

13

These limitations of medicine and the frustration with them that she had expressed to Yorikuni led Ginko to take an interest in Christianity, and she began attending a church in Hongo. The pastor there was the Reverend Danjo Ebina.

The year before, in October 1884, she had attended a speech on Christianity at the Shintomi Theatre in Kyobashi. Until then she had considered it a rather mysterious, unpleasant religion that had originated in a foreign country and had little to do with her. She had known a few believers at the Tokyo Women's Normal School, but they were treated with suspicion by the other students and considered almost a race apart. Ginko herself had been somewhat wary of them and never got too close. Besides, her whole focus had been on securing good grades and getting a step closer to her goal of becoming a doctor.

She had attended the lecture at the Shintomi a couple of weeks after passing the first of her medical licensing examinations. She still had another test to take, but she was full of hope and had begun to relax ever so slightly. Her impression of Christianity at the time had been that it was all new and rather astonishing. She had arrived thirty minutes ahead of time to find the enormous auditorium already full. The programme began with organ music. She had never heard anything like it before, but it sounded quite dignified. It was followed by a long succession of Christians taking to the stage to expound on the wonder of their faith.

Eventually the themes turned to biting criticism of Japan's social system. After many had spoken, a foreigner with blue eyes stood up. And he spoke in Japanese. Ginko was stunned to hear someone from another country, the sort of person she had always been fearful of, speak in words she could understand. Not only that, but she found herself agreeing with every word he said. Ginko was particularly moved by the notion that all people were God's children. Regardless of whether they were male or female, or what sort of work they did, they were all equal in God's eyes. She had only had a taste of Christianity at this event, but she felt almost drunk with the stern integrity of the speakers and the reverent atmosphere of the hall.

"Christianity is the only religion that acknowledges the status of women. Spreading Christianity would help to improve the lot of women," said Shizuko Furuichi excitedly to Ginko, whom she had invited, at the close of the event. Ginko still felt as if she were in a dream. "That religion could provide the basis for change in Japan!"

As she listened to Shizuko, Ginko squeezed the tiny Bible she had been given. Underneath that black cover, she was sure, were words of wisdom and courage. As inspired as she was, however, she still had her second medical licensing examination to study for. She had gone back to her books, prepared for and passed the test, and then had immediately set up her practice. Every once in a while, she recalled the speeches she had heard and read her Bible. The lettering was tiny, so she began copying out the entire text, both so she could learn it and so that she'd be able to reread it later in larger print. By the time her first summer as a doctor rolled around and she had begun to get used to the work, she had finished copying the Bible.

The Japanese Congregational Church had been established that same year, 1885, in order to facilitate evangelizing nation-wide. This had necessitated a major restructuring of the workings of the organization, which was comprised of thirty-one congregational churches, forty ministers and 3,465 members. The Hongo church was in fact not a church but a preaching post, and just a ten-minute walk from Ginko's clinic in Yushima. In the new system, it came under the pastorship of the Reverend Danjo Ebina, a minister who had been extraordinarily successful in Joshu, the present-day Gunma prefecture.

There were three groups within the Japanese Protestants at that time. One came out of the Yokohama Evangelist School, and supported a traditional form of theology. Another was from the Kumamoto Western School, which had a Japanese classical tendency. The last was made up of graduates of the Sapporo

Agricultural School, who had a strong individualistic orientation and eventually became the "Non-Church" movement of Kanzo Uchimura. These groups had one thing in common: they were all from samurai families, and they established a Christian faith that was a combination of East and West, training many evangelists.

Danjo Ebina was one of the most talented of the second wave of the Kumamoto group, and was just thirty years old when he first arrived at the preaching post in Hongo.

Whenever Ginko walked past that small Hongo church, she could hear the mysterious sound of the organ playing and hymns being sung. At those times she remembered how excited she had felt at the Shintomi Theatre. Beneath the wooden cross displayed at the entrance of the preaching post was a sign reading: "All are free to enter here".

Should I go in? Ginko wondered one day as she walked past. The next day, on her way back from making house calls, she took a detour past the little church just as the believers were filing out, gentle smiles on their faces. Ginko was still unsure whether she should approach them, however, and hurried on her way. The next day the church was quiet. Maybe the music had already finished for the day. Ginko wondered what the inside of the building might look like, but continued on.

The next Sunday morning, Ginko walked to the church and stood before it. Two or three people chatting together went inside. The door was partly open. She could see people inside sitting on long benches, their backs to her.

"Would you like to come in?" Hearing herself addressed, Ginko spun around and found herself face to face with a large man with a beard and white-framed round glasses. "The service is about to begin. Let's go in." The man put his hand lightly to Ginko's back, and Ginko moved forwards obediently. The small church was no bigger than a normal house, but it had a larger, more open entrance, and wooden floors rather than tatami. "Everyone will be glad to see you."

Ginko felt herself being drawn in. She was uneasy and confused, but she could feel a much greater power pulling her along. She took off her *geta* and stepped up inside. The room had been made by removing a wall to create a single, large open space. There were long benches lined up before a lectern at the front. The only two things that Ginko recognized were the cross on the wall behind it – a symbol of the saviour called Jesus Christ – and the instrument to the left making the mysterious-sounding music: the organ.

"Please have a seat." The man spoke in a quiet voice that seemed almost incongruous with his large frame. Shortly afterwards the organ stopped playing and the man moved to a seat in the front row. That was when Ginko realized he must be Danjo Ebina, the minister of the church whose name was on the sign out front.

Ebina may have spoken about Westerners such as Washington and Lincoln, and the apostles Paul and John, and of course Christ, but he himself was the personification of a traditional Japanese man in kimono, *hakama* trousers and *geta*. He had been born and raised in Kyushu, and his personality reflected both his country upbringing and his scholarly accomplishments.

"Normal, everyday people can never become first-generation Christians. They have to be extraordinarily intelligent, or extraordinarily ordinary, or extraordinarily strange in order to endure the obstacles and criticism and still maintain their faith." This quote from Ebina's writings is very much like the man himself: full of confidence and bluster, yet setting forth an essential truth. This was not an age when ministers could don their clerical robes, close themselves up in their churches and devote themselves to giving sermons. Ebina was not so much a righteous man of faith as he was a man of action with worldly ambitions. For this he was criticized by the social historian Aizan Yamaji: "Your heart is like hot, flowing wax. You never stick to any particular idea for long. You head in the direction that looks best to you on a particular day, always moving from one idea to the next. Ebina, you are imprudent."

But Ebina viewed Christianity as a practical science more than a mere belief. He also considered the traditional Japanese standards of loyalty, patriotism and filial piety to all be part and parcel of Christianity. This way of thinking had an extraordinary effect on his missionary work, and preached by him, Christianity no longer appeared to be a foreign religion. The fact that Ebina had been on hand when Ginko first became interested in Christianity had a profound influence on the rest of her life. Within a month, she was visiting the church as regularly as the rest of the believers, and she began to close her clinic on Sundays.

The other church members were interested in Ginko too, knowing she was the female doctor who lived in the neighbourhood. Although all believers were considered equal, it did make an impact when someone who was well known joined the congregation. Reverend Ebina kept his eye on Ginko, but did not pressure her in any way. He knew that it was only a matter of time until she would ask to be baptized.

One Sunday early in November, Ginko found an opportunity to have a long talk with the minister. He was five years younger, but Ginko considered him her superior in many ways. She told him about the discrimination she had endured on her path to becoming a doctor, and how she had felt that she was the only one who had had to suffer such trials.

"But now I finally understand that this was not the case. There are many people in the world with far greater problems than mine. Many of them suffer merely because they were born under the wrong star, and most have given up on improving their lot in life. Medical science alone cannot help these people. They face obstacles beyond its scope."

Reverend Ebina nodded silently to encourage Ginko to talk more about how she felt.

"I've never thought about anyone besides myself," she continued. "All I ever thought of was becoming a doctor so that I could look down on the people who hurt me. On the surface, I wanted to save other women patients from the humiliation I suffered, but deep down, I wanted revenge. I wanted to get back at all the men who made me suffer, and the people who treated me as an outcast – my family and relatives, the town I grew up in, and even myself. I thought that knowing more and being more accomplished than anyone else would solve all my problems. I would have the high social status of a respected physician. It just proves what a small person I really am."

Now it was Ebina's turn to speak. "I was the same. Right before I was baptized, I was captivated by the commanding presence of military officers on parade. I couldn't decide whether to go into the army or follow the path of God. After I was baptized, I was determined to throw away everything of this world so that I could give everything I had to God. The more I tried, however, the more I was overwhelmed by the ambition, political aspirations and thirst for knowledge that were fostered in me as the son of a samurai family. I tried my best to overcome these, but the effort left me exhausted. Yours is a very common struggle."

A figure of Jesus Christ hung on the wall just behind him, and Ginko felt Christ's as well as Ebina's eyes on her. "Do you think it's possible for someone as self-centred as me to become a true believer? Might I not fail in the process?"

"Don't think too deeply about it. Commend yourself to the care of God. Become his child."

"A child?"

"That's right. I wanted to become a loyal retainer to God. But that was a selfish, foolhardy task. It only made me miserable. The best I could do was to start out as a child, an infant. It took me ten years to realize that, and it was such a relief when I finally did. It's simple and requires no philosophy or discussion, yet it's a notion that's at the very root of both philosophy and theology."

Ebina's voice was hoarse from days of street evangelism, and this lent added weight to his words. Ginko was able to talk to him with complete honesty. "I never thought of anyone but myself until I achieved my goal. And once I did, all I noticed were people's imperfections. Behind the misfortune of every single woman was the tyranny of a single man, and I hated every one of those men for it. That was how I looked at people."

This was no longer a conversation; Ginko was confessing her sins and asking for salvation. Ebina reassured her, "Humans are not completely rebellious against God. They cling to Him even as they sink further into sin. It's at times like these that humans truly yearn for God. Ours is a personal God, full of love, and this is when we are able to join Him in a relationship like that between a parent and child."

It was Ebina's belief that no matter how many mistakes we made, we could still come to God. The relationship would not be one of a lord and a vassal, but that of a god and a child, the only possible relationship. The natural progression of this idea was that Jesus Christ was not Ebina's Lord, but his brother. Faith did not entail a great leap or change in life – it was merely a single stage of development, that required understanding the distinct religious definition that one had as a human being. There was no atonement to Christ in this way of thinking. It meant being enlightened and influenced by the cross of Christ, knowing that one would die in sin, but that it would lead to eternal life.

"Entering into a relationship with God as his child will lead to a mysterious state in which we are one with Him." All of Ebina's ideas were based on his own experience and were unmistakably liberal. Basically, he did not envisage a fundamental reform of man based on the gospel, but an acknowledgment of the reality and the importance of loyalty, patriotism and filial piety, which he believed would lead to bonding and integration in a deeper state of Christianity. There was nothing in this way of thinking that suggested confrontation or change. It was a notion of comprehensive absorption, and he skilfully used the ideas of the age and the logic of others to develop his style.

Ebina's inclusive approach persuaded Ginko, and she made the decision to become a Christian. Ebina baptized her in November 1885, along with other new believers including Ukichi Taguchi, a well-known private-sector economic critic and politician, and Professor Hajime Onishi, a famous Meiji-era philosopher. At about this time, the congregation outgrew the old preaching post, and they rented a larger house, only to move again the following March to still roomier quarters in Hongo Kinsuke. Ebina's skill as an evangelist was undeniable.

As if moving in tandem with the Hongo church, the Ogino Clinic also began to outgrow its location. In the autumn of 1886, the clinic moved from Yushima to Ueno Nishikuromon.

There was a combined reception desk and pharmacy dispensary as well as a waiting room, and the new examination room was sufficiently spacious to have a section partitioned off for use as a dressing room. There were also three rooms for Ginko's private use. In addition, there was a second floor with four rooms that Ginko reserved for any patients requiring hospitalization.

Ginko also employed another nurse, by the name of Tomiko Sekiguchi, and a rickshaw driver for her exclusive use, so that the Ogino Clinic's list of employees now included one doctor, two full-time nurses, a handyman, a maid and a rickshaw driver. The clinic itself continued to be crowded with patients, and Ginko also graciously acceded to requests for house calls both early in the morning and late at night. Ginko's reputation continued to grow, yet it was during this time that her interest began to shift from the work of a doctor to the social activism of a Christian.

Each night, by the time Ginko had returned from her round of house calls, eaten dinner and bathed, it was already nine o'clock. She would then go to her room and read. She had a figure of Christ and a cross on her desk along with her Bible, and had now started reading the Bible in English, looking up words in the dictionary as she went along. She never went to sleep before two or three in the morning. Ginko's night-owl habits had started at the Tokyo Women's Normal College, and had not changed even now as she approached forty.

When Ginko tired of reading the Bible, she would shift to recent Japanese publications. Her bookshelves included such titles as *Learning for Modern Women* by Koka Doi, *The Subjection of Women* by John Stuart Mill, translated by Uchiki Fukama, *Social Statistics* by Herbert Spencer, translated by Tsutomu Inoue, *Japanese Women* and *Male and Female Relations* by Yukichi Fukuzawa and *Women's Rights in the West* by Horyu Yunome. These were all written during the first twenty years of the Meiji era, and all had a major influence on the emerging women's movement.

Ginko no longer had to watch the amount of money she spent on either lamp oil or books. She could read as long as she liked, and while that usually meant until the early hours of morning, sometimes it was until sunrise. She had no more tests to take, nor did she have to worry about making a living. She could study anything she liked as much or as little as she pleased. The more she read, the more interesting a subject became. One of the advantages of being a doctor was that she could also study people from all walks of life, and be privy to both what they allowed others to see and what they wanted to hide. Now that her finances were also on a firm footing, she became an even more fervent Christian, and within six months of her baptism, she was one of the leading members of the Hongo church.

Ginko's widening reputation as a doctor also influenced other women, inspiring more and more to become physicians. Female medical students even travelled in from outlying areas and appeared on Ginko's doorstep, expecting to be housed and fed by her. Ginko welcomed them all, and let them stay in the empty rooms above her clinic. In that autumn of 1886, a second woman passed the medical licensing examination, and was soon followed by others.

14

It was also in the autumn of 1886 that another important development for Japanese women and for Ginko personally took place: the founding of the Japan Christian Women's Organization (JCWO). This was one of the early beacons of female social action in Japan. The plain-spoken leader of the group was Kajiko Yajima, a native of Kumamoto, who was one of the first female educators in Japan, having set up a Christian school for girls in Kojimachi, Tokyo, together with Maria T. True, five years previously in 1881.

The original Women's Christian Temperance Union was first established in Ohio in the United States in 1872. In 1884, after Frances Willard was elected president, the group began to expand its organization overseas, and it had a major influence on the Japanese women's movement. In 1887, Frances Willard came to Japan, causing a stir and bringing more attention to the activities of the JCWO.

Ginko was one of the original members of JCWO, and served as Chief of Manners and Morals. The organization's first order of business was to decide which social issues to pursue. Yajima began with a statement: "First of all, let us declare our ultimate goal to be establishing a society free from conflict." There was no objection from the assembled as she continued, "Alcohol is the greatest cause of discord in society. I propose that we begin by working to prohibit alcohol." The Sino-Japanese War was still eight years away, and war was not yet a threat. Liquor consumed by males was by far the biggest source of distress to women and disruption to society.

One of the other members spoke up. "When you say prohibit alcohol, do you mean that even a drop is unacceptable, or will a certain amount be allowed?"

"The ideal, of course, would be the complete prohibition of liquor. But since that would be difficult to achieve, initially, at least, we should start out by making it illegal for minors, women and abusers to drink." This was exactly what the other women were hoping for, and there were no objections.

"Well then," said Yajima, "it's settled. The primary objectives of the Christian Women's Organization shall be peace and the prohibition of alcohol. Let us now consider the steps we will need to take to achieve them."

"There is another matter I would like the organization to consider." A small woman on the right-hand side of the table stood up. It was Ginko. "I believe that the root of evil in this society is the existence of brothels and prostitutes. Men restrict the freedom of women and use them as sexual playthings. Human beings should not be allowed to do this to one another." Ginko's voice carried clearly through the meeting room. "Prostitutes are the source of social diseases. Men get infected and then spread them to their innocent wives and children. Countless women suffer because of this. How can we ignore this issue when we know the source of these horrible diseases? I believe that the first job of the Christian Women's Organization should be to root out prostitution." Ginko was much younger than the other women, but she spoke with firm conviction. "May we please add it to the other fundamental objectives?"

Coming from a doctor, Ginko's plea was convincing. Of course none of the others realized that she was also speaking from personal experience. They unanimously agreed to her proposal, and the goals of the JCWO were henceforth "Peace, Abolition of Alcohol and the Eradication of Prostitution".

The JCWO travelled throughout the country to meet with women, recruiting members and building up support for its causes. At first they spoke in churches, but eventually they moved out onto the street and spoke alongside the Salvation Army. Whenever Ginko had a few moments free from her practice, she went around to churches and narrow alleyways, any place where women gathered, to promote the three pillars of the JCWO.

In October 1887, about a year after the Japan Christian Woman's Organization was established, a woman sought refuge in the Hongo church. She appeared to be a prostitute, judging from her fancy hairstyle and brightly coloured kimono, both considerably dishevelled, yet she could be no more than sixteen or seventeen years old.

"I came here because I heard there were people here who would help me," she said, as she looked uneasily around the inside of the church. The girl explained that she had been born in Kawagoe and had been sold to a brothel in Fukaya the year before, but she hated the work demanded of her and had decided to run away. Ginko went straight to Kajiko Yajima and the other JCWO members to discuss how they should deal with the situation.

The young woman had risked her life to leave the brothel. During the Edo era, a woman would have been dragged back as soon as she was found, and whether she then lived or died was left to the discretion of the owner. Anyone who tried to protect or assist such a woman would also be subject to retaliation. Matters had improved with the cultural enlightenment of the Meiji years, but no one doubted that things would be bad for the girl if she were discovered and returned to the brothel.

"We must protect her at all costs. If we are unable to do so, the Christian Women's Organization will be a laughing stock. No one will ever believe again that we are capable of accomplishing anything." Ginko gestured with feeling as she spoke. Kajiko Yajima and the other members all nodded in agreement, but they also realized that just a few brave words and the fervour of the moment would not suffice in this case.

"We can't just leave her in the church." The young woman had only the clothes she wore.

"And hiding her would be dangerous."

"What about the police?"

"They would treat her like a criminal. Who can we possibly entrust her safety to?"

"We can't send her back to the parents who sold her to the brothel."

"I'll take her." Ginko had silently listened to the others, but now she spoke up. "I have room for her to stay, and she can work in the clinic."

"But—"

"She can stay with me until the excitement wears off. I'll hide her for the time being."

And so it was decided, but it was not long before danger presented itself. Five days later, three disreputable-looking men showed up at Ginko's clinic. They had a sharp glint in their eyes and scars on their cheeks, and they spoke roughly. It only took a glance to know they were from the brothel.

"Don't try to stop us, it won't do you any good," said the largest of them, rolling back his sleeves to reveal the tattoo of a dragon. The men had clearly heard that the girl was in Ginko's care. "Where's she hiding? Bring her out. Now!"

It was evening and the few patients remaining in the waiting room ran into the examination room, leaving Ginko alone to deal with the unwanted visitors. The nurses and servants, too, huddled in the next room, waiting to see what would happen.

"Are you the President of the Women's Organization, or whatever they call it?"

"No, I am the Chief of Manners and Morals."

"You've got a nerve. You're the ones talking about not drinking and letting women go, aren't you? Damn fools! I hope you know what you're asking for by hiding that girl." One of the men put his foot, still in its filthy sandal, onto the floor of the clinic. "If you won't bring her out, we'll have to go in and look for her ourselves."

"This is my house, and if you enter without my permission that will not be the end of it for you." Ginko kneeled on the floor glaring at the three. She was used to men with no respect for women, thanks to her years at Kojuin Medical School, and she was not about to retreat. This time, however, she was dealing with criminals with no respect for life.

"You want to hurt our business, don't you?"

"Of course I do!"

"We bought her. She's ours. You don't look like you know what that means."

"The business you run is wrong. There is no proper business that involves buying women."

"Our business is one of the oldest there is! It's not against the law."

"It has been illegal to buy and sell human beings since the Edo era."

"We have proof that she's ours."

"It has been illegal to sell women to brothels since 1872."

The men were no match for Ginko when it came to debate. "If you won't hand her over, we'll tear this place down looking for her!"

"Go ahead and try." Ginko was risking her life. She kept her eyes on the men. Her patients, knowing they would not be examined today, had escaped through the back door, and word quickly spread on the street that there was a confrontation at the Ogino Clinic. The front gate was crowded with neighbours who had come running to see what the trouble was about. With this many witnesses, the intruders were now at a disadvantage.

"Bring her here!" they yelled, but Ginko did not move. The men knew they were dealing with a doctor, a pillar of the community, and they did not want any trouble with the police. They had obviously been told to do no more than threaten Ginko, but it was having little effect. "Hurry up and bring her out!" They were running out of patience. "We'll break your arms and legs," one of the men growled, and made a move to step up into the clinic.

"I'm much better than you at cutting off arms and legs," Ginko replied calmly.

The men glanced at each other uneasily. The lady doctor was beginning to scare them and the crowd outside was growing by the minute. Staying any longer would not be to their advantage. "We won't be as easy on you next time!" they threatened. Then they all spat wrathfully on the floor and ran out.

The immediate danger had passed, but it was clear that it would be unwise to keep the girl any longer. Ginko consulted with Kajiko Yajima and they decided to ask the police to return her to her home town. And although the matter had come close to being disastrous for Ginko, it brought the JCWO into the public eye. Even male opinion leaders, who had given little credence to the campaigns of the group before, praised them for the courageous action they had taken.

The men from the brothel, no doubt humiliated by their defeat, returned once to harass Ginko by leaving a large barrel of mud at the entrance of the Ogino Clinic, but that was the last Ginko heard from them.

The movement to abolish prostitution drew even greater attention the following year when the Yoshiwara red-light district was largely destroyed by a fire. Ginko watched the flames from her clinic and gleefully commented that it would make the work of the JCWO much easier. Just as she predicted, not only the Christian Women's Organization, but other women's groups and social leaders came forwards to object to plans to rebuild the Yoshiwara district. Support for their movement grew.

As the activities of the JCWO took shape and broadened in scope, Ginko made sure to attend all the meetings no matter how busy she was with clinic hours and house calls. The busier she was, the better she felt. But as if that was not enough, it wasn't long before she was recommended for the post of secretary of the Japan Women's Health Association.

"There must be someone better qualified for the office," Ginko demurred, but in reality there was no one better qualified than herself, none who had the extensive knowledge of women's health that she did. Despite her protests, Ginko was eager for the appointment. She knew that she was stretching her limits, but she was confident that she was the most suitable candidate.

This, however, was not the last of the roles she was asked to fill. The next year, in 1889, she was asked to teach health and physiology at the Meiji Women's School and to serve as school physician as well. Teaching such subjects to women was a matter of urgency, and it was only practical to have a female doctor at a women's school. Ginko agreed to do both.

Whether she liked it or not, Ginko was now at the forefront of society, living and working in the limelight.

In February of the same year, the long-awaited Constitution of the Empire of Japan was decreed. Among other things, this provided for the creation of an Imperial Diet, which was to be elected by popular vote, and thus for the first time offer nominal public participation in government. In honour of the occasion, the government declared an amnesty for political prisoners, including some from the Freedom and People's Rights Movement, a clever move to capture the sympathy of the general populace and garner support for the new government. A report in the *Tokyo Nichi-Nichi* newspaper described throngs of people of all ages before the Emperor's Palace all waving flags, pulling floats and cheering: "Banzai! Banzai!" on the day the constitution was announced.

The constitution was the final step legitimizing the Meiji government as a modern state, and the first Imperial Diet was to be held the following year, in November 1890. Nevertheless, it soon became clear that the country was being run by the same bureaucrat factions as before. The government was constitutional in name only. Not only that, but the law providing for elected officials did not give women the right to vote and arbitrarily forbade women political expression as well. The majority of the population considered this to be only natural. Even the Freedom and People's Rights Movement raised little objection. The only dissenting voices were those of women themselves, and even then, only a few and not very vociferously.

During the preparations for the long-awaited Imperial Diet, however, it transpired that a new law had been enacted specifically prohibiting women from even observing Diet sessions. Ginko had already been incensed by the failure to award voting rights to women, and when she found out about this new law, she went straight to the Ministry of Justice for an official interpretation. However, the Ministry merely confirmed that women were not allowed to watch the Diet proceedings.

Ginko next went to Kajiko Yajima and called a meeting of Christian Women Organization leaders to inform them of what she had learnt. "All males are allowed to attend, be they teachers or students, stable boys, old itinerant pedlars or hired farmhands. No one will be turned away. The only men who are not allowed to attend are those who are intoxicated or carrying weapons. Women are banished for no reason other than the fact of their gender. Logically this means that all women are no better than drunkards or weapon-bearing thugs."

Ginko continued, "Women are unable to vote, and now we have even been deprived of the right to observe proceedings. We have never had a voice in government, and now we have been robbed of the opportunity to know what the government is doing. Female pursuit of academic study and knowledge has been rendered meaningless."

Ginko was resigned to the denial of women's suffrage if only because she was well aware of the low level of female learning. Nevertheless, refusing to allow women to be present at Diet proceedings was clearly crossing the line. She was sure that it would sabotage the enthusiasm women were finally showing for learning. "I believe the JCWO should take action on this matter," she concluded. As the Chief of Manners and Morals, it was not Ginko's place to initiate social action, although everyone knew she had suffered more than anyone because of discrimination against women. "I think we should petition the government directly."

Agreeing, the group decided to contact the main government party, the Taiseikai (Great Achievement Association), and demand the recall of the new law. Kajiko Yajima used the opinions of Ginko and the other women to draft the petition, which was signed by twenty-one women, including Kajiko Yajima and Ginko herself. It was successful, and won the right for women to observe Imperial Diet proceedings. Not only did Ginko achieve her goal, but this was the first successful political action by a women's group in Japan.

Ginko became more and more widely known among the intellectual classes as Japan's first female doctor and an enthusiastic Christian. The Ogino Clinic, on the other hand, was not doing so well. When it had moved to its new quarters, there had seemed to be no end of patients, but the number quickly plateaued.

"I heard people talking about how they don't feel confident with a female doctor. How could they be so ignorant? I couldn't say a word, I was so disgusted." Nurse Moto had come back from shopping in a righteous fury.

Her nose in the Bible, Ginko only smiled at her indignation.

"Just because we've lost a patient or two because they found some other place that's more convenient! It doesn't matter."

"What are we going to do with a doctor like this?" Nurse Moto huffed in return.

Ginko spoke without malice or regret. She was no longer interested in fighting over patients or trying to expand her practice. She had her mind on greater things.

Since the clinic's move, there were always two or three female medical students who lived and ate there for free, attending classes and helping out with the work. They stood in for Ginko whenever she was out, filling in patient charts and prescribing medicine. Ginko inspected all of the records closely after she got home, correcting their spelling and noting any questions she had about medications prescribed.

"And why did you diagnose the patient with German measles?"

"Fever, runny nose and runny eyes."

"Did you check the membranes in the mouth?"

"Ahh..."

"I see. You didn't. Then you can't diagnose German measles. You've missed the most important thing." Ginko was merciless. She crossed out the writing on the chart. "Let me see this patient if she comes in tomorrow." So saying, she would return to her study. She never scolded the students or admonished them to study harder. She dealt with them rather coldly, leaving the girls only with charts that were black with corrections.

"She's like that with everyone," Nurse Moto would say soothingly, hiding the annoyance she felt towards Ginko. She felt the doctor should either give them a scolding or encourage them to try a little harder.

Ginko, however, had her own ideas. "If you want to get on in academia, you can't rely on people encouraging or indulging you. You are doing it for your own improvement." This was what Ginko herself had done. The fact that she had worked harder than anyone made the mistakes of others all the more difficult for her to endure. Like many geniuses, she could not bear to discuss matters in detail, because she knew she would only become more irritated at the ignorance of the person she was dealing with.

It would have been easier for the women working for her if she had confined her concerns to academic matters, but in the evenings she also taught needlework and flower-arranging to the nurses and maids. Their efforts were a source of grave disappointment to her.

"I've already explained that!" Ginko hated having to repeat herself. Not only were her pupils poor learners, but they failed to maintain the proper sitting position. In those days, chairs were almost unheard of. Men were allowed to sit cross-legged in less formal situations, but women were expected to kneel with their legs folded neatly beneath them. Stretching them out even slightly to the side was considered disrespectful.

"Legs!" she would yell, and smack a nurse with a yardstick. Her patients would never have guessed that the thoughtful, quiet doctor who treated them could be so strict. Shocked by the blow, the young nurse would make even more mistakes, but when she made the same one twice, Ginko would refrain from commenting, saying merely, "I'm finished," as she headed back to her study.

"She's much too accomplished for her own good," Nurse Moto would try to comfort the others. "She knows everything in all the books, and can write poetry, sew, do tea ceremony and flower-arranging, not to mention classical singing. It's hard for her to have to deal with normal women like us. You must understand that she is being as patient as she is capable of. She was raised in a good family and brought up properly. That's why she's so strict with us. She is kind at heart. Anyone else as busy as she is would never even take the time to try to teach us sewing."

The others understood what Nurse Moto was saying, but they could not help considering Ginko a different species from themselves. She made life miserable for everyone who worked for her, reprimanding them even for activities that had nothing to do with work or lessons. On their days and evenings off, everyone who worked for Ginko was required to explain where they were going, what they would be doing and what time they would be back. It was customary for them all to ask for her permission whenever they left the premises. If they wanted to go out while Ginko was gone, they had to make a request ahead of time. Once Nurse Moto had gone out without consulting her and had the misfortune to return home late, after eight o'clock.

"What have you been doing wandering around town at this hour?" Ginko sat rigidly straight and her voice was chilly with anger. "Tell me where you went and what you were doing!"

"I've been to the Ekoin Temple in Ryogoku." Moto mumbled.

"The anniversary of Buddha's birth, I see." It was 8th April, and the occasion was celebrated at the temples of most Buddhist sects. Ekoin offered one of the grander celebrations. "And who were you with?"

"Sawa." She mentioned the name of a young female clerk at the local umbrella shop.

"What did you do?"

"I offered hydrangea tea to Buddha and prayed." She carefully left out the parts about visiting the various stalls, eating candy and watching the trained monkey.

Ginko, of course, was on to her. "Girls should not be out on the street watching street performers and buying things. It makes you look loose, and men will start following you around." Ginko reminded Moto of the occasion, not six months before, when she had been followed home from the public bath by a strange man, and that there were dark, dangerous spots near the Ryogoku Bridge and along the river.

"And out so late! What would you do if a man took advantage of you, and you still an unmarried girl? I don't know how I'd be able to answer to your mother! If you can't mind what I tell you, I'll have to send you home immediately."

"I won't do it again. Please forgive me!"

Whenever the young women apologized, Ginko always put both hands on her knees and closed her eyes.

"Please!" Moto pleaded.

Ginko refused to accept the apology so readily. She could never understand why so much scolding was necessary. She felt responsible for the women who lived and worked in her

215

clinic, even though she knew it would be easier to think of them as other people's children, and blame mistakes on their upbringing. She knew her employees would like her better for it too, but her personality would not allow such a thing. She had to have everything done properly. Her temper had become even shorter since she had opened her clinic and had a household to run. It was this temperament that had enabled her to complete her schooling and overcome every difficulty men set for her, but now it was turned on her employees. It must have been difficult even for her.

Ginko had still not accepted the apology, and Moto, waiting with her head hanging, timidly leant forwards and held something out. "I bought this while I was out." From her sleeve Moto pulled out a small bamboo tube containing hydrangea tea. It was said that if you dripped it onto an ink stone, mixed it with ink, and wrote the character for "insect" on a piece of paper to hang in the toilet, it would keep bugs away. "I'll go and get an ink stone," Moto added in a virtuous tone of voice, but Ginko was having none of it. Neither did she believe in such superstitions.

"Don't think you can get away with it like that! Throw it away!"

A Shinto festival was to be held on the twenty-fifth of the month, and that evening Nurse Tomiko asked for permission to attend. Ginko had been sitting at her desk copying out a book. "And who are you going with?"

"With Otayo." Tomiko gave the name of the new servant girl.

"Be back before dark." Ginko looked up as she spoke, and her expression quickly reflected her dissatisfaction. "But you're not going out like that!"

Startled, Tomiko sat back down and looked at Ginko, seemingly unaware of what the problem was.

"What sort of hairstyle is that?"

"Hair?" Tomiko reached up to touch her ornamental hairpin.

"Don't you know?" Ginko was furious. "That is not a style

worn by decent girls. Only prostitutes have the *shimada-tsubushi* coiffure. Do you want people mistaking you for a girl like that?"

"But…" Tomiko had spent an hour doing her hair. The style might once have had disreputable associations, but it was currently all the rage in downtown Tokyo.

"I can't let you go out looking so vulgar. Take it out."

Ginko was a leader of the movement to banish prostitution. She and her colleagues may have insisted that prostitutes were equal to other women, but they were nevertheless scornful of their posturing and their attire. This was Ginko's natural inclination as the daughter of a good family, and it had become even more pronounced after her divorce.

"Go and redo your hair right now!"

Nurse Tomiko knew there was no changing Ginko's mind once she had made it up. Her employer's neat and proper appearance struck her as unbearably cold and sterile. Ginko did feel close to the people who worked for her, but it was difficult for her to express her affection in words and gestures because of her upbringing. She was too reserved for that. It had taken Nurse Moto a full year to get used to Ginko's ways, so it was impossible to expect the newer nurses and medical students to do so any more quickly.

Ginko was becoming better known among the new intelligentsia of the Meiji era, and her contact with them broadened. She had not specifically sought this attention, but it was inevitable. She had been born into a well-known family, was a beauty, and had a first-class education as well as the supreme social rank of doctor. She had saved women from humiliation as patients, and was now spearheading the struggle for their broader rights. Ginko appeared to be bathed in light and assured of a shining future. If things had continued as they were, she would surely have been one of the most famous figures of the Meiji era. But fate can change everything.

In the spring of 1887, at a meeting of the Kanto area branch of the Japan Congregationalist Church, Ginko had become acquainted with the Reverend Shinjiro Okubo and his wife from the Omiya church. Though they had met through their shared Christianity, it turned out that Mrs Okubo was also very interested in women's rights, and the two women had quickly become close. Whenever Mrs Okubo came to Tokyo, she would drop by the Ogino Clinic, and the two would talk all night long.

In the spring of 1890, Mrs Okubo stopped by to see Ginko while on a trip to Tokyo with her husband. The two spoke about the church, and then their conversation turned to social problems of the day. Since the women had talked until late, Mrs Okubo was invited to stay at Ginko's home that night. In anticipation of this decision, the maid had already made up the guest room on the second floor.

As the two women stood up to retire to their separate rooms, Mrs Okubo said, as if suddenly remembering something, "Would you consider putting up a man this summer vacation?"

"A man?" Ginko often had guests and female medical students staying with her, and as long as she knew the person introducing them, she enquired little about their background or family. However, she had never had a man stay overnight before. The only men to be found around the Ogino Clinic were the husband of one of the kitchen maids, the old man who took care of odd jobs and the rickshaw driver.

"Don't worry, he's safe," Mrs Okubo added. "He's a student at Doshisha, and he's an active congregationalist."

"A college student?" This, and that he was a Christian, was reassuring to Ginko.

"He's stayed with me three times before, and he's going to join my husband evangelizing in Chichibu. He's twenty-six and he's still single." Mrs Okubo thought for a few moments, and then laughed. "He's quite a large man, and he doesn't always seem to be focused. Once, half as a joke, I asked my daughter what she thought of him, and she said that the new, phlegmatic type was not for her."

Ginko was relieved. He didn't sound like he'd be the sort to cause any problems with the nurses.

"He wants to stop in Tokyo on his way back to Kyoto from Chichibu, and I've been trying to think of somewhere he could stay. It would certainly be the ideal situation for him here."

"We'll be delighted to have him."

"He's from Kumamoto, you know."

"Then he must know Reverend Ebina?"

"Yes, they know each other well."

Ginko was all the more relieved to hear this.

"He's been living in Kyoto for years, but Tokyo has so many things that will be new to him. Not only that, but he's a fan of yours."

"You're joking, surely!"

"No, it's true. Two years ago when he was with us, we talked about you and he said he'd read about you in the newspaper. He's terribly anxious to meet you."

"I find that hard to believe." Ginko was outwardly dismissive, but the very idea made her feel a little bit younger.

"He'll be here during his summer vacation. It ought to be easy now that the Tokaido Line is running."

"I hear that the train from Kyoto only takes fifteen hours now."

"We should try it sometime."

"What is the name of this student, then?"

"Oh, of course. It's an unusual name – Shikata. Yukiyoshi Shikata."

Ginko got the impression that it was a difficult name to remember, and by the next day she had forgotten the matter entirely.

Ginko's sister Tomoko came to visit her in the middle of June. Tomoko was just four years older than Ginko, but life in the countryside had aged her considerably. Her slim figure and the shape of her eyes, however, still made it patently clear that she and Ginko were sisters.

"I'd heard that the city had grown," said Tomoko, "but what a surprise!" Tomoko had only been to Tokyo once, with her husband right after she was married, back when it still went by the name of Edo. She was amazed by the changes of the ensuing twenty-plus years. "I guess I'm just a country woman who knows nothing outside Kumagaya."

Tomoko had been widowed ten years before. She had

converted one of the family storehouses into a pawnshop in order to support herself and her four children. Her three daughters had been married off, and her only son had taken a wife and now had children. Tomoko had finally finished raising her family.

"Thank you for all your help for so many years," said Ginko. The money Tomoko had sent her during her time as a struggling student had amounted to a sizeable sum. Ginko had paid her back as much as she could in the first two years that her clinic was open, and there was little financial debt left. However, the emotional support she had gained from knowing that Tomoko would always send her something to get her by had been an enormous comfort, and was a debt she could never repay. Especially after their mother had passed away, Tomoko had been the person Ginko relied on most. It was distressing for Ginko to see Tomoko looking so old now.

"How is Zen?" she asked about her sister's son.

"He's fine, thanks," Tomoko said shortly. Ginko saw that she did not want to talk about her family. Tomoko had raised Zen, but he was the son of her husband's first wife, and the current position of mother-in-law to her stepson's household was clearly not a comfortable one for her. Tomoko was not given to complaining, but Ginko understood how she must have felt.

"And Tawarase?" Ginko tried a new tack.

"You would never know it. Someone else owns the back fields and the mulberry trees now. All that is left to the family is the house and the land as far as the irrigation canal. It's awful." Tomoko sipped her tea, and tried to hide her vexation about the matter.

"Is Yasuhei idling his time away?"

"He comes up to Kumagaya from time to time, but there's only so much there for him to spend his money on. It's all Yai's fault. Everyone knows how she's frittered away the family fortune. She orders all her kimonos and accessories from famous shops in Tokyo. And she hates to work too. It's no wonder that the family is in such straits, with a wife like her keeping house."

At the time Ginko left Tawarase, Yai had only been married a few years, yet already acted as if she were in charge. Now she was driving the family to ruin. "But things wouldn't be so bad if Yasuhei had control, would they?"

"You know he's incapable of that. His only virtue is his quiet nature."

Ginko had never expected much of her eldest brother, but she had hoped he would protect the land he had inherited from their parents. The Ogino family had once owned everything you could see as far as the banks of the Toné River. Now their holdings only reached the irrigation canal.

"Once things take a turn for the worse, it doesn't take long, does it?" Tomoko sighed.

Since the Meiji Restoration, Ginko had seen countless families fall into ruin. How many times had she heard of the wife of a former retainer to the shogun going to work in some restaurant or other? It wasn't unusual to hear about land being sold off either. Maybe it was too much to ask for that the Ogino family would not have to change along with the rest of the country. Life in Tokyo, where people were ruled by money and power, made it easier for her to accept the change in her family's fortunes.

It was much more difficult for Tomoko, who lived close to her ancestral home. "I can't imagine what Mother and Father would have said."

Ginko had to admit that it was painful to think that her parents had once owned more land than any other family in northern Saitama. They had been widely respected too, and she recalled with chagrin the old local saying: "Learn from the Upper Oginos". It had all ended with her mother's death.

The sisters were silent for a time. Finally Tomoko spoke, as if trying to clear the air. "I saw Kanichiro not long ago."

Surprised to hear the name, Ginko looked up. She knew that Tomoko had remained in contact with the Inamura family, but it was still an unpleasant shock to have the memory of her former husband revived.

"The family is still well-to-do, and I hear that Kanichiro is going to open a bank. He'll be the first president of it." Tomoko meant nothing by bringing up the subject; she was merely trying to find something the two of them could chat about. She knew that nothing to do with Kanichiro could affect Ginko in her present secure position. "He told me that he'd heard about you opening your own clinic. He was as pleased as if you were still a member of the family."

It had been more than twenty years since the divorce, but Ginko could remember him clearly. She suddenly had a vivid image of what he must look like now, what he was thinking and what he was trying to do. He was intelligent and educated. It was entirely possible that, as a young man, he had gone into the entertainment district on a whim – maybe a friend had invited him. He could not be held completely responsible for her becoming ill, any more than he could for the burden the Inamura family had been to her, and the stifling way she had been treated by her mother-in-law. He might not have been as bad as Ginko had made him out to be. *But still…*

Ginko quickly brought herself up short. Just because he had made only one bad mistake, it did not mean she had to forgive him. No matter how good he might be, that single wrong he had done was capable of erasing it all. If Ginko had been in her present position at the time it all happened, she might have been able to forgive him. But she had been an inexperienced girl of sixteen. She had had no recourse but to entrust her life to him.

"He told me that he comes to Tokyo occasionally." Tomoko was merely reporting the facts as she had heard them. "He said that he had even thought of asking you to come back. But it had been so long. Now all he does is pray that you will continue to be successful."

Ginko told herself that she had never thought of Kanichiro. Not once. *I would never have gone back even if he had asked.*

"When I go back home, I'll give him your regards," Tomoko continued.

"No, please don't!" Ginko looked at her sister with fire in her eyes. She had never hoped for any sort of reconciliation with Kanichiro during the past twenty years. She had erased him from her memory, and she wished for nothing more from him. Time had cured her of the pain she had felt, but she had no intention of having anything to do with her former husband. "Don't say anything on my behalf."

"All I meant was—"

"Just don't use me as a topic of conversation."

"Gin!" Tomoko's hair was already turning white. She was quickly becoming a lonely old woman, and the only thing left to her was her pride in her sister.

Ginko realized she was asking too much and finally apologized. Then something occurred to her. *Can I really claim to have washed my hands of Kanichiro? I am what I am today because of what happened with him. If I hadn't endured that sadness and humiliation, I never would have become a doctor, or even a Christian.* She could not deny it. On the other hand, she still had inside her the wound that Kanichiro had inflicted. The disease was in remission, but every once in a while it flared up to remind her of its presence. Even though her mind had nearly forgotten him, her body never would. This was something that Ginko could neither forgive nor resign herself to. She would always be a woman and, as such, susceptible to harm from men.

Tomoko stayed three nights. On the fourth day, she left bearing two bundles of presents. Ginko took Tomoko to Ueno Station and stood watching as she boarded the Takasaki Line train. Tomoko stowed the gifts from her sister in the net over her seat, and then bowed to her once more.

"Thanks for everything."

"Take care of yourself."

As the train pulled out, Ginko realized sadly that Tomoko was unable to look out for her well-being any longer. Their roles had been reversed and Ginko was now the one in the position to do favours. Ginko had prayed for years that this day would come, yet now that it had, she only felt chilled and lonely.

15

That year the rainy season dragged on longer than usual, and when it did finally end, the July heat seemed more powerful than ever. Shopkeepers put up bamboo shades and sprinkled water on the ground to cool the air.

"Get your ices here! Ices from Hakodate!" The voice of the street vendor selling bowls of flavoured shaved ice seemed energized by the prospect of brisk business.

Ginko came home that evening from making house calls to find Nurse Moto waiting for her in the entrance hall.

"There's a man here to see you!" the nurse whispered urgently.

"Who could it be?" Ginko looked at the shoes lined up by the front door. There was a pair of *geta* that looked about twice as large as a woman's. Imprints of the owner's feet, black with dirt, were clearly visible, and the supports had been worn down at an angle.

"He says his name is Shikata."

"Shikata?"

"He claims to be a student from Kyoto."

"Oh, I see. He's from Doshisha." Ginko recalled Mrs Okubo asking her three months previously to put him up.

"Do you know him?"

"I've never met him. He's a friend of the Okubos." Ginko went around to the kitchen to wash her hands and feet, Nurse Moto hard on her heels.

"He's really big, and he has a strange smell."

"Smell?"

"Yes."

"What kind of smell?"

"I don't know."

"Clean the guest room on the second floor. He'll be staying tonight."

"Staying here? I haven't even given him any tea yet."

"What have you been doing since he got here?"

"Um, I thought he was a salesman or something."

"So, where is he?"

"In the waiting room."

"You silly girl! Take him into my sitting room." Ginko dried her hands and feet, then headed directly for the room where guests were received, remembering at the last moment to stop and check her reflection in the mirror before she went in. She used very little make-up, but she had recently begun to apply a little powder. Her skin was beginning to lose some of its firmness and she had more freckles than before. She was anxious not to disappoint the student who had come so far to meet her.

When Ginko walked into the room, Shikata was kneeling with his back ramrod straight and his hands resting formally in his lap. She got her first glimpse of him from behind, and he looked like a huge rock.

"Thank you for waiting," she said. "I'm Ginko Ogino."

Startled, Shikata turned around and bowed deeply, bumping his head on the low table. Undeterred, he bowed again and introduced himself.

"I'm Yukiyoshi Shikata." He sounded as proper as a soldier at attention. "Thank you very much for agreeing to take me in, even though I know you are extremely busy."

"Not at all. I've got the extra room, and someone might as well use it."

"Thank you!"

Ginko looked at his large, sunburnt face. His hair appeared to have been cut recently, but his chin was covered in stubble. Despite his size, his features looked almost childlike. "Please, make yourself comfortable," she urged.

Shikata nodded, but remained seated properly.

Ginko had to smile at his nervousness, and she also noticed that his forehead was turning red where he had bumped it. "Your forehead," she said, indicating it ruefully with her eyes.

"It doesn't hurt a bit," Shikata insisted. His large shoulders seemed to spread out like wings, and his arms stuck out at angles. "I'm so sorry."

There was no reason why he should apologize to Ginko, and she thought that he was certainly a strange character. Nurse Moto finally arrived with tea. She placed the cups and coasters on the table, and then bowed to take her leave. As she did so, she gave a meaningful look at the bundle placed at Shikata's side. Ginko followed her gaze, and realized Moto had discovered the source of the strange smell. Shikata noticed Ginko looking at the bundle and reached out to open it. Moto, who was on her way out of the room, stopped to see what it could be.

"I brought this as a gift," Shikata said.

"What is it?" asked Ginko.

"Sweetfish. I caught them this morning in the Tama River. The river was full of fish! Practically all I had to do was reach in and grab them."

Now that the mystery was solved, Ginko wanted to laugh out loud, but the earnest expression on Shikata's face stopped her. She accepted the fish and thanked him.

Ginko was having Shikata stay in the guest room furthest from the stairs on the second floor, separated from the room that Nurses Moto and Tomiko shared by one other room. After Ginko and Shikata had exchanged some more formalities, he picked up his few possessions and climbed the stairs.

By the time Ginko had finished seeing patients and putting away the charts for the day, it was half-past seven. Shikata had already had dinner and a bath. After Ginko had her dinner, she instructed Nurse Moto to ask Shikata if he would like to come downstairs and chat. Moto went upstairs, but hastily came back down, clutching her stomach with laughter.

"When I opened the door, he was wearing nothing but his loincloth!"

"He was naked?"

"He was sitting there reading out loud from the Bible!" All of the women at the table burst out laughing, a rare happening at the Ogino Clinic.

Ginko went ahead and had her bath. She changed into a light summer cotton kimono and then met Shikata in the inner room. By then he had changed back into the same *hakama* trousers he had worn that afternoon. They still smelt of sweat and fish.

"Why don't you let me wash those *hakama* for you?"

"No, I couldn't possibly—"

"We run a clinic here and there is always lots of laundry to do. Do you have anything else to wear?"

"Just my sleeping robe."

"Well then, please change into that."

"Thank you." So saying, Shikata stood up and climbed the stairs again. He came back down wearing a light cotton sleeping robe that was several sizes too small for him.

Ginko finally persuaded Shikata to cross his legs in a more comfortable sitting position. The doors onto the garden were open, but the night air had still not cooled down. The rainy season was over, but the air was humid and close. Ginko sat opposite Shikata at a small, round table, the lamp in the centre lighting the left side of Shikata's face and the right side of hers. They could hear the maid in the next room, cleaning up and getting ready for the next day.

Before she could say any more, Shikata launched into a formal self-introduction. "I was born in Kutami in the Yamaga district of Kumamoto. My father's name is Yukihiro, and my mother was the fourth daughter of the Umehara family. My father was from a samurai family, but he died when I was thirteen. It was during the Satsuma Rebellion. Almost every night we could see flames in the sky and hear the sound of cannon fire."

At the time of the Satsuma Rebellion, Ginko had been at the Women's Normal School. Shikata had still been a child. She was amazed to think that someone so young was sitting here having a conversation with her. Shikata continued his story, sounding as serious as if he were under interrogation from the police.

"I planned to go into the army. I left Kumamoto when I was fourteen, and went to live with my married sister in Kobe. I learnt English there. Then I went to officers' training school in Osaka, but I was expelled after two years because of a weak stomach. A relative who was a captain in the army insisted that I go to Doshisha, the school established by Joh Niijima."

"When were you baptized?"

"In the autumn of 1886. A friend of mine invited me to attend services, and I was baptized by Professor Niijima himself that same year."

"That was about the same time as I was baptized."

"Who baptized you, Dr Ogino?" asked Shikata respectfully.

"Reverend Ebina."

"I know him well. He's from Kumamoto too, and he's back at the Kumamoto church now."

"You're like him in that you wanted to a soldier, but decided to dedicate your life to the Church."

"Yes, if I had gone into the army, I'd be wearing a uniform and carrying a sabre by now. I would never have changed paths if it hadn't been for Professor Niijima. You never know what's going to happen or how your destiny will change, do you?"

Ginko felt the same way. There was no sense trying to understand why things happened as they did. What she did not yet know was just how much this chance meeting with Shikata was soon to change her own fate.

The air was heavy, oppressed by dark, unmoving clouds. The wind chime tinkled softly now and then. The maid finished her work in the kitchen, served Ginko and Shikata some fruit, and went upstairs.

"I have the greatest admiration for your courage," Shikata said. "You pioneered the path for women to become doctors. And I know you're involved with the Japan Christian Women's Organization."

It was obvious to Ginko that Shikata wasn't merely trying to flatter her. He seemed so open and honest that she was sure he was incapable of doing such a thing. He was obviously thrilled to be able to meet in person this great woman who was so famous even in Kumamoto.

"For a long time, I've wanted to meet and talk with you."

Ginko was amused at the youthful ardour of this man and the way he praised her. After a while, she was tempted to tease him. "And how do you feel about the activities of the JCWO?" she asked.

"I agree with the JCWO on everything. Prostitution should have been banned years ago."

"But won't it be awfully inconvenient for you men not to have prostitutes available to you?"

"Of course not! The Emperor believes in monogamy, but Japanese society views male and female relations as no more than a way to maintain households in a samurai society. It is a discriminatory system that does not respect the rights of the individual. There is no reason to treat women any differently from men."

"The government wouldn't even allow women to view Imperial Diet proceedings, let alone give us the vote."

"I heard about the JCWO's petition. This government is so anachronistic! The government should be looking for talented women and making use of them. In the West, the number of prominent men is still greater too, but there are many countries ruled by queens. Catherine, Elizabeth, Maria Theresa, Victoria... and China has His-t'aihou. There are women who are economists, such as Harriet Martineau, and philosophers like Madame de Staël. Poets and writers like Elizabeth Browning. You know, it's interesting that before the seventeenth century, before the industrial age, there were almost no prominent women. It was during the seventeenth century, when academic learning became more widespread, that we began seeing them."

Ginko decided that Shikata had done his homework. She knew he was passionate, but she doubted he was always quite so articulate.

He went on, "Japan's time has finally come. And you, Doctor, are at the forefront." Shikata gestured with his hands as he spoke, and Ginko could not help catching glimpses of his plump arms from the openings in his cotton robe.

"But women have a drawback, don't they? They get pregnant and bear children." Feeling herself drawn into the discussion, Ginko decided to play devil's advocate.

"Yes, I've always wondered why it is that women have this important but strenuous duty to bear. It says in the Old Testament that Eve ate the forbidden fruit of the tree of knowledge. God punished her and all of the women who came after her by giving them the duty and pain of bearing children.

But even before this happened, men and women had different bodies. I'm convinced that the idea that childbirth is a divine punishment is no more than a myth that was created by the ancient Israelites. To think otherwise is to believe that females of all species – animals, insects, fish, even trees and other plants – all committed the same sin. I think it's a waste of time and energy to go back to the beginning of time to try and find out why women have had to bear such a burden. It's ridiculous to rob women of their dignity and their rights because of it."

"I agree with your conclusion, but I am not so sure that pregnancy and childbirth ought to be considered an unfortunate burden."

"Of course. If women refused to propagate the species, our society would be long gone. There would be no future for mankind. Women have an illustrious role that men can never fulfil. The fact that this is a basis for men to ignore the rights of women, reserving high positions for men only, is proof that our society is still immature. Even in this age, when learning and science are making such great strides, men still insist on dominating women with their physical strength. We are still primitive in our emotions. Men of the nineteenth century must admit to their mistaken way of thinking and make amends for it." Shikata's face was flushed, and there was a thin layer of perspiration on his forehead. Ginko was impressed with his fervour on matters about which she herself felt so strongly. "In modern society some degree of discrimination based on ability is inevitable, but there is no reason to discriminate merely because of sex."

"So are you saying," asked Ginko, "that you consider it acceptable for women to go out into society and work, rather than stay at home to raise children?"

"Of course. Women must have occupations if they are to become independent and think for themselves. There are plenty of professions that would be better filled by women than men."

"For example?"

"First of all, teaching. Female teachers are patient, thoughtful and gentle. They are the most suited for that job. I've heard that in the West, female teachers far outnumber male. Medicine is also an appropriate profession." Ginko was embarrassed that he appeared to be speaking of her. "Women are keenly sensitive, and they are able to see through a person at a glance. And they remember everything. Women are supremely suited to identifying different types of disease. And in particular, women are the most suitable for treating diseases unique to women. Which is what you do, Dr Ogino."

"Are there any others?" she prodded him.

"Telegraph operator. And I hear that in Scandinavia, women are superior in their jobs at bank insurance companies."

Now Ginko was convinced that he had studied up on women's rights and female occupations in anticipation of meeting her. She considered his efforts rather charming. And the more he talked, the more she wanted to tease him. "I don't suppose you would ever consider marrying a woman with a profession, now would you?"

"Getting married means knowing everything there is to know about your spouse. You ought to marry someone who matches you and whom you love. The most important thing is to recognize the other person's talents, respect their position, and not infringe on it. Marriage in Japan is in a sorry state. To have two young, immature people, who have never even met each other, married through the offices of an intermediary and to fulfil a promise made by their parents is badly out of date. That's the way aristocrats did it in ancient times, but it's truly laughable nowadays."

This rang painfully true to Ginko.

"Marriage should be the way two people are linked when they agree to spend their lives together, in good times and in bad. In order to achieve this, two people must know each other well before they agree to marry. Without such mutual appreciation, marriage is no different from buying and selling merchandise."

Shikata's strong words were a great surprise to Ginko. He had opinions that were so revolutionary for the time as to make the listener doubt that the speaker could really be serious. They had obviously been nurtured in the halls of Doshisha, where much time was devoted to debate. "So, am I to believe that you plan to do exactly as you profess?"

"It is only natural that one should carry out what he says."

"Which means your ideal woman would be?..."

"If I tell you, will you promise not to hold my own deficiencies against me?"

"Of course."

"Someone with a superior mind, an occupation of her own and a beautiful face and heart."

"Physical beauty is important, I see."

"I would be lying if I said it wasn't. Women have a much better appearance than men. It is not because they have any special essence. It's a matter of evolution. Men choose beautiful women."

"I suppose you'd have to say that I was a little late in the evolutionary scheme of things."

"Please, don't make jokes." Shikata was adamant in his denial. "You, Sensei," he said, slipping into the familiar way of addressing doctors, "are as evolved as one could be."

Ginko had to stifle a laugh at this unusual way of telling a woman she was pretty. Shikata's face had turned red and he had dropped his head in embarrassment. *He couldn't possibly be interested in me!* Ginko quickly reminded herself that a young man in his twenties would never feel attracted to a woman thirteen years older, and she directed her gaze outside.

By this time there was finally a cool night breeze, and the wind chime under the eaves began to ring softly. Just outside the room was a narrow ledge on which to sit and enjoy the tiny garden. There was dense foliage beside the fence at the end of the garden, which backed onto an alley leading to the street. At night, almost no one walked down that alley, which came to a dead end two or three houses beyond Ginko's clinic. But if anyone had been passing by, they would have been able to see through the fence and into the brightly lit room. The neighbours were impressed with Ginko's life, which seemed so devoid of men, but they imagined that she must get bored at times. They would have been astonished at this scene.

When Ginko looked up again, she saw that Shikata had turned his attention to the garden. Ginko picked up a fan, and its breeze picked up what might have been the scent of a man, although she finally decided it was probably perspiration. In the distance she heard the cry of a soba-noodle seller.

"Are you hungry?" she asked.

"No, I'm fine." Shikata turned towards Ginko, picked up the glass of water on the table and drank it down in a single gulp.

"Will you work for the Church after you graduate from college?"

"That's what I plan to do. I believe the Church is about to enter a difficult period."

"I agree." During the last two or three years, starting with the new constitution and the Imperial Rescript on Education, a nationalistic backlash had been rising against the Westernization of the government that had been welcomed with open arms during the initial years of the Meiji era. With this backlash, the Church was coming under renewed pressure as a "foreign" religion.

"The government is only looking out for its own interests." Once again Shikata spoke with conviction. "It used the educational side of Christianity to help modernize the country, but is now objecting to its influence."

"But there's more to it than that," added Ginko. "The farmers in the middle and upper classes were supposed to help support the spread of Protestantism, but now those people have reached a level of security where they don't care any more."

"It's true that evangelism in agricultural villages is becoming more difficult."

"The main problem is that people these days are satisfied as long as they can own land."

"I think you might be right."

"Is it the same in the Kyoto area?"

"There are even some people who are calling for the eradication of foreign religions."

"There is too much prejudice against Christianity."

Shikata stared into the lamp as he spoke. "There is one thing that I want to do after I finish college."

"What's that?"

"I'd like to leave this overcrowded society."

"Leave?"

"My dream is to go somewhere with wide open spaces. I want to create a utopian Christian community. A natural paradise for believers. Christians should be able to lead a self-sufficient life far away from this land of fussy bureaucracy. Just like the pilgrims did when they took the Mayflower to America." Shikata spread out his arms and gently swayed, as though seeing images of his dreams as he spoke.

"Where do you intend to go?" Ginko was interested.

"Somewhere with a lot of land. But I don't know where that might be yet. That's what I've got to start thinking about. There must be somewhere, and it can happen if believers decide to come together. We'll be able to live out our beliefs. Don't you think it's possible?"

Ginko did not, but she was envious of the daring dreams of this young man.

"I'll do it!" he declared. "I'll show everyone that it is possible to have a Christian paradise on this earth." Shikata's dark pupils were enormous. Ginko saw her own face reflected in them and felt as though she were being drawn in.

The clock on the wall struck ten. The house was quiet except for this one room. All of a sudden Ginko heard the low sound of a bell. Had she heard four peals? But the only bell in the area was Kaneiji Temple in Ueno, and it only rang at six in the morning. What could it be?

Shikata fell silent when he heard the bell. The lamp created a circle of light in the room, casting shadows of the two against the paper shoji. It *had* been a temple bell. It began to ring again, this time at short intervals.

Ginko looked at Shikata, who finally spoke. "It must be a fire."

They both stood up and walked over to the ledge overlooking the garden. The sound was now unmistakable, but there were no signs of flames.

"We'll be able to see it from the second floor." Shikata headed for the stairs, with Ginko close behind him.

Shikata slid open the shoji door of his guest room and motioned her in. In the dark, she could see his bundle of

235

belongings next to the pillow on the bedding that the maid had laid out for him earlier that evening.

"Look, it's over there."

They could hear the bell clearly through the open window, and they now spotted the soft red glow of flames on the horizon.

"What is that area?" he asked.

"It's to the west. It must be Ushigome or Koishikawa."

"Three peals." The bell rang three times in succession, and then rested for one beat. There were several patterns that told people in the area how close a fire was. If the fire grew closer, it would ring continuously.

The two heard the footsteps of neighbours rushing towards the scene. Ginko watched the fire for a while, and then turned to leave.

"Where are you going?" asked Shikata.

"I should wake the others."

"It doesn't seem to be that big a fire." Everyone else in the house had finally gone to sleep. It did not sound as if anyone had been roused. If the bell had sounded any later, even the two of them would not have heard it.

"I hope it won't spread." Ginko had learnt about the danger of fires after she moved to Tokyo. Out in the country, a fire meant no more than the loss of a single house. In the city, though, houses were built so closely together that a single fire could quickly destroy an entire neighbourhood.

She had witnessed the Kanda fire of 1880, and the Matsueda fire of 1881, when ten thousand houses had burnt. A fire in Ushigome or Koishikawa was not too worrying, but it was not so far away that she could just ignore it. And the flames they could see showed no signs of growing dimmer.

"Why don't we keep watch for a while longer," Shikata suggested.

"Do you think we should?" Ginko looked up at Shikata.

"The wind is blowing in the opposite direction." There had not been even a hint of a breeze earlier in the evening, but the wind had picked up and they could see the direction the flames were moving in. "I don't think it will come this way."

"I certainly hope not."

"You know what you want kept safe if anything should happen, don't you?"

"Just some books and my medical equipment."

"I'll carry it all out for you. There's no need to worry." Shikata spoke over Ginko's head.

I'll be fine as long as he is here with me. As this thought occurred to Ginko, the tension left her. She looked up at the sky again. "What could have caused a fire in the middle of summer?" The neighbourhood fire watch had stopped making rounds during the rainy season, and fires were not common during the summer.

"It might have been arson," said Shikata. Ginko felt troubled at the notion that someone might have deliberately set a fire during the peaceful time that they had spent talking together.

They could hear people's voices on the street, but no one was running and there were no signs of possessions being removed from homes. The two continued to stand at the window and watch the sky in the west. Gradually the flames began to dim, and a short while later, the peals of the bell rang further apart. Ginko took a deep breath and looked at the eaves over the first floor. The tiles shone black with dew.

"It's all over," Shikata assured her.

"I'm glad of that." Ginko nodded and turned around to face Shikata's broad chest. His face was far above hers, but she could tell that he was gazing at her. She found it suddenly difficult to breathe and felt a need to escape, but her legs refused to move. Her body seemed no longer hers to control. She stood there and stared at his chest.

"Sensei," Shikata whispered hoarsely.

She saw his face right in front of her own. Even in the dark, his eyes shone. Ginko's hand, resting on the window sill, could feel Shikata's hand next to hers, and she could almost feel his blood running through it. Ginko wondered for a second about what was happening, but in the next her mind rejected it.

"I…" he tried to continue.

Ginko used every ounce of power she had to turn away from him at last. "Well then, goodnight," she said.

"Dr Ogino!"

But it was too late. Holding her collar together with both hands, Ginko fled the room. She ran back downstairs and into the sitting room, where she closed the door and finally took a breath. Her heart was still pounding. She put her hands to her hair to smooth it, and leant out of the window to look outside. The reddish glow had nearly faded from the sky.

She went into her room to sleep, but the harder she tried, the more awake she became. Even her soft bed seemed to be working to keep her awake. She picked up the latest issue of the magazine *Women in Academics* to make herself drowsy, but it was no use. Her eyes were glued to the print, but her mind refused to comprehend it.

Maybe it's because of that fire, Ginko thought, as she stared at the ceiling. It did not quite ring true, but she stoutly refused to consider any other reason for her inability to settle down. She tried to close her eyes.

Ginko got up the next morning at seven, unusually early for someone who tended to stay awake late into the night and then sleep in.

"Good morning!" The clinic staff greeted her, obviously flustered at this change in routine.

Ginko washed her face and then went back to her room to apply some make-up. She thought her skin looked refreshed for someone who had had so little sleep. She applied some powder and wondered if she might use lipstick. She tried a dab and liked the effect.

Looking at her face, though, she felt restless. She had not used colour on her lips in years, but she knew it was not the only reason. She was too old for such things. Ginko deliberately wiped her lips clean.

She stood up, clapped her hands and called for Kiyo, the maid. "Go to the room of our guest and bring me the kimono he was wearing yesterday. Make sure you don't wake him up."

Kiyo bowed and left the room. While she was gone, Ginko got out her sewing box. Kiyo soon returned and Ginko asked whether the young man had noticed her.

"Oh no, he was fast asleep with both legs poking out of the covers."

Ginko nodded without changing expression. She had noticed yesterday that he had a small tear in his sleeve. Ginko pulled the edges lightly together and began sewing. As she worked, she smiled at the thought of Shikata sprawled out in bed, fast asleep. He must have been exhausted.

Everything that had happened the night before seemed unlikely, thinking about it now in the light of day. Had there really been a fire? Had the two of them really stood there and watched it together? It must have happened, because here she was sewing his kimono. She was a little perturbed that despite it all, and without giving her a second thought, he could lie there fast asleep. Ginko cut the thread with her teeth and handed the kimono back to Kiyo.

"Please put it back, and be quiet about it."

"Yes, ma'am." Kiyo had the hint of a smile on her face. She could not decide which was more amusing, Shikata obliviously asleep or Ginko sewing a man's kimono.

Shikata finally came downstairs after ten. Ginko could hear his feet on the stairs from her sitting room. She tried to maintain her composure and continued reading the newspaper. Finally the door opened and Shikata stepped in. As they exchanged greetings, each looked into the other's face as if to confirm what had happened the night before.

"Did you sleep well?" Ginko asked.

"Yes, thank you."

They both spoke formally, with no trace of the intimacy of the previous evening.

"Do you have any plans for the day?" she enquired.

"I've promised to meet Reverend Kozaki at the Reinanzaka church about noon. Then I'll take the three o'clock train to Takasaki."

Ginko nodded. She wondered whether he would stay another night if she asked.

"My kimono has been mended," he said.

"I'm not very good at sewing," she said, "but I thought it would be better than leaving it as it was."

239

"I'm sorry to have troubled you." Shikata looked at his sleeve and bowed again.

"You'll be with Reverend Okubo in Takasaki?"

"Yes, I'll stay there one night and then go on to Nagano, then home."

"When will you be back in Tokyo?"

"I won't be back," he answered, and then added, "Would you mind if I wrote to you?"

"Please do."

"I'll write when I reach Kyoto."

They were back to normal. The night before had been a dream after all, Ginko decided. They had been strangely affected by the passionate discussion and the fire, but now they were back to normal and it was all for the good, Ginko told herself.

Nurse Moto spoke up as if suddenly remembering. "There was a fire last night." She told them that it had started in Ushigome and spread to Kaitai and Yamabuki, but had been stopped by the rice fields there. The area had large estates and a great deal of open space, which had kept the fire from spreading further. Only about a hundred homes had been destroyed, a small fire by Tokyo standards in those days. "So it didn't amount to much," she concluded.

Ginko nodded as she listened to Moto, but her mind was still on Shikata.

16

Shikata had said he would write after he returned to Kyoto, but in fact he wrote twice on the way – once from Takasaki and once from Nagano.

The first letter was to thank her for letting him stay, ending with "I'll remember your kindness for the rest of my life". The second letter was longer, recording something of his impressions while on the road, to which he had added "In spare moments between mission duties I recall you, Sensei, and feel acutely aware of what is lacking in myself".

What on earth did he mean by "I recall you"? What was it about her that he recalled? Normally such words would sound like a confession of love, but Ginko was hardly inclined to interpret them as such. There was no way a man thirteen years her junior could be in love with her. It was simply impossible – and even if it were possible, it was not acceptable. Perhaps they had experienced a momentary misapprehension, a shared dream from which she had already awoken, while he was still asleep.

Or maybe she was reading more into his words than was there. Being such a direct and frank young man, Shikata could simply be saying that he had enjoyed the night they had spent talking together and that it was now a memory he recalled with pleasure. But what if, by some chance, his words *were* a declaration of love? What would she feel then?

Ginko recalled Shikata's large, self-effacing figure. Everything about him sprang readily to mind: the way his eyes reddened with tears in the midst of a discussion on a subject close to his heart, how his right hand trembled slightly... his broad chest, which had been close enough to touch... all of these were burnt vividly in Ginko's memory. His presence had soothed her even as they watched the fire reddening the sky in the distance. She had not felt any fear at all. She knew that it was because Shikata

had been there, but she was surprised at herself for feeling that way.

Ginko had never before relied on a man, let alone relaxed in the presence of one. Men had more often been her bitter rivals, and she had spent many years developing a veneer of invulnerability. She had always been prepared to defend herself against anybody. But that night she had been comfortable, entirely at ease. Perhaps some male instinct in Shikata had sensed that her guard was down. *Something about me must have led him on.*

What did she feel for him, though? Ginko asked herself once more, searching her mind and heart. *Nothing in particular*, she insisted to herself. He was simply someone passing though, with whom she'd spent an evening in conversation: that was all. But at the same time she could hear another small voice. *Could it possibly be that I like him more than that?*

Ginko concluded that mental and physical exhaustion were causing her to let her thoughts run away with her.

August came. Nurse Moto sprinkled water in the yard in front of the clinic to settle the dust, but it dried as soon as it hit the ground. From the clinic windows, Ginko could see a colourful array of parasols as pedestrians walked by the fence, and even they looked wilted. It had been several weeks now since she had heard from Shikata. Without realizing it, Ginko had got into the habit of waiting for his letters. She would forget about him while she was busy with people or examining patients, but in between examinations and on her way to house calls he would come to mind. Whenever she had a free moment, she would find herself thinking of him.

There were even times when the nurse would call for her attention two or three times before she would finally notice and look around in surprise. "Did you say something?"

"There's a request for a house call in Matsutomi."

"Let's go, then."

Ginko realized her reply had been slower in coming than usual, and noticed that the nurse was looking at her curiously. Were the nurses catching on? She had spent an evening in conversation with a male guest, and the next morning she had mended the sleeve of his kimono. No one would think there was anything between them from just that, would they? She was sure her employees never thought of her in any capacity other than as doctor and mistress of the house.

The employees, however, had noticed a change in Ginko. Recently she had become kinder and more patient with them. Before, when the clinic was crowded with patients and they ran out of sterilized cotton cloth or other supplies, she would fling her pincette into the kidney basin in a fury. Or if the nurse making up the medicines made a mistake, she would whack her on the hand with her pestle, demanding to know how she could work like that and expect to consider herself a nurse.

Ginko missed nothing and she attended to every detail as diligently as ever, but these last couple of months, the tongue lashings had decreased. It was not that she had become lax – she just did not fly into rages any more. "Maybe she's getting old," Nurse Moto and the others whispered behind her back. Neither she nor they realized that her feelings towards Shikata were mellowing her.

The new school term began in September. Shikata should have returned to Doshisha by then, but still no new letters arrived. *It was just a passing youthful infatuation after all, then*, Ginko decided. At night, alone in her room, she considered this and realized that she felt no anger. He had not done anything wrong. They had enjoyed a stimulating conversation, and he had looked at her with passion in his eyes. It was Ginko herself who had interpreted that as love.

"At my age I should have known better," Ginko chided herself.

The heat continued into September, and the anticipation of cooler weather made it seem all the hotter. With such high temperatures, there was a constant stream of children suffering from the effects of spoilt food, and the Ogino Clinic was filled with their wails.

Ginko was extremely busy outside the clinic as well. One day on her way back from a committee meeting of the Japan

Women's Health Association, Ginko stopped by Shinobazu Pond to enjoy the cool air there. As she crossed Mitsubashi Bridge and climbed the slope back towards Ueno, the noise of Tokyo fell away. The benches were crowded with all kinds of people, from students to grandmothers with children in tow. She had come here occasionally while she was a student at Kojuin, but this was the first time since she had opened her clinic. She wondered vaguely why, despite her busy schedule, she had suddenly felt the urge to come here now.

Ginko settled herself on a bench near a bridge leading to a Buddhist statue of the smiling goddess Benten on a small island in the middle of the pond. The island and the surface of the water sparkled gold in the sunlight. Ginko watched some people as they made their way over the bridge, illuminated by the golden light: a merchant's wife, then an elderly man, and following them, a large man, with his wife carrying a child on her back. They moved unhurriedly, pointing at the water and chatting about something.

Ginko snapped back to attention and looked more closely. It was her former teacher Yorikuni Inoue and his wife Chiyo. They had stopped near the middle of the bridge and were now looking at something in the water and laughing together. As Ginko watched, Yorikuni started walking leisurely in her direction. She stood up and quickly set off back towards her clinic.

Another two weeks went by. Ginko was too busy to think of Shikata very often. One evening towards the middle of September, when Ginko was in her room reading after dinner, Nurse Moto came rushing in.

"Excuse me, but Mr Shikata..."

"What about Mr Shikata?"

"He's at the front door."

Ginko hastily got up and headed for the door, thinking it was impossible. However, Shikata was indeed standing at the entrance. He looked exactly the same as before, with his large frame reaching almost up to the lintel, the faint growth of stubble on his boyish face, and his broad shoulders.

"I'm sorry I didn't let you know I'd be coming." He stood in his *hakama* trousers, his feet planted slightly apart, his head bowed.

"But since you are here, you might as well come in!" There really wasn't anything else she could say.

She led him into her study. On his previous visit, they had used the formal sitting room in the back, but now she hesitated to invite him there for fear of creating a similar atmosphere of intimacy as before.

As he seated himself on the tatami floor of the study, Shikata looked around in wonder. There was a small low desk by the window, but the rest of the walls were entirely covered with bookshelves. Since opening her clinic, Ginko had built up quite a library. Her dream was to amass a collection comparable to that in Yorikuni's study.

"Are you here on Church business this time too?"

"No, I'm not."

"Oh. For your studies then?"

"No." Shikata shook his head, his face pale and stiff with tension.

"What is it, then?"

Nurse Moto came in, bringing chilled barley tea and a sweet snack. Shikata waited for her to leave before answering, "May I stay here tonight?"

"Certainly. But your university?..."

"I've quit."

Ginko noticed that Shikata appeared to have lost weight, and that his cheeks were sunken. "Why?"

Shikata squeezed his eyes shut.

"Why so suddenly?" Ginko repeated.

"Sensei," Shikata bowed low with both hands pressed to the tatami, and continued. "Will you marry me?"

"Marry you?"

"Yes! Please marry me!" Shikata raised his voice. Then his strength seemed to drain away and he bowed his head again. Ginko was reeling from his words. She had no idea how to respond, and was not even entirely sure this was actually happening. "Please," Shikata repeated. "I've come here to propose to you."

245

"But—"

"If you turn me down, I've got nowhere to go. I left school and my lodgings and got rid of everything before coming here. *Please.*"

This was outrageous! Ginko had heard of women throwing themselves at men, begging to marry them, but never the other way round.

"Well, for now…" even the unflappable Ginko was at a loss. The fleeting sweet vision of two months ago had suddenly thrust itself upon her as reality. "Let's continue this conversation later. You must be tired." Ginko desperately wanted to be left alone to regain her composure. "Please rest in the room upstairs."

"Does that mean you accept?"

Ginko did not answer, and Shikata rushed on, "From Takasaki to Nagano, and then all the way back to Kyoto, I couldn't think of anything but you. You filled my thoughts. I couldn't concentrate on my studies or focus on missionary work. I beat my head, ran until I was exhausted, drank even though I never drink – I did everything I could to forget you. I turned to the Bible and tried to read it with my whole heart. But nothing worked. This is the only answer."

He intended to persuade her that he had thought his actions through, but to Ginko he sounded impulsive and reckless. "Let's consider this matter when we're a little more cool headed."

"I am cool headed! I've come to this decision after calm deliberation!"

"But what about me could make you—"

"I love your mind, and the way you've sought knowledge. I love your elegance. It's always been my dream to be with a woman of intelligence, and now I've finally found my ideal partner." Shikata had always had a weakness for intelligent women, ever since the age of twelve, when he had had a terrible crush on a teacher.

"I'm thirteen years older than you."

"That doesn't matter as long as we're in love."

"But what will people think?" The faces of Ginko's friends and relatives flashed through her mind. Ginko quailed, thinking of what they would say if she married a college student.

"The most important thing is that two people decide to marry each other, isn't it? Mutual consent and understanding. Isn't that the biggest – the *only* – thing?"

He had a point. Previously they had both agreed that marriage should be by mutual agreement, and his eyes seemed to be questioning her, asking whether she was going to back out on that now.

Those eyes, Ginko thought. It had been his eyes with their unwavering conviction that had swayed her last time. She could see that she would soon be under their spell again.

"Could you love me?" He was unflinching on this, the essential issue for him.

"I... Please let me think about it."

"Then I will await your answer upstairs." Full of passion, Shikata looked at her for a few moments before leaving the room.

The entire encounter had lasted no more than a few minutes, but it left Ginko feeling as though a wave had crashed over her. Alone once more, she felt no calmer or clearer about anything.

She thought back to their first meeting in July, which had been at the request of Mrs Okubo. She and Shikata had talked late into the night, then watched the fire blazing in a neighbouring district. She had found him to be a friendly and agreeable young man. They shared the same views on many things: women's rights, love and marriage, the future of Christianity – everything. Ginko had felt utterly at ease with him, and had found his presence soothing. She had been caught off guard too, to find that she felt lonely after he left. She had waited and hoped day after day for his letters to arrive.

With hindsight, she realized that of course they had been love letters, and that she had reciprocated unreservedly in her responses. But she had not been prepared to take the next step, and his sudden strong-arm proposal was an unasked-for inconvenience. It was outrageous for him to come barging in with no warning, demanding an immediate answer! He was thoughtless and inconsiderate of a woman's feelings.

So I should just turn him down.

247

But even as her mind told her this, her inner voice insisted otherwise. *He's so sincere.* When he chose a path, he pursued it wholeheartedly without calculation or guile. It made her happy that he was so taken with her. And it was rare for a man to be able to speak so directly. She cherished that about him too. A part of herself that she had suppressed and hidden began to question her resolve. *Must I turn him down?*

Whichever way she looked at it, it was an impossible proposition. They would be a laughing stock. But to turn him down for that reason alone – wouldn't that be cowardice? Not only cowardice, but it would be rejecting her own heart.

Competing thoughts jostled for dominance in her head, vying to gain the upper hand. She had to admit that she had wanted to see Shikata again. She had hoped Shikata would declare his love for her, and now what she had hoped for had happened. Would it not be selfish to back out now just because she was scared?

Kiyo slid the door open slightly and asked, "Will your guest be staying here tonight?"

"Yes," Ginko replied. "Will you please prepare him something to eat?"

Kiyo waited a moment longer, expecting further orders, but when none came, she left.

But, Ginko thought to herself as she listened to Kiyo's footsteps receding, *will he make physical demands of me?* She was seized with an almost forgotten fear. She had not thought about it until just now, but of course it was obvious.

Shikata doesn't know my secret. He doesn't know that the woman of his dreams has gonorrhoea. The woman doctor, the devout Christian, a leader in the Japan Christian Women's Organization, has a venereal disease. At the moment Ginko's disease was in remission, but she could never know when it would become active again and infect him. *I would have to warn him. Loving each other means telling the truth.* But what was to be gained in telling him? Would it not merely sadden and discomfort them both?

No, I can't marry him! Ginko tried to convince the irresolute part of herself that was insisting there might be some hope.

* * *

Three days later, Ginko accepted Shikata's proposal. Until then he had stayed in the upstairs guest room, waiting for her answer. Both had stepped quietly around the house during that time, with bated breath.

"I will walk the path of the Lord with you," were Ginko's carefully chosen words. They showed that her decision was firm and also reflected her shyness.

Shikata raised his thick eyebrows, and his eyes lit with fire as he embraced her. Buried in his big chest, feeling his hands on her back and neck, he was all she could see or smell. She felt utterly at peace. *This is what I've been longing for.*

Now that they had decided to marry, they saw no reason to wait. Ginko told her clinic staff and the congregation at her church a few days later. Her nurses listened with wide eyes and did not even attempt to nod understanding. And they were not the only ones – everyone was against it. It was as though they had all discussed the matter in her absence and agreed on their response.

Ginko's sister Tomoko wrote: "Naturally I am opposed, but if your decision is firm, then of course I cannot stop you." Tomoko understood Ginko better than anyone, and knew that once she had made up her mind, she never wavered from it, so her objection was voiced with no apparent expectation that she could change her sister's mind.

Her older brother Yasuhei, his wife Yai, her sisters Sonoe and Masa, and of course all the other relatives, were incredulous: "A woman of nearly forty with a student of uncertain background and thirteen years younger?" Ginko's friends, including Ogie, were more circumspect in their wording: "You and Shikata seem so poorly matched – isn't it a waste?"

Since leaving Tawarase, however, Ginko had had almost no contact with her siblings other than Tomoko. They may have been linked by blood, but since she had been practically disowned when she moved to Tokyo, she was under no real obligation to listen to their complaints. She was prepared for their criticism, and ignoring it raised no fear of repercussion.

Shikata's parents had passed away, but his older sisters and brothers-in-law were also vociferous in their opposition, although their objections were precisely the opposite of those from Ginko's side: "She's too old, and her status is too high for a woman."

By now though, the two were so in love that nothing could stop them. If anything, the opposition from all around merely served to strengthen their determination to proceed.

"Shall we ask the Okubos to be our witnesses?"

Since the minister and his wife had been the ones to bring about their meeting, this seemed the most appropriate plan. Shikata had no objections, being content to follow Ginko's lead. To their dismay, however, the Okubos wrote to say that they could not do it:

Shikata is still a student and ignorant of the ways of the world. His consideration of matters is overly hasty and though his ideals are lofty, we do not believe the passion of the moment is sufficient to make a lifetime together. Your status is too high for him, and we believe the age difference is such that it would be a mistake and a blot on your future happiness. We regret to say that we cannot take on the responsibility of this role.

Shikata and Ginko had not expected to be turned down quite so flatly.

"Everyone thinks it's a waste for someone of your talent to be with me."

"But they only ever discuss matters of status. That's hardly something to worry about." Ginko felt that everyone's unwillingness to accept the person she had chosen amounted to taking Ginko herself lightly, and she wanted to shield Shikata from this.

"Are you regretting agreeing to marry someone like me?"

"Why would I have regrets? What a strange thing to say!"

"I don't care what people say about me as long as I can be with you."

Ginko loved Shikata's single-mindedness. Men, to her mind,

were mostly selfish and tyrannical beasts, and Shikata seemed like an entirely different species. He was big, sweet and easy-going, and he assuaged her years of loneliness without hurting the pride she had built up over that time.

"But just because it's me, no one will stand up with us."

"There's no need to have anyone of high social standing as our witness. We are going to be wed in the sight of God, and that is sufficient." Ginko tried to think of other Christian acquaintances she might ask, but she knew it would be no good. Everyone was opposed to them marrying.

"I'd like to be married in Kumamoto," Shikata ventured tentatively.

"Let's do that," Ginko agreed immediately.

Shikata's birthplace was in Kutami, near the city of Kumamoto, where he had been raised and converted to Christianity, and he still had many relatives there. Upon marriage, a bride was usually removed from her own family register and entered into her husband's, and it was therefore natural that the wedding be held where the groom's roots ran deepest. Even if the marriage had elicited only disapproval, the couple would still be expected to make the rounds of the groom's family to pay their respects. In Tokyo, Shikata had neither connections nor social standing, and Ginko was embarrassed to realize that she had overlooked that fundamental point.

"Would you really go there?" he asked.

"Of course I'll go. And Reverend Ebina is there too."

"I'd be obliged." Shikata's response was humble, but only natural in the circumstances. Ginko would officially be marrying into his family, but the reality was that he was a free lodger in her house and she would take care of the expenses for travelling all the way south to Kumamoto and for the wedding itself.

They wrote to the Reverend Ebina immediately to ask him to officiate at the ceremony, feeling fairly confident that he would agree. To their surprise, however, his reply was the same as the Okubos: "I wish I could congratulate you on the occasion of your marriage, but I regret to say that I cannot approve or do as you ask." Reverend Ebina's refusal stung all the more because it came written in his elegant calligraphy.

"With all their talk of modernization, the Japanese view of marriage hasn't changed at all!" Shikata flung the letter down on the table in despair. "They're all taking me for a fool."

"No, it's just because I'm too old."

"That's not true. No one wants to see you married to someone as worthless as me." The knuckles of Shikata's clenched fists were white. It was the first time Ginko had seen him angry.

"I really don't think so," she disagreed. "I think they just have our best interests at heart and are offering well-intentioned advice."

"More like sabotage!" Shikata shot back.

"Well, we don't need to worry about them."

"But we're not getting anywhere like this!"

"Let's ask a foreign minister to marry us," Ginko suggested. "A foreigner won't fill our ears with objections the way the Japanese do. It's foreigners who brought Christianity to Japan, so wouldn't it be best that way in any case?"

And so, on 25th November 1890, Ginko Ogino and Yukiyoshi Shikata were married in Kutami, Kumamoto prefecture, with the Reverend O.H. Gulick officiating.

17

Ginko and Shikata saw in the 1891 New Year as a married couple. Ginko was busy as usual with patients, the JCWO and the Women's Health Association. Shikata was working as a minister at the Hongo church, having received an introduction from Shinjiro Okubo.

Though Ginko was now married, everyone still called her Dr Ogino, and her clinic name remained unchanged. Shikata, however, was addressed as "Mr Shikata", using the most basic level of politeness. He gave no sign of noticing or minding this, but Ginko decided at least to bring it up with her staff.

"From now on please refer to him as 'the master'."

Nurse Moto nodded silently in assent, but by the next day all the staff had, as though in agreement, dropped his name completely from all conversations. The maid would inform Ginko: "You are being called" or "You've been asked to look at this". Occasionally Ginko would ask in reply: "By whom?" upon which the maid would glance upwards towards Shikata's room on the second floor with a mumbled "Um…"

While they all liked Shikata well enough as a person, Ginko's staff were unwilling to acknowledge him as her husband. Since no one was actually using his name, it was difficult for Ginko to complain, although she insisted on leading by example: "Please take this to the master" or "Go and ask the master of the house about this and let me know".

Ginko also made a point of discussing even the smallest matters with Shikata and asking his opinion.

"I wonder if we should change the cover on the examination table to a leather one?"

"That sounds good."

"We'll do that, then."

Shikata of course had no experience with the practice of medicine, and the question from Ginko was only a formality

– the decision had already been made. When members of the staff requested time off too, she would answer: "Let's ask the master." Ginko was doing her best to shore up the position of her young husband, but her efforts were largely futile.

What worried Ginko most, though, was her disease. She had given herself to Shikata for the first time the day after their wedding in Kumamoto. They had had no relations during the month preceding, even though Shikata had been staying in Ginko's house. Though he had occasionally sent a burning glance in her direction, he had never tried to press or force himself on her. For her part, Ginko would not have been inclined to give in if he had made a move. There was her position as a Christian and a leader in the Christian Women's Organization, but there were also the constraints of the live-in staff and the responsibility she felt to be an example to them.

Since she had opened her clinic, her disease had been under control. She had occasionally felt a slight ache in her lower abdomen, but it had always settled back down within a few days. The illness was in remission, but she never knew when it might flare up again, leaving Shikata vulnerable to infection. Shikata being the faithful man he was, if he ever came down with a sexually transmitted disease, there would be no question of where it had come from.

"I've had occasional fevers and stomach pain ever since my days at the Women's Normal School. Please forgive me if I need to rest when that happens," Ginko had whispered into Shikata's chest after their first night together. To her young husband, who rarely felt fatigue, it was all she had to say.

"Don't worry, I'll take care of you." Shikata did not know any of the particulars, but he saw that she was embarrassed about it and, protective of his bride, he hugged her tightly.

Their lovemaking was not particularly pleasurable for Ginko, as Shikata was driven rather than skilled. Ginko had not experienced any physical pleasure during her previous marriage either, so despite her having been married once before, they were beginning on an equal footing. She had not had sexual relations of any kind for twenty years, so it was rather uncomfortable at first, but their enjoyment gradually increased. Nevertheless, Ginko was always fraught with worry and guilt.

254

Two months later Shikata still showed no signs of infection. The doctor in Ginko watched him closely for any symptom of the disease, and the wife in her could not rid herself of the feeling that she was deceiving him.

One evening at the end of February, Shikata summoned Ginko to his room on the second floor soon after returning from church. Ginko had finished examining patients and was organizing the charts, but she immediately handed the job over to Nurse Moto and ascended the stairs.

Shikata was kneeling formally at his desk with his hands thrust into his sleeves. Ginko had not seen him in such a stiffly formal posture since the day she had accepted his marriage proposal, and she felt a sudden uneasiness.

"I'm thinking of going to Hokkaido." Shikata had recently started using the more blunt and authoritative manner of speaking typical of husbands of the time, and this was voiced without preface or softeners.

"Hokkaido?"

"Yes," he answered, his face stiff and unmoving.

"Why?" Ginko was used to Shikata's unexpected pronouncements, but this time she was taken aback.

The northern island of Japan had recently had its name changed to Hokkaido, but inhabitants of the mainland still referred to it by the old name "Ezo". All that most mainland residents knew about Hokkaido was that the sea bordering its southern shore was a good place to catch herring, and that it was otherwise a cold, barren land under snow for much of the year. Other than isolated settlements of migrant fishermen, it was largely undeveloped. Rebel samurai loyal to the former shogun had fled there when the Emperor was restored to the throne, and criminals seeking to avoid justice eked out a living there. Otherwise it was the territory of bears, wolves and the Ainu people. There were only a few settlements that could be called towns, primarily Hakodate, Matsumae and Sapporo, but none of these were considered suitable places for decent and upright citizens. This was the land where Ginko's husband was proposing to go.

"It looks like we can get virgin land there."

"And then what will you do with it?"

"That's obvious, isn't it?" Shikata gave her an endearing smile. "We'll build our utopian Christian community there."

"Are you serious?"

"Yes, I am. I've been discussing it with Maruyama and the others from Doshisha all month, and it looks like it will work out."

"You mean you'll be able to get land?"

"Professor Inukai has a large tract of land in Hokkaido."

"And that means?"

"Kendo Tanaka, who was a year ahead of me at Doshisha, approached Inukai about it, and Inukai offered to hand it over to us just like that."

"He's not asking anything for it?"

"Right! It's ours to clear and develop as we like." Shikata's chest puffed up with pride.

In the early years of the Meiji government, it had been determined that the two most effective strategies for opening up Hokkaido were to have the military clear land for development, or to sell off large tracts of ownerless, virgin land for people to develop as they wished, no strings attached. This second option had been instituted from 1886 as a strategy to create privately owned farmland, and a single applicant could receive a plot of about eighty acres on loan. Once they had succeeded in developing it, they would be allowed to buy it at a fixed price.

It was under this programme that in March 1891 Professor Tsuyoshi Inukai and seven of his associates formed a group in order to receive a huge tract of land to develop – almost a quarter of a million acres – on the Toshibetsu plain by the south-west coast of Hokkaido. They had planned to set up and manage a large-scale farm, to which end they had immediately imported all the necessary agricultural equipment from the United States. They had intended to use their farming profits for political purposes. However, they had not counted on how thickly forested the area would be, and they ran into further trouble with a dishonest manager. After running into one setback after another, their ambitious plan was eventually shelved. *This* was the land that Shikata was in line to receive.

"We would never be able to get a piece of land this big on the mainland. We'll clear it, make some fields, and it'll be ours, just like that. All we have to do is work for it."

Dazed, Ginko remained silent.

Shikata went on, "Here on the main island, Christianity is always being persecuted as though it were a tool of Western domination. Instead of tiptoeing around and always keeping a careful eye on this unenlightened government, it would be better to have the space to live freely and spread our wings. In Hokkaido there's no one to restrict or oppress us. The land and water will be ours to do with as we please. I think this land is a sign of God's blessing and protection, don't you?" Once again Shikata's eyes were brimming with emotion.

With effort, Ginko asked, "What about us?"

"I'll go first. I'll get the area cleared and under cultivation. Then when it's habitable, I'll send for you. It probably won't take more than a year."

"But what about the clinic?"

Shikata nodded, then shifted his gaze away from Ginko's as he answered. "You will probably have your own thoughts about that."

Ginko remained silent.

"But I would be happy if you would join me there."

"You mean, close the clinic?"

That was in fact what Shikata meant, but he could not bring himself to say it. Ginko knew that Shikata's dream had been to build a utopian community, and she had never been opposed to the idea. Nevertheless, this was such a drastic change in their situation that Ginko was unable to organize her thoughts. She did not even know where to start or how to determine if this was a positive development or not.

"I'm sure this is not good news for you," Shikata offered, seeing Ginko's expression of shock. "But I'm not getting anywhere here like this."

There was some truth to that. Having dropped out of Doshisha, Shikata was only able to work as an assistant minister at the Hongo church. And even if he was nominally the master of Ginko's house, there was nothing for him to do there beyond handyman duties such as weeding the garden and mending the fence. Whatever the power of the love and disregard for the future that had brought him to Ginko, he would not be able to continue like this for long. His self-respect would not stand for it.

"I want to see what I can make of this opportunity. There will be plenty of time later to decide what to do about the clinic. For now it will just be me going up there, whether anyone else follows later or not," he said, his voice low but determined.

Ginko stared at him, appalled. Shikata was not looking at her, however, but at some point in the darkness, like a man possessed. She knew he would go no matter what she said. She had thought they were close, but her husband seemed suddenly far away. He had seemed to be hers to hold, but now he was leaving her.

18

In May 1891, Shikata set sail for Hokkaido with Yojiro Maruyama, the younger brother of a former classmate at Doshisha.

The tenth of May brought with it a hint of summer as Ginko went to Yokohama harbour to see him off. Shikata stood on the pier in the new clothes Ginko had ordered to be made for him. Beside him was a single wicker trunk and a large cloth-wrapped bundle similar to the one he had brought with him from Kyoto.

Along with his Bible, these contained a set of woollen under-clothes, two sets of long cotton underwear, two changes of winter clothing, a cloak, split-toe socks, boots, Shikata's favourite bean-jam-filled sweets and crackers, and carefully labelled packets of medicines to treat vomiting, stomach aches, fevers, infections and cuts, plus cotton and bandages.

"Time to go," said Shikata, as a gong announced the final warning for the ship's passengers to board.

"Take care."

"I'll be fine." Shikata's sunny expression showed no trace of unease at leaving his wife and heading off to an undeveloped territory. Ginko watched his broad back as his rolling strides took him up the gangplank. He reached the deck and turned once more to give her a big wave. "Stay well for me!"

Ginko wanted to say the same, but instead she pulled her shawl more closely around herself and followed Shikata with her eyes. The ship's gong sounded once more before it pulled slowly away from the pier.

"Take care!" Shikata shouted again, his voice carrying over the water to her. The ship took a wide turn to the left and headed towards the harbour exit. Shikata's figure on the deck grew smaller and smaller, finally becoming a point of black against the early summer light.

So here I am alone in Tokyo, a wife without her husband, Ginko thought, as she watched the silhouette of the steamship disappear over the horizon.

The ship took Shikata and Yojiro from the Boso Peninsula up along the eastern Tohoku coast, and then detoured around the Shimokita Peninsula before entering Hakodate harbour. They rested there a day, then chugged up Hokkaido's west coast via Kumaishi and Ota, before docking in Setana harbour. It had been exactly ten days since they had left Yokohama. They had run into stormy weather twice on the way, first just past Shimokita Peninsula, and then off Kumaishi. The second time they had taken on water at the stern and narrowly avoided being shipwrecked.

The town of Setana was one of the herring fishing ports dotted along Hokkaido's western coastline. It had been established in 1593, when Toyotomi Hideyoshi granted Yoshihiro, the fifth-generation head of the Matsumae family, jurisdiction over the province of Ezo. Originally inhabited by Ainu, Setana was now full of fishermen from the town of Matsumae and the Tohoku area, attracted by the herring industry that had been thriving since the 1790s. Just a little inland from this hubbub, though, the Toshibetsu plain was all undeveloped wilderness, with no trace of human presence. Further inland still, the settlement of eastern Setana had just over a hundred people living in a total of eighty-two residences scattered around the densely forested area of the huge Toshibetsu river basin.

The name Setana was derived from the Ainu word *setanai*, meaning "dog stream", which referred to the sighting of dogs, later thought to be wolves, swimming down the Baba River that flowed through the town.

Shikata and Yojiro rested in the port for a day, and took the opportunity to ask some of the settlers, hailing originally from Tokushima, about the conditions of the land upstream along the Toshibetsu River.

"No one's living there. A year ago five or so folks from Tokushima came up here and tried to go inland, but the trees were so big and the forest so thick that it was dark even in the daytime. It wasn't ten days before they came running back and went home."

"How's the soil there?"

"They said it didn't look bad."

Shikata nodded, his eyes on the surface of the river, swollen with melted snow. If the soil was fertile, they could probably manage somehow, he thought.

"Are you serious about going in there?"

"As far as Nakayakeno."

"You'd be better off giving up on it."

The settlers tried to dissuade them, but having come this far, Shikata and Yojiro could not give up. They had come knowing that things would be difficult. Shikata later noted his impressions of their two-day journey along the river from Setana:

We took the route suggested by our guides, going upstream on the Toshibetsu River with three light boats. That night we slept in the open. We finally reached Nakayakeno, the area on the Toshibetsu plain to be developed, about three in the afternoon the next day. It took two days from Setana travelling upstream, but it would be a distance of twelve kilometres by road. The river has salmon, trout, lamprey eels, cherry salmon and more. I don't think humans have ever been here. Huge trees lie across the river. Cutting off branches to pass under them, and hoisting the boats over the ones we could not get under, was no easy task. The river bottom was filled with large freshwater mussels. The land showed no signs of human presence, being so thickly forested that no one could ever get through. The vegetation on the plains, forests and fields is so rich that the land must be quite fertile.

They had made it to their destination, but now, armed only with saws and hatchets, they faced a dense primeval forest of enormous trees and waist-high bamboo grass. It took an entire day to fell a single tree, remove its stump and clear the land around it. They were not short of fish, which were so abundant they could practically catch them with their bare hands, but their stocks of rice, salt and miso would soon run low.

During the day sunlight filtered in through the skylight afforded by the clearing they had opened in the trees, but after the sun had passed its peak and night fell, the thick forest would once again be pitch black. It was a two-day journey back to Setana to replenish their supply of matches, candles and lamp oil, and they were unwilling to waste that much time. They were therefore unable to read in the evenings. First thing in the morning, as the light gradually penetrated the forest, they would devote a short time to reading the Bible, but at night, all they could do was listen to the calls of unfamiliar birds and the howls of wild dogs. It was a primitive lifestyle.

That was not to say they had time to be idle, however. With unpractised hands, the two of them took up their shovels, wielded their saws and trod the first steps of their slowly forming road.

Summer arrived. Southern Hokkaido was cool during the nights even in high summer, but daytime temperatures matched those in Tokyo. Along with the heat came hordes of mosquitoes. They were big and black, a kind not seen on the main island, and their wings made a different sound from other mosquitoes as they swarmed in to attack. Swatting had little effect and the next moment the men's faces were again black with them. It must have been the first scent of human blood these mosquitoes had ever had, and it seemed to send them into a frenzy of delight.

Unable to bear it, Shikata dunked a sheaf of straw in water, hung it from his waist and lit it to set it smoking. Yojiro never lost sight of him in the woods because he was always surrounded by rising smoke. This did indeed keep the mosquitoes at bay, but inside the cloud of smoke Shikata's eyes were red and swollen.

"I think I'll follow suit," Yojiro announced after another couple of days, and he too adopted the smoking-straw mosquito repellent.

So the two figures toiled in the wilderness, belching smoke. Their columns of smoke came together when they moved the huge, fallen trees, and moved apart again as they set about chopping them up.

Shikata had the habit of muttering under his breath, "Take

that! And that! And that!" as he wielded his axe or shovelled dirt. Once in a while, when he straightened up to wipe off sweat and stretch, a faint smile would cross his face.

"What's up?" the sharp-eyed Yojiro would ask.

"What? Oh... nothing," Shikata would reply.

"You're thinking about your wife, aren't you?"

"Huh? No, no, not at all," he would deny, flustered that he had been seen through so easily. Sometimes while his mind was on Ginko, he would look up to realize suddenly that he had nearly cut through a tree, and was in danger of having it fall on him.

As the sun sank low, the pair would scrunch down in their sleeping bags out of reach of the mosquitoes, and Shikata would think of Ginko and ache with longing to see and hold her.

Each day followed the same pattern, with Shikata and Yojiro doing battle with the huge trees, cleaning up the roots and clearing the bamboo grass, without ever taking a day of rest. September arrived and with it the end of summer, yet they had managed to clear less than an acre of land. Furthermore, the land was still rough and far from ready for cultivation.

"We'll end up starving," Shikata said to Yojiro near the end of September. There was a chill autumn breeze blowing through their clearing, and the mornings and evenings were cold. They would not be able to plant anything until the following year now.

"Once the snow falls, we'll be stuck here," agreed Yojiro, looking up at the distant autumn sky.

"We both look a sight," Shikata observed aloud.

Only their eyes glinted through their bushy beards. If they were seen like this in Tokyo, they would be taken for vagrants or beggars.

"I wonder when it'll start snowing?"

"November is what I heard – and it'll last until the end of April."

"Wonder how much it piles up?"

"They said it comes to a man's height here, but that it's not much compared to the rest of Hokkaido."

Yojiro went quiet. They were surrounded by nothing but the earth and the sky. There was little left to say to each other.

"It's a long way…"

"Mmm?"

"Oh, nothing." Shikata looked up at the sky. He was wondering how Ginko was getting along. He had mailed a letter to her on each of his monthly trips to Setana, but he wondered how many had actually reached her. He had received a reply from her only in August to a letter he had sent in May. That was the last letter from her that had reached him.

"What should we do?" asked Yojiro.

"Hmm." Shikata knew what he was getting at. "It'll probably be impossible to get through the winter."

"So, you want to go back?"

"Yes, and then come back in the spring."

This would mean a major setback for their plan, which had been to establish the foundations for self-sufficiency within the first year, and be ready to bring twenty or thirty believers up to join them during the second.

"We'll have to go back by mid-October then. Any later than that and sea travel will be too dangerous." Even in May, when the ocean had been calm, the sea route had been perilous.

"So that leaves us a month."

"I'll stay here," Yojiro said suddenly. "I'd rather do that than make that trip again. I don't know how much it'll snow, but I'll probably be able to manage somehow if I go down to Setana with you and buy a store of food to get me through the winter."

"But, on your own—"

"I'll do some carving. At least there's plenty of wood."

Yojiro had been apprenticed to an engraving studio in Kyoto. He had met Shikata purely by chance when visiting his older brother Dentaro at Doshisha, but had decided to accompany him after hearing of his plan. Since they had been up here, he had made the most of their occasional breaks to make carvings, which he had been able to sell for cash in Setana.

"Well, then I'll stay too."

"No, you go back. Please go and meet the others who are waiting to come up, and tell them what Hokkaido's like and explain what kind of preparations they should make. And besides…" he paused and then went on, "your wife is waiting for you."

"But what if something goes wrong while you're alone?"

"It won't make any difference whether it's one or two of us. If the cold and snow are bad enough to kill, two people will be frozen as easily as one. And actually, it'll be easier to survive if there's just one mouth to feed. If I just stay put in camp there's probably nothing that'll kill me. Really, don't worry about it. Actually, I'm going to be more worried about you going on the sea route."

Shikata was silent as he thought this over.

"With a whole winter I bet I can get a good bit of carving done." Yojiro gave a faint laugh, but they both knew it was a whistle in the dark.

At the end of October, Shikata left Yojiro Maruyama in Hokkaido and returned to Tokyo. Ginko closed her clinic for the day and went to meet him off the ship at Yokohama.

It had been just six months since they had seen each other, but to Ginko it had seemed more like years. Shikata, a head taller than the other passengers disembarking from the ship, came towards her with long strides. Ginko ran to meet him.

"Sensei."

"Welcome home!"

Shikata placed his big hands on her shoulders and Ginko added, "You're back safely." She gazed up at his suntanned face, studying the changes there. His frame was as solid as ever, but it was as though the meat had been whittled off him. The old Shikata was gone, and in place of the youthful dreamer was a man who had been honed by hardship.

He rested for a few days at Ginko's house, but within a week he was on the move again. He went around to the churches first, paying his respects and collecting donations. Then, soon after the beginning of the New Year, he departed for Kyoto to meet with Yojiro's brother Dentaro Maruyama, and the others who were planning to join them in Hokkaido in the spring.

"Welcome back." The thirty or so members who had gathered at Dentaro's house for this meeting looked closely at Shikata's sharpened features.

"So, what kind of shape is the settlement in now?"

"Well, it's more or less liveable."

"What do you mean by that? What's the land like?"

"It's hard to describe it all precisely in a few words." There were so many things he needed to tell them, he was at a loss about where to begin.

"What's the climate like?"

"It's pretty much like here during the daytime, but it cools down quickly at night. The summers are definitely milder."

"Are food and water available nearby?"

"They certainly are! The Toshibetsu River's no more than a mile or so away. Pure, cold, clear water. It's filled with *ayu* sweetfish and cherry salmon, and in the autumn salmon swim up it. If you smack a pole in there you can catch all you want – it's so easy it's almost a game. And you can get all the udon and butterbur sprouts you want just by bending down and picking them. There's mugwort too, and flowering ferns, and a lot of wild grasses we don't know the names of – but there's no shortage of them, at any rate."

"What kind of houses have you got?"

"Well, there's tons of wood, and reeds we can use for thatching. If we just use trees that we've felled in the clearing work, we can put up some huts pretty quickly."

"How about animals?"

"Apparently bear and deer are around, but I've only seen bear tracks once and I've never met one. I did see a deer running once. Sometimes a jackrabbit runs into our clearing. They make good soup."

Listening to Shikata, the men envisioned a relaxed life amid pastoral beauty. But he had simply been answering their questions. The pastoral beauty was there, but he could not bring himself to tell them about the other side – their bitter struggle on the undeveloped land.

"What was the hardest thing?"

"The mosquitoes. We must be the first humans they've ever tasted, so they come in swarms."

"That's the worst?"

"Yes, that's it."

The others looked at each other, a little deflated. If the hardest thing about pioneering this wilderness was the mosquitoes, then where was the adventure? But they would never know the reality until they themselves went up there.

"And how much land did you clear these past six months?"

"Well, I guess about a couple of acres or so." Shikata could not bring himself to tell them it was less than an acre – so little to show for six months' labour.

"So, you've started planting, then?"

"Yes, some potatoes." This was not true either. Shikata faltered, then added more confidently, "Anyway, we've got a huge area."

"Right – nearly a quarter of a million acres, isn't it?" someone agreed. They were all imagining a plain that stretched as far as the eye could see. In reality, however, there was no view there at all. Whichever direction you looked, there was nothing to see but dense forest and the little patch of sky above their clearing.

"So what should we bring with us?" asked Yamazaki, who was planning to set out for the settlement with his wife in April.

"Hmm." Shikata thought this over with his chin in his hand. As many clothes and as much bedding as they could carry. Saws and hoes, and other utensils and tools. Medicine, rice... the list was endless, he realized.

"Well, money is the main thing, really." If they at least had money, they could buy almost anything they needed in Setana.

"And that's really all we need?"

"Well, actually you don't really need anything."

"Pardon?"

"You just need the will and spirit to establish a new land, your body, and the desire to work as God's servant. The rest will work out."

Shikata's words were met with startled silence.

"Here, see my hands, from the hatchet and saw." Shikata thrust his palms out in front of his listeners. There was a line of hard white calluses across each one. Shikata moved to conclude the meeting on the right note. "So in April, let's get as many people together as we can to go to that pure land and start a new life!"

After the gathering had dispersed, Dentaro moved closer to Shikata to have a private word. "Shikata, what you were saying wasn't all true, was it?"

"Not true?"

Dentaro looked Shikata in the eye and nodded. "It's not what I've heard from my brother."

"Oh, well, that could be... I just gave you my point of view."

"But you've got them believing in a dream."

"It's not just a dream. It really will come true! It *is* coming true, little by little."

"I hope so."

Dentaro said no more, but Shikata felt ill at ease for the rest of his visit.

After Kyoto, Shikata went down to Kumamoto to fetch his elder sister Shime and her husband, who were also planning to go to Hokkaido with him in the spring. On returning to Tokyo, he set about meeting with potential backers to ask for their support, and making the rounds of the Tokyo branch of the Hokkaido Development Commission, the Defence Ministry, the Home Ministry and others to arrange for equipment, tools and food rations.

It was February by the time everything had been arranged, and Shikata was scheduled to leave for Hokkaido in April.

"I'll come with you if you like," Ginko told Shikata one day late in February, on a rare occasion when they were relaxing together at home. She had felt for some time that she should say this, but she had been putting it off, day after day. This was partly because there had been no opportunity to converse at leisure while Shikata had been out on his rounds, but it was also true that her will was wavering and she could not bring herself to speak up until her conviction was firm. In fact, she had not yet made up her mind to close the clinic, but Shikata accepted her words at face value.

"You stay here, please."

"But even your sister is going. There's no reason for me, your wife, to be staying behind."

"There would be nothing for my sister to do if she stayed behind in Kumamoto. It's a whole different matter with you, though."

"I'm not attached to Tokyo and I don't mind quitting my medical practice. If you tell me to come, I will. You know I'm a believer too." Ginko silently marvelled at herself for being able to voice these protestations despite her still truly mixed feelings.

"I understand how you feel," Shikata answered, "but it's still too early. I want to make it a little more habitable. Then I'll send for you."

"But I can work at clearing the land too. I can handle a hoe and saw."

"No, it's not fit for you to go to yet. It would be pointless – you'd just ruin your health."

"But you're going."

"I'm a man. You know I'm much stronger than you. Furthermore, I'm the man who's organized and planned it all."

Ginko knew how soft-hearted Shikata was and it emboldened her to probe further. She did not yet have the sense of urgency that she would have if she was truly due to go there any time soon. "Is it really that horrible a place?"

"Setana's one thing, but you can't go where we're working."

"But you're so enthusiastic about recruiting everyone else to go."

"It's what I have to do."

Ginko tried to picture the huge trees and the snow, but all she could summon were vague images of a vast wilderness.

"Truth be told, I was shocked when I went up there and saw it for myself. I can't tell the others this, but even now I'm not sure that it'll work out. You know, everyone coming with me this time could easily decide to leave once they get there. But I'm the one who started it, so I've got to see it out."

"In that case, you must do your very best." Secretly, however, Ginko wished he would give up on it.

"If I quit now, it'll mean that all the work we did last year will be for nothing. And it wouldn't be fair to Yojiro up there on his own. We're making a community where we can worship God, so we can put up with some suffering to build it."

"Yes, of course."

"Anyhow, I do want you to come. But not yet – for the moment, please." Shikata hesitated, then seemed to come to a decision and said, "I'd appreciate it if you could stay in Tokyo for a couple more years and continue working to raise as much money for us as you can."

"Me?"

"Yes. If we just had a little more money, the work up there would go more easily. We could get better tools, eat rice, and use lamps at night—"

"You mean you haven't had any rice or even lamps?"

"That's right."

Ginko scanned his face again, and noted how much the single year had aged him.

"The tools the Hokkaido Development Commission is loaning us to clear the land and the food rations aren't enough. There's no question that if we had more funds we could get the land cleared more quickly and have a harvest to look forward to."

"In that case, I'll certainly do what I can."

"I'd appreciate that."

"Not at all." Ginko understood that she herself was the only person who could really help her husband now. At the same time, she could not help recalling how two days earlier she had been recommended as a candidate for the next head of the Japan Christian Women's Organization.

In April 1892, once the snows had melted, Shikata again set out for Hokkaido, this time accompanied by five people, including his older sister and her husband. The previous autumn had seen the completion of a railway from Tokyo to Aomori on the northernmost tip of Japan's main island, and so they travelled by train. From Aomori they boarded a ship to Hakodate in Hokkaido and from there they travelled overland to Nakayakeno.

Shikata kept detailed notes of their itinerary for this portion of the trip, which took four days, in a guidebook for use by future settlers.

Yojiro Maruyama was still alive and waiting for them when they arrived at Nakayakeno. In his nearly six months of isolated privation, he had sculpted more than twenty statues of Daikokuten and other Buddhist deities.

"If I hadn't enjoyed sculpting so much, I'd probably have gone mad and died," he said cheerfully, but his cheeks were sunken, and his face, which had been tanned nearly black at the end of summer, had bleached grey over the winter months.

"The worst problem was the lack of food," he continued. "In the autumn, I went for forty days just eating butterburs boiled in salt. Then from January on, I got along for two weeks at a time on a watered-down cup of rice." He devoured the sweets they had brought him from Tokyo as he related this.

Their band now numbered seven and they set to work clearing the land once again. Around the same time, a group of seventy families from distant Tokushima prefecture began a settlement at nearby Osabuchi, halfway between Setana and Nakayakeno. Soon afterwards, in May 1892, twelve people from Fukushima prefecture settled a little upstream from Osabuchi, even closer.

Densely forested as it was, the soil of the Toshibetsu River basin was so fertile that even novices like Shikata and his group managed to enjoy a harvest of rye and potatoes by that autumn. A crop of rice was still beyond them, but for the moment at least their group would not starve, and the seven of them would be able to get through the winter there.

The New Year of 1893 arrived, and in the spring three more of Shikata's comrades arrived, including Yojiro's brother Dentaro. Within three months, they had each summoned their families to join them as well.

In June of that year, a group of Episcopalians from Kumagaya, Saitama, came to explore the possibility of moving a band of pioneers from their church up to Hokkaido. Their leader, Kozaburo Amanuma, had already heard from the Doshisha Professor, Inukai, about Shikata's settlement, and now he proposed that they merge their forces.

Shikata and his cohorts were at a point where any extra hands were welcome, and Shikata moved quickly to bring the matter to the other members of his group. "Apparently there are more than a dozen of them. But they belong to the Episcopalian Church. What do you think?" Shikata's group was from the Congregational Church. Although they shared the same religion, their doctrine and rites differed. In this unpopulated wilderness, however, they did not feel they had the luxury to quibble.

"Whether they're Congregationalists or Episcopalians, Christians are Christians. And if both of our bands work with the same aim to settle this land, it's good enough, isn't it?" Yojiro answered, and everyone else immediately agreed. They all wanted more help. As a result, in June, Amanuma's group, numbering fourteen households in all, moved up to join them from their borrowed lodgings in nearby Datemonbetsu.

At the same time Shikata's band of Congregationalists was also slowly growing. In August of that year more had arrived from Hyogo prefecture, and then in 1894, some came from Setana, followed by yet more from Hyogo. By the end of the year they could count fifty families in the Nakayakeno settlement.

Furthermore, a road from Setana eastwards to Kunnui was opened in the summer. It was a humble road, only wide enough for a single wagon, but they no longer needed to fear getting lost on the route inland from Hakodate.

Now that their population exceeded fifty households, the makeshift name Nakayakeno no longer seemed appropriate. Shikata's group held discussions with Amanuma's Episcopalians and they all agreed on the biblical name Emmanuel, meaning "God with us". They also settled on the principles for the charter of their settlement:

Anyone of the Christian faith, regardless of denomination, shall be entitled to join us and to have 15,000 tsubo of land to cultivate, upon success of which he shall donate a tenth of his profits to the church.

All settlers shall abstain from alcohol and observe the other moral precepts of Christianity. Failure to adhere to these

*precepts shall result in dissolution of their contract with the
settlement.*

*All holidays and all Sundays shall be days of rest and a time
to worship and deepen our faith.*

*If continuing misfortune should occur, we shall endeavour
to help and aid each other.*

Falling into credit and debt is forbidden.

*All settlers shall endeavour to the best of their abilities to
become self-supporting.*

Shikata's ideal Christian farming community finally seemed to
be succeeding.

It was now two years since Shikata had last been in Tokyo.
Ginko had received a letter from him every month, and was able
to get a fairly good idea of how the community was developing.
Shikata's letters invariably ended with "Everything is going
according to plan". Knowing how idealistic he was and that he
was too considerate to worry her, Ginko did not take his words
at face value. She sometimes wondered if she ought to be letting
Shikata live on his own like this, and she in turn ended each
letter she wrote to him with "Please don't overwork yourself.
There is no need to rush things, and I know you are doing your
best, I pray daily for your safety".

During these two years Ginko's surroundings had undergone
some changes as well. Japan was on the brink of war with
China, and just as Shikata had foretold, Christian missionary
work on the Japanese mainland had begun to lose momentum
in the mood of impending national crisis.

Near the end of 1893, Ginko's elder brother, Yasuhei, passed
away at the age of forty-seven. The cause of death was cerebral
haemorrhage. At Tomoko's urging, Ginko decided to visit
Tawarase, ostensibly to pay her respects at Yasuhei's funeral,
but also to make a long-delayed visit to her parents' graves. If
she was to join Shikata in Hokkaido, this would be her last
opportunity for many years – possibly for ever – to visit her
family home.

The road she had raced home on in a rickshaw ten years

previously was now a railroad line. As the train brought her closer to Tawarase, memories of that last visit washed over her, and her heart grew heavier and heavier as she recalled the grief she had felt over her mother's death, and the cold eyes of her relatives and the villagers.

But Tawarase had changed. There was no more coldness towards her, and in its place she was treated with curiosity and awe. Dozens of people appeared by her seat at Yasuhei's wake to exchange greetings and talk with her. Some were distant relatives whose faces she recalled, while others were people she had completely forgotten. Even the newly widowed Yai had warmed to Ginko.

Tomoko whispered, "Everyone's got their eyes on you."

"Why on earth is that?"

"They're saying you're the female doctor, and the famous Christian."

"Oh, for Heaven's sake."

"They respect you. They're probably a little curious about you too."

"They're just toying with me."

"It's certainly a big change from last time, when Mother died and they all treated you like some sort of insane woman. Our poor, dead Yasuhei here included."

The bleak scene came back vividly to Ginko. Without exception, they had all viewed her as the disobedient, unfilial and disowned daughter.

"You're rich and famous now, so the world sees you differently."

"How silly."

Ginko was ill-disposed to listen to this, although she could see that what Tomoko said was true.

Most of the guests departed at eight o'clock, leaving only the Ogino family, their relatives and the neighbours who were helping them with the funeral preparations.

"Shikata still hasn't returned from Hokkaido?" Tomoko asked Ginko when they finally had a few moments alone.

"No, he hasn't. He refuses to give up on his project."

"And are you going up there too?"

"It's possible I will have to at some point."

"Don't!" Tomoko's tone was unusually strong. "What is the benefit to anyone of you going?"

"Benefit?"

"Hokkaido is for people who can't make a living here, or who have some other reason for leaving. They've all been driven there. Just because you're a believer doesn't mean you have to go. You're doing plenty of great things now, working as a doctor in Tokyo."

Ginko was silent.

"There's no need for you to be dealing with uncouth men, cutting and clearing trees, and living in a hut set in the mud. The only thing you'll accomplish by going to such a place is to shorten your life."

"But I'm Shikata's—"

"Wife? And what exactly has Shikata provided for you as a husband? You've paid for everything from the wedding costs to the living expenses, and he's just been living off you. Then he decides to leave and go to Hokkaido, and now he wants to force you to go up there as well?"

"His intention has simply been to build an ideal Christian farming community, that's all."

"It's ridiculous. He may be full of talk about an ideal community, but it's really just clearing a hole in the woods, isn't it?"

"He told me before we married that this was his dream. Now he's just making it come true, little by little."

"Well, then it's his dream and he can go up there and pursue it. But you worked so long and hard to become a doctor. Why should you have to abandon your dream to follow his?"

"Well, it's something that we'll decide between ourselves as a couple," Ginko snapped back coldly. Tomoko lapsed into silence and Ginko felt a sudden sense of foreboding.

Yasuhei's son, Sanzo, succeeded his father as head of the Ogino household, but there was little left to inherit, since both the land and the family's prominence were long gone. Even Yasuhei's funeral was a much more sparsely attended affair than one would have expected. He had been a weak person and had let the family's fortune slip through his fingers, so it could be said that this was his just reward. Nevertheless, Ginko did not think of him as a bad person, and it was in this spirit that she laid him to rest.

"It wouldn't have been like this if Mother had been here," said Tomoko, looking at the altar set up for Yasuhei, remarkably poor and unadorned compared to that of their father all those years before. "This may well mark the end of the Ogino family."

Sanzo, the chief mourner and new head of the family, was now twenty-three, but he had always been a sickly child and had never shown any interest in farming.

"Well, there's probably no need to keep the property in the family any more, is there?" Ginko said, recalling that she had overheard Sanzo mention that he wanted to move to Tokyo and find work there.

"But a family's successor has a duty to protect and maintain the family home as best he can."

Tomoko may have been right, but Ginko did not feel inclined to force this view onto the young Sanzo. That she and Tomoko differed on this made her think that perhaps they were indeed growing further apart.

"Oh, and did you see him?" Tomoko changed the subject suddenly.

"See him? Who do you mean?"

"You didn't know? Kanichiro was here."

Ginko looked hard at Tomoko at the mention of her former husband.

"He came and greeted me, so I thought that surely you'd spoken as well."

Kanichiro and Ginko had long been divorced, but as the Inamura and Ogino families had shared prominent positions as wealthy farming households in northern Saitama, formal relations between the families had continued. It was only to be expected that Kanichiro would come to pay respects at the funeral of the head of the Ogino household, even if it was a household in decline. He was, after all, a former relative by marriage, and from a household separated from theirs by less than twenty-five miles.

"I suppose he must have come and gone without approaching you, then."

"I didn't notice him at all."

"But I'm sure he saw you."

During the wake Ginko had been seated near the edge of the gathered relatives. Perhaps that was why she had failed to notice him. Or maybe she had seen him as he had approached the front to offer incense, but had failed to recognize him from behind. It was almost twenty-five years since she had last seen him.

"He's the President of a bank now, you know."

Ginko could not picture the pale, silent young man she had known as the head of a bank.

"He was surprised when I told him you'd married a student, thirteen years your junior."

"Tomoko, I really don't want to talk about this!" Ginko stood up abruptly.

Yai came over and tried to motion Ginko into the next room where the men were eating and drinking. "Won't you have some sake with us? There are so many people who want to talk with you. You're the pride of the Ogino family."

"Oh, let's join them for a bit, then," Tomoko chimed in.

"That's very nice and I hate to miss the chance, but I have an early start tomorrow morning." Ginko turned away with a heavy feeling of irritation weighing her down. *The countryside never changes*, she thought. *It's as unbearable as ever.*

19

Ginko had been resigned to the idea of going to Hokkaido ever since Shikata's last visit to Tokyo, and the question was only of when. She prepared herself mentally to leave the moment Shikata sent word to join him. Would it be this spring? Or in summer? She waited for his summons – but it didn't come.

Shikata's letters continued as always to arrive once a month. Every month without fail he informed her that they were fine and that the development was progressing little by little. Never, however, did he give any hint that he wanted her to come.

Shikata's elder sister, Shime, was there at the settlement, and his companions Takabayashi, Dentaro and the others had all called for their wives to join them. Shikata alone made no move to do so. He only repeated again and again that he was fine. She gradually became convinced that he was holding back because he did not want to make her live in the rough conditions there.

I'm a believer too, and I'm in agreement with Shikata's plan. Whether he calls for me or not, I should go. Besides, I'm his wife. I've just been taking advantage of his reticence. Takabayashi and Dentaro Maruyama have their wives there, so it's not like it's a place where women can't survive. Because I'm a doctor and have an important position in society, I keep thinking I'm different from other women. That's what makes it possible for me to stay in Tokyo with a clear conscience. In reality, I've been unbearably conceited.

Once this had occurred to her, her conviction only intensified. She was mortified to think that she had been using her privileged position as an excuse. *All believers are equal before God.* There was no reason for Ginko alone to be living a life of ease. She began to lose sleep, and one night, with the wind banging on the shutters, she composed a poem:

Woken from sleep by a midnight storm
I imagine how cold it must be
On the Toshibetsu plain.
Even when the wind disperses the clouds
I wonder about the morning and evening sky
Over the Toshibetsu plain.

Falling asleep once again, she saw Shikata in a dream. He was standing alone in a snow-covered field. Around him she could only see cut, bare trees. Shikata said nothing. He simply stood stock-still, holding a hoe. But he was looking in her direction. "You want me to come, don't you?" He did not answer, and she asked again. This time, ever so faintly, he nodded. Then he lit up with that smile that was his alone.

When Ginko opened her eyes, the storm had subsided. It was a bright Tokyo morning.

"I'll go."

Now that she had definitely made up her mind, she was even a little annoyed with Shikata for holding back for so long.

In June 1894, Ginko set off for Hokkaido and her waiting husband. She had closed the clinic and divided up the furniture and household goods between Nurse Moto and the other staff.

"You're really going after all?" Nurse Moto had come to see Ginko off at Ueno Station, but she still could not believe that Ginko was truly leaving Tokyo for Hokkaido.

"Yes, of course I am."

"But..." Unable to say any more, Nurse Moto looked down. Ginko had been a hard taskmaster and Moto had been on the verge of quitting more than once, but now she looked back almost fondly on those times. Ginko had taught her so much about so many things. The strictness had been Ginko's way of looking after her, she realized now. "Take care of yourself," she finished sadly.

One after another the people who had come to see Ginko off approached and bowed their heads, grasping her hand. Kajiko Yajima of the Japan Christian Women's Organization, the Okubos, who had unwittingly introduced her to Shikata, the ministers from the Hongo and Reinanzaka churches, young women doctors she had mentored, the Chairman of the Tokyo Medical Association, journalists and others from the press, and her old friends Ogie Matsumoto and Shizuko Furuichi. Many were well known, but even a number of her former patients had turned up as well. It was a grand send-off entirely unlike Shikata's modest departure.

Amid the throng, Mrs Okubo whispered to her husband, "It's such a waste." As a Christian, what Ginko was setting out to do was nothing short of praiseworthy. As the wife of a Christian too, it was laudable. Mrs Okubo knew she should be fully supportive of another Christian setting out on a road that she believed was right. Yet if she had stayed in Tokyo, Ginko's fame not only as a doctor, but also as a social reformer was bound to have spread, and she regretted that Ginko would lose out on that particular future. She could not bring herself to say goodbye to Ginko the way she had to Shikata, and she could not shake off the feeling that their marriage had been a terrible mistake. Nobody there on the platform voiced their misgivings, but all were in agreement with Mrs Okubo's sentiments.

It was time for Ginko to board the train. She settled herself into a seat by the window, but kept her face resolutely forwards and her eyes down.

"This will break my heart," whispered Mrs Okubo to her husband just as the bell sounded for the departure.

"Goodbye!"

"Take care!"

The assembled crowd voiced their best wishes in a chorus, but Ginko could not allow herself to look out of the window. She felt sure that her eyes would meet some familiar face. And if she locked eyes with that one person, it would be an inadvertent slight to the others who were seeing her off.

Everyone went quiet, watching the train go. Suddenly Nurse Moto wailed, "Doctor!" and ran down the platform after the train. As she reached the end of the platform, she called once more after Ginko, but Ginko could no longer hear her. The train pulled away from the station, gathering speed. It was only after Ginko had crossed the Arakawa River and was approaching Kawaguchi that it sunk in that she really was alone now, and on her way to Hokkaido.

20

Ginko had thought she was prepared for life in the settlement, but it was a challenge nonetheless. The hut she and Shikata lived in had an entrance area with an earthen floor and two tiny rooms with wooden-plank flooring. Everything else was outside, including the well and the communal outdoor toilet.

"You're shocked, aren't you?"

"Not at all. It's exactly as I imagined." Ginko did her best to appear unconcerned, but deep down she was indeed shocked. She could never have imagined such living conditions from her comfortable life in Tokyo. Now she understood why Shikata had been reluctant to call for her.

They laid out their bedding on top of straw spread over the wooden planks. It had been two years since they had slept side by side. Everything – the floor beneath them and all that was around them – felt unfamiliar. "We'll only have to bear this for another two or three years," Shikata murmured, holding Ginko in his arms. His skin carried the scent of grass and earth. It had probably sunk into him these three years. *With time it will probably sink into me too*, Ginko thought. She closed her eyes and tried to drive away her uncertainties by focusing solely on her happiness at being with Shikata again.

Their settlement was populated entirely by Christians, who all kept to the principles set out in their founding charter. All rested from work on the sabbath, and all worked to raise funds to build their church.

This work, however, did not always go smoothly. The health of most of the settlers had been compromised by the heavy labour, and many suffered severe bouts of diarrhoea, possibly caused by the drinking water. What really tormented them, however, were the swarms of mosquitoes. Shikata's belt of smoking straw proved effective for some, but the faces of those with sensitive skin were constantly swollen from mosquito bites.

Still they had the will to continue working together for their common goal. All of them without exception were first-time farmers, but they were fortunate to have been given fertile land to work. In a little over a year they had managed to harvest a hundred sacks of potatoes, as well as some rye and millet. This was more than they had dreamt possible.

"It's going to work!"

The settlers felt renewed confidence and with it a glimmer of hope for the future of their settlement. Other problems persisted, however – not least the differences of opinions between the denominations.

Shikata's Congregationalists and Amanuma's Episcopalians were living together in Emmanuel, with the huts of the former clustered around a small hill to the east, and the latter near the edge of the clearing to the west. Their shared work of clearing the trees and cultivating the land had gone well, but in periods of rest when the talk turned to matters of religion or ideology, the hoes would stand idle and the fervent discussion would eclipse all else. There were times when the confrontation would last until sundown, and their work, already behind schedule, would be set back even more.

Ginko's life in Emmanuel could not have been further removed from her life in Tokyo. She rose at seven, dressed and ate breakfast, and at eight she began work with the rest, joining whatever group she had been assigned to. The women would set to the laundry and cooking. At noon they would clean up after lunch and take an hour's rest, then work until four in the afternoon, when all members gathered for a prayer of thanks. On the sabbath they assembled by the eastern slope at ten in the morning for worship, after which they spent the afternoon relaxing or carrying out maintenance and repairs to their respective homes.

Ginko had left her family home in Tawarase over twenty years previously. Though her life since then had often been very difficult, she had always lived and worked according to the pace she set for herself. Group living was not easy for her.

"Women don't really have to attend the morning meetings," Shikata said, knowing Ginko was a night owl and a late sleeper.

"But I shouldn't be sleeping when everyone else is out working!"

"The morning meetings are just a way we've worked out to unify the denominations and smooth the relationship between the Episcopalians and ourselves."

"Well, in that case maybe I will sleep in a little longer."

"That will be fine. And we've got plenty of lamp oil now, so please do use what you need," Shikata added, pointing to the jug set in the dirt by the door to their hut. Each household received set rations of oil, but Shikata had gone to Setana to purchase more especially for Ginko, knowing that she loved to stay up late reading. Even now, she was working through the English text of the Bible.

Ginko appreciated Shikata's concern for her happiness. While she hesitated to take him up on the favour, she feared for her sanity in this wilderness if she were unable to read. There had been an incident, about a month after Ginko's arrival in Emmanuel, when the wife of Yamazaki, one of the Congregationalists, had suddenly tossed her baby aside, run out of her hut, and collapsed near the well where the other women were gathered. The women had called for Ginko, who was soon at her side. The woman lay with her leg exposed from ankle to thigh, groaning and tearing at her chest.

"Is it malaria?"

"Her eyes have rolled up in her head."

"She's frothing at the mouth."

"Can you help her?"

Ginko sat in silence surrounded by worried settlers, who had come running at word of an emergency, and watched Mrs Yamazaki groan in agony.

"Doctor, please do something for her," Yamazaki pleaded. It was a source of pride for all the settlers of Emmanuel that they had a qualified doctor in their midst. This set them apart even from Setana, and was one of the things that helped them bear their lives in this rough place. "What should we do?"

"Please carry her back home."

"But what about medicine?"

"Please boil some sugar water and have her drink that. For today, make sure you stay by her side and see to her needs."

"Is that all?"

"There's no need to worry. The rest of you too, please lend a hand."

Dubious but obedient, they lifted the woman.

Ginko returned to her hut and Shikata followed. "Are you sure that's enough?" he asked.

"She's not a believer, is she?" Ginko returned flatly.

"Yamazaki is, but I guess maybe she isn't."

"She can't understand why her husband is determined to follow the will of God in this great undertaking. Maybe he didn't explain it to her well enough. At any rate, she's clearly unable to bear the isolation of this place, where there's no one for her to turn to."

"Are you saying that it's made her go mad?"

"She can't take the loneliness and she's become hysterical. She purposely collapsed in a place where people could see her, she was clawing at her chest, and even as she fell she chose a soft place to land – it's a classic case of hysteria."

"Now that you mention it, I heard Yamazaki complaining that lately she's been melancholic and has given up on the housework and minding the children. He's been doing everything from the laundry to the nappy-changing himself."

"The wailing and appearance of insanity is an attempt to get herself sent home." They could no longer hear the woman's wailing, so perhaps she was drinking the sugar water her husband had made for her. Instead, they could now hear a child crying in Yamazaki's hut. "If you're not a believer, following someone here to pioneer the land is probably too much to ask."

"That could be," Shikata nodded his head, looking out beyond the fields, where the settlers were burning brush on newly cleared land. "It isn't enough just to be the wife of a believer."

Having been in Hokkaido only a month herself at that time, Ginko was in no position to speak harshly of anyone. She could not be certain that she herself would not end up like Yamazaki's wife, and there were others too who were suffering severe homesickness.

Now, six months later, the settlement was running out of funds. They were out of miso, soy sauce and even salt. Yojiro went to Setana to sell some of his carvings, and returned with miso purchased with the money he had earned. It had taken him two days to travel the twelve kilometres downstream in a dugout canoe, sloshing through water up to his knees through swamps where the canoe could not pass. As for vegetables, they made do with what grew wild. The situation was becoming increasingly uncomfortable, and as summer waned, some voiced doubts about the validity of their mission.

"Have you all forgotten what we pledged at Doshisha? And how Shikata and Maruyama worked themselves almost to death for us back in 1891? Commander Fukushima rode alone on horseback to Siberia, didn't he? Lieutenant Gunji went to the deserted island of Chijima and became a guardian saint, didn't he? Are we such shameless weaklings that we are going to lose heart over such minor difficulties as these?"

During the morning and evening leisure hours, a member of their group by the name of Takabayashi would try to encourage his wavering comrades, but at times even he felt like giving up on the project and running away. His exhortations were not only for the benefit of the others, but an attempt to firm up his own resolve.

Their Sunday morning worship was what held them together. They took turns holding the assemblies at their homes, and there they prayed, encouraged each other and reaffirmed their pledges to cooperate and help one another. "All as one under God" summed up their promise and their bond.

Ginko contributed to the work as well as she could, now as Shikata's wife rather than as a doctor. She was not able to take down the huge trees or lop off the roots, but she could help cultivate the land they cleared for farming. On occasion, group members were hurt at work too, and Ginko's experience as a doctor was then put to use. Her general medical training benefited the settlement at times like those.

The majority of the settlers struggled on, but some fell sick or lost heart. Starting with Yamazaki, who had been troubled for so long over his wife's hysteria, five households comprising twelve people left the settlement. Emmanuel's population had risen for two years in a row, and this was the first drop in their numbers.

Then in early October, just one month after the twelve had left, a typhoon blew in from the sea of Japan and swept over Hokkaido. The normally placid Toshibetsu River rose and flooded its plain, burying the crops the settlers had sweated over for an entire year in rocks and mud. As if this disaster were not enough, ten days later they were hit by a frost.

These setbacks were all the more bitter for the optimism they had been feeling at the prospect of a good harvest. Now the doubts of those who were wavering became all the more pronounced. "This happened all the time in Tawarase. The more often the river overflows, the more it enriches the land on the plain." Ginko tried to encourage the other settlers, but her explanations fell on deaf ears for those with no farming experience.

Recriminations began to fly over falling behind schedule. Worse, winter was almost upon them. Due to the flood, they now had almost no food stored away. The prospects for making it through the winter on their slim rations from the government looked bleak. Simply believing in God would not be enough. At the first sign of snow at the end of October, half of their group, twenty-eight people in all, decided to leave Emmanuel.

"This test too is given to us by God. If we just bear with it, in two or three years things will take a turn for the better." Shikata tried to dissuade them from leaving, but the families that had resolved to go gathered in one of the huts to read the Bible and beg the forgiveness of God for leaving. Then they departed in silence. There was nothing more that Shikata and the others could have done to keep them there. Indeed, if they had convinced them to stay, the meagre store of rations remaining would clearly not have got them all through the winter.

"Why do we have to bear all this suffering?" asked Shikata, standing with Ginko on the bank of the Toshibetsu River, watching the figures of the departing believers grow smaller in the distance. In the three years since Shikata had come to work on this settlement, his rounded face had become angular and he now looked older than his years.

"You swore to me when we first met that this was your plan, and you are working hard on it. You have come a long way." It was now Ginko's turn to encourage Shikata, exhausted from pioneering and almost ready to give up.

Snow covered the river and plain in solid white. In the depths of the winter, Shikata's sister Shime gave birth to a baby girl, whom she and her husband named Tomi. The child was healthy, but a difficult labour, compounded by inadequate nutrition and the fatigue of hard work, slowed Shime's recovery from childbirth. Then a sudden cold snap hit and she came down with pneumonia. Ginko and Shikata nursed her day and night for a week, but two months later Shime passed away.

This was the first death in the settlement. After a cremation in Setana, they buried Shime's remains in the north-eastern corner of Emmanuel and built a marker for her there. *Did she come to Hokkaido just to die?* wondered Ginko, staring at the white marker.

"How about taking in Tomi?" Shikata suggested, watching Ginko's expression carefully. It was a month after Shime's death. "It's impossible for a man to raise a baby daughter alone on top of the work he's doing here," he added. Shime's husband, aged thirty-one, was making daily trips to a distant wet nurse he had found.

"We... the child?..." Ginko was momentarily confused by this sudden proposal.

"Yes. Let's adopt her."

"Would he agree?"

"We spoke about it five days ago and he said that if we would raise her, he would give her to us." So Shikata had been thinking about this for a while. "What do you think?"

Ginko was unsure how to answer. She had never particularly liked children. They seemed cute enough, but she was sure this was mostly a ploy to curry favour with adults, and it annoyed her no end. She had even said as much to her old friend Ogie, who had tactfully replied that children did this instinctively and should not be held responsible for their actions. Ginko was forced to agree, but it did not make her any more anxious to have a child of her own. And now suddenly she was faced with the prospect of raising one.

"I'll help look after her too. And perhaps when we have more money, we could hire a nursemaid."

Ginko was silent, not sure if she was for or against this idea. She could never have become a doctor or taken on activist roles in society if she had had a child. But was this really why she found the whole idea disagreeable? Then it occurred to her that maybe because she was unable to bear children, she had closed herself off from thinking about them. Eventually her strategy had become ingrained and she had lost interest in them, and her familiarity with them as well.

"I'm the child's only other blood relative here."

He had a point, Ginko thought.

"And anyway, it doesn't look like we are going to have children ourselves."

Ginko gasped as a sharp pain shot though her.

"That's right, isn't it?" he prodded.

She nodded. Shikata's eyes were imploring her, but there was no need – she had already given in.

The band of Congregationalists had seen their numbers severely depleted, but with spring came some new arrivals and with them, fresh hope for Emmanuel. With the extra members, all of strong will and deep faith, their work proceeded smoothly.

Partly in order to avoid further wavering of faith in the group, Shikata was more determined than ever to build a church, and that summer the members built the thatched Toshibetsu church, where they worshipped each Sunday. Additional contributions of money and labour also enabled them to build a small school that autumn. It was a rudimentary structure, but sufficient for their needs. The elders of the community, for whom heavy labour was impossible, were appointed as teachers of reading and arithmetic. That year too, on 25th December, Shikata and Ginko invited the community to their home for their first

Christmas celebration. All who attended promised to make it an annual event.

The settlement in what had been densely forested wilderness was gradually becoming a village. The nearest government office in Setana took note, but refused to register it under the name Emmanuel. Most local place names had originated from the Ainu language, but the Hokkaido government had decreed that all conform to the kanji characters favoured by the mainland Japanese. Emmanuel's foreign-sounding name went against this policy of making names sound as Japanese as possible.

"But this name isn't from the Ainu language – it's from the Bible, and we Japanese have chosen it," the settlers protested.

"Names of foreign origin are impermissible. The village name must either be rendered in kanji or changed." Now the settlers were getting a taste of what it was like to be treated by bureaucrats as outsiders in their own country, just as the Ainu were.

"But we have chosen a name that is a symbolic expression of our religious faith. We can't just change it!" Shikata and the others were outraged, but they were up against the powerful, inflexible bureaucracy.

"What if we just change the name for the government, but we continue calling it Emmanuel? A superficial change will be enough to satisfy them," Ginko pointed out to the infuriated Shikata. Realizing she was right, the settlers chose the name Kami-ga-Oka: "God's hill". The government accepted this as the area's official name, but to this day the settlement is referred to locally as Emmanuel.

Settlements like Emmanuel were gradually springing up around Setana, each recorded by the local government. Elsewhere in Hokkaido, too, similar development was also taking place. Settlers were coming from all over Japan, and the names they chose for their settlements were generally derived from either the names of their group leaders, the places they had come from, or local Ainu names adapted to Japanese. Many of the settlers were fortune-seekers, some having found themselves out of favour after the Meiji Restoration, while others were simply the younger sons of farming families with no inheritance to count on. Few were like Shikata's group, pioneering purely out of religious motivation.

Many of those early settlers are now revered figures in the towns they founded, but the truth is that the majority had been unable to make a living on the mainland, and had nowhere to return to.

In April 1895 the mood in Tokyo was ebullient after the signing of the treaty concluding the Sino-Japanese War of 1894–95, but in Hokkaido the settlers' unremitting battle against the wilderness continued. Just a year later, however, in December 1896, a new bill went before the Diet. Entitled "Disposition of Undeveloped Hokkaido Lands", the bill was a major revision of the 1886 "Regulations for Sale of Hokkaido Lands", which had been in force for ten years.

The adoption of this bill into law meant that all tracts of land previously distributed in Hokkaido, including the land that Tsuyoshi Inukai had ceded to Shikata's Congregationalists, would revert back to government ownership. All settlers would have to reapply directly to the government for the lease on the land they were working. This meant that all the land not yet cultivated by the Emmanuel settlers was repossessed by the government for reallocation to other settler groups. The prospect of non-believers settling in the vicinity completely upset Shikata's dream of a thriving community built exclusively by and for Christians, undisturbed by wider Japanese society.

Furthermore, the friction between Shikata's band of Congregationalists and Amanuma's Episcopalians was worsening. It was about two years since Amanuma's group of Episcopalians had joined with the original Emmanuel settlers. The settlement's charter and governing issues since then had been decided by both groups in council, but in reality the Congregationalists had the balance of power, partly because they had been there first, and also because they had outnumbered the Episcopalians.

But many of the Congregationalists had departed after their crops had been destroyed by the flood, and those that remained were now outnumbered by the Episcopalians. The issue had remained in hibernation over the snowbound winter months, but it resurfaced as the spring thaw brought new development work. The contrasting positions and rivalry became increasingly hard to smooth over, and were all the more painful since they shared the same basic Christian beliefs.

It was just a matter of time until the headstrong and impulsive Shikata, driven into a corner by this reversal of power, fell out with Amanuma. The spark came when Amanuma's group stopped worshipping with Shikata's group at their Toshibetsu church. The differences that had been held in check for so long erupted all at once in a bitter confrontation that quickly grew out of control.

Shikata knew that he was outnumbered and could not possibly win. It had been a mistake to merge with Amanuma's group, but it was too late for regrets now.

In the summer of 1896 Shikata made the decision to leave Emmanuel and move to Kunnui, thirty miles to the east.

"There's a manganese mine there. I've always wanted to try my hand at that." Shikata had been sweet-talked by a speculator. Mining was no enterprise for an amateur, but his enthusiasm had already been ignited for the new project.

"What about your religious goals? This has nothing to do with them, has it?" Ginko asked.

"There's no point in me staying here, is there?" He had come to Hokkaido with the lofty ambition of building an ideal Christian community, and his dream had been strong enough to mobilize other people too. As a Christian herself, Ginko had been able to agree with and support him. But now he was talking about developing a newly opened mine, and using the remainder of the money Ginko had brought from Tokyo for it. "He says I'll be able to recover the full investment within two years."

"If we have to move from here," she suggested gently, "why not return to the mainland?"

"I could never go back there like this." Shikata had his pride. "This time I'll make it work, and then with the profits I'll buy land and build a new town."

"Aren't we deciding this in too much of a rush? Please calm down and think it over carefully."

"I've already thought about it enough! I've thought it through completely and I've made my decision."

"You can't succeed on passion and will alone, you know." Ginko understood Shikata's fervour. Her own ambition to become a doctor had appeared equally reckless and far-fetched. However, she could not understand the way his ambitions changed.

"I know that, but there's no point in staying here any longer."

"I'd be happy to start again somewhere and open a clinic."

"No. I'm going to Kunnui and that's that." *I'm the man*, Shikata seemed to be saying. "I'm just asking you to go along with what I say for once. I'm begging you." Shikata put his hands on the floor and bowed low.

Ginko was forcibly reminded of the occasion six years earlier, when Shikata had begged her to marry him. His pose now was precisely the same as it had been then. *Wanting to marry me was no different! He's in a headlong rush about everything*, Ginko thought.

Now she understood why everyone who knew Shikata had opposed their marriage. Their counsels had indeed been only natural and well intentioned after all. Yet Ginko had no regrets. She had been happy back then. She had needed Shikata; it had not been a mistake. And she still needed him now, and he needed her.

Shikata tied their daughter Tomi, now nearly two years old, on his back, and left the community on horseback, with Ginko following on her own horse. Slung over the saddles were their possessions – just the barest household necessities.

As they were crossing Yakumo Pass, they came across a bear, only managing to avoid being attacked by banging on pots and pans. They passed through Imakane and upstream to Yurap in single file. The large figure of Shikata and the smaller one of Ginko wove along on horseback through the thickets and brush of the pass leading to Kunnui. Hardly a trace remained of Ginko Ogino, the doctor who had been among Tokyo's leading female intellectuals.

They arrived safely in Kunnui that evening.

Mining for manganese in Kunnui had begun in the late 1880s, as it had in many of the mines in the surrounding mountains. Shikata arrived with no experience and little more than the expectation that he could make a success of it. With the profits he was certain he would earn, he planned to build a new town for Christian believers.

Just as Ginko had foreseen, however, this new venture ended in failure.

21

The following spring saw Shikata and Ginko clearing out of Kunnui, and heading once again with Tomi over the mountain pass and across the Toshibetsu plain back to Setana. Once they had got over the highest point of the pass and reached a convenient bamboo grove, the three of them stopped by the wayside for lunch.

"You must be tired." Shikata observed Ginko with concern as he bit into a rice ball. "But we're through the worst of it now."

Far away, past the sea of trees, the blue ocean sparkled in the distance. A white ribbon of water threading in and out through the trees below them was the Toshibetsu River, which led to Setana on the small flatland and then poured into the ocean.

"Aren't you going to eat?" Ginko had only eaten half of her rice ball. She would have expected herself to be hungry, but she found she had no appetite. It was always like that for her when she was riding horseback. "Want some water?" Shikata poured her a cupful from his bamboo holder and held it out to her.

Ginko understood painfully well why he was being so solicitous. His plans for Emmanuel had fallen through, and now the manganese mine had ended in failure. Shikata was finally beginning to realize that chasing one dream after another was not an acceptable way of life for a man with a wife and child.

"The house is near the harbour, so it should be a lively place, and we won't have anything to worry about." Shikata talked about the place they would be renting in Setana, no doubt hoping to cheer Ginko up. It was a small house rented out for one yen a month by the owner of a dry-goods shop next door. It would not be easy to accommodate a working clinic in such premises, but the money that Ginko had saved and brought with her to Hokkaido three years earlier was now gone. They were in no position to ask for much.

"We'll need to find a nurse and cleaning staff," continued Shikata.

"No, we won't need any." Ginko did not even have a desk, examining table or medicine chest, so hiring help was not high on her list of priorities.

"I'd like to help if I can."

"But you'll be busy with missionary work, won't you?" Ginko answered, aware of Shikata's loss of confidence in himself, and protective of his pride. Resuming his missionary work in Setana, building a church and starting a Sunday school was the one path left for him.

"I'll have free time between preaching jobs. I'll help," Shikata answered, his expression clear. He balanced Tomi, now almost three, on his knee, and helped her eat her rice ball.

By now Setana had a permanent population of nearly a thousand fishing households, swelled by an additional three thousand fishermen, who came up when there was work. Nestled among cypress-covered mountains in south-western Hokkaido, it was a major fishing port, and the bustling town was now at its peak. Not long after Ginko and her family arrived, however, the herring industry supporting the area went into a gradual decline.

Ginko opened her clinic specializing in gynaecology, obstetrics and paediatrics in the Aizu neighbourhood near the centre of town. There were already two other clinics open in Setana, but she assumed the population was large enough to accommodate one more. However, the situation was very different from when she had opened her clinic in Tokyo. In this far-flung northern corner of Japan, no one knew that she was renowned as Japan's first woman doctor and as a social reformer. In Tokyo, her accomplishments and activities had been a source of popularity for her, but in this rough fishing boom town, people were not ready to trust a woman doctor, much less an opinionated one.

Ginko focused pragmatically on her work and refused to waste time on what people thought of her. With no savings left, worry was a luxury she could not afford. During their first month in Setana, the family was reduced to buying their rice by

298

the cupful. It would have been unseemly for a doctor or even a missionary to be seen stooping to that level in public. Thus it was left to little Tomi, barely old enough to play outside, to go out with their order written on a slip of paper.

They knew no one, and Ginko did not have any regular patients. They were starting again from scratch. If asked to make a house call, no matter how far away, she would don her favourite black kimono overcoat and head for the door. Shikata, with a newly grown beard and wearing tall boots woven from straw, would accompany her, leading her horse. Barely out of town, they would find themselves on a narrow path surrounded by nothing but forest and striped bamboo grass. Occasionally they would see deer or even bears. When they arrived at their destination, Ginko would dismount and Shikata would wait outside, sitting on a tree stump until she returned. Helping her mount the horse once again, he would then lead it back into town.

No one could have guessed on seeing them that Shikata was Ginko's husband.

As 1897 drew to a close, Ginko and Shikata were becoming accustomed to the town. Ginko's clinic had been open for about six months and the number of patients was gradually increasing, so their financial situation was a little more secure. Town leaders and intellectuals had discovered Ginko too, and were beginning to consult her on various matters. Meanwhile the fishing town and surrounding mountains provided the family with a sense of calm.

The following spring, Ginko formed a new women's association, the Womanly Virtues Society, and served as its first president. Now that she had finally settled down, her innate desire to improve the lot of women began to reassert itself. All the ladies of prominent families in this rural town attended, from the mayor's wife and the police chief's wife to the wives of the chief priest at the Kotohira Shrine and the proprietors of the fancy-goods store and the kimono shop. Though Ginko had devised this group along the lines of the Japan Christian Women's Organization, its goals were focused less on women's rights and the betterment of society than on mutual friendship between the members and enriching their general education.

Ginko taught the women crafts such as needlework and flower-arranging, and gave lectures that ran the gamut of matters that modern women needed to know, from feminine deportment to female physiology and hygiene, and even the proper treatment and bandaging of wounds. She particularly emphasized the significance of gentlewomanly conduct and the virtue of chastity.

Many of the men who had fled north to this area at the beginning of the Meiji era were largely uneducated, as were the women they had brought along with them. But the women thirsted for knowledge and listened seriously to what Ginko tried to teach them.

"What is a gentlewoman?" Ginko would ask them.

"The possessor of high-minded sentiments is a gentlewoman. It is unrelated to any distinction of rank or name."

"And what is a noblewoman?"

"A noblewoman is one who holds beauty in her heart. It is unrelated to a woman who wears beautiful clothing."

The ladies would answer as Ginko had taught them, in chorus. The men started to notice that their wives had begun to learn some strange things of late, but they respected Ginko.

As Ginko became busier lecturing and training the women in her group, she tended to be out of the house more. The daytime was generally occupied with examining patients, so the group usually met in the evening. Shikata would always accompany Ginko when she had to travel any significant distance. This meant that Tomi was often left at home alone. At first she cried from the loneliness, but Ginko saw no reason to indulge her.

"Auntie has important work to do, and it won't do for me to stay home just for you," she would chide Tomi when the little girl protested. Then she would leave, closing and locking the door behind her. Little Tomi thought that Auntie's work must be something fearsome.

By the time Tomi went to grammar school, she had already memorized the two phonetic Japanese alphabets, and could do simple addition and subtraction. Ginko had taught her all this with scoldings and sometimes blows.

Shikata usually arrived home ahead of Ginko after accompanying her to a lecture or meeting, and would spend the free time playing with Tomi. Often he would take the little girl by the hand and they would go together to see the harbour or the view of the three huge rocks jutting out of it. He would give her piggyback rides or imitate a cat miaowing to amuse her. Consequently, the loneliest times for Tomi were when Shikata was gone.

The first foreigner appeared in Setana in 1894, when Father Andres, a missionary for the Episcopal Church in the nearby city of Hakodate, passed through on his way to Emmanuel. Three years later, a Congregationalist missionary named Roland came on his district rounds, and not long afterwards, in 1898, the missionary Takekuma Udagawa urged the Emmanuel Congregationalists to build their own church separately from the Episcopalians, thus clinching the split between the two camps in the settlement.

In 1900, Roland returned to Setana at the invitation of Ginko's group, the Womanly Virtues Society, to deliver a lecture on Christianity. The society organized everything from preparing the hall to ushering for the event itself, and even Tomi, who was about to enter elementary school the following year, helped by posting notices advertising the event.

Afterwards, Roland was resting with Ginko and Shikata in their house. Turning to Ginko, he commented, "You can read and write English. How about learning to speak it as well? If you could speak English, you could go abroad and learn a lot of new things." As if Shikata were not even in the room, he continued enthusiastically, "It's a waste having you buried in this backwater town. If you're going to have a medical practice in Hokkaido, why not try Sapporo? It's the capital and it has the agricultural college, and people of your level who you could talk to. I'll introduce you to a missionary friend of mine there. In a place like this you'll forever be giving with nothing in return."

Listening to Roland, Ginko's memories of the lively days she had spent in Tokyo came flooding back. Back then, all eyes had been on her and everything she said or did was reported in

301

newspaper or magazine articles. And then letters from readers would come fluttering in almost daily to editors or to her directly. But that had been Tokyo; it was the centre of Japan.

"The Japan Women's Medical College has been founded by someone named Yayoi Yoshioka. And next year Tokyo Women's University will be opening."

"A women's university?"

"The times are really changing. It's pointless for you to be hibernating in a place like this."

Three years earlier a women's suffrage alliance had been formed in Tokyo. This year, a school to teach women English had opened. A medical school for women had been founded, and now there was to be a women's university as well. It all seemed like a dream come true. Ginko thought about Tokyo, how it was always in motion. She could be a part of that again if she chose to.

"Anyway, please think about it. I'd be happy to assist in any way I can."

Roland stayed that night in Setana, and then early the next morning departed for Emmanuel. From there he took the overland route back to Hakodate.

"What do you think about trying out Sapporo?" It was late that night, after Ginko and Shikata had gone to bed. Ginko tried to discern the expression on Shikata's face as he spoke, but he was hidden in darkness. "You should probably do as Roland said."

"I am perfectly satisfied with my life here," Ginko lied.

"You should go." This time Shikata was more definite.

"But I've finally got the clinic here running smoothly."

"You can leave everything here as it is, and just go to Sapporo for a year or so to try it out."

"And what would you do during that time?" She could not justify dragging him along with her like a manservant, but leaving him behind here alone was unthinkable.

"I was thinking I could go back to school."

"Doshisha?"

"That's right. I never graduated; I was thinking about going back to finish."

"Would they let you do that?"

"I don't know for sure, but they might be willing to work something out."

It had been ten years since Shikata had left Kyoto, when he had dropped out of Doshisha to ask for Ginko's hand in marriage. The young man of ten years ago, single-mindedly pursuing the love he was burning for, was now nearly forty. His thick black hair was streaked here and there with grey, and his forehead showed the beginnings of lines, like the growth rings of a tree.

"Well, if you are absolutely certain that's what we should do..."

"I am. I'm fed up with leaving everything I do half-done."

In early summer 1903, Ginko took Tomi and went to Sapporo, continuing to pay the rent on her clinic and leaving a "Temporarily Closed" sign on the door. Shikata left at the same time for Doshisha University in Kyoto.

The acacia trees outside Sapporo Station were in full bloom and white petals fell on Ginko's and Tomi's shoulders as they passed beneath them. Ginko rented a small, three-room house bordering an apple orchard behind the agricultural college. They attended the Kitaichijo church, where Ginko tutored a missionary in Japanese and received lessons in English in exchange. The sense of possibilities opening before her, and new hope, filled her in much the same way as when she had first obtained her medical licence.

Taro Muya, a former Associate Professor of internal medicine at Kojuin during Ginko's time there, was now head of a ward hospital in Sapporo. A week after arriving, Ginko went to see Muya at his hospital. He had already heard rumours that Ginko was in Setana and would soon be coming to Sapporo. They talked for a while about Kojuin. As tough as those three years had been for Ginko, she found that, twenty years later, she could look back on them fondly.

Two months later, she visited Muya once more to inform him that she was planning to open a clinic in Sapporo. She had thought he would be supportive, but instead he frowned and sank into thought.

"Sapporo might be rather difficult for you," he finally offered, reluctantly.

"Yes, I'm prepared for that."

"So Setana doesn't have what you want?"

"Well…" She explained how isolated she felt there.

Muya nodded, and then said, "I hope you don't mind me speaking frankly, but you studied medicine twenty years ago, and left Tokyo ten years ago. So much progress has been made in that time that it is embarrassing to think about what I used to teach at Kojuin. The medical techniques we used back then have become obsolete, and young doctors nowadays know so much more. It's been all I can do, studying constantly, to keep from falling behind them. I don't mean to be rude, but with all you've been through these ten years on the settlement and moving around, I doubt you've been able to keep up with new medical developments. You might get by in a rural area, but I do think it would be difficult for you to start up a practice here in Sapporo."

Ginko looked at the floor, lost for words. She had never thought of this before. Muya was pointing out something she had failed to think about. *I've been careless. I got caught up in my own complacency.*

"I hate to say it, but the fact that you were an excellent medical student twenty years ago is not going to be enough." He had been one of her teachers back then, and felt no need to mince words now.

"You're right. I haven't thought this through enough." She was deeply embarrassed for even having brought her plans to him and having forced him to set her straight like this.

"No, no. I'm certainly not saying that you cannot open a practice here. There are others still practising the old ways in Sapporo. But naturally enough, people tend to give them a wide berth. And then there's the drawback of you being a woman. Medicine is much more of a science these days, and women are not as hesitant as they used to be about being examined by male doctors, so it's no longer such a big advantage being a female doctor."

Ginko was chagrined at how little she knew about the changes that had taken place while she had been at Emmanuel and in Setana. "I understand completely."

"Well, it's just my own professional opinion. Of course, if you go ahead, I'll do what I can in my circle to support you."

"Thank you. I truly appreciate your concern and am very grateful for your advice."

Ginko took her leave as soon as she could, but once outside she felt no better. Her face reddened in shame at the thought of her own overconfidence. *I guess I lost touch with the world without even realizing it.* The chill autumn wind of Sapporo was beginning to blow as she walked through the city, and she felt older than she ever had before.

At the end of September, Ginko left her rented house in Sapporo and returned to Setana. She had been away for just three months. Her English had not yet reached a satisfactory level, but she decided to give it up. Her primary purpose in going to Sapporo had been to explore the possibility of opening a clinic there, and improving her English-speaking ability had been secondary. Now there was insufficient reason for her to remain in Sapporo. She had overreached herself, and felt a fool.

Looking out of the window of the train at the autumn sunset over the fields and scattered trees of the plains, she saw neither houses nor any signs of people. It looked like the fields would stretch on for ever. She and Tomi had eaten the packed lunches they had bought in Otaru, and now Tomi was asleep next to her.

If I hadn't gone to Sapporo and met Muya, I'd still believe I was capable of anything. I leapt at outlandish advice when it came in a random encounter because I was overconfident and full of pride. But I've fallen behind the times and my day is probably over.

She could see the end of the fields now, as they headed towards the dark forest.

Ginko opened her clinic in Setana once again. Medical practice might have changed over the years, but she had no other way to make a living. For the moment, she would work and forget about both Sapporo and Tokyo.

The following spring, Shikata graduated from Doshisha and returned to Hokkaido as a fully qualified minister. After only ten days in Setana, however, he was sent to pastor a church in Urakawa, a post he took up alone. Now that he was a minister, he and Ginko were destined for separations like this, but they comforted themselves with the thought that at least this time they were both in Hokkaido.

Ginko and Tomi continued their unexciting but peaceful life in Setana. As always, letters arrived from Shikata at the rate of about once a month, and Ginko's replies were sent at more or less the same rate. The Russo-Japanese War had broken out in February 1904, and once again the country was focused on conflict. Ginko's daily life, though, was largely unaffected. She treated her patients and during her free time she read the Bible and studied English. She also pursued her activities with the Womanly Virtues Society as before.

In July 1905, Shikata quit his church post and returned to Setana to work on developing a self-supporting ministry based in the area of cypress-covered mountains around Setana. From the end of August, he set out alone visiting remote settlements, preaching and handing out Bibles.

Halfway through September, Shikata returned from a ten-day trek in the northern part of the region complaining of chills, and he took to his bed. In more than ten years of marriage, Ginko had seen Shikata confined to bed only once, when he had suffered a bad cold during the winter they had spent in Kunnui.

Ginko took his temperature and found he had a low fever. She quickly mixed up some medicine for him and prepared an ice pillow, then told him to rest. The next day his fever was down somewhat, but he felt lethargic. However, a gathering of Emmanuel's Congregationalists was planned for noon, and Shikata got up to go.

"You should stay home," Ginko told him.

"I can't. Everyone's waiting for me."

"But what if you get worse?"

"I've never taken time off for something as trifling as this!"

Shikata laughed, confident as always in his strong body, and went out.

Later that afternoon, Yojiro Maruyama brought him home on horseback, his face red and his eyes glazed. Ginko could see at a glance that he had a raging fever. She quickly spread out his bedding and made him lie down. Shikata closed his eyes, looking exhausted. His temperature was high and his pulse racing. Ginko gave him an injection to reduce the fever and relieve the pain, but the fever did not respond. His breathing was fast and shallow and appeared laboured. When she listened to his chest, she could hear fluid in his lungs. Ginko thought it was pneumonia, but she could not be sure. This was not her medical speciality and, alarmed by someone so close to her being ill, she could not trust her own judgement.

Yojiro went to fetch Dr Nomura from the clinic opposite Tomi's elementary school. Dr Nomura's diagnosis was acute pneumonia, and he gave Shikata another injection and more medicine. Ginko set herself to boiling water and warming Shikata's chest with wet towels.

Ginko stayed by his side throughout the night, changing the hot compresses every hour. Shikata's eyes remained closed and eventually he slept, but his breathing stayed shallow and fast.

In the morning his fever was down slightly, but that afternoon it shot up again. Shikata was badly weakened. His eyes were sunken and his cheeks hollow, and his hair looked whiter than before. Occasionally, when he coughed, there was blood in the phlegm. It was as though his body, which had endured so much over the years, was being consumed all at once. Ginko kept changing the hot compresses and making him take medicine, praying all the while.

In the afternoon of the fourth day, Shikata slipped into unconsciousness.

He just whispered, "It hurts," and raised his hands a little, as though reaching for something in the air. Then he called "Sensei?" into the darkness around him.

"Isn't there anything we can do?" Ginko pressed Dr Nomura. But Nomura did not answer. His eyes were on Shikata's face, and a frown furrowed his brow. "*Please* do something for him!" she pleaded, forgetting that she was a doctor herself.

Shikata died a little after eight that evening, on 23rd September 1905. Ginko shook her suddenly lifeless husband, calling his name, but he would not wake. He was forty-one years old.

Ginko laid Shikata to rest on a hill at the northern end of Emmanuel. From there he could look down over the settlement he had borne such hardships to clear, and at the shining white Toshibetsu River.

22

Ginko had always been a woman of few words, and after Shikata's death she had even less to say. She stopped going to the Womanly Virtues Society meetings, and after she had finished with her patients each day, she kept to herself at home, spending her time reading the Bible or in prayer.

Living quietly with Tomi, Ginko thought about Shikata. They had spent much of their marriage apart. He had gone off to Hokkaido without her, returned to Doshisha University and served alone at the church in Urakawa. Probably half their married life had been spent apart. She had thought she was used to living without him. However, this time he would not be coming back, and it felt entirely different. The hole left by his absence was much bigger and much deeper. She no longer wished to leave Setana — she wanted to stay where Shikata was and be buried next to him.

Ginko did not confide her loneliness to anyone. It was not as if talking about it would help, she thought. No matter what the circumstances, she was still disinclined to rely on others.

Three months after Shikata died, Tomoko began asking Ginko to return to Tokyo, where she was living in a small rented house, after leaving her own home in Kumagaya a year before. Sharing a household with her stepson and his wife had not gone well, and so Tomoko had moved out. The sisters were now in similar circumstances, both alone and getting on in years. The heir to their Tawarase home, Sanzo Ogino, had also moved to Tokyo and was employed at the Omori post office. His mother Yai, Yasuhei's widow, had joined him there.

"It would be so nice if all of us lived together in Tokyo!" Tomoko wrote to Ginko.

But Ginko did not wish to move back to Tokyo now. She finally felt settled in Setana. She wrote back to Tomoko telling her this, but Tomoko would not give up and continued to write regularly, asking Ginko to come and live with her.

"If I returned to Tokyo, Shikata would be all alone here," Ginko wrote, almost as if trying to convince herself to stay.

Soon after Shikata's death, Ginko came down with a cold and slight fever. It was not severe, but it was accompanied by a dull pain in her lower abdomen. Her urine was cloudy as well. She closed the clinic and went to bed.

The cold had lowered her resistance, and now the long-dormant gonorrhoea had flared up again. It had been mostly in remission for almost forty years, and seeing its symptoms show themselves again after all this time sent an undeniable chill through Ginko.

While she was confined to bed, Tomi, now eleven years old, took care of all the cooking and cleaning. When patients came, she even followed Ginko's instructions and prepared their medicines herself. Tomi was Ginko's sole support.

After a week, Ginko was able to get up, but the cold had taken something out of her. Her back would tire after a couple hours of sitting in a chair, and she no longer felt up to making house calls around town in the afternoons. Just as each rainstorm deepens autumn, Ginko's ability to recover was slowing.

A new year began. The Russo-Japanese War had ended the previous September with the Treaty of Portsmouth, and the ebullient mood of victory reached even this far-northern town. Setana, however, was otherwise under a pall of gloom.

The Setana coastline saw little snow, and by March it was usually gone. The return of the herring usually foretold the arrival of spring, but the catch had been declining year by year, and that spring the haul was particularly disappointing. Setana had been built around the herring industry, and without the usual catch the town began to lose its vitality.

The whole western coastline of Hokkaido was feeling the pinch. Overfishing was partly to blame, but there had also been a change in the ocean currents. People waited with a vague expectation that things would eventually improve, but no effective strategy had been developed to deal with the decline. The years had thus drifted by without any change for the better.

Ginko's routine, however, was much the same as it had always been. Her clinic was open every day, and she was back to making house calls, except for Sundays when she went to church. In her spare time, she was again participating in Womanly Virtues Society activities, and she studied English late into the night. As ever, she was a night owl and a late sleeper. Her latest project was writing a diary entry in English each night before turning in.

Summer passed, and the autumn breezes began to blow in from the ocean. Under the autumn sky, the three huge rocks standing in the harbour off Setana cast black shadows on the surface of the sea. A second winter without Shikata was approaching. Ginko had got used to the loneliness, but every once in a while she was visited by a vision of her husband, covered in sweat and dust, returning from his missionary work. As though she could sense it too, Tomi would sometimes announce, "I saw Uncle in a dream last night."

As the cold closed in, Ginko's lower back and legs began to ache. These past few years she'd felt some discomfort every winter, but this year was markedly worse. The cold mornings were the hardest for her, and Tomi would get up first to light the stove and cook the rice before heading off to school. Ginko would rouse herself later, rinse her mouth, wash her face, and check the mirror. Then she would comb her hair, counting the hairs that fell out as she did so. Her complexion had dulled and wrinkles stood out on her once-beautiful face. After her nurse arrived, the day's work would begin, and Ginko would concentrate on her patients, forgetting her own troubles for a while.

Late one early December afternoon after work, Ginko walked through the snow to the town hall. In the meeting room on the second floor she was to give a talk to young women on marriage. There was a big pot-bellied wood stove in the centre of the medium-sized meeting room, with thirty young women squeezed in around it.

311

"Marriages must be made based on mutual consent and understanding between adults healthy in body and mind." Ginko was feeling older these days, but her voice was as clear and carried as well as ever. Near the conclusion of her lecture she felt a slight dizziness. Her head felt rock heavy, but she wrapped up her remarks as scheduled, and then stepped down from the podium.

"You look a little pale," commented one of the employees at the hall.

"I suppose I'm just tired," said Ginko. She declined to join the tea reception, and set off on her ten-minute walk home.

It was bitterly cold and the snow had settled in a fine powder on the dark street. Only the sound of her feet sinking into and pulling out of the snow accompanied Ginko as she walked. She turned at the corner where she could see the lit lamps serving as markers, went another half-block, and came to a standstill to catch her breath and rest. Her body felt as heavy as lead. After a couple of deep breaths, she lifted her head. Beyond the town's roofs loomed the Toshibetsu mountain range, like the dark back of a beast at rest.

Shikata is sleeping just over there, Ginko thought, and then felt a sharp pain lash through her back to her chest. An instant later her small body sank slowly into the white snow.

I must get up, she thought, but snow was under her back and on her face. Barely conscious, she saw Tokyo, then Emmanuel, then Tawarase. Beyond a field of rape blossoms shining bright yellow in the sunshine, she could see the Toné River. A white-sailed ship was sailing silently by, bound for Edo. Ginko heard a voice and turned to see a figure coming towards her from the embankment. Her mother Kayo was beckoning to her. Whether she was smiling or crying Ginko could not be sure, but she was looking directly at her. Ginko began to run to her, but then remembered something and looked back. Shikata was there, looking lost.

"Is everything all right?" Ginko asked her mother, but Kayo did not answer and just stood looking at her. Behind Kayo now stood Tomoko, Yasuhei and his wife Yai. Looking closer, Ginko could see Ogie, and next to her, her old teacher Yorikuni.

Ginko felt a moment's puzzlement that all of these people were gathered by the Toné River, but then their figures became less distinct. As the whole scene darkened and faded, Ginko felt as though she herself was floating leisurely towards that unfinished scene.

About thirty minutes later, a passerby found Ginko lying unconscious in the snow. She was taken to a nearby hospital, and they discovered that she had suffered a heart attack. Miraculously, she survived. However, she remained weakened and unable to resume making house calls.

At the end of 1906, no longer confident of her physical strength, Ginko finally returned to Tokyo, accompanied by Tomi. There she opened a clinic and practised until she passed away on 23rd June 1913, at the age of sixty-three.

Acknowledgements

The author is indebted to Gotaro Matsumoto's *Ginko Ogino*, published by the Hokkaido Medical Association, and *The History of Japanese Women Doctors*, published by the Japan Medical Women's Association. *Imakane Town History* and *Eastern Setana Town History* were used for reference. He is also indebted to Ginko Ogino's adopted daughter Tomi Takenoya, and other relatives, including Ikuo Tsunemi, for their assistance.

The translators are indebted to Deborah Davidson and the Menuma Historical Society for invaluable information and insight. We also greatly appreciate the assistance of Kiyo Hoshino of the Japan Literature Publishing Project, Shigeko Fujita, Ginny Tapley and Manna Iwabuchi.

The publisher wishes to acknowledge the help and support of Chris Braham of J-Lit Center in the preparation of this work.